Siren's Song

Wyrd Love: Book 1

Cynthia Diamond

To Brianna,
Welcome to the Wyrd!

Artwork by Lynne Anderson

Publisher's Note: This is a work of fiction. Names, characters, places, and incidents are a product of the author's imagination. Locales and public names are sometimes used for atmospheric purposes. Any resemblance to actual people, living or dead, or to businesses, companies, events, institutions, or locales is completely coincidental.

Siren's Song/ Cynthia Diamond. -- 1st ed.
ISBN: 9781731337214

To my real life Wyrd sisters: Jen, Ace, Stacy, and Ty.
To my true sister Lisa, who will always be my hero.

Special thanks to Doug Chastant for breathing life into a cranky old dragon. Jack would still be just a vague idea without his help in his creation.

Contents

Chapter 1

Five days tied to a dirty mattress in what probably was an abandoned crack house wasn't ideal vacation time for Adelle. She was glad Valerie found her before her life was sucked out completely. The five skinny, pale vampires had scurried out the window when her sister broke down the door. Adelle watched them run like rats from a sinking ship. They were fast little buggers, dashing out of sight before she could blink. She wished Valerie would have caught them. Hell hath no fury like a Valkyrie scorned. Judging by the furious battle scream that reverberated from down stairs, Valerie was indeed pissed and would have torn through them like paper. Adelle really wished Valerie had. The scorching need for vengeance burned deep down in Adelle's gut, scalding the back of her throat with bile. Instead of giving into the rage, Adelle pushed it back down, keeping her siren's anger in check. She felt like hell. She looked like hell too. The side of her throat was bitten raw, stinging in agony, sticky and crusted over with her blood. The blood had poured down her neck, staining and stiffening the collar of her purple paisley shirt.

Dammit, that was a nice shirt, she thought.

These blood suckers were a messy group of eaters. It was expected from freshly turned vampires. The youngest was probably a mere few weeks in. His weak gag reflex at the site of her blood was a dead giveaway.

Adelle's arms were bound tightly over her head to the rickety metal headboard with plastic zip ties, her ankles and knees tied together with twine. She couldn't feel her appendages anymore, and what precious little she could feel was ice cold and tingling with pain. Ethan and his asshole friends had drained her of so much blood that she could barely keep her eyes open to watch Valerie burst into the room.

The Valkyrie's huge shimmering broadsword was unsheathed from her back, black hair flowing, dark eyes blazing in rage as her skin glowed with an intense light. All six feet of her sister's lean muscle was on edge and ready to crush what got in her way. Not many women could make a pair of jeans and a T-shirt look like battle armor just by walking into a room angry. Adelle never noticed how awe-inspiring her sister was going into battle until she saw it from the front. Usually, she stood behind her. She would have to mention that when the dirty rag in her mouth was removed. Right about then, Adelle realized that blood loss and the last of the vampire venom weren't helping her think logically about her current situation. Logically, she should have been in tears. Unfortunately, her emotions would have brought on a certain amount of destruction to the neighborhood. It was best to swallow it down and think about Valerie's intimidating visage instead.

Adelle let out a pathetic moan through the crumpled cloth stuffed in her mouth. It caught Valerie's attention and she spun on her heels, sword raised and ready to slice. She lowered the gleaming blade as soon as she saw her sister tied to the bed. With an expression halfway between relief and disgust, Valerie strode over and yanked the gag out of Adelle's mouth. Adelle choked out a cough, raking her dry tongue across the roof of her mouth to remove the lint and dirt that had moved in.

"Thanks," Adelle said, voice dry and weak.

"Did they turn you?" Valerie asked, her dark brows furrowed together.

Adelle understood the concern. She was pale enough to look transformed into a vampire but her heart was still beating. She was pale, clammy, but still alive. They wanted her alive so they could feed. It explained why they kept shoving crackers and water in her mouth. They forced her to eat, it forced her to heal faster, and they would start all over again.

"No. Still have a pulse." She tried to give Valerie a reassuring smile. Her lips stung as they cracked open and bled. That didn't help soften Valerie's pained face. A quick arc of the sword and the blade expertly cut through the zip ties and twine. Blood rushed back to Adelle's fingers and her skin prickled, adding to the pain. Her wrists were rubbed raw and burned with a fury. Feebly, she shook her hands and hissed. Valerie ran to the window, hoping catch up with the escaping vampires.

"They ran the minute they heard you coming up the stairs," Adelle said. "Out the window. No offence Val, but announcing that you're going to trounce some fuckers when you got here may not have been the stealthiest way-"

"Goddammit, Dell shut up!" Valerie said.

She turned and kicked the closet door open, gave it a quick search, then peered under the bed that Adelle laid on. There weren't any other places to hide in the sparse room. Just the bed, the closet, and some bloody towels on the floor. Valerie padded around the room on the balls of her feet, a spring in her step and a tense rise in her shoulders. The Valkyrie needed to spill blood, to give chase. But vampires were faster than Valkyries. With their head start, there was no way she could catch up. Once the realization hit her, the light of her skin dimmed. Valerie slammed a fist on the wall, shaking the room.

"Dammit!" she cried.

Adelle sighed, shame wrapping about her. She didn't blame Valerie for her anger one bit. It was her own fault she had gotten into this situation. Her sister had told her over and over how dating a vampire was bad news.

Well, that prophecy came to fruition, Adelle thought.

She rolled onto her side, pressing a hand to the punctures that ran down her neck. It took a groaning effort for her to get that far. After Valerie walked over and took her by the shoulders, she found herself sitting up right.

"Thanks," Adelle said. She pursed her lips, and then raised her bloodshot eyes to her sister. Dirty red curls shadowed her face. "I'm beginning to see your point about Ethan."

"You should have blasted him," Valerie said. 'Why didn't you blast him?"

Adelle only shrugged in response, hunching over her knees. Adelle had siren's blood in her. She could have easily used her powers. She could have blown the entire house away with a single scream. One solid punch to her throat had solved that problem for Ethan though. The hypnotic gazes and venom from their fangs had done the rest. But even during the brief moments of lucidity between feedings, Adelle had been too frightened to try to use her voice against her captors. If she had tried even the slightest scream, the whole city block could have crumbled to dust. That scared her more than being kidnapped.

Valerie grabbed Adelle by the shoulders, giving her a sharp shake. The sudden jolt forced Adelle to look her sister in the eye. The Valkyrie wasn't taking any of her sister's pouty bullshit tonight.

"Why didn't you blast him?" Valerie repeated. Her voice quivered in anger, dark eyes glassed over with furious tears.

"Val, there are other houses on this block," Adelle said. "They have families in them. If I just cut loose they all would have-" A dry cough strangled the words from her mouth.

"I don't care about those other people, I care about you," Valerie said.

Adelle wiped the spittle and blood from her lips. "Yeah, well I happen to care about those other people."

"When you get in trouble you fucking use your fucking powers!"

"Easy for you to say. You don't make shit explode when you raise your voice."

Valerie threw her hands up. "Man up, Dell! I'm sick of saving your pathetic ass when you can save yourself!"

Adelle flinched at her sister's rage.

Sticks and stones may break my bones. But Val's words hurt the worst.

For five days, Adelle had been beaten, bitten, and drained dry. For five days, a crazed Ethan had threatened her with the death of her two sisters if she didn't cooperate. For five long days, she had known she could have lit all those little freaks a blaze, but was too afraid to do it. Now the sting of Valerie's words shook her core. She sighed, brushed some of her dirty curls from her face, and looked down to her feet. Her now bare feet. Ethan had taken her shoes.

That blood sucking little shit.

Adelle pressed a hand against her wounded neck and shut her eyes tight, teeth grinding hard. Her hands shook, her throating closing as her calm crumbled. Raw emotion welled up inside, threatening to consume her. With a dry gulp of air, she shoved it all back down into her gut. Dammit, she was not going to cry. She couldn't cry, especially with her sister here. They both would be crushed in the rubble. Adelle would hang on to that last shred of control she had left if it killed her.

Just keep calm, her mind whispered. *Just keep calm.*

The mattress dipped beside her, and she felt Valerie put a warm hand on her shoulder. “Dell, we already lost Mom. I’m not losing you too.” Her voice was kinder now. “Please.”

Adelle shuddered and bit her trembling lower lip. Mentioning Mom didn’t help Adelle with her struggle for composure. Four years, and the hurt never went away. Only held at bay when Adelle could keep her mind off of it.

If only I had been there...

With a sharp shake of her head, she whipped the memories from her mind.

“Is Phoebe all right?” Adelle asked, her voice a dry husk.

“She’s fine,” Valerie said. “She doesn’t even know there was trouble.”

“She never knows when there’s trouble. She doesn’t even know what we are. What she is. What we do.”

Valerie sighed. “Is this the time to bring this up again?”

“Yes. It’s keeping me from going completely bonkers right now.” Adelle took a deep breath, to strengthen her walls, and then asked, “What did you tell her this time?”

“When you vanished, I told her that you had to go to a conference for work.”

Adelle turned to Valerie, eyebrows raised. “I’m a receptionist.”

“Yeah... A receptionist... Conference.” Valerie shrugged when Adelle stared at her. “Oh come on, it's not like she’ll really know any better.”

Adelle snorted a little laugh then lowered her head to look at her dirty bare feet. The levity was fleeting and soon she felt her facade cracking again. “Can we get the hell out of here? Please?”

Valerie stood, slung her sister’s arm over her shoulders, and dragged her to her feet. Adelle felt her knees buckle as she rose. The room swirled, her head filling with air. Only Valerie’s strong arm kept her from completely keeling over. Swallowing hard, Adelle forced herself to walk out of the room and down the stairs of the dilapidated house.

"It would be easier if I just carried you," Valerie said.

"Not a chance in Hell, Val."

Adelle heard her sister chuckle.

At a steady pace, they reached the front porch, the skies inky and clear over San Diego. Adelle had lost track of time after her first day in captivity, having blacked out before dawn. It was the dark hours of the morning when Valerie helped her outside. Adelle's feet felt like lead and each step was like trudging through thick mud.

As they stumbled down the porch, Valerie paused. Slowly, she lifted her head, one of her dark eyebrows arched. Her hackles rose as she listened to the still air.

"What?" Adelle asked, hanging from her shoulders.

No sooner did she speak when something slammed into Adelle's chest. The blow forced the breath out of her lungs and she fell backward. A whoosh of air, the wet sound of metal hitting flesh, and the head of one of the vampires hit the pavement before she did. Adelle landed on her side with an "Oof", now eye to eye with the blood sucker's severed head. He looked shocked; red eyes wide in horror, mouth slightly open for a scream that never came. That one was Andy. Andy was a dick, if she recalled correctly. He would giggle like a mad man while he poked her in the side with a sharp stick. A dull thud followed, announcing that Andy's body had hit the ground too. She raised her eyes to see Valerie standing over her, sword raised. The blade glittered with blood turned deep black in the moonlight.

"At least I got one of those little fucks," Valerie snorted.

She wiped the sword clean on her jeans and slid the blade into the sheath strapped to her back. The leather swallowed the blade as it transformed into a plain, brown shoulder bag. Valerie reached down, grabbed Adelle by the arm, and hauled her back to her feet.

"He get you bad?" she asked.

"Just pushed me down," Adelle wheezed, leaning on the Valerie for support.

They both looked down at the twitching body, knowing it would turn to ash by sunrise. Adelle scowled, and then kicked the body in the gut for good measure.

Valerie snorted. "I got to hand it to you Dell. You're tougher than you look."

Adelle smiled, her dry lips cracking. "Part of the charm of being in the Constance family."

The drive back home was fast. Get Valerie behind any wheel and she turned into Mario Andretti. Get her into her beautiful 1977 Pontiac Firebird -which she nicknamed Freya- and she turned into Mario Andretti being chased by hungry tigers. Adelle was poured into the front seat and Valerie was flooring it all the way home to Old Town, San Diego. The swift movements of the car tied Adelle's stomach into knots. They probably broke every traffic law in the state, but Adelle was just too tired to scold her sister, even if Freya's speed wanted to make her barf. The passing headlights would shine into Adelle's eyes, shaking her out of the encroaching velvet blackness of sweet oblivion with a sharp stab to her sockets. Luckily, the passing cars at that time of night were few and far between.

Adelle was just about to doze off when she heard Valerie say, "I'm sending you away, Dell."

Adelle's eyes snapped open. "What do you mean?"

"It's best you go out of town, lay low until this Ethan business simmers down."

Adelle struggled to sit up, anger throbbing in her temples. "I'm not running away, Val. I'm not hiding," she said.

"You know Ethan threatened to take Phoebe, right?" Valerie's voice turned cold. "He sent notes saying that if I came after you, he'd take her too. It was stupid of him, yes. He is a wimp at best, yes. But I don't take any threats lightly." Her knuckles whitened as they clutched the steering wheel. "If this was just your fight I'd say stay and fight. But now it involves her. She doesn't even know about all this supernatural bullshit. She thinks you're at a receptionist conference, and I'm a grave yard shift rent-a-cop, for God's sake."

"We could just tell her," Adelle said.

"Not until her powers start showing. She wouldn't understand the business."

"What's there to understand? We hunt down the Wyrd rogues and spank them. That's about it."

Valerie shook her head. "That's what Cybil did with us. It's what we're going to do with her."

Adelle let out a frustrated groan as the same old argument resurfaced. "You just want me to tell her."

"That's beside the point," Valerie said.

Adelle croaked out a mirthless chuckle. "Whatever, Val."

"Whatever, nothing, Adelle! You're not dragging Phoebe into all this crap before her time just because you have issues being a siren!"

She pursed her lips, her angry gaze fixed on the road. Adelle felt the car accelerate. She was pretty sure Valerie just ran a stop sign and swerved around a cat. It made her stomach lurch.

After she swallowed down her rage, Valerie muttered, "You can head up to Washington and stay with Wendy."

Adelle shuddered at the thought. Wendy the mind mage, otherwise called Wendy the mind fucker. The most convincing argument she could form was a whiney sounding, “Val, really?”

“She may not be the most reliable cousin we have, but she’s the furthest away,” Valerie said. “I’m giving you two choices. Stay here and use your powers or go up to Washington. There are no other options for you now.”

Adelle went silent again. She hated ultimatums. She especially hated Valerie’s ultimatums because Valerie always followed through with them. She pressed her forehead against Freya’s door window, the glass cool against her aching skin. Too tired to answer, Adelle wasn’t going to justify that ultimatum in the car.

After a long droning silence, Adelle whispered, “I’m scared.”

“Of what?” Valerie asked.

“Of myself. Of what I can do.”

Valerie pursed her lips. “Well you better get over that shit, quick.”

Adelle said no more, her eyes cracked open to watch the dark houses zip by rhythmically. Valerie’s sigh echoed in her ears. “Think on it a bit, or I will make the decision for you.”

The Constance house was tucked away in Old Town, not far from the historical tourist area. It was large but it felt cozy despite its size. An elegant home painted in sage green with white gingerbread trim, nestled behind a lofty peppercorn tree. It was three stories of Victorian elegance, with a wraparound porch that looked out onto the quiet neighborhood. The large grassy front yard was unkempt due to the sisters never having time to mow the lawn, much to their neighbor’s chagrin. It was their home, their shelter, and a damn noisy structure to sneak into.

The porch steps creaked, the door squeaked, and every little noise amplified tenfold in the dead of night. That’s what one got with high ceilings. The two sisters crept into the house as silently as it would allow them, wincing at every noise their tiptoeing made. Adelle hung from Valerie's shoulders, her hand pressed against her stinging neck as her feet dragged across the floor.

"Be quiet," Valerie whispered. "Phoebe is a light sleeper."

"I was being quiet. Why are you telling me this?" Adelle whispered back.

Because..." Valerie paused then scowled. "Don't question me. Come on, we'll get you to bed and wash you up."

They were almost to Adelle's bedroom when the living room light clicked on.

"Sheesh Val," The squeaky voice of their baby sister, Phoebe called.

She walked into the living room, clad in her fuzzy Phineas and Ferb pajamas, looking blurry eyed. The twenty five year old ruffled her short blonde hair and turned her mouth up into a pout.

"It's three in the morning. Are you bringing another guy home?" Her voice faltered as she took a good look at Adelle's bloody, battered state and the red stains all over Valerie's jeans. Valerie and Adelle stared back, frozen in mid step. The three gawked at each other for a long while before Phoebe screamed, "Oh my God! What happened to you, Dell?!"

"Oh, hey Pheebs," Adelle said, trying to sound casual. "Are those new pajamas?" The hairs on Phoebe's arms were raised and tears welled up in her blue eyes. A lump formed in Adelle's throat and she swallowed hard, cursing under her breath.

"Are you bleeding?" Phoebe said. "Oh my God! Did you get attacked by a cougar?!"

"Yeah. About that," Adelle said.

Valerie hoisted Adelle up straighter. The sudden jerk sent a sharp pain circling up her spine. When Adelle let out a yelp, the windows shook with a violent fury. She snapped her teeth shut.

Phoebe's eyes widen to the size of dinner plates as the hanging lamp in the living room swung back and forth over head.

"Ah well, Pheebs," Valerie interrupted, "You know those receptionist conferences? Totally cut throat."

"Ohhh cut throat, yeah!" Adelle roared in pain. The walls of the living room rattled. "Really got to get to bed, Pheebs!"

Phoebe glanced around the shaking room slack jawed then back at her older sisters. "I... I don't understand. Was that an earthquake?"

Valerie spun towards Adelle's room. "Go to bed. I'll explain in the morning." She pulled Adelle along, her bare feet dragging feebly along the hardwood floor and repeated, "Go to bed!"

"Okay... Good night?" Phoebe said before the door was slammed on her. Adelle suspected Phoebe was catching on. It would only be a matter of time before she would confront them both on their secrets.

Valerie rolled Adelle onto her bed. The soft clean smell of fresh sheets enveloped her and she buried her face into her downy pillow, inhaling deeply. Safe at last. Valerie rushed out the door to the bathroom to wet a towel, and snag the first aid kit. She dashed past Phoebe who was still standing dumbly in the middle of the room.

"Go to bed!" Valerie snapped as Phoebe just gawked at her. She kicked the door closed with her foot and sat herself beside Adelle's bed.

"God, I need a shower," Adelle groaned.

"You can't even stand on your own. No shower," Valerie said, pulling Adelle's jeans off and tossing them to the side. She propped Adelle up with steady, careful hands, yanking off her blood encrusted blouse. Every grimy muscle in Adelle's body screeched as she was undressed.

"Can you toss me in the bathtub then?" Adelle said. "I'll just sit there."

"You're going to have to settle for a wipe down until tomorrow, Freakzoid," Valerie said. "You should be able to stand by then." The warm, damp cloth that Valerie swiped across her skin soothed Adelle's aching body. "You may knock your Wyrd blood, Delly, but you'll be thanking it when you heal up fast."

"Yeah, yeah," Adelle moaned as Valerie lowered her back onto the bed. Her sister had a point, damn her. At least one good thing came with her siren's blood.

Soon, Adelle was cleaned and bandaged. Not as great as a shower would have been, but beggars can't be choosers. Adelle was just grateful the stinging from the bites and her raw wrists were easing down. She shut her eyes.

"I think I now hate vampires," she groaned.

"Don't let Reina hear you say that. She'll slap you silly," Valerie said, sitting down on the bed beside her.

The warm towel ran across her forehead, mopping up the last of the crusted dried blood from her hairline. Nothing felt better than that towel, save the soft mattress beneath her. Adelle sighed in appeasement.

"All right then, I hate shit sucking junky vampires. Vampires like Reina are still cool," she said.

"How many were there?" Valerie asked.

"Five. Well, four now."

"Ethan's pals?"

"That's my guess. Either that or they paid him for a hit off me."

Valerie's fingers tighten around the towel as she kept wiping Adelle's face and neck clean. "I swear, Dell. If I find that little asshole, I will pop his head right off."

"Not if I get to him first." Adelle opened her tired eyes and smiled. Her sister's dark expression softened.

"Oh my. Suddenly so fierce." Valerie chuckled.

"I don't like being taken off guard. I trusted him. I had him meet family for God's sake." Adelle sunk her teeth into her lower lip as rage started bubbling again. The voice of Cybil echoed in her head.

Just keep calm, Adelle. Keep calm.

Valerie rose to her feet and tossed the towel into the wicker hamper. "Get some rest. Tomorrow we'll get some food in you. I left a glass of water on your nightstand in case-"

"I'll go," Adelle said. "I'll go stay with Wendy."

Valerie blinked in surprise. "Really?"

"Yeah."

"You're okay with it?"

"No, actually I'm not. I don't like Wendy, and I like running away even less." Adelle let out a long breath as the anger burned away from her face. "But you're right. We can't let Phoebe get hurt, and I can't use my powers."

"You mean you won't use your powers."

Adelle winced at Valerie's truth. "Either way, it's safer for everyone."

Valerie looked down at Adelle sprawled out on her bed, pale and weak. Her sister's gaze was full of pity, lips pulled into a grimace. Adelle hated when she looked at her like that.

"It probably won't be long. I'll book you a flight and give Wendy a call tomorrow," Valerie said.

"Ten dollars says she tries to pawn me off on someone after a week," Adelle said.

Valerie snorted. "I give it two."

"You're on."

Valerie reached down and pulled the blankets over her. "Get some sleep. I'll stand watch just in case."

"Working on it." Adelle clumsily reached over to her nightstand and clicked off her light. Her weak voice whispered, "Val?" Valerie stopped in the doorway, her tall shadow silhouetted in the moonlight, waiting for Adelle to finish. "I love you, Val," Adelle said.

She could sense Valerie's smile. "Love you too, Freakzoid."

Valerie's footsteps faded out and Adelle felt herself begin to slip into sleep. The first true sleep she'd had in five days. Soon, she would be on a plane soon heading to Washington State. She'd need all the rest she could get.

Chapter 2

She has a lot of balls, making me wait for her. Like I'm a goddamned lap dog.

Despite the rumblings and grumblings in Jack's mind, it was a good day to sit around with a black coffee and brood. But that was what Jack did best on the weekends ever since Wendy had dumped him. Considering he was one of the older, crankier dragons living in the U.S., Jack felt he had earned a right to brood out of seniority. Dragons never took rejection gracefully. He may or may not have set a few fires in the forest outside of town after getting the boot a few months back. It was just to blow off some steam. Things were calmer and the rage was now just an angry smolder. But if he was going to meet with his ex today, coffee was definitely in order.

Whiskey would be in order later.

It was a typical autumn day in Washington; grey, blustery, and cold. Orange and red leaves dappled the trees and occasionally a nice icy wind would whisk through the streets of town adding an extra chill. Jack didn't mind the cold. In fact, he welcomed the colder seasons. He was hot blooded enough. Summer months were a pain in the ass when you were more or less a walking furnace.

When he strode into *What a Grind*, a small mom and pop coffee shop in his little town of Whitmore, a few people peered up from their newspapers and conversations to watch the large man seat himself. He was used to it.

Clocking in over six feet tall and over two-hundred and fifty pounds of muscle as a man, Jack wasn't a delicate creature in either form. Add in the black fingernails and his strange amber colored eyes, he was someone you wanted to look at in case you needed to give his description to the police later. Luckily, Whitmore was a small town where a good chunk of the population was of the Wyrd. Most folks in town were familiar with his intimidating presence and others knew he was a dragon in human guise.

Whitmore was tucked up north in the Cascades, earning its income as a ski resort town to the tourists in the winter and a party town to the college kids in the summer and spring. The vampires, the shape shifters, the landed merfolk, among many other types lived there to get away from city life. Jack had managed to find a niche of his own there. As long as his human form stayed true, things were hunky dory.

After some grumbling and growling, a coffee was ordered and Jack sat in restless silence. There he was, one of the most feared creatures in the Wyrd waiting like a sad little puppy for his ex and resenting every minute of it. He glanced out the window, looking for any sign of the angel faced beauty. Nothing yet.

More waiting.

More grumbling.

It sucked.

Three months ago, Wendy gave him the boot. After meeting her, Jack thought he had finally found his mate. When he decided it was time to stake his dragon's claim and say the bonding words to her, she had unceremoniously dumped him with the "It's not you, it's me" speech.

He was over Wendy. Well, when they were apart he thought he was. But whenever they were thrown together, Jack found her intoxicating all over again. He winced.

Infatuated? That was an understatement. He was absolutely twiterpated. The sweet, willowy blonde had come out of nowhere and hit him like a speeding Buick.

Wendy had called Jack last night, asking him to meet her. It wasn't the first time she had asked for a favor after their break up. This time it sounded urgent. Her sweet feminine voice had pleaded with him over the phone; "Please Jack, you're the only one I trust with this".

Damn his weakness for damsels in distress. He remembered the "good old days" when they were more appealing considered as a snack. Then he started sleeping with his snacks and it was all downhill from there.

Jack sipped his black coffee and leaned back in his chair. His eyes fixed on the window as he waited for Wendy. She was always fashionably late. Soon, a black Ford Mustang pulled up out front and she stepped out of the passenger side. Most of his hot coffee was finished before she came through the door.

The bell over the coffee shop door tinkled and in she walked. The delicate smell of daisies filled the shop upon her arrival. Wendy had an aura that drew every eye in the room to her, causing men and women alike to stammer, stare, and hang on every word. Jack felt his heart stop, and he swallowed hard as she approached. Dammit, she still made him falter when he looked at her. She flipped the length of her sunny blonde hair over her shoulder, her cornflower blue eyes twinkling as she smiled.

Wendy's high cheekbones and willowy frame could easily pass her off as a fae if it weren't for her lack of pointed ears. Despite the heart shaped face that spoke of innocence, Jack knew she had a wild streak. Experience with her in the sack told him so.

Wendy made eye contact with Jack and smiled in her usual gentle manner, giving him a wave of her slender hand. Jack felt himself smile at the ethereal beauty and gestured for her to take a seat across from him.

"Wendy," he said. He tried to stop that grin from coming but couldn't.

"Good to see you Jack," Wendy replied. She sat herself down, smoothing out the skirt of her blue floral print dress with a prim touch of her hands. "You look good."

"I always do," Jack leaned back in his chair.

Wendy let out a giggle which made his mouth twitch upwards again. "Always so confident, yet you still hide that devilish accent of yours."

"I'm not hiding it. I've been around here long enough to have it fade."

It wasn't a total lie. His Scottish still dusted his gravel scratched tones but was hardly noticeable. Sometimes it slipped out when he was tired or distracted. Now a days, Jack only broke out his full brogue for ladies who found accents sexy as hell. It was an instant panty dropper in most cases.

"I'm sorry to call you out of the blue," Wendy said.

"No you're not. But I can't stay mad at you."

He took another sip of his coffee, annoyed that he spoke the truth. He'd get mad, and then see her again and all the anger would fly right out the window. That's what he got for dating a mind mage. They had a way of sneaking into your head and sticking with you.

"I wouldn't have contacted you if I didn't think it was important. I need your help." Wendy bit her lower lip and folded her hands on top of the table. She raised her pensive blue eyes to him like a helpless kitten. It could have been an act. Wendy was damn good at the distressed pouty act. Jack bought it every time. Today was no different.

He waved a hand, pretending he didn't care what she had to say. "It's okay. Just say it."

"Remember my cousin, Adelle?"

"Yeah, I remember. The redhead, right? She dropped in a few years back to help you move."

He vaguely remembered her. It was a while ago. Wendy had a couple of cousins in San Diego that popped in on rare occasions. One was a tall dark haired woman with a loud mouth named Valerie. Her younger sister, Adelle had spent most of her visit telling Valerie to stop checking out Jack's ass. Jack didn't talk much to Adelle. She spent most of the time hiding from him. But it was hard to forget that bright flaming red hair and how he wanted to bury his hands into it. He always did love redheads the most. Still, Wendy's cousin was off limits then and still was if he had any common sense.

"What about her?"

"She's moved to town. She's new, she doesn't know a soul, and..." Wendy trailed off as Jack let out a long groan and crushed his empty paper cup. His cheeks burned with annoyance.

"Oh, Christ. Are you fixing me up?"

"I'm *not* fixing you up."

"Then what?"

"This is different. It's a bit more... dire."

"She direly needs to get laid?" Jack smirked. "Because if that's all-"

"Jack, I'm being serious!"

"So am I." He grinned at her.

Wendy paused and shut her eyes, taking in a long deep breath. She was counting to ten. Jack had seen her do it before. She did it often when they had conversations.

"She needs someone to look out for her," Wendy continued, curbing her temper. "And I figured since you and me-" She wrung her hands, teeth sinking into her lower lip. "Well since we know each other, she's more apt to trust you."

Jack scowled at the pretty creature across from him. "Know each other. That's one way to put it."

"You know what I mean."

Jack looked down to his fist clutching the crushed cup. The half sip of coffee that was left had dribbled through his fingers, scalding his skin. He growled loud enough that the people at the far table gave them a worried glance, then turned to Wendy, jaw clenched. Once he met her sweet cornflower blue gaze, all the anger rushed from him.

Dammit! She always does that!

A sigh escaped his lips and he murmured, "I'll be more than happy to help, Wendy."

"So you'll help my cousin?"

"Sure."

"And you'll protect her?"

"Why not?"

"You promise?"

"I promise."

Wendy smiled, took his large hand into hers, and gave it a squeeze. Electricity tingled up his arm at her touch. The dragon suddenly felt like a sucker.

"So, where is this cousin?" Jack said.

Wendy turned and waved out the window. "Just outside," she said.

Wendy kept her eyes glued to the grey blustery streets and the Mustang parked out front. The door opened and Steven stepped out. The sight of the vampire creased Jack's brow with jealousy. Steven was tall, lean, and extremely handsome. He was blessed with movie star good looks and everything else that made women fantasize at night.

Two hyper good looking people together at last.

Wendy and Steven were the new power couple of Whitmore. At least Steven was a half-blood, giving Jack one advantage over him. Poor Steven. He managed to start a transformation into a vampire, but never finished for some reason. That created a beautiful, solemn man who could stand in the sunlight but lacked all the extra abilities that came with being a full blood vampire. While he was faster and stronger than a human, Steven would never be as powerful as the real deal.

Jack hated him, regardless.

He didn't really know Steven other than he was the one Wendy dumped him for. That was all he needed. Why she went for a half-breed vampire over a manly, full-blooded dragon was baffling. So, Jack just blamed all those T.V shows on cable. Blood sucker mystique was all the rage these days. The only reason Steven was still alive was because Wendy asked Jack nicely not to kill him. But there had been days. Jack was about to say something snarky about his rival when Steven opened the passenger door and let Wendy's cousin out. Most women didn't stop him short of a smart ass remark but this one did.

Jack sat up, spine rigid, nerves alert, as Adelle stepped out to the sidewalk. The woman had luscious curves that could stop a city bus on a dime. Her blue jeans and that fitted paisley shirt sang their praises with every step those black ankle boots took. Waves of fire red curls streaked across the grey streets of Whitmore when a sharp gust of wind took the locks from her shoulders. Her oval shaped face was fair with light freckles dusting her cheeks and her neck was long and slender, accented by long sparkling gold earrings.

Jack bit his lower lip and suppressed a low groan as she passed by the coffee shop window. For a brief moment, Adelle glanced through the plate glass, her gaze locking with his. Those round, green eyes were the stuff of sonnets; green with webs of gold and brown laced in. They reminded him of sea moss and ivy. Adelle lost her footing a moment as their eyes met, cheeks flushing. She caught herself and, just as quickly as it happened, she turned away, breaking their electrified connection.

Looks must have ran in Wendy's family. Wendy was definitely a work of art, an other worldly beauty from somewhere beyond. Adelle lacked that pixie land bullshit and had an earthy, real quality to her. Someone you could touch and taste. A lady you wanted in your bed, not on a pedestal.

When Jack recovered from his first solid glimpse of Adelle, he noticed the angry scowl cutting across her pink lips. All the sudden fantasies about her vanished from his mind as he recalled why he was here meeting her. She didn't look too keen about it either. Jack had a sneaky suspicion he was walking into a trap.

Oh this is going to be a joy, he thought with a groan.

Steven escorted Wendy's cousin into the coffee shop like a gentleman, holding her elbow as they walked in. Adelle didn't seem to like the formal gesture, judging by the heat in her eyes. For a moment, Jack was tempted to swat Steven's hand away from her.

Wendy turned to Jack with a mild smile then stood beside her cousin. "Jack this is my cousin, Adelle. Adelle Constance, this is my friend, Jack."

He gave her a cool nod of his head but Adelle didn't make eye contact. She only folded her arms, pursed her lips, and fixed her big green eyes on the ceiling.

Oh yeah, a real joy.

"Adelle," Wendy warned. "Be nice."

"I am being nice. I didn't say anything bitchy, did I?" Adelle said in a flat, unamused tone. The corners of Jack's mouth turned up into a small grin.

This one has a bit of a bite.

Wendy sighed. "Adelle, don't do this."

Adelle fixed Wendy with a glare that could melt glass. After a tense second, she let out a sigh then offered a hand for Jack to shake. "Hi," she murmured, finally looking at Jack's face.

Her lips parted in surprise when they made eye contact again. It was his eyes. It was always his eyes. The human form could hide most the scales and all of the wings but his amber colored eyes always gave away that he wasn't human. Most people were a bit shocked at first. Surprised or not, Adelle's grip on his hand was firm and fearless.

"Hey there. I'm Jack. Obviously." The dragon arched a brow once again looking her over. Yup, all curves. At least the view will be enjoyable. "So, what? We're going to the movies or something?"

Adelle's mouth screwed up into a little smirk. "Apparently, you're going to be the new jailer this round." Wendy elbowed her so hard that Adelle almost fell over. She caught herself on the chair and shouted, "Hey!" ready to let loose a string of curse words a mile long.

Wendy turned a sharp glare on her, eyes blazing. The tirade was dashed before it began and Adelle winced hard, grabbing her forehead. Jack knew that move all too well. Wendy was having a few words with her cousin inside her head. She had done it to Jack a couple of times before, like when he chewed out that smart ass waiter or told Steven his ass looked big in khakis. Slipping into thoughts was a mind mage's sneaky way to argue in public. It gave the victim one hell of a headache too.

After a moment of silent glaring, Wendy turned away, the serene expression returning to her perfect face. Adelle let out a sigh of relief. She rubbed her temples and said, "Sorry. That was uncalled for."

"I've said worse," Jack said with a little grin. It gave him a sense of smug satisfaction to see someone make Wendy lose her cool. Jack figured he was the only one who could.

A feisty red head. Maybe this wouldn't be too horrible.

Wendy stepped over to Steven, her ever stoic and eternal Ken Doll of the night. She took his arm and looked between the two. "Well, I'll let you both get acquainted. Adelle, I'll bring your bags over to Jack's place later tonight."

That's when Jack jumped to his feet, waving his hands. "Whoa! Wait, wait. Bags? As in she's staying with me?"

Adelle just put her hands up to him in defense. "Dude, I tried to warn you but I got brain frozen."

"Jack," Wendy said in a sweet voice. "You *promised* you'd help. And you're a creature of your word."

"Help as in show her around the town. Not as in get myself a roommate and-" Jack clenched his fists as his face grew hot with anger.

Son of a bitch, she got him.

Promises weren't taken lightly in the Wyrd world. All were bound to their word. You break a vow, and that vow would break you. Jack said the words 'I promise'. Now he was bound to Wendy's favor. The tingle he felt when they grabbed hands had sealed the deal. Wendy must have used her mind juju too, so it wasn't noticeable when he accepted.

"Wendy, you told me you'd never screw around with me like this!" Jack snarled.

"I'm not screwing around with you! You promised!"

Wendy's lips turned up into a pretty pout. When Jack growled, Steven clenched Wendy against him, eyes turning a fierce red. Just when Jack was about to start world war three in a coffee shop, Adelle stepped in.

"Okay, let's all relax here," Adelle said, putting her arms out between them all. "Look, Jack. I need a place to stay. I'm sorry Wendy left that important part out but..." Her eyes lifted towards the ceiling as she tried to find her words. "As melodramatic as this sounds, I'm not safe at Wendy's place. At least not now."

"Not safe?" Jack said "What do you mean?"

"It's a long story."

"Then why should I let you into my house? So whoever is looking for you can break in and kill me?"

Adelle answered him with a smirk and a cock of her hip. "Really? You're worried about that? You?" Her hand gestured to Jack's large physique.

All right, so she had a point. Only an idiot would come looking for trouble with dragons. Her acknowledgement of Jack's strength soothed the bruise Wendy left on his ego.

Adelle's expression softened. "Look, I don't like this anymore than you do but please." She gave him a helpless sigh. With an offer of her empty palms towards him, she pleaded, "I got nothing, man."

Jack set his jaw tight as he looked over Adelle, and her gesture of humility. Her brow was knitted with wounded pride. The sight nudged at his heart just enough to weaken his resolve. She needed an ally and lord knew he could use one against Wendy. That didn't make Wendy's trickery sting any less but maybe he could calm his ire by ganging up on his ex-girlfriend at a later date.

With a nod he sat himself back down, a nasty scowl on his lips. "Well it doesn't matter anyways." He glared at Wendy "I'm *bound* now."

Wendy shuddered at the venom Jack spat with his words. When Steven stepped in front of Wendy to shield her, it only pissed him off more.

No maiming. Not in public.

"Fine. I got a spare room. You can stay with me for now, Adelle," he said.

That didn't make Adelle look any less uneasy. In fact, she seemed to be even more uncomfortable than before. For some reason her uneasiness irritated him far worse.

"Thank you," Wendy said. Jack's anger started to simmer down to a low boil at the sound of her voice. She turned to Adelle. "Be good, please."

Adelle just nodded and sat down as her cousin took Steven's arm and walked out. The bell over the coffee shop door tinkled and there was silence. That's when Jack noticed everyone was staring at them. With a grunt, Jack ignored the audience, folded his arms and stared across the table at Adelle. She in turn, did the same thing.

More awkward silence followed before Jack finally said, "Yeah, this is going to be fun."

Adelle pushed some of her fiery curls from her face and pursed her lips. Her nervous eyes darted around the room.

Even more silence followed.

"You know," Jack continued. "Talking, is always an option to explore." A hint of mirth touched his voice. He could have sworn he saw her crack a smile. That encouraged him.

"So." Adelle's gaze kept moving around as she grasped for a topic. Eventually she found one. "You got dumped by my cousin, huh?"

Jack gaped at her, eyebrows raised. Adelle paled. She covered her mouth with her hands as if trying to shove the words back in.

"Okay, maybe not! I didn't mean…!" She stammered, trying to claw her way out of the social faux pas pit she had fallen head first into. "But you had a fling. You... flung with... umm."

"Yeah. Didn't work out," Jack replied still staring at Adelle, mouth hanging half open.

The redhead bit her lower lip again then groaned, "Aw hell!" and flopped her head down onto the table with a thud.

"You're not good with people, are you?"

"I'm out of my element," her muffled voice said from beneath her arms. "This is going to be an awkward relationship I can tell."

"No kidding." Jack looked down at her, eyebrow cocked half up. "So, who and when was your last date?" Adelle lifted her head and glared at him. That seemed to answer his question. "Ah. I had a feeling."

"Don't rub it in." She sat up, straightening her jean jacket as she tried to recover with grace. "I'm sorry. I didn't mean to say that. I'm just a nervous wreck right now, thanks to my cousin."

"And I'm your current jailer huh?" Jack asked. "What was your last jailer like?"

"I didn't have one." Her cheeks grew pink. "I was just being dramatic. I um, I ran into some trouble down south so my sister, Valerie, thought it best that I come up here and stay with Wendy and out of the spotlight for a bit."

"Down south where and what kind of trouble?"

"San Diego and I don't really want to get into it right now."

"Ah. I'll ask again. What kind-"

"I don't want to go into it right now." Adelle's voice went hard as stone, eyes narrowing.

Startled by the change, Jack didn't press further. At least not yet. He had to admit he was impressed that she was sticking to her guns. Eventually he'd intimidate it out of her but right now, he liked her spirit. If he wasn't so sure she would be a pain in the ass later, he'd find that stubborn streak kind of sexy.

"No one is going to come beat you up if you're indeed worried," she said.

Jack gave her a toothy grin. “I’m never worried about that.”

“Yeah, I figured.” Adelle laughed a bit, the sound melodic and all too brief. “This is all Wendy's idea. She claims I’m too easy to find at her place. Honestly, I think she just doesn’t want me to cramp her sex schedule. I decided it’s best to just comply with her hack plans and keep her out of my head."

Jack watched the skittish creature rub the palms of her hands together as she spoke, her eyes jumping from him, to the wall, to the window, then back to him. With Wendy gone, he had a moment to sit back and appreciate Adelle and her amazing ability to fill out a fitted shirt and jeans. She had a body that Jack was convinced was built for sin. And those eyes... She couldn’t be fully human. No full human looked like that.

"Look. I don't need a babysitter," Adelle said.

"Who said I was a babysitter?" That earned him yet another bitter look. He leaned forward and said in a low voice, "Listen Adelle, I’m bound by word to this and even if I wasn’t, I owe Wendy a few solids.”

“Meaning you’re still carrying a torch for her.”

Jack clenched his jaw, vowed to himself not to eat her, and continued. “It's clear you don't want to be in this mess. Neither do I. So, what say you and I get out of here, keep her happy for a while, and you get some free room and board? Once we make it clear to her that you don't need a guardian, Wendy will release me and we'll both be off the hook."

Adelle narrowed her eyes at him, her lips thinning into a tight suspicious line.

"Come on. We'll go get some pizza," he added.

Adelle sighed. “'I’d rather just go. I’m sure you’re a good guy Jack but this is ridiculous. Sorry about the trouble."

She got to her feet to leave only to find Jack standing in front of her, his body obstructing the way to the door. Jack grinned as

Adelle gawked up the length of him, noting how very large he was compared to her. She swallowed, laughed, and then tried to sidestep him. Jack only widened his stance and planted his booted feet in place, blocking her exit.

"Not that simple, Buttercup," he said. "I let you walk away and my vow is broken. A broken vow is a big no-no for me. Plus, I'll never hear the end of it from Wendy. So we're stuck with each other for a while. I'll drive you to my place; we'll order a pizza then wait for Wendy to drop off your stuff, deal?"

Adelle shifted from one foot to the other, twitching like a cornered cat. "I won't tell her that you left your post."

She was bargaining?

Why do all the damsels feel the need to bargain?

"Right," Jack said. "What are the odds on a mind mage not finding out the truth anyways?"

Adelle opened her mouth to retort then paused. A light of realization ignited behind her eyes and her shoulders slumped. "Touché, sir," she groaned.

"Come on. It's a short walk to my car." Jack put a hand on her shoulder to guide her to the door.

"You don't take no for an answer, do you?" Jack's reply was in the form of a sly grin and nothing more. Adelle took two steps then suddenly dug her heels into the floor. "What If I refused?"

His grin got even wider. "Find out."

"Jeeze, you're a real chest thumping caveman, aren't you?"

"Chest thumper, yes. Man, no. Now can we go?"

"You didn't answer my question."

Jack rubbed his forehead and grunted. "Adelle, there are three places to ride in my car. The front seat, the back seat, and the trunk."

Her green eyes widened. "Duly noted."

"And now we're communicating!" He gestured to the door with a grand sweep of his arm. "Ladies first."

Adelle sighed and started walking. But before she passed, she swung around and wagged a finger in his face, giving the tip of his nose a delicate thump.

"We'll negotiate this later," she said then turned on her heels and walked out, chin raised high. The bell over the door rang furiously. Jack growled under his breath.

"Wendy, you owe me big time," he muttered.

Chapter 3

Adelle sat in the front seat of Jack's cherry red '67 Chevy Impala, silent as the grave. She shifted, the black leather seats squeaking under her backside. The engine purred like a kitten and the ride was hardly bumpy even if it was way too fast for surface streets. Her sister, Valerie, was a terror on the road so Adelle was used to speed. Besides, when driving a red Impala, one had to have the "need to speed". That was probably a natural law somewhere. It wasn't surprising that the dragon drove a vintage muscle car. In fact, it was downright appropriate.

Jack didn't seem to be all that bad of a guy. He had even made her crack a smile earlier. She expected a strutting macho douche that would stop at nothing to grab her ass. Most Wyrd males she met were of that ilk. Jack was only grumpy and stubborn. She couldn't really blame him for the grumpy part, considering the circumstances. Still, Jack seemed to be the type who always expected to get his way. Adelle predicted many an argument, knowing how hard she dug her heels in when pushed.

I might as well suck it up and try to make friends with Mr. Crankypants McGee, she thought.

"So," Adelle's voice lifted over the Impala's mighty engine. "You have a guest room?"

"Nope. You'll have to sleep with me," Jack said, never taking his eyes of the road. "Beware. I spoon."

Adelle's stomach dropped and cold chills dashed across her back. She'd have to make sure her hands remained in her pockets while she slept.

As if sensing her sudden panic, or possibly seeing her eyes bugging out of her head, Jack added, "Yes, I have a guest room. Don't worry; I'm safer than I look. And you haven't told me what you want on your pizza yet."

Her cheeks flushed. *Of course he was kidding. Are you an idiot?*

"Mushrooms," Adelle said.

"Anything else?"

"I'm not picky."

Jack nodded and continued to drive.

Silence reigned again.

Long live the silence.

Adelle was apprehensive about starting another bout of small talk. The first round was an epic failure. Foot in mouth disease ran rampant with Adelle when she was nervous. Chances were she'd say something along the lines of "So, my cousin showed me you were one helluva guy in the sack" which would probably go over as well as the first time she had tried to initiate conversation. Besides, she already knew everything about him. Well, everything Wendy knew at least.

Before dragging Adelle to the coffee shop, Wendy performed one of her "mind dumps" on her. Wendy was always keen on mind dumps. They saved her time. The blonde beauty had put her hands against Adelle's forehead and whoosh; Wendy's memories snatched Adelle's brain like a vice. Every last detail about their relationship, including the things she didn't really want to know, flooded her. Jack was a dragon, he was pretty dang old, he owned his own business which was a gym, he howled like a dog in heat when Wendy would touch the back of his…

Ew, Ew, EEEEEW!

The mind dump also gave sensations and emotions which sent Adelle straight into squicksville. Seeing her cousin doing the bedroom bop? There went those cold chills again. Suddenly, she understood how Phoebe felt whenever Valerie started in on her sexual conquest stories, out loud, in detail, and in public. She'd never scoff at her baby sister again.

Adelle remembered Jack from a few years ago. The memory had hit her as soon as she saw him sitting in the coffee shop. It was hard to forget a guy like him. She and Valerie had come to Washington to help Wendy move into her new apartment. Of course, Wendy's new boyfriend, Jack was helping as well. And Jack just oozed masculinity to distraction.

Strongly built with a rough deep voice like thunder, Jack was not what a lady would call cute or boyish. But cute and boyish didn't make Adelle's stomach somersault. Jack sent her belly right onto the Olympic gymnastics team. He was all man and muscle poured into a tight t-shirt and blue jeans. That butt in that weathered denim?

Yowzah.

His square jaw was dusted over with stubble and a thin scar traced his right cheekbone under his eye. And his eyes were just... Well, no human had eyes that color. They were an amazing combination of gold, yellow, and brown, swirled together in an intoxicating galaxy. Eyes the color of whiskey poured into a crystal glass.

Adelle had avoided him the rest of that moving day. Both to keep her hormones in check and to secretly curse her cousin for snagging such a masculine specimen. Much to her chagrin, Adelle had found herself wondering all day what his shaggy golden brown hair would feel like in between her fingers, how his skin felt, and what his mouth tasted like. Chances were he could break most of Adelle's ex-boyfriends over his knee if he wanted. She found that strangely comforting.

Adelle dated her fair share of pretty boys but it was the big manly guys that turned her crank. Yet, she shied away from their ilk and stuck with the boys. Now, she had ended up right in the lap of a red blooded beefcake.

Oh, awkward.

On occasion, Adelle snuck a glance over at Jack as they drove. She had had a feeling he wasn't human when they first met years ago, but had never had the nerve to ask. Those eyes were a telltale sign that he was indeed from the Wyrd, like herself. There were other things beyond that; such as the black fingernails which were not painted on if you took a good look and a golden red hue that shimmered under his skin when the light hit him just right. Cybil had trained Adelle to detect those things. Tells, if you will. Every full blood had at least one. Jack seemed to have three so far.

Jack must have felt her staring at him. He flicked a glance to her, eyebrow cocked. An electric tingle warmed her belly as she locked eyes with him. Adelle smiled, shrugged her shoulders, and turned her head to look out the windshield.

Oh, so very awkward.

After a short, strained drive, Jack pulled into the parking lot of a gym. It was just a square of a building with a simple sign announcing *Jack's Gym*. Well, he was no marketing genius by any means with a name like that. She looked through the large picture windows that traced the front of the building and found a decent amount of people inside, despite the dull name.

Jack slipped out of the car then walked around the front of the Impala to open her door for her. It was an odd gentlemanly gesture coming from the grumbling hulk. Adelle hesitated then got out and to her feet, brushing some unruly curls from her eyes.

"You live in a gym?" she asked.

"I live upstairs above the gym."

Jack pointed to the tall stairway that stretched up to a small porch and single door. By the looks of it, his living quarters were about the same footprint of the gym which, while simple, was pretty spacious. When Adelle looked back at him, Jack had already started up the stairs, fishing keys out of his jeans' pocket. She had to sprint to keep up with his long stride. The keys jingled and he opened the door stepping aside in that lady's first way that continued to baffle her. She eyed him a moment, jaw set into place. The dragon sensed her discomfort and sighed.

"What?" Jack said. "I was a kid in the age of chivalry. Old habits die hard. Will you get inside already?"

She peered through the doorway of his home. Thresholds were powerful devices. They were designed to make uninvited guests "uncomfortable". On top of that, many warded their thresholds with strong magic for double the safety. Even the Constance house had one, set to only welcome in those they invited. She always regretted inviting Ethan over for dinner before their break up. He never could have snuck into her bedroom if she hadn't. That was just the beginning of the mess she was in.

Adelle held her breath as her toes slid across the doorway. She didn't explode and no magical rabid dogs came to tear her apart. Her breath was released with a smile and she stepped inside. The sound of an amused snort made her look back at Jack standing behind her.

"Most folks know not to mess with my threshold," Jack said, explaining the lack of extra magical wards. He gave her another cocky grin before closing the door. Yup, there was no turning back now.

The home was a rather neat and open floor plan. The walls were painted a warm white and it was sparse in furniture. What furniture Jack had appeared to be old, worn in, and nothing matched. There was a Victorian style table beside a midcentury modern recliner in front of an Ikea bookshelf and so on. Judging by the eclectic look of every piece, he had to be a sucker for garage sales and swap meets. Jack had several bookshelves, all different in style, all overflowing with hard covered books and dog eared paperbacks.

But what intrigued Adelle the most was the colored glass scattered around the house. Jack had quite the collection. Various soda and liquor bottles lined bookshelves. Small abstract sun catchers hung in the windows, spraying bands of colors across the white carpet. There were apothecary jars full of broken bits of shimmering color, as well as chips and shards that sparkled in small bowls on the coffee table.

Dragons were like ferrets but bigger and meaner. They couldn't resist shiny objects and usually got attached to a specific kind. In Jack's case, he had an affinity for all things clear and colorful. Adelle's mouth curled at the idea of big bad Jack searching the sidewalks for bits of broken bottles; carefully cleaning and collecting each piece so he could stare at it for hours.

"What?" Jack's gruff voice cut through her day dream.

Adelle shook herself when she felt a silly smile twisting her lips. "What, what?" she asked.

"You look... amused." His amber eyes narrowed as they bored right into her with an agitated glare.

"You have a nice place." Adelle smiled at him feigning innocence. No, she was not just imagining him being adorable. Not her.

"Yeah," was all Jack replied, suspicion drenching the word. Apparently, he was guarded when it came to his obsession. Adelle said nothing more about his decor. "All right, the guest room is the door on the right. Bathroom's at the end of the hall. Use it all you like. I got my own in my bedroom." Jack flipped the lock on the front door and strode into the kitchen. "Mushrooms, right?"

"Yup," Adelle said as she strolled through the living room, hands tucked behind her back.

She peered up at the musty old books then down to the sparking cluster of broken glass in a plastic candy dish beside the couch. Carefully, she reached down and picked up a chunk of a brown *Budweiser* bottle. It twinkled as she held it up to the light.

"Hey!" Jack snapped.

Adelle dropped the shard back into the bowl with a sharp clink. He was peering out from the kitchen doorway, brows jutting down over his eyes in a hostile V. The phone was still held up to his ear as he glared mental bullets at her.

Encroaching on dragon territory, Dell! Stand down, stand down!

A wiggle of her fingers at him proved they were completely empty. "Mushrooms," Adelle said, giving him an apprehensive thumb up.

Jack retreated, creeping back into the kitchen, his gaze on her the whole way. As soon as he was out of sight, Adelle flopped herself onto the couch and sighed, rubbing her temples.

All right, so maybe he isn't the teddy bear I hoped he'd be.

After a couple minutes, Jack returned from the kitchen. He peeled off his leather jacket and hung it on a hook by the front door. That olive green t-shirt was practically painted on him, defining every chiseled muscle in his chest and shoulders. On his left forearm was a tattoo of scales that ran from his wrist all the way to his elbow. Each crimson scale was shaded to faultless accuracy, gold tinging the round edges, shimmering when the light touched his skin. It was perfect in every detail. Too perfect, actually. Adelle wondered if it was really a tattoo or actual scales that he couldn't completely transform into flesh.

Tell number four.

He must be a magnificent creature in true form. Not that he wasn't one in his human disguise. Was Adelle staring? Yes, yes she was.

"Should be about forty-five minutes," Jack said. The hulking dragon sat across from her in a worn leather armchair and studied her yet again, stretching his long legs out. "I'm probably going out on a limb here, but I'm going to assume you're not normal."

Normal. The word slapped Adelle in the face. *Nice way to put it, jackass.* She pretended it didn't hurt. "No one is normal, Jack."

"Ah. Cute. By normal I mean not human."

That one hurt even more. She tried not to wince and said, "You're assuming correctly."

"You're a mage like Wendy, huh?"

"Mage?" *I only wish I was that normal.* She sighed. "No. I'm a genuine Wyrd article. Well, I'm half the genuine article at least."

"And you're a half of what? Fairy? Nymph? Perhaps some sort of mer... thing?" Jack leaned back in his chair, his black fingernails dragging across the stubble on his chin as a devilish smile spread across his mouth.

His amber eyes raked up the length of her, taking her all in. She could feel the strength of his gaze caress every inch of her. Adelle squirmed in her seat. Her pale cheeks flushed pink as he continued to stare. He was trying to intimidate her. It was working.

Intimidation was nothing new to Adelle. Working in the family business meant she was used to posturizing. But just because she had seen it before didn't mean Jack wasn't damn good at it. He wanted her to spill her guts, tell him all her dirty details with just a look. But Adelle didn't like talking about what she was. She hated the fact that she wasn't just a plain ol' human. And she'd be damned if she let this joker squeeze it out of her.

All three of the Constance girls were half-blooded. But while Valerie and Phoebe had Wyrd *being* blood, Adelle had the blood of a beast. Adelle was a siren.

Since she was a child, Adelle had wanted to be a singer. She practiced her vocals constantly, honing her musical talent into something grand. Her beautiful voice brought music teachers to their knees. Choir teachers grappled for her attention. She was one scholarship away from Juilliard. But her siren's blood was too powerful to be contained. On her eighteenth birthday, she sang in the church glee club and almost brought down the house, literally, on the entire congregation during her solo.

That was the birthday Adelle manifested.

No more Juilliard. No more singing. After that it was all cross bows, spell slinging, and discovering that she had some rather unruly powers. Adelle continued to study music at a lesser college to get her fix by focusing on piano. But knowing she could never sing again crushed her.

The older she got, the more powerful she grew. Soon, it was more than just her singing that was a problem. Any cry or shout would cause mass destruction if loud enough. More than once she had set a car or building a blaze just by shouting "Fuck!"

Adelle had had to become the Zen master of her feelings to keep her family safe. But there were days when she'd spiral all out control. Cybil seemed to be the only one who could calm her when the emotions grew wild. But Cybil was gone now.

"You're grinding your teeth," Jack told her.

Adelle looked up, realizing she had completely zone out. "I'm what?" she said.

"Grinding your teeth. I can hear you across the room."

Adelle opened her mouth and felt the tight joints in her jaw pop. Yup, she was definitely grinding her teeth. "Sorry."

Jack leaned back in his chair with a shrug. He steepled his fingers together under his chin and said, "Apparently I hit a sore spot so, moving on."

Adelle ran with that cue, drawing the attentions off of her. "You're a dragon?" she asked

"Looks like Wendy briefed you on me."

Oh in ways you wouldn't want to know, Jack.

"Yeah," she said. "She gave me the basic info. I kind of feel horrible for Wendy doing this to you."

"She's done worse to me, I assure you."

I wouldn't doubt that.

"Still, I'll stay out of your way. You won't even know I'm here."

Once again, Jack looked her up and down, eyes a burning liquid gold as he raked her in. Then he waved a cavalier hand in the air. "Meh, I won't notice you either way."

Being dismissed made Adelle bristle. Was he going to run hot and cold all the time? She scowled.

"So about this trouble you're in," Jack said.

And we're back to being a nosey jerk.

Adelle stiffened her spine. "I told you, I rather not go into it," she said, voice clipped.

Jack leaned forward in his chair. His shoulders puffed up as he straightened, pulling himself into a larger bearing than before. Adelle felt dwarfed in his shadow. Then he grinned again, a sinister glint in his eye.

"It makes it easier on me if you just put it all out on the table, Buttercup."

Adelle straightened her own posture, looked him right in the eye, and repeated, "I'd rather not go into it." She narrowed her eyes at him; fingers digging into the couch cushions.

Bring it on, Puff.

The two stared at each other, locked in an intense battle of wills. Jack's brow lowered, mouth forming into a grim line. He was waiting for her to wilt under his gaze. Jack was downright scary when docile. If he tried, he probably could make a grown man wet his shorts and everyone else kowtow to whatever he wanted. Dammit, she was not going to let him win. She was not going to be his doormat. Adelle raised her chin, wrinkling her nose at his glare. The lengthy staring contest was interrupted by the doorbell ringing. Both wavered a moment at the sound.

"Pizza's here." Adelle refused to even blink.

"No shit, the pizza's here," Jack replied, still staring hard.

The doorbell rang again. Jack twitched. The more irritated he grew with the doorbell chimes the more she smiled.

"It's your house, man. I can't answer that," she told him.

Two doorbell rings and a knock later, Jack groaned and got to his feet, stomping to the door.

Victory!

Adelle restrained herself from fist pumping. After a curt exchange of money and words with the pizza boy, Jack returned, tossing the box unceremoniously onto the coffee table in front of her.

"You don't screw around, do you?"

"I do not screw around."

Chapter 4

Jack knew he was in for trouble. Well, if not trouble then at least handfuls of annoyance every day for an indefinite time. That female stared him down. Him! A dragon, started down by a girl. He used to eat girls when he was a child. Essentially, he was stared down by a hamburger.

Well no, not really. He never ate a human but still, he'd be tempted to!

First Adelle touched his glass, and then she challenged him in his own home. After that brief humiliation, Jack turned the T.V. on so he wouldn't have to continue any more conversations with the infuriating redhead. He consumed most of the pizza out of spite, leaving her one piece, and went to bed.

A couple days had passed since their staring match. The only time he saw Adelle was in the morning when he'd make coffee. The rich smell of dark roasted beans would waft through the house and lure her out of the guest room. It was like watching those Looney Tunes cartoons where Porky Pig would float on the smell of a freshly baked pie. Other than that, Jack avoided her, busying himself down in the gym. That left Adelle to her own devices in his house, much to his ire. He just knew she spent the day getting fingerprints all over his glass collection. She had no idea how much time went into cleaning all those bottles and shards.

All right, so she did clean up the house. When Jack got home from work, the dishes would be washed and put away and the carpet vacuumed. But as soon as he'd give her credit for cleaning, he'd remember she dug through his belongings to find the dish soap and the vacuum. That would send him spiraling, and he'd go to bed fuming and tense.

Adelle seemed to take it in stride, ignoring his moods and retreating to the guest room when he'd start griping. That made her even more infuriating, her damn calmness. Maybe he wouldn't feel so hostile if she threw a dish at him or something.

It was another morning that Jack woke up with a crick in his neck and a tension headache. Grumbling and growling, he pulled himself out of bed to drag his tired backside to the kitchen, neck burning and cranium throbbing with a rhythmic *Boom, Boom, Boom* every step of the way. A flick of his wrist and he turned on the coffee machine, waiting for the dark roasted witch's brew to lure Adelle from her sleep. The guest room door remained closed.

The creature from the bitch lagoon must have had a late night.

"Hey! Coffee's coming up!" Jack shouted a little louder than he needed.

Yelling made the icepick in his brain twist more. But there was an off chance Adelle may still be sleeping and well, whoops! He was just a little too loud. Jack pulled two mugs out of the cabinet, while rubbing his aching forehead.

There was no response.

"Yo! Sleeping beauty!"

Still nothing.

With a sigh, Jack stomped across the carpet toward the guest room, wearing only his boxer shorts. He stopped, looking his scantily clad self over. Modesty tugged at him. After all, he had had the decency to put on some pants when greeting her in the morning. He snorted. If seeing him in his underwear was too much for her delicate sensibilities, too bad. He shook it off and continued on his way.

Jack peeked into her room. For a fleeting moment he felt like a creepy old man. What if she was getting dressed? Well, seeing her nude wasn't necessarily a bad thing in his books. Hell, it was something he wanted to see a few days ago so why not now? Still, he wasn't sure about her reaction to him hovering in her doorway half naked. She'd probably scream. Scream and throw something. At least he'd finally get a reaction out of her. The thought made his headache go from dull roar to full jet engine squeal. He pushed open the guest room door the rest of the way.

The bed was made, and her suitcase was sitting neatly on a dresser, zipped up but there was no sign of Adelle, naked or otherwise. Jack furrowed his brow, stepping into the room to give it a good look over. Nothing. Just as he turned to leave, Jack noticed the bathroom door was closed. A couple quick steps and he was knocking there.

"Hey, Buttercup," he said. "Coffee."

No response.

He pushed the bathroom door open to find that empty as well. His teeth gnashed with a whistling creak. Now, he was getting concerned.

There wasn't any other place for Adelle to go other than his bedroom. Jack was pretty positive he'd remember if she came in there. She could have gone down to the gym, but Jack hadn't gone downstairs to open up yet. Besides, Adelle didn't look like the type to enjoy early morning workouts. More like the type who would lounge in bed with a good book.

Had Adelle's trouble snuck into his house and spirited her away? Doubtful. He would have known if someone had invaded his domain. It was hard to get a drop on a dragon. Jack sighed. His temples pulsed in agony and the crick in his neck developed into a sharp stab. For a moment, he considered just leaving it be. If she had run off and gotten into trouble, so what? He hardly knew her. Let the damn girl rot and be done with it. The hand he shook with Wendy tingled with pins and needles as a sudden reminder of his vow. Unfortunately, it was his problem now. If he blew this off, a wave of bad karma the size of the Space Needle would come crashing down on him, probably kill him, or at least maim him.

"Well, fuck!" he roared.

Jack stormed across the room, snagged his keys off their hook, and headed out the front door, boxer clad and barefoot.

Five blocks and several bewildered looks later, he spotted Adelle walking up the street, sipping from a paper coffee cup and reading a book that was clenched in her free hand. She was probably drinking a latte or one of those stupid fancy drinks that women like. Jack clenched his fists and charged up to her. By the time he reached her, his face was flaming scarlet with rage.

"Where the hell did you go?!" he bellowed.

Activity on the street came to a screeching stop. A man on his bike hit a bush and flipped over. Dogs began to howl. Somewhere, a baby cried. Adelle slowly raised her eyes from her book. They traveled up the length of him then back down and she went slack jawed as soon as they rested on his crotch. That didn't stop him from snatching the book from her hand.

"You just took off, huh?" Jack said. "After telling me you're in danger, you just take off without a friggin' note?"

Adelle continued to gape at him. "You're...You're not wearing any pants," she said.

"That's not important!"

"It might be to everyone staring down the open fly of your boxers."

Jack glanced to the side to see a mortified mother covering the eyes of her ten year old daughter. "I'll be embarrassed later!"

"Look, I was just getting a coffee and taking a morning walk. It's all right." Adelle used that infuriating calm voice. It was like nails on a blackboard and made him bristle.

"No actually, it's not all right. You damn well know I'm bound by my word and you just wander off after I vow my protection-"

Adelle swept the air with her hand, cutting his words off. "Wait. Protection? Since when? I just needed a place to stay."

"I made a vow!"

"To give me a room."

"And to protect you!"

Adelle cocked a shapely hip, planting her knuckles on it and she glared. "Since when?"

"Wendy said you needed someone to watch out for you," Jack growled. "She made me vow to protect you. Funny enough, I take that pretty damn seriously, Buttercup!"

"Oh, for God's sake." Adelle threw up her free hand again, the other clutching her drink in a death grip. Her usual calm tone started to crack. "I'm sorry I didn't leave a note, okay? But I do not need a bodyguard. Am I going to have to ask permission to use the bathroom too, because that is not going to fly. And *you have no pants on!*"

The loud words jabbed into Jack's ears and right up into his aching brain. Their fight and his half naked visage were achieving quite a crowd of gawkers, which only added to the torment. Enough was enough. He grabbed her wrist and tugged.

"We're going home," he said.

"Wait a minute!" Adelle tried to pull her arm away but Jack held her tight and fast.

"We're going home!" His voice was hard as he tugged her a couple steps towards him.

Adelle locked her knees and pulled back on his grip. "The hell we are!" Her calm demeanor cracked further with her snarl, the angry tremble in her voice growing with every breath.

Angry and nearly nude with a throbbing headache does not a happy dragon make. Jack snatched Adelle by the waist, and she let out a surprised squeak through clenched lips. Her coffee cup flew into the gutter as he spun around, exploding onto the pavement in a splash of light brown liquid. He slung her over his shoulder like a sack of flour and trudged back up the street.

"What do you think you're doing!?" she said.

"My friggin' duty," he grumbled and hauled her off down the street.

It wasn't until Jack kicked his front door open that he felt satisfied with Adelle's safety. Of course, as soon he dumped her onto the couch, she started sniping again, making him wish he could tear his own head off so he could stop listening.

"What the hell was that all about?" Adelle snapped.

No appreciation!

Jack spun around on her, thrusting a finger into her face, centimeters from her nose. "I am not in the mood!"

He slammed his fist down on the arm rest. The couch shuddered from his blow and Jack regretted that move the minute Adelle cringed. Adelle stared at him wide eyed then took a deep inhalation through her nose. Seeing her fear, he backed away.

Jack paced the carpet and rubbed his temples. "It was about you being stupid," he said.

"I was just getting a coffee," Adelle said, her voice low and strained through her teeth.

"You were going out unescorted after giving me the impression that you were in danger."

"So you ran out to the streets in your underwear to save me from my latte?"

"A latte! I knew it!"

Adelle stared at him in confusion. "What?"

Jack just waved her question off with a wild arm gesture. "What would you do out there if you bumped into a werewolf? Its mating season and those guys are bastards during mating season!"

"Jack," Adelle said. "I know how to defend myself against randy werewolves."

"Well, you could have given me that little tidbit of info last night!" Jack bellowed.

"Could you please not talk to me like I'm stupid?"

"Well smart people don't stumble into danger!"

"I'm sorry, okay!" Adelle's cheeks burned pink. Her voice grew loud and shrill as she shouted, "Don't be such a jackass!"

Jack's head pulsed with agony from her shout, feeling like it was about to burst. He turned to her and roared, "Then don't be an idiot!"

Adelle's hand clutched her ears, face red, teeth clenched. Jack took a nervous step back when her eyes flashed a blazing white. "I am not an idiot! So stop yelling at me!"

Her scream reverberated off the walls, shaking the room. With an explosive crash, three bottles on Jack's bookshelf shattered in a blaze of shimmering shards and steam. Both jumped at the sound and watched as the wreckage crumbled to the floor. Jack turned his slow gaze to Adelle, eyebrow arched. She sat on the couch, her hands clutched over her ears, eyes wide, and mouth hanging open.

Jack's jaw was starting to hurt after all that clenching. He was going to need a crowbar to undo the damage. He glanced back to the pile of broken glass, now nothing but tiny, sparkling slivers of color and powder. There wasn't even anything left to glue back together. They just disintegrated. When his gaze returned to Adelle, she was in full panic mode, huddled in corner of the couch, hands still pressed against her ears. Her eyes were big as dinner plates.

Jack wanted to be angry. He wanted to rage and roar and set furniture on fire. Then he wanted a beer. Instead, he closed his eyes and counted. By the time he reached ten, the rage had mostly subsided and he sat himself down across from her.

"Did you do that?" he asked, gesturing to the shiny mess on his carpet.

She nodded and replied with a quivery, "Yup."

Another nod and Jack fell quiet. His large hand rubbed the back of his aching, stiff neck as he contemplated this sudden turn of events. Adelle shattered glass when she screamed. There were only two creatures that could do that; sirens and banshees. Adelle had a pulse so that left only one option.

"So," Jack said. "That means you're a-"

"Yup." Adelle cut him off as if not wanting to hear the word siren. Then she added "Half," as if that would make the word hurt less.

He nodded. *Why didn't you warn me?!* his brain screamed but instead he said, "You don't see those around much these days."

"Nope," Adelle said.

Knowing he'd only get one word answers from her, Jack didn't interrogate further. But it did put some of her puzzle pieces together. Sirens were elusive beasts. They rarely mated outside their species. Even then, sirens couldn't bear children on a regular basis. Adelle was unique.

Half-bloods were not just rare but also powerful. One could take down a city block with a single scream if provoked. There were a lot of people out there who would like to get their hands on someone like Adelle and harness that power. So, that was the trouble. No wonder she was so tight lipped about her bloodline. It also explained why his headache was worse after she yelled at him. The discovery made him bury his face in his hands.

"I'm sorry," Adelle said, breaking the awkward silence. "I should have left a note."

"Meh," Jack muttered, rubbing the back of his neck.

"And you're right. I am in trouble. I should take it more seriously," Adelle said.

"Meh," he repeated.

"Would it help if I told you why I'm in trouble?"

Jack peered up at her. "A bit, yeah."

Adelle let out a sigh. She hugged her knees to her chest then took a deep breath and spilled out the truth. "All right then. I dated this vampire named Ethan and-"

"Oh God, a vampire? "Jack groaned. "What is it about women and vampires?"

Adelle frowned at him. "Can I continue or are you going to question my taste in men further?"

The flat look of unamused irritation she wore made Jack purse his lips. He gestured to her to continue.

"So, I dated Ethan," she said. "And he was all right for a while. It wasn't love or anything. I guess I was lonely and he was lonely. He was changed against his will and not happy about it. He didn't feed off me until he found out that I was a... you know."

"A siren," Jack finished for her.

Adelle made a sour face. "Yeah, one of those. He heard that vampires could get high off their blood. So, he asked me once out of curiosity. I said yes." Jack opened his mouth but Adelle held up a hand. "This was *before* he told me about the whole getting high part. After that, he started feeding off me all the time. I broke it off with him when it became too much. Unfortunately, he was a junkie by then." She looked up to the ceiling again, her cheeks flushed pink. "Instead of taking our breakup like a man, he kidnapped me and kept me zip tied to a bed with a rag in my mouth. He and his vampire buddies binged. After five days, my sister Valerie managed to find me." She stopped as her brows knitted. Her eyes grew glassy and she pressed a hand against her face. "I was such an idiot," she whispered before, once again, falling silent.

Jack gazed at the woman as she tried to gather her thoughts. Adelle was quite the big talker before; cool, collected, and ready to stare down a dragon to keep her secrets. Now, she looked so vulnerable, huddled on his couch as her big green eyes stared up at the ceiling to avoid his gaze. When she brushed her hair over her shoulder, he could see the healing pink scars of bite marks running up one side of her pale neck and behind her ear. Jack's knuckles cracked as he balled his fists.

Damn douchebag vampires. Nothing but trouble.

Her sudden vulnerability pressed up against his heart, much to his chagrin. God help him, he wanted to walk over there, wrap his arms around her, and tell her everything was going to be fine. He fought back the urge.

"Anyways," Adelle continued. "When they started threatening my baby sister, Phoebe, Val and I thought it best I relocate for a while and lay low." She snorted. "Okay, well Val felt it best. So, I ended up in Washington at Wendy's place. I mean, I doubt he'll find me up here but-"

"So why didn't you blast him?" Jack asked. Her eyes darkened as she looked at him. It didn't stop Jack from pushing further. "Let me guess. Still had feelings for him?"

"No. I'd beat the crap out of him if I could. I just..." Adelle squirmed in her seat and rubbed the palms of her hands together. "I just don't like using my powers. I can't control them so I'd rather roll over than kill innocents."

"You just said you could defend yourself."

"I can! With a crossbow. And a sword sometimes... Maybe by throwing a chair." She looked at him then shrugged in defeat. "Okay, I am pretty useless at times."

"No offence, Buttercup but you better start liking your powers pretty soon if you want to survive in this world."

Adelle opened her mouth to retort, puffing up like an angry bird. It didn't last though. Soon she deflated at his words. "You're right," she said, running her fingers through her long red locks. 'You're right. I have a complex, and I need to get the fuck over it."

Jack grinned just a wee bit at her. "You're kind of cute when you curse."

He was greeted with a smile that she tried to twist into a smirk.

Better than nothing.

Now that she had proven to be a little more passionate than advertised, maybe Adelle was worth giving a leg up to in this crappy situation. If a gang of blood suckers were after her, and she had no control over the amazing force she held, she'd need all the help she could get. Besides, Jack had made a promise to protect her. It was a vague promise, so he could protect her in any way he saw fit. Maybe, if he taught her to defend herself like a proper siren, this sister of hers would let her come back home. Then Jack would be off the hook and could go back to brooding in peace. Say what you will about bonding words, they did sometimes have loop holes.

Jack cleared his throat. "Look, I'll help you learn control."

It was Adelle's turn to do a little brow arching. She shook her head, "You're serious?"

"I'm serious. I've been around. And lord knows I've been kicked in the balls by sirens before. Unpleasant? Yes. But I can survive."

"I may take your head off."

"Bull shit. I'm a tough old bastard. I didn't get to live this long by being stupid." He started to get up. "Sleep on it if you must but it's an open offer and-"

"Okay, fine."

That was a quicker response than he was expecting. "Oh, yeah?"

"Yeah. Wendy may be a bitch sometimes, but she trusted you enough to dump me in your lap. That's a decent reason for me to trust you too."

Not only did she say he was right, not only did she trust him, she also called Wendy a bitch. The proper use of the b word made him preen.

This might be a good partnership yet.

He grinned at her and nodded. "It's a deal then?"

"Yeah... It is." Adelle offered him a slight smile that made her face light up. For a split second, Jack's pulse fluttered.

"You still have no pants on," Adelle said.

"I know. Consider that a bonus to this conversation." He turned and headed into his room, in search of a pair of clean jeans.

Chapter 5

There was a quiet truce in Jack's house the following week. After the street side underwear skirmish, there was no need to raise their voices at each other. While Jack went to work, Adelle watched T.V. and cleaned up. Then they'd have dinner when he got home. Then it was bedtime. It was routine but routine kept Adelle calm and in control, just how she liked it. Hell, Adelle was even starting to like the big lug past the point of eye candy.

Even if he was an occasional jackass, Jack did make her laugh. He had a sharp sense of humor and a quick wit that kept her on her toes. Adelle had grown up with two sisters who you could not show weakness to, lest the teasing be merciless. So when Jack started in with the smart ass remarks, she shot them right back with ease. Their conversations were like tennis matches, both of them slinging words back and forth at each other. At first, Adelle wasn't sure if that amused Jack or just bugged him. But then, she'd catch him grinning afterwards, as if he enjoyed having a good sparring partner. Still, sitting idle most of day made her feel like a useless lump. The idleness made her mind wander to Jack's offer.

The crazy bastard wanted to help her control her powers. Adelle had never had anyone volunteer to jump on that grenade. Even Cybil didn't have enough knowledge about sirens to train her. She had hoped Adelle would grow into her powers, like Valerie had. Not that Jack said he was an expert on sirens. Expert or not, Adelle took the offer before she chickened out. It was an opportunity she couldn't pass up. But the dragon was taking his sweet time starting these lessons and it was driving her bonkers. Chances were Jack was waiting for Adelle to come to him, head held high, singing *Eye of the Tiger*.

Adelle peeked out of her room to find Jack reclined on the couch after a long day at work. His legs were draped over the armrest, the rest of his massive bulk taking up every inch available on the cushions. The T.V. was blaring but his half-closed eyelids proved that he wasn't paying attention to it. Soon, deep snores rolled from his chest and wisps of smoke curled from his nostrils. Oh yeah, he was out for the count.

Never wake a sleeping dragon. Her mother once told her that. But if she didn't wake this one, nothing would get done.

Put your big girl panties on and ask him, Dell.

Adelle bit her lower lip, hovering in the hallway, then took a deep breath and marched over to the couch.

"Jack?"

Adelle peered over the top of the couch to find him sleeping and shirtless. Jack was all hard muscle and scars with chiseled arms and broad shoulders designed to grab a hold of. He had a light dusting of golden brown hair across his chest, trailing into a line down his taut belly and under the waistband of his jeans. Slashed scars of past battles puckered the skin on his stomach. Adelle pressed a hand over her mouth to keep from gasping.

"Oh, sweet mama-jama," she whispered between her fingers.

Her gaze raked across every last inch of him as her mouth watered. Adelle was aware that Jack was a well-built male but how well built took her by surprise. Before she realized it, she was reaching out, her fingers brushing soft against his stone hard abs. Jack jolted with a snort the second her fingertips touched his belly. She yanked her arm away as a barrage of Gaelic curses flew from his lips.

"What dumb shite woke me?!" he choked in a thick Scottish brogue.

Jack was Scottish? His low rumbling voice sent tremors of arousal quaking between her thighs. Valerie used to call Scottish accents instant panty droppers. Adelle never understood what she meant until that moment.

He sat up, ramrod straight, teeth bared until his gaze fell on to Adelle. Then his shoulders went slack and he rubbed his face with an annoyed grunt.

"Oh. It's only ye, lass." If he kept talking to her in that accent, she'd wake him up every chance she'd get. He coughed then added in his regular voice, "What is it, Buttercup?"

"What?" Adelle shook herself from her lustful filled thoughts, hiding her incriminating hand behind her back. "Oh, yeah. Lessons. I'm ready to get started."

Jack glared at her through a haze of sleep, ruffling his golden brown hair with his thick fingers. "Now?"

"Well no, not right *now*."

"Then couldn't this have waited until after I woke up?"

Adelle let out a long breath then shook her head. "No, actually. It couldn't."

Jack's amber glare studied her for a short, yet uncomfortable moment. He seemed to read the determination on her face as he rubbed the stubble on his chin. A nod, then a sigh marked his compliance.

"All right, then. Tomorrow." he said, lying back out onto the couch.

Adelle watched his powerful body recline, each muscle rippling as he stretched his arms behind his head and closed his eyes. Adelle pressed a hand against her chest, her heart thudding in an erratic rhythm.

Everything was going to change now. Either she was going to finally take control of her powers or kill both of them in the process. She looked back at Jack, worrying her lip. Well, hopefully he was strong enough to withstand her powers. That delicious body spoke of his strength.

"If you're waiting for a show, I won't be taking my pants off until later," Jack said.

Adelle's face burned. She slunk away towards the hall. "See you tomorrow, then."

Adelle's sheets were yanked off her, waking her from a deep sleep. She snorted, hands groping for the blankets blindly as all that comforting heat evaporated into the chilly morning air.

"Wakey, wakey," Jack's low voice chirped.

She cracked her eyes open and saw his blurry outline standing over her bed, fully dressed, and appearing far too cheerful for this time of day. Thank god she had worn pajamas to bed that night.

Adelle groaned and covered her face with her hands. "I knew it. You've finally come to kill me. Let's get it over with so I can go back to sleep." She curled up into a ball and rolled onto her side but Jack rolled her right back into place.

"You wake me up, I wake you," he said. "Come on."

Jack's strong arms hooked under her armpits and hauled her upright. Adelle flailed like a sad rag doll as he plopped her on her feet beside the bed. When he reached over and pushed some of her mangled morning hair from her face, she glared at him, the dark blue circles under her eyes darkening further.

"Aw, look at you," Jack chuckled. "You're not wearing any pants."

"They're sleep shorts, you ass," Adelle snarled.

Jack grinned in delight. "Don't care. I'm enjoying this moment. Get cleaned up and dressed. We're going out to start working on your powers."

He turned to walk away, giving her behind a firm swat as he passed. The sting jolted her back into the land of the wakeful and she growled through her clenched teeth, rubbing her left butt cheek.

Adelle glanced at the clock on the wall. Her jaw dropped when she noted the hour. "At four in the morning?" she said. "When you said tomorrow I didn't think first thing in the morning!"

"I have to get the gym open by seven so yeah, first thing in the morning. Move it, Buttercup. I only have three hours to spare you."

Adelle watched with hazy eyes as Jack sauntered out of her bedroom. As soon as he was gone, she stomped to the shower, grumbling under her breath the entire way.

A half hour car drive later, Jack pulled up to an isolated chunk of forested land. There were no houses or other buildings, only miles of tall, beautiful trees stretching their green limbs into the steel grey skies of early dawn. Adelle peered out the window, admiring the view. She was a city girl and had spent most of her life in San Diego proper. Oh, there were trees in Southern California of course, but nothing quite like the vast expanse of greenery that stretched before her. It was breathtaking.

When she came to, Jack had already pulled over and exited the driver's seat, rounding the Impala to get her door. She stepped out of the car before he could open it for her. Jack frowned a moment, letting out a little snort. The crisp morning air nipped at Adelle's cheeks and a chill hit her flesh, raising a flock of goose bumps on her arms. She shivered under her denim jacket.

"Wow. It's beautiful out here," she said.

"Yeah, not too shabby. Scotland is more impressive but it's pretty nice for the New World."

Adelle giggled which only earned another scowl from the dragon. Phrases like 'the New World' gave his age away and that seemed to irritate him.

With a wave of his hand, Jack tromped off the road, his snake skin boots crunching under the dirt and brush as he went. Adelle followed. He lead her deeper into the thick clutch of green sweet smelling trees. They walked along a narrow dirt path for about half a mile until Jack deemed their location remote enough.

"Seems like a good spot," he said.

"Is this when you remove your shirt and expose your glittering skin to me in all its glory?" Adelle laughed. Her laughter died when she saw the utmost confusion on Jack's face. He tilted his head, eyebrow cocked, waiting for an explanation of that reference.

"Um... Never mind." Adelle grimaced, rubbing the back of her neck. "So, my powers?"

Jack walked away about twenty paces then turned and held his arms out. "Okay, hit me," he said.

Adelle's eyes almost bugged right out of her skull. "What?"

"Come on. Hit me with everything you got. I can take it."

"Are you out of your damn mind? I'll kill you!"

"How am I going to assess what you got if you don't show me what you got? I've been hit by a full blood siren both barrels before so what harm can a half-blood do? I need to see what your raw talent is. Besides, you're a tiny girl. "Jack gave her a cocky smile and Adelle felt her blood boil. "You're not going to kill me."

Adelle folded her arms tight across her chest as her cheeks heated up. With a long deep breath, she pushed the anger back down into her gut. "You are insane."

"And you're a wimp for just standing there, balking." His mouth curled into an arrogant smile. That stupid grin only poked her ire more.

"I am not going to unleash the beast on you."

Keep Calm Adelle; he's just trying to rile you up on purpose. Unfortunately, Jack just kept on smiling which started to put a sizable crack in her calm.

"Chicken," Jack said.

Adelle took another deep breath, the teasing seeping under her skin. Who the hell was he to judge her courage? "I'm serious. Don't make me," Adelle said through clenched teeth.

"You are really cute when you're angry."

"Stop pissing me off! It's only making it worse!"

"Your nose scrunches up in the most adorable way and you turn a delightful shade of pink-"

"Jack!"

It was when he started clucking like a chicken that she lost her temper.

Adelle let out a scream that bent the treetops backwards and sent birds skyward into a panic flight. A wave of shimmering blue energy ripped through the air, bashed Jack right in the chest, and sent him sailing backwards. She would never forget his expression when the force hit him. It was a delightful cross between utter shock and complete regret. After knocking down three young trees, Jack dropped fifty feet away, leaving a deep groove in the dirt where he landed.

Wide eyed, Adelle held her breath; afraid that maybe she had killed the poor guy. When Jack's legs twitched out from the hole he lay in, she inhaled in relief, the irritation returning.

Serves the arrogant ass right.

Adelle strolled over to where Jack was half buried and looked down at him. Lazily, she cocked her head to the side.

"I warned you," she said.

After a high pitched groan, Jack spit up some soil and coughed. He wiggled like a turtle on his back before Adelle offered a hand to help him to his feet. His pride wasn't so bruised that he didn't accept it.

"Holy shit, you pack a punch," Jack said.

"Well, you were right. I didn't kill you."

He tightened his gaze at her. "You were holding back, weren't you?"

Adelle bit her lower lip and blushed, raising her gaze to the sky.

Jack's amber eyes widened as he gaped at her. "Holy crap. You were."

"Maybe just a little bit."

Jack dusted off his jeans and rubbed his lower back, letting out a painful sounding grunt. Adelle was certain he would have one hell of a road rash on his magnificent ass after that crash landing.

"Well, now that I know what damage you can do. I suppose we should talk about control," he said.

Adelle sighed. "Which I have none of."

"Wrong. You could have killed me, but you didn't." Jack rubbed his lower back again and winced. "So, what makes you feel in control?"

Adelle smirked at him. "Not using my powers."

"Ha ha. Adorable. What else?"

"Not a whole lot else when it comes to this."

"There's got to be something." Jack walked around in a tight circle, back half bent. With every step, his posture straightened a bit. Then he shook his head. "Let me rephrase. What out there makes you feel both passionate as hell and in control of everything?"

Adelle pursed her lips in thought. It really wasn't that hard of an answer to find. "When I sing." Jack's bewildered expression almost made Adelle giggle. She smiled back at him. "Yes, I sing. I'm full of surprises."

"Singing, huh? You love it?"

"With a passion."

"You're good at it?"

"If I may toot my own horn, yes, I used to be great at it."

Jack ran his tongue over her bottom lip then nodded. "All right then, try a few scales and phrases. See if you can use that as your catalyst."

Adelle's stomach dropped like a brick and went cold. "Jack, singing is what got me into this problem in the first place. The last time I sang, people almost died."

"It's something you love right?" Jack asked. "You feel passionate about it enough that when you sing, stuff goes boom? And you're a trained singer?"

"I have a bachelor's in music. But I haven't sang in-"

Jack pointed at her, wagging one of his large fingers under her nose. The gesture silenced her, quick. "So you know how to use your voice."

"Well yeah but-"

"No buts, Adelle. Do you or don't you know how to use your voice?"

Her thoughts wandered back to the horrible birthday she manifested. During the emotional second verse of Ave Maria, the whole church began to shake. Plaster crumbled from the ceiling in white puffs of dust. People screamed "Earthquake!" and dove under their pews. Adelle didn't even know it was happening, so entrenched in the music. It wasn't until Cybil grabbed her by the shoulders and shoved her out the doors that she noticed something was wrong. Her voice, the one thing she cherished most about herself, could demolish buildings and make heads explode. Luckily, only a little structural damage was done to the church and just some people walked out with splitting headaches.

Since that day, Adelle had assumed singing was the problem, not the key to control. But the ins and outs of music were as in tune with Adelle as much as breathing. Music was just another part of her, another limb, and another heartbeat. It flowed through her veins and gave her life. When she stopped singing, a small piece of her died. God, she'd give anything to sing again, to break from the numbed existence she had been living for ten years. If she could channel her power through her song, maybe there was a way.

"Yes. I do know how to use my voice," she said. "I've just been... afraid."

Jack nodded and raked his black fingernails through the stubble on this chin. "Well, it's safe out here. Maybe you should act like your species, sing a tune or two, and cause some mass destruction."

Adelle quirked a little smirk. "How do you know so much about sirens?"

Jack grinned, wiping some dust from his cheek with his sleeve. "I don't. I'm just assuming that it's along the same lines as learning to breathe fire."

"So, you're about as clueless as me."

"Yup, we're going to die." He patted her on the head and walked stiffly away, his large hand pressed against his tailbone. Actually, it was less of a walk and more of a limp. "We probably still got a good hour left before I have to get back. So fling some notes around and we'll see where this goes. Um, maybe aim for the trees this time and not me."

"All right, let's just assume I don't know anything about breathing fire, because I don't." Adelle's shoulders scrunched up into a shrug. "How do I get started?"

Jack ran a hand across his chin as he made her way back towards her. His eyes squinted as he struggled to put his thoughts to words. "Close your eyes," he said.

Adelle did so, feeling a little too vulnerable. Her hands balled into tense fists. She didn't like being caught off guard and who knew what lurked around in the woods. The warm touch of large calloused hands pressed over her wrists. Jack's thumbs smoothed over her knuckles, making her breath catch in her throat.

"Jeeze woman, relax," Jack laughed.

Adelle was about to snap back at him that she was trying but getting snippy would just be counterproductive. Instead she wiggled her fingers, forcing her hands to hang down by her sides. Eventually, Jack let her go. The disappointment she felt irked her.

"Good, now take a deep breath." The dragon's low rolling voice smoothed over her like warm honey, soothing the tension from her shoulders. Adelle inhaled, the woody smell of earth and the sharp chill in the air filling her lungs.

"Good, Buttercup," Jack purred. "Now, stand on one leg."

Adelle popped one eye open, fixing him with a glare. Jack's lips pressed together as the snort of a mischievous giggle escaped his nostrils.

"Sorry. Just making sure you were listening."

Adelle let out an exasperated sigh and closed her eyes again. It only took her a moment to fall back into her earlier relaxed state. She shook out her wrists lifted her chin, and waited for instruction.

"All right," Jack voice grew fainter as his footfalls backed away from her. "Now concentrate and do your thing."

"That's it?" she asked.

"That's it," Jack said.

Hesitant at first, Adelle began with soft scales. Tree branches swayed and pebbles rustled through the dirt. Not much, but it was a start. Jack nodded to her when she glanced at him, encouraging her to push further. Adelle put more power behind her scales, causing the ground to shake beneath her feet. The vibrations pushed her further. A wispy soprano Adelle was not. She had a voice most performers would kill for; strong, clear, and powerful. It was a voice that brought grown men to their knees and made women weep.

It had been so very long; that delicious old feeling of power and expression dancing over her skin, igniting every nerve ending, bringing her back to life. Passion. That's what it was. A feeling she hadn't experienced in years. For so long she had kept herself calm, composed, numb to the world. Now passion heated her veins and pulsed through her body, raising her skin into goose flesh and curling the hair on the back of her neck.

Soon, there was a full force gale whipping through the forest around both her and Jack. Panic welled for only a moment before she reminded herself she was in a safe place. Adelle shut her eyes, losing herself in the joy of her song.

The wind whipped her hair into her face and she stopped, the storm coming to an abrupt halt. Slowly, she opened her eyes. She took a deep breath, her head swimming. A heavy hand pressed down onto her shoulder. Adelle turned to see Jack standing right beside her, his warm fingers squeezing her arm.

"You all right?" he asked.

She nodded. "Yeah, I'm fine. A little overwhelmed but fine."

Jack's lips curved upwards. "And you didn't blow anything up. Look at you go, Buttercup."

Adelle looked about the practice spot. Other than some fallen leaves and a few misplaced pebbles, he was right. Nothing blew up. Of course, it could have been a fluke. Maybe her powers were weak from years of neglect and that is why nothing was damaged.

But what if it is *me controlling it?*

Her lips parted and a soft gasp of surprise whistled from her.

“So, what was the difference between now and then?” Jack asked.

Adelle pursed her lips then answered, “I was calm... and singing.” She looked to Jack who smiled from ear to ear.

"I think we're onto something," he said. That was enough to convince Adelle that the dragon knew what he was talking about.

Chapter 6

The second body fell before Ethan, charred black and smoldering. He started to panic. That was Marcus. He was only a few months into vampirism. Since Marcus was a junky before he was turned, like himself, it had been easy for Ethan to convince him to buy into the feeding frenzy on Adelle. One hundred bucks later, Ethan had no idea Marcus would end up a pile of blackened meat at the hands of a sadistic mage.

The smell of dead, burnt flesh spiraled into his nostrils and Ethan bit his tongue, trying to keep from vomiting all over his lap. All of this was bad. So very bad. Ethan knew that every choice he had made since feeding on Adelle had been a dreadful mistake, but he never knew it would lead to this.

It was midafternoon, not a good time to be awake when you were a vampire. The barn that they were chained up in had slivers of yellow sunlight peeping through the wooden boards, spattering the dirt floor. Occasionally a beam brushed against Ethan, making his skin sizzle and pop in agony.

All three vampires laid on the floor, arms bound behind their backs with slender lengths of silver chain. The metal rendered their strength useless and no amount of struggling brought freedom. There was an eerie lack of urban sounds from outside. No cars, no other voices, no hint of civilization. Ethan had a feeling the mage had dragged them out east, getting them as far from the population as possible.

All three vampires were simpering, cringing from the streams of illumination that crept closer as the day moved on. The mage paced in front of them, circling Marcus's remains, eyes locked on the quivering Ethan. The smile he wore never touched his eyes.

"Ethan, Ethan, Ethan," he purred. He wiped the black remains of Marcus off his hands into a white handkerchief, "We had a deal."

"I know," Ethan said, voice trembling. "I know, Anthony. And I'm so sorry. I didn't mean to screw up. I just needed some of her. Just a bit before I went totally crazy."

Anthony stopped in mid pace. A brow raised as his dark eyes bore down on him. "Five days' worth of feeding isn't just a little bit, Ethan," he said. "You were aware I needed her alive, were you not?"

Ethan shook his head hard. "We weren't going to kill her."

"Alive and in peak condition," Anthony added. "But instead you almost kill the siren then put the Valkyrie on your trail. Not smart, Ethan." He kicked Marcus's burnt body out of his path and back into the sunlight that poured through the open barn doors. The corpse hissed, twitched, and then dissolved into ash. "Now the siren is gone and the Valkyrie is on the warpath." Anthony sighed in disappointment. "I don't think I can trust you anymore. It's best we end this relationship."

Ethan tried to gulp but his throat closed. He wasn't expecting any of this to happen. He had his problems, becoming a vampire being the top one, Adelle now a very close second.

When he met first Adelle, he truly did find her to be a nice person. He had stumbled upon her in a local bookstore, rather taken with all that fiery red hair and those amazing green eyes. They hung out, she introduced him to her sisters, and they even kissed a couple times. It never went further than that. The two spent more time confiding in each other than anything else- stories about family, friends, and how much it sucked being in the Wyrd.

Ethan hadn't expected to feed off her.

He hadn't expected it to be so amazing.

He hadn't expected to want more.

How was he supposed to know that a siren would affect him like that? It was just some stupid rumor he had heard. A rumor that had gotten him more than curious one day.

The first moment Adelle's rich, intoxicating blood dripped onto Ethan's tongue, the world melted away. He felt invincible, strong. The taste filled him with an ecstasy better than the hottest sex he had ever had, the highest high he had ever felt with meth. The bliss would roll on for hours.

Now, without a hit, Ethan was nothing but a pathetic junky. He had the shakes, his stomach howled at him in agony every minute, and the only thing he wanted every second of his unlife was another taste of Adelle. Knowing that he was immortal only made the agony greater.

Adelle had tried to talk him down, told him he needed to detox but it never worked. Nothing was going to take away the pain but drinking from her again. The memory of her sweet blood would flood his senses and he was lost again, forcing himself onto her, using his powers to entrance her and sink his teeth into her throat.

When Adelle left him, Ethan went crazy. Threatening notes were sent to her house. He hovered around her work outside on the rooftops hoping to intercept her if she worked after sunset. Since she once invited him in, he managed to slip into her house and hide under her bed. As soon as she closed the door, he was on her, begging and pleading for just one more taste. Just one more and he'd leave her alone. A knee to the groin told him that she wasn't willing. Undead or not, a nut shot still hurt.

Adelle had screamed in his face that night. His ears felt like they were on fire as he flew across the room, cracking the far wall with his head. Then her older sister, Valerie had rushed in. The beating was severe. Ethan was lucky enough to pry himself free from her iron grip and crash through the front door for escape.

That should have stopped him from pursuing Adelle further. It didn't. Ethan continued to plot ways to get more. Adelle was a decent girl. He didn't particularly like torturing her, but his addiction forced him too. Besides, it was her fault. She said yes that first time he asked for a taste then she took it away from him.

She said yes. She had it coming.

That's when the mage showed up. He was a tall and lean man with short black hair, handsome face, and high cheek bones. He looked rather young, possibly pushing his late twenties though most mages looked younger than they were. He introduced himself as Anthony and that he needed a favor.

"We seem to know some ladies in common. I need help procuring one of them," Anthony said. His voice was smooth and confident. He said he was impressed that Ethan managed to stay so close to Adelle, even after she refused him. That's why he needed him. Anthony promised Ethan a large cash sum, a pint of Adelle's blood after delivery, and set him back on the hunt.

Ethan caught her as she left from work. Adelle tried to scream but that only infuriated his already hunger crazed state. A firm punch to the throat silenced her and a yellow eyed stare made her complaint to carrying her away. But when Ethan had Adelle prone in his arms, he couldn't deliver her. One more hit. That's all he thought he needed. What harm would it be if he got his fix? What harm would it be if he invited a few friends over for profit? It would only be one night. That one night had turned into two nights, then five.

When Valerie broke down the door, they ran like hell. Ethan took to the sewers, living off rats for three months, and hoped that the mage would forget him. By then, he was half crazed with hunger from the shitty rats' blood and still suffering from withdrawal after his five day binge on his ex-girlfriend. He got sloppy, crawled out of the muck through a storm drain, and attacked the first mortal he saw. That mortal happened to be in front of a popular nightclub in downtown San Diego.

Ethan was identified almost instantly and Anthony found him the next day while he slept. Then he collected the remains of his crew. Given the choice, Ethan would have chosen to fight the Valkyrie over the mage. At least she would kill him quick. Now he was here, mere inches from the daylight, and facing his demise. Ethan didn't welcome it like he always thought he would.

Anthony strolled to Chase, another one of the vampires who had fed on Adelle. He was a skinny kid, a weak little vampire. It didn't take much effort for Anthony to grab him by the back of the shirt and drag him to the barn doors. The spindly vampire screamed and thrashed about, fighting against the silver chains that held him.

"Wait! Wait! Fucking wait! I didn't know!" Chase screamed. "I didn't know about any of this, man! Oh, God! Please!"

If Ethan's heart could beat, it would have been racing. If he could sweat, his shirt would have been drenched. Brett, the last of his friends, was sitting on the other side of him, whimpering as Chase continued to beg for mercy.

Anthony unceremoniously dropped Chase in the afternoon sunlight and strode away, letting him writhe like a bug under a magnifying glass. Chase's flesh bubbled and popped, growing bright crimson. His shrieks grew frenzied. Blood poured from his eyes, nose, and mouth as he choked. It felt like hours before Chase's wails became sad gurgles. Soon, his skin blackened and crumbled into grey cinders. Nothing was left of the skinny creature but a vague Chase shaped pile of dust surrounded by loose silver links.

Silence rang in Ethan's ears as ice cold tears streamed down his cheeks. Anthony grabbed a hold of his chains. Hysteria strangled him and Ethan went rigid. He opened his mouth to speak but nothing came out other than high pitch squeals of horror. He could still hear Brett whimpering from his corner, unable and unwilling to help. Ethan kicked his feet, gouging the dirt with his heels, trying to toss himself from Anthony's strong hold. He only succeeded in buzzing up dry clouds of dust.

His mind raced in terror. There had to be a way to save himself maybe a tidbit of information about Adelle and her sisters to entice the mage to keep him alive. Something tucked away in his dumbass mind. Anything. Memories whizzed through his brain in a blur and then stopped on the image of a beautiful blonde relative Adelle had once shown him.

"I know where she is!" he screamed.

Anthony stopped a mere foot before the barn doors. He looked down to Ethan, raising his eyebrows. It was a bluff really. He wasn't sure at all. But if it made Anthony pause, it gave him a way out.

"I... I know where she is," Ethan said, panting. "Adelle. I know where they sent her."

"You could have volunteered this information about two bodies ago," Anthony said, sounding much put out.

"It just hit me." Ethan's voice trembled. "They have a cousin. Up in Washington State. They had to have sent her there."

"You know about their family?" Anthony released his grip and kneeled down to meet his eyes. His icy stare tore into him. "Keep in mind Ethan. I know the Constance girls rather well. Which cousin are you referring to?"

His mind raced. *What the fuck was her name again? Something with a W.*

"Whitney! No! Fuck! Wendy! Wendy is her name!" The silver chains wrapped around him rattled from his tremors. "Wendy. She moved up to Washington. Adelle told me all about it."

Anthony's expression was impossible to read. He rubbed his chin, his gaze like fire.

"Please, you got to believe me," Ethan sobbed. "Wendy in Washington. Please! I can go hunt her down! I can go find her for you!"

With a sigh, the mage rose to his feet. His surveyed the piles of ash left behind by Ethan's former pals. "They do indeed have a cousin named Wendy. Wendy something or other. It's surprising that she moved. Unfortunately, it is a moot point now," he said. Ethan lowered his head and started sobbing again.

"But," Anthony continued. Ethan gulped down his sobs. Hope tingled over his cold skin. "I suppose it couldn't hurt to try." He rolled Ethan away from the sunlight with a soft kick of his well-polished shoe. "You boys will head up to Washington, find her, and bring her back to me. Three weeks. That's all I can give you. I'm on a tight schedule."

"Three weeks?" Brett wailed. "To search a whole fucking state?!"

The glare Anthony shot him shut him up.

"It's called the internet, dear boy. Perhaps you should look into it," Anthony replied.

He knelt back down beside Ethan, who was gasping for a breath he didn't need. The mage curled his fingers around a clutch of Ethan's dirty long brown hair and pulled his head back. His scalp burned as Anthony jerked his fist.

"Three weeks. Deliver me the siren, and we'll call it even. I'll even let you take a bit of blood before you go back into your holes."

"We'll find her. I promise," Ethan said.

"I'm sure you will," Anthony said. "But just in case..."

Anthony punched his fist into Ethan's chest. The mage's knuckles sunk through his skin and tore through his ribcage, fingers feeling around inside his guts, clawing and scratching so hard that Ethan arched back and howled in agony. His body lit up with scalding pain, every inch of him throbbing for mercy. A distinct tick tick-tick-tick of a watch echoed in his head.

After some grotesque exploratory groping inside his torso, Anthony released him. Ethan shook his head as green spots of nausea swam before his eyes. The ticking remained pounding through him, echoing with loud insistence.

"What the fuck, man?" Ethan groaned. "What did you do to me?"

"Just planted a little insurance inside you," Anthony said, "You try that stunt with the siren again? You run away and not return to me in three weeks? You explode. That simple."

A pat was placed on Ethan's greasy hair as he passed. He blew on his immaculate fingernails and walked towards Brett. Soon his tormented screams filled the barn as Anthony shoved his fist through his chest as well.

Anthony walked towards the barn doors, knocking the dust from his slacks. He stopped and looked at the two writhing on the floor like pathetic dogs. With a snap of his fingers, the chains fell from their bodies, setting their arms free. The chains slithered across the dirt floor until they undulated up the mage's leg and into his open palm. Anthony tucked them into his coat pocket.

"You may want to wait a few hours before venturing outside," Anthony smiled. "I wish you good luck gentlemen. Don't disappoint me."

And with that, he strolled out the door, leaving Ethan and Brett trembling and waiting for night to set in.

Chapter 7

It was a quiet Thursday afternoon. The sun was peeking out from behind the usual dense cloud cover of autumn which gave Jack a bit more spring in his step than usual. Dragons weren't solar powered but today the warmth of the sun brightened his usual crusty mood. It had to be that. Not the redheaded siren he was housing. No, not at all.

Jack had to admit, Adelle wasn't as much of a pain in the ass as he thought she would be. Actually, she was pretty dang simpatico with him. She had a smart mouth, yes, but she kept the bathroom clean and hell, she even cooked dinner every once in a while. She wasn't the best cook and most of her meals came from a box but it was still one less thing he had to deal with after work.

The clock read noon and the gym was bustling. His small staff had things under control which allowed him to take a longer lunch break. Most of the time, Jack didn't feel the need to even take one. Work kept him from getting broody and he had been overworking himself since Wendy dumped him. But today he didn't feel like brooding or working. Since he was in such a great mood he figured why not take the rest of the day?

Jack checked out with his manager then headed up the stairs. Chances were Adelle was sitting on the couch, watching cartoons and shoveling Cheerios into her mouth. It was her modus operandi these days. Sitting idle in the house was giving Adelle a bad case of cabin fever. She didn't say anything to Jack about it, but her expression around the house was grim. Maybe he'd drag her out for lunch today. It was the least he could do. She liked pizza with mushrooms. That would probably cheer her up.

When he walked in the door, Adelle was exactly where he expected her to be, sitting cross legged on the couch, watching cartoons, and holding a half empty bowl of Cheerios in her lap, the spoon stuffed into her mouth. She looked over to him when he entered. Today, she had managed to get out of her pajamas and into jeans and a bright yellow t-shirt. Usually when he came home, her curvy form was still clad in pale green pajamas, hair sleep tousled in that cute sexy way.

Jack caught himself staring at her more than once these days. The fiery curls of her thick mane, the luscious curves of her hips and breasts, and that sparkling smile that was uniquely hers sent a tingle up his spine and some rather ungentlemanly thoughts right into his brain. All right, so he stared at her. Any red blooded male would stare at that delicious woman.

"You're home early," she said, voice muffled around the spoon.

"Taking the day," he said, "Don't eat another bite of that crap. You're coming with me to lunch."

Adelle blinked at him in surprise then put her bowl and spoon down on the coffee table. "Adelle is going walkies?" she said. A broad smile split her mouth, and she clapped her hands like a child. "Can we go to the park? Can you throw a ball and I go play fetchies?"

Jack rolled his eyes. He headed to his room to change out of his gym clothes. "I'm sorry you've been stranded here."

"Eh, not for long." Adelle stretched out on the couch with a smug grin on her face. "I found a job."

Jack froze mid step. "A job?"

"Yup."

"Why would you go and do that?"

Adelle sighed. She swung around, hooked her knees over the back of the couch, and dangled her head off the seat, her flaming hair pooling on the carpet below her head. "Because I am bored as shit, Jack," she confessed.

She was sitting upside down on his couch. He'd agree with the boredom.

"I'm one of those types that need to keep busy or my brain goes into overdrive. Before you know it, I will have cleaned every single piece of your glass collection with a toothbrush." She folded her arms, and frowned at him. "Do you want me to touch your collection again, Jack? Do you?"

Jack could feel a grimace screwing up his mouth. "When did you go interview for a job?"

"This afternoon."

"And how far did you go?"

Adelle laughed, the sound smoothing Jack's ruffled scales. "Down, Simba. I just was down the street. Well within screaming distance if something happened. Jolene's Pub needs waitresses. I saw the help wanted sign and walked in. Just part time but better than nothing. I used to wait tables in college and I'm figuring the job hasn't changed all that much." Adelle wiggled her feet at him.

Jack cracked a smile at the sight and chuckled. She had cute feet; petite, pink, and blue painted toenails. He turned and leaned his arms on the back of the couch.

"What hours do you work?" he asked.

"The night shift unfortunately. I'm working from six at night until one in the morning."

"And you start when?"

"Tonight."

Jack rubbed the stubble on his chin thoughtfully. With a nod, he rounded the couch and flopped into a sit beside her upside down visage. "Works for me. I work mornings, anyways."

"I figured I'll eventually work my way up to day shifts..." Her voice trailed off as Jack's words began to sink in. She lifted her head off the floor. "It works for you?"

"Perfectly."

Adelle fixed on him, a suspicious frown on her face. "And this matters, why?"

"You think you're going out alone at that hour after me explaining to you, repeatedly I might add, that I made a vow?" He reached up and gave her dainty foot a wiggle. "How delightful you are."

With a groan, Adelle righted herself on the couch, sitting in its far corner. "Working the gym all day and sitting in on my shifts at night. Don't you think the staff will find that creepy?"

"Chances are people in the pub are Wyrd and understand the seriousness of a vow."

"And when do you plan to sleep?"

"Whenever I damn well please. Look Buttercup, don't argue with me on this."

Adelle put up her hands in surrender. "Fine. I'm not going to argue. Last time I argued I ended up being carried like a gunny sack back to your place in front of a crowd."

Jack grinned. "Yeah. Good times. "

"For you, maybe."

He eyed her a moment, a devilish grin curling his mouth. "Are you saying you didn't like being slung over my shoulder?"

He loved it when she blushed. She would turn red from toe to head, like a thermometer. When the color of her skin grew flushed, it egged him on to tease her more.

"There are dishes to do," Adelle announced, picking up her bowl from the coffee table and rushing to the kitchen.

Jack leaned his head back on the couch and called after her, "Big manly dragons carting off fair maidens to do unspeakable but amazing things to them in their cave!"

"*So* many dishes to do!" He heard the clumsy clinking of plates and cups echoing from the sink.

"Lots of thrusting action!"

"Can't hear you! Sink's on!" And a gush of rushing water followed.

A low rumble of Jack's laughter echoed in from the living room.

Adelle never figured Jolene to be an Irish name but who was she to judge? The staff was friendly, and even though Adelle came home with swollen feet and beer stained jeans, she was happy as a clam to finally be doing something other than sitting on the couch all day. The pub was homey, all dark wood and dim lighting. A huge bar on one side of the room, tables and booths scattered about, with one pool table that was constantly populated. Guinness posters decorated the walls along with other various *Kiss me I'm Irish* style decor.

That first night was a bit awkward. Jack hovered in the darkest corner of the pub, eyeing every customer Adelle encountered. His intimidating glare scared off more than one man just trying to order a beer. When the manager called her over, Adelle assumed her return to waitressing was over before it began.

"The uh, gentleman in the corner," her manager asked. "Is he with you?"

Adelle sighed rubbing a hand across her face. "Yeah, he kind of, sort of is. He's here for…"

Her voice trailed off as she scrambled to think of an excuse that a human would understand. The only two she could come up with were, “He’s my ride” and “He’s currently writing a book on the behaviors and habits of the part time night waitress”. Neither sounded convincing.

Just when she opened her mouth to stammer some more, Adelle noticed the pointed ear tips tucked under her manager’s shaggy blonde hair. Adelle paused, looking for other tells on him. Pointed ear tips, slender tall build, and ice blue eyes. Oh yeah, he had to be an elf. The tells were subtle, and she had almost missed them.

Jack wasn’t kidding when he said the staff could be Wyrd.

Sensing her gaze, her manager brushed some of his hair over his ear, self-consciously. Adelle scanned the pub, noting how perfectly blended the Wyrd and human numbers were. Vampire, werewolf, human, elf, human, another vampire, human, human, human. Whitmore was turning out to be more densely populated with Wyrd than she originally thought. It was a small town and small towns did love their secrets.

“Jack’s a dragon and he’s under a vow for me,” Adelle blurted out.

The manager’s icy blue eyes widened, and then he nodded. A relieved laugh gurgled from his throat. “Ah, say no more. I was worried how to tell you that a dragon was stalking you. Good. So you know, Jack?”

“Oh, yeah. We’re roommates,” Adelle said.

“Thank the Gods. I did not want to fight a dragon tonight. Especially that one. Just let him know that the glares aren’t helping business, okay?”

Jack eventually stopped the glares and let Adelle work. If it was anyone else, Adelle would have found the whole experience creepy. Instead, Jack’s presence was comforting. Comfort was welcomed after a year of looking over her shoulder. She was grateful Jack walked her to and from work, especially on those dark nights when two blocks felt like two-hundred miles on tired, swollen feet.

The first week passed and the staff of adorable waitresses began to grow accustomed to his presence. They fawned over Jack, rewarding his regularity with free potato skins and beer. He ate up the attention as fast as those potato skins. Jack holding court amongst flirty waitresses and tipsy pool players. It was a sight to behold.

At the beginning of Adelle's third week, Leah, the sexy slender hostess leaned across the bar towards her. She lifted her pointed chin towards Jack's booth and whispered, "Is that your boyfriend?"

Adelle almost dropped the water pitcher she was pouring. "My boyfriend?"

She looked over to Jack seated in his usual spot, enjoying a large platter of nachos. He crunched on the chips and cheese in delight, engrossed in his free food.

Damn, did he have a hollow leg?

His handsome amber eyes glanced up, shooting over Leah's head and fixed on the shelves of backlit liquor bottles on display. They glazed over as the twinkling glass hypnotized him. Adelle smiled, warm amusement spreading over her. That was the third time she'd caught him drooling over the bottles. Then she shook her head.

"No. Just a friend," she said

Leah beamed. "Oh good! I'm taking a crack at him."

"You're... What?" Adelle tried not to frown. Her mouth trembled as she forced its corners back up into a smile.

"You said he was fair game." She leaned forward, tossing some of her brunette hair over her shoulder. "Besides, he's looking right at me. See?"

The dragon was looking all right. Right over Leah's head and at the bottles behind her. It gave Adelle a bit of solace.

"I don't know if he's looking directly at-" Adelle began but was cut off when Leah reached down the front of her little black dress and fluffed her "girls" into primo presentation. That caught Jack's attention and his eyes snapped to Leah's new found cleavage. Adelle's frown started winning the battle.

"Wish me luck!" Leah started to rise from her bar stool.

Adelle 'accidently' elbowed a glass of water into Leah's lap sending her dashing towards the bathroom. Adelle winced at the bitchiest move she'd ever made towards another woman and walked stiffly over to Jack's booth.

"Sorry!" she called over her shoulder.

Jack watched the exchange with a cocked eyebrow, jaw set. "You're bright red," he said as soon as Adelle was close enough.

"It was an accident."

Jack shrugged in reply, much to Adelle's relief.

"So," Adelle said. "How's the king of the potato skins doing?"

"I'm expanding my kingdom and claiming nacho territory," Jack said, making a grand gesture across his half-finished plate. "Play your cards right Buttercup and you could become the duchess of guacamole."

"Wow. A title all for me. So generous, my liege." Adelle leaned across the table, resting her elbows on its surface. "So... Which one do you like?" Her tone was low and conspiratorial as she jerked her head towards the bar.

Jack shoved a nacho into his mouth, chewed, then shrugged. "The brunette is nice, even if she's all wet right now. Actually, that's a plus."

"Not what I meant." Adelle placed a hand on his chin and turned his sights to the bottles lining the back of the bar. "Which one do you like?" she repeated.

Jack laughed. It didn't sound very convincing. "You think I'm sitting here ogling bottles and not women?"

"Oh please, don't give me that macho BS. You've been staring at those shelves all night."

Adelle found herself twirling a lock of hair around a finger. Jack's vision fixed on the movement and he bit his lower lip. His thick fingers reached up, taking the lock of hair and smoothing them down the curl. The devilish smile he flashed made Adelle's knees wobble.

"That's because the soggy brunette is standing in front of them," he said.

Adelle leaned in closer, her lips almost brushing his ear. That rich scent of smoke and sandalwood wrapped around her. "It makes it easier on me if you just put it all out on the table, darlin'." she whispered.

Jack folded his arms, sinking into his seat like a scolded child. Adelle used every ounce of her willpower to not giggle at him.

"The St. Germaine bottle is nice," he grumbled.

Well, it was a pretty looking bottle, tall, shimmering, and cut at interesting angles. Adelle assumed he had picked that one because it caught the light so well. She smiled and ruffled his hair. "I'll see what I can do."

His eyes lit up, despite the fake frown. As she walked away she heard him call, "The Grey Goose Vodka bottle too, while you're at it!"

Adelle headed back to the bar, plastered with a silly grin. It wouldn't take much to ask the bartender for his empties. Besides, it was the least she could do for Jack. After all, he'd been watching out of her, teaching her, even gave her a place to stay. She rounded the barstools, the memory of his fingers smoothing down her hair on constant repeat. A shiver crept up her back and she pressed a hand over her mouth to stifle the bubbling giggle.

The girlish thoughts came to a thudding halt as she felt an arm hook around her waist.

A frumpy gentleman in a rumpled business suit yanked her off her feet with a cackle and into his lap. Adelle managed to brace her hands against the bar before she did a complete header onto the floor. His stench of cheap whiskey and cigarettes made her nose wrinkle in disgust and she pushed a hand against the drunk's stubble encrusted face.

"Let go!" Adelle shouted. The bottles behind the bar rattled from her anger and she snapped her mouth shut, fear pooling in her stomach.

"I bet you taste good!" the drunk slurred at her, taking a healthy handful of her breast. He was stronger than he looked. The harder she struggled, the tighter his grip on her grew. Adelle bit the inside of her cheek to keep from screaming.

Jack had already jumped to his feet, smoke curling from his nostrils. When the drunk ran his tongue up the side of her face, his huge hands balled up into fists and he started his way over.

With a furious growl, Adelle reached behind her captor, snagging a server's tray. She flipped her tray over in her hands and cracked the drunk hard across the jaw. He released his grip and Adelle stumbled to her feet. Another crack and she whacked the tray over his head, forcing him out of his barstool and to the floor.

"Back. The fuck. Off," Adelle snarled, holding the tray over her head.

The drunkard slunk back. He squinted at her as he staggered to his feet, rubbing his face. "Bitch," he said, teeth bared.

After a quick look over, Adelle was relieved to discover he was just a regular obnoxious human. The last thing she needed was a fight with a drunken werewolf or fae.

"Oh, I'll be more than a bitch if you don't pedal your ass out that door," Adelle said.

He took a step towards her then stopped after noticing that the entire pub was watching him. He snorted, wagged a thick finger at her, and then stumbled out the door. The pub burst into applause at his exit. Adelle lowered her tray, and took a deep breath when a warm hand rested on her shoulder. She craned her neck up to see Jack beside her.

"You okay?" he asked.

Adelle gave him a nod. "I told you I could defend myself," she said, raising her chin.

"I especially loved the wind up and the pitch there. Very good form." Jack smoothed a hand down the length of her hair before heading back to his booth. If she wasn't mistaken, she could have sworn that was a proud smile he wore.

Around midnight, Adelle took her final break. Only a quick ten minute one but even ten minutes of out of the noisy pub was a relief on her ringing ears. She slipped outside, passing a few of her coworkers as they headed in for the final push. The din from the dining room and kitchen was reduced to a dull roar as soon as she stepped out the door. Adelle sighed, rubbing her temples. There were a couple chairs set outside the kitchen's back door so the wait staff could sit or smoke, whatever they deemed fit when the weather permitted. She flopped herself down into one of the chairs and took a deep breath, the stillness of the night unknotting her shoulders.

Even though her feet pulsed with heat, a smile touched Adelle's lips. It felt good to be doing something again. So what if it involved swollen feet and the occasional cranky customer giving her grief? She could handle that. She also could raid the bar of its empty bottles for Jack. Adelle squeaked out laugh as she thought of his frown. It was adorable to see a dangerous brute pout like a three year old, then grow giddy when he got what he wanted. She grew giddy herself. A sharp shake of her head whisked the giddiness away but it didn't stay away for long. Jack had a presence that she couldn't keep out of her mind. Adelle didn't want to admit it but she was growing rather attracted to her gruff roomie. And it was getting worse every day.

No. This was a strictly platonic thing. Roomie and roomie. Teacher and student. No matter how many times she told herself this, the hard corded muscles of his glorious, battle scarred chest flooded her mind. Adelle was sliding into dangerous territory. Her daily quips were becoming more flirtatious. She even leaned in super close to whisper to him tonight. Close enough that her lips brushed the top of his ear, making them tingle. Close enough to catch his mouth watering scent.

Was I really twirling my hair at him?

Not only that, but she spilt water on poor Leah when she mentioned asking Jack out. Was she jealous? After a long moment of agonizing contemplation, Adelle slapped a hand against her face and groaned.

Crap, I am *jealous.*

If she did decide to throw caution to the wind and jump into bed with that sexy dragon, her nasty habit of becoming emotionally attached to who she slept with would rear its ugly head.

Adelle didn't want to be someone's conquest. It had happened once to her in high school. She and that cute basketball player in the back of his pickup truck after homecoming. He never spoke to her again. The entire situation was humiliating. Not the best way to lose one's virginity. That led Adelle to a string of sensitive boys who latched onto her like a child and were lukewarm in bed at best. She didn't want to risk the heartache this round.

While Jack seemed to enjoy her company, there was a good chance he was just making best of a crappy situation. He had a vow to keep. Yet, Adelle wondered about how serious he was about it.

Earlier that week, a rather handsome customer had chatted her up. Judging by his five o'clock shadow and side burns, he was probably a werewolf. He asked Adelle when she got off of work and if she'd be interested in getting a drink or two. Adelle enjoyed the attention but when her eyes glanced over to Jack, he was glaring daggers from his corner booth. The werewolf gave Adelle's arm a flirtatious squeeze and Jack started to get to his feet. Instead of starting a species grudge match, Adelle declined the offer.

Jack was just being overprotective.

Or he could have been jealous.

Someone snagged her arm with a sharp yank. Adelle yelped in shock, falling from her chair to the ground. The spill knocked the wind right out of her. She clutched her belly, struggling for a breath. Before she could roll to her knees to rise, a body landed on top of her and a hand slapped over her mouth. The drunk from the bar pinned her down in the gravel parking lot with his flabby bulk. Adelle's heart pounded, and her stomach went ice cold. He must have been lurking in the parking lot, waiting for her to come out.

The drunk's jaw was red and swollen, turning purple from the blow she gave him earlier. Greasy dark hair hung in his rage filled eyes as he stared down at Adelle. Tiny rocks pressed into her back, scratching and scraping through her t-shirt as she struggled. No matter how hard she tried to push him off, he wouldn't budge.

"Stupid bitch thinks you can hit me?!" His breath stank of whiskey. A glob of spittle landed on her cheek. Adelle tried to bite the fingers that pressed hard against her lips, but couldn't get her teeth to catch.

Blast him.

Rage rose from deep in her gut. It spoke to her in a faint hiss.

Yes, blast him. Melt him into the ground. He deserves it. It will satisfy you.

White haloed her vision and Adelle took a deep breath, ready to unleash her fury. But the scream caught in her throat. That all too familiar feeling of dread overtook the rage.

No! reason screamed. *Too many people close! You're right next to the pub! You'll take down everyone around you!*

Frantic to rope in her emotions, Adelle shut her eyes, shaking her head hard from side to side.

"Yeah, I figured you were speechless," the drunk cackled. "I bet you'll taste good. I bet-"

He screamed as his body was wrenched up into the air. Adelle sat up, coughing and wiping her mouth. She scooted back on her rump across the gravel as Jack gripped her attacker by the neck and slammed him against the pub's cement wall, shaking the building.

"Who the fuck?!" the drunk bellowed.

"Hi, I'm Jack, and I'm going to be the one putting you in the hospital tonight." Jack pulled back his fist and hit the drunk in the jaw hard enough to spring two teeth loose.

The drunkard's eyes rolled back into his head. Blood trickled from his mouth and he slid down the wall into a sprawled sit, unconscious. After nudging the man with his boot, Jack turned and offered a hand to Adelle.

"You all right?" he asked, worry curling around his words.

"Yeah," Adelle said in a trembling voice.

She was shaking head to toe as she took Jack's hand and pulled herself up. His fingers wrapped around hers, warm and secure, steadying her as she stood. Adelle willed her hands to stop, afraid her fear would escalate to panic, then to explosions.

"Thanks. How did you-"

"Heard you went on break and didn't want to leave my post." Jack must have felt the tremor in her fingers. His grip tightened. "You sure you're all right?"

"Yeah, I am." Adelle swallowed the shake in her voice. For a moment, she managed to still her body. She looked Jack right in the eyes and slapped on a fake grin, resting her hands on her hips. But her casual smile melted and she started to crumble. She pressed her hands against her face. "I just hate being taken off guard."

Keep calm, Adelle. Keep calm.

Jack's strong arm slipped around her shoulders and pulled her against his side in a gentle embrace. The shakes started to subside. She closed her eyes and pressed her cheek up against his shoulder, his warmth and strength lulling Adelle down into a place of stillness. She wasn't sure how long she stayed like that. If she had the choice, she'd stay there all night. For the first time in years, Adelle felt true comfort and lost herself to the beautiful void that shrouded her thoughts.

The low rumble of Jack clearing his throat brought her back to earth. Adelle pulled away and smoothed her hair back from her face, cheeks flushing pink.

"I think I'm going to get inside," she said.

Jack glanced over his shoulder to the man on the ground then cracked his knuckles. His brows lowered over his eyes as they glinted with violence. "Hang on, not done yet. He's still got unbroken bones."

Adelle's jaw dropped open. She gave herself a mental reminder to never piss off a dragon as she stepped in front of him. "Whoa, whoa! Don't kill him!'

"I'm not going to kill him. I told him I'd put him in the hospital, not the morgue. Are you telling me I can't break any more bones?"

"That's exactly what I'm saying!"

He paused, looked down at the guy, then back to Adelle. Jack's scary visage melted into a sad puppy dog frown. "Not even a rib?"

Adelle's mouth opened to let loose a paragraph of curse words when she caught the cheeky smile he was trying to smother. She narrowed her eyes.

"He's unconscious," she said. "Are we done peacocking?"

Jack snorted out a little giggle.

Adelle rolled her eyes. "You're horrible."

"He's worse. He deserved it."

Adelle couldn't argue with him. The jerk off assaulted her. If Jack was serious about breaking a few more of his bones, she would let him despite her protests. But Jack didn't need to know that.

She turned to head back into the kitchen, and then paused. Her hand slipped into Jack's, giving it a tender squeeze. In turn, his fingers laced with hers. The touch of his hand brought back that beautiful comfort she found herself craving.

"Thank you," Adelle said. "I better get back to work."

"All right, I'll be in in a minute." As soon as he saw the resulting frown on her face, he held up his hands defensively. "Kidding! Really! I'll call the cops."

Chapter 8

Adelle was pressed against her mother, chin resting on her shoulder after the tears began to dry. So much for a happy birthday party. Valerie had already retreated, cleaning up the birthday cake and ushering Phoebe out of the living room.

"I know it's a lot to handle," Cybil said as she touched her soft red curls.

"It's more than a lot, Mom," Adelle said.

She pulled the birthday hat from her head and looked to the older woman, tear tracks still sticky on her cheeks. Her heart was thudding hard against her chest. Her hands were shaking.

What Valerie said couldn't have been true. She had to have been lying. But when Adelle looked up into Cybil's soft brown eyes, and the older woman furrowed her brow, she knew it was the truth. Anger boiled over and she pushed her mother away, scooting back on the couch as far from her as she could.

"Why didn't you tell me before? Why didn't you warn me?" Adelle said.

"Because you weren't ready," Cybil said.

"Then how come Val knew about her powers when she was 16?"

"Because that's when they manifested." Cybil sighed. She reached for her daughter, but when Adelle put her hand up in warning, Cybil retreated, hands in her lap. "It's hard to understand now. But I wanted you to have a normal life for as long as you possibly could."

Adelle put her hands over her ears. The more Cybil talked, the more she wanted to scream. Her skin grew cold as a strange pulse throbbed through her veins. Her fingers curled into her hair, yanking hard as she bit back the fury.

"Mom," Adelle said, straining for control. "Crossbows? Sword fighting? That's normal when you're a kid? I just assumed you wanted us doing something athletic or maybe we were joining a historical recreation society!"

"You and your sisters need to be prepared. You need to be trained to-"

"You were training us?!"

Adelle's shrill shout shook an entire shelf of books to the floor. She slapped a hand over her mouth, her wide eyes staring at the pile of paperbacks in horror. When she looked to Cybil, her heart sank even further. The pity in her mother's eyes tore through her heart like it was paper.

"Did I do..?" Her voice trailed into a squeak when Cybil replied with a slow nod.

"You love singing. I couldn't take that away from you," Cybil said.

"So the church roof." Adelle swallowed. "That was my fault?"

Cybil answered her with silence.

"Oh my God." Adelle felt the sobs returning. She locked them back down into her throat afraid of what might happen if she let them loose. "I could have killed everyone."

"No." Cybil grabbed a firm hold of her shoulders. "No, you wouldn't have. We wouldn't have let it get that far."

"I could have killed Val and Phoebe! I could have killed you!"

"Sweet Pea-"

"And you let me sing knowing I could do this?!"

Cybil gave Adelle a little shake. The jolt pulled her out from her panic spiral.

"There was no knowing how your powers would have manifested, Dell," Cybil said. "They could have cropped up in any way. But now that you have them, we'll teach you a way to control them."

With a violent shake of her head, Adelle snapped, "I'm never going to use them!"

"Adelle."

"I'm a monster! Mom, what's wrong with me?!"

The windows rattled. Adelle's stomach lurched as anxiety tied itself around her throat and pulled tight. She slapped her hands back over her mouth. No matter how deep a breath she took, it just wasn't enough. Only the touch of her mother's strong hands on her flushed cheeks calmed the terror.

"You are not a monster," Cybil said with conviction. "My girls are not monsters. They're not killers. They're not freaks. Do you understand me?" Her thumbs brushed away the tears rolling from Adelle's eyes. "No one is allowed to call you that, including you."

Adelle looked at her mother, lower lip quivering. Light from the windows haloed around Cybil's curly brown hair through her tears. She buried her face against her chest and shuddered.

"We'll find a way for you to control it," Cybil murmured into her ear.

Adelle wiped her cheek against Cybil's shirt. "How?"

"I don't know yet, Sweet Pea. But we'll find a way." Cybil hadn't called her Sweet Pea since she was ten. She only used the nickname when Adelle was beyond distraught, like now.

"What if we don't?"

"We will." Cybil wrapped her arms around Adelle's shoulders in a fierce hug, as if she was trying to squeeze the fear out of her.

"I was going to go to college. You promised. I can't go if I'm this... thing."

Cybil sighed, resting a cheek on the top of her head. "You girls are special. And it will take some adjustment to become who you really are. We'll work something out." She heard Cybil swallow nervously. "You won't go through this alone. Until then, just keep calm."

Adelle could hear the uncertainty in her mother's voice. Her heart twisted. She tightened her arms around Cybil, but they passed right through her. Adelle's eyes popped open as her mother's form crumbled into dust, spilling over her arms and down her shirt in grey flecks.

"Mom!" she screamed.

The walls rattled. Plaster crumbled and fell, burying Adelle in heavy piles of debris. She clawed at the air, desperate to dig herself out before she was crushed to death. The tortured screams of her sisters echoed in her ears, pouring in with sharp pangs of agony. They wailed her name over and over, coughing and retching as the house collapsed upon them.

"No! No Please!" Adelle cried. The harder she begged, the louder her sisters screamed.

"All your fault," a voice hissed. "It's your fault. She's dead because of you. They'll be dead because of you, too. You're a monster. All your fault."

As it hissed its venom, dread crashed down in on her. She was hearing the sound of her own voice.

"Mommy!" Adelle screamed.

"Please keep calm," Cybil's voice whispered.

"Rise and shine, Buttercup!"

Adelle shot up in bed, skin hot and clammy, sweat staining the collar of her pajamas. She pressed her hands against her chest, trying to push her heart back into her ribcage.

"Wakey, wakey, sleeping beauty." Jack didn't notice her distress as he yanked the blankets off her, just like he did every morning. "It's play time."

She replied with an eloquent, "Huh?" and blinked her sticky eyes, her tangled hair hanging in her face. The nightmare still pulsed in her brain and the whispers of "all your fault" haunted her ears.

It was just a dream, Adelle. Don't think about it. Think about the dragon who is currently rummaging through your underwear drawer.

She concentrated on Jack, her eyes boring into the back of his head. She took in his hair, the muscles tensing in his neck, and the curve of his shoulders; anything to push the terror away.

After a deep inhale, the crisp morning air sobered her up. Another breath and Adelle realized that she did not slumber well at all. She rubbed her sleep swollen eyes, shoulders creaking with morning stiffness. That was enough to distract her from her fear. Her eyes flickered to the clock. It read 4:51 am. Her shift at Jolene's had ended at one in the morning.

Three hours of sleep? He wants me to practice on three hours of sleep?

"Now?" Adelle said.

"Hey, I gave you an extra hour of sleep today, "Jack said. He tossed a pair of jeans and a sweatshirt on the bed at her feet. "Get dressed; I only have two hours to spare you before the gym opens."

Adelle groaned, scrubbing her face hard with her palms. "Please, just let me sleep in this morning. It was a rough night."

Jack tossed her bra into her head. "Sleep when you're dead, Buttercup."

"Come on, Jack."

"We're burning daylight!"

Adelle glared daggers at him. “I really hate you right now.”

“Good! Motivation!” He gave a toothy grin as he headed to the door. “I’ll wait in the car.” Jack managed to close the door before the jeans Adelle threw could hit him.

“Just keep calm,” she growled through her teeth.

The fog was thick but showed signs of burning off in a few hours. Tall tips of green trees poked up through the cottony blanket of grey that coated their practice spot. Jack stepped out of the Impala and stretched his arms over his head. The cold air felt wonderful as he took a deep breath, cooling his lungs.

“Nothing like an early morning in the woods to get your blood flowing,” he said.

Adelle dredged her way out of the car, slamming the door behind her with a strained growl. “It’s five in the morning, Jack,” she said. “Five. In the morning. I went to bed last night at one thirty.”

“Training under duress is a good way to learn,” Jack said.

Adelle ran her hands through her messy hair, her curls sticking up at every which angle between her tense fingers. “I barely had time to wash my face and grab my purse before you dragged me out.”

“So? It’s not like you need your wallet and you smell fine.”

She turned her puffy, tired, and very enraged sights to him. “Why are you doing this?”

Jack rolled his eyes, lifting his wide shoulders into a shrug. “Because I’m an asshole,” he said.

Adelle grumbled a line of curse words as she stomped past Jack, heading to the dirt path. Jack shoved his hands into his pockets and followed behind her. He watched Adelle as she stumbled along, her mouth fixed into a wicked frown and surge of protectiveness filled him. After seeing that drunken bastard tackle her to the ground, he was overwhelmed with a rage that set his blood on fire. The drunk was lucky he walked away with his cock still attached.

"If you want the real answer," Jack said. "It's because of what happened two nights ago. You didn't even try to defend yourself."

Why didn't Adelle use her voice? After what Jack witnessed from their practices, she could have cooked the asshole with ease. But she didn't. Was she still afraid of her powers? If she was, he would step up their practices until she could defend herself properly.

"I'm not sure if you noticed but he had a hand over my mouth," Adelle said.

Her flippant reply needled his already souring mood. "He was a human. You could have burnt through his hand in two seconds if you wanted to. But you just laid there like a dead fish."

Adelle stopped in mid step. With a whirl of her red curls she spun towards him, green eyes blazing. She marched over to him, fists clenched and said, "Are you seriously criticizing me on how I handed being *assaulted*, Jack?"

Jack opened his mouth to retort, then stopped himself before the angry words escaped. One look into her glossy eyes exposed the fear she kept locked down inside her. Adelle wasn't a damsel in distress. She had made that perfectly clear to him the night she stared him down. But that night at Jolene's shook her to the bone. She had been caught off her guard, had forced herself to remain powerless just to keep others safe. And he just berated her for it. Jack swallowed hard, a lump settling in his stomach.

"Sorry," Jack replied, casting his eyes to his feet. He couldn't look at her anymore. Shame made blood rise to his cheeks. "I..." His thoughts swam through the guilt, trying to form a cohesive sentence.

I was terrified you were hurt. I was worried what would have happen if I wasn't there. I was so enraged that he dared touch you that I wanted to tear him in half. I can't bear the idea of losing you.

His last thought stopped his racing mind short. Did he truly fear losing her?

"I'm a jerk," he said instead.

After an agonizing moment of silence, Adelle stepped towards him and took his arm, expression softening.

"You're not a jerk," she assured him.

"No. I was being a Grade A asshole. I shouldn't have said that. It was a dick move on my part and I didn't mean it." Jack raised his eyes to see a faint smile on her pink lips.

"Apology accepted," she said. "Come on, we have practice to do."

Jack released a breath as relief washed over him. Carefully, he pressed a hand over hers and walked with her down the dirt path to their practice spot.

The small clearing had grown in circumference after weeks of Adelle taking her emotions out on the foliage. What was once a lush patch of grass, was now a burnt playing field. She did her best to not eradicate the entire woods but their presence was evident with all the tumbled down trees and charred shrubs that circled them.

As Jack scanned the circle, he began to realize how much fear Adelle must have felt all her life. So much fear, anger, and sadness trapped in such a delicate body. She might as well light a candle with a flamethrower. No wonder she was scared to death of herself.

Adelle slid her purse off her shoulder then turned to look at him. "You said you had a siren attack you once," she said.

"Yeah," Jack said. "But I deserved it. I was a little shit when I was a kid."

Adelle laughed. "You? A shit? Say it ain't so."

"I know. Shocking," Jack said with a grin. "I was young and sniffing around a siren's nest I found on the cliffs of Orkney. Sirens are territorial and when I got too close, boom."

Adelle nodded. She pursed her lips a moment then ventured to ask, "So what are they like?"

"Sirens?"

"Yeah. I- well, I don't know anything about them."

"They're beautiful." Jack rubbed his jaw in thought. "Bird like. Their hair is long feathers, their arms are huge magnificent wings, but the rest is all human."

The memory was still fresh in Jack's mind, even after all these years. Jack had clawed his way up the pale cliffs, curiosity egging on his young mind even after his father roared at him to stop. That's when he found a round nest of twigs and seaweed and the enchanting creature that sat upon it.

She was breathtaking. Her golden feathers streamed from her head and wings. A delicate face and wide set green eyes, pale bare breasts and thighs, flawless and shimmering in the rising yellow sunlight. Jack had just stared, unable to move, paralyzed by her beauty.

His sudden snort of steam caught her attention. The siren turned her head towards Jack, startled and wide eyed. She seemed so innocent and defenseless in her surprise. The young dragon managed to squeak a gasp before she released a scream that knocked him off the cliffs and deep into the sea. His father had had to come fish him out before he drowned. She was beautiful but deadly. A beast Jack couldn't help but admire.

Jack could see a siren's features gracing Adelle's face; the large eyes, a straight aquiline nose, and small pink lips. He caught himself smiling as he gazed at her. When she turned to face him, he turned his head away with a cough.

"They're dangerous, private, and beautiful," he said, rubbing the back of his neck. "A lot like you."

A blush touched Adelle's face and Jack felt giddy. At that moment, he promised himself he'd make her blush as often as he could.

"And what about dragons? What can you tell me about your kind?" she asked.

"Eh, there's plenty about me out there. In children's books mostly."

Adelle laughed giving him a skeptical look. "So I should just go camp out in the kiddy section of the library? Dr. Seuss and Grimm's fairy tales?"

"I'm still trying to figure out how that Peter Dickinson guy got all his info."

"Are you serious?"

Jack pointed a finger at her firmly. "*Flight of Dragons* is not a kid's book."

Adelle folded her arms across her chest with a cockeyed grin. "The entire dragon race was unveiled by a children's book, huh?"

"Hey. Don't mock. That stuff is important."

Instead of continuing their conversation, Adelle shrugged with a smile and stepped towards the center of their circle. She kicked off her boots, peeled off her socks, and dug her toes into the dirt. Jack sat himself down on a fallen tree trunk, puzzled.

"Um, what are you doing?" Jack asked.

Adelle shrugged again as she straightened her posture. "Just a hunch. Might not do anything."

A hunch? Adelle wasn't the type to act on hunches. Apparently, she was getting reckless after the time she spent with him.

I must be rubbing off on her.

He watched her, rubbing the palms of his hands against his jeans. "Not plugging in today?" Jack asked. Adelle had been singing along with her iPod lately, using some of her favorite songs to fine tune her power.

"Not today," Adelle said.

No shoes, no socks, no iPod. The creature of habit was breaking all the rules.

Adelle's toes scratched deeper divots into the earth. Jack was ready to smugly warn her of the dangers of catching a cold when she closed her eyes and took a breath. His snark was overpowered by his curiosity and he remained silent.

Nothing happened for a long moment. The wind in the trees rustled, dried leaves twirling down around Adelle. She stood quiet, eyes closed, shoulders relaxed as her breath rolled in and out with the rhythm of the wind. She lifted her hand and snapped her fingers with a slow steady beat.

Jack's ears perked as he heard a faint whistle on the breeze. A chilled gust swept through the clearing. It caught Adelle's hair and whisked it off her shoulders in a tornado of flame red curls. Thin white and blue currents of light coursed through the ground. They were small and faint at first but sparkling rivers grew brighter and brighter, pulsing to the rhythm of Adelle's snapping fingers. More luminous veins of power flowed from the rocks, the trees, and the air as she called them to her.

Adelle lifted her face to the sky, eyes still closed, fingers still snapping. The bands of power seeped up through the soles of her bare feet and into her body, illuminating the webbed veins under her pale skin. She absorbed the power from the earth, her body now a nimbus of blue fire glowing so bright that Jack had to shield his eyes from the glare.

Light shimmered around her, through her, rippling under her skin, practically bursting from her. Adelle's eyes popped open. The vibrant green was gone, replaced with white flame. Her lips parted and she belted out a long powerful note that ripped through the air.

The tree across from her burst into a blue fire with a deafening roar. As soon as it ignited, it snuffed out, leaves and bark charred black and smoking with a soft hiss. Jack leapt behind the fallen tree he sat on, ducking for cover. All the light rushed from Adelle's body and back into the earth where it once hid. With a sharp inhale, she bent in two, her hands resting on her thighs as she clamored for breath. Jack rounded the fallen tree, catching her shoulders before she pitched over.

“Adelle?” He couldn't hide the fear in his voice.

Adelle lifted her head to him, a little smile on her face as she breathed hard. “Sorry. Anything happen?”

Jack blinked in disbelief. “You're joking, right?” He helped her straighten, still holding her shoulders steady. “Dammit, Adelle, you better be joking.”

“Only partially,” she chuckled and leaned against him. "I mean, I couldn't see what was happening from my angle. But man, could I feel it.”

The hairs on her arms were raised into goose flesh, and she trembled in excitement. The scent of electricity covered her skin, a strange mixture of earth and sulfur, like someone had set off a dozen roman candles at once.

“But you're all right, right?” He tried to sound casual. In reality, his heart had stopped at least forty times during that display.

“I'm more than all right, Jack.” She pointed at the still smoldering tree. “Do you see that? I did that. I did that to the tree and nothing else around it. You're not on fire, I'm not on fire. If that's not an example of control I don't know what is!” Her delighted laughter rose into the air and Adelle flung her arms around his neck in a tight hug.

Jack froze as her warm soft body pressed itself against him. He closed his eyes, wrapped his arms around her waist, then lifted her off her feet and spun her in a circle, laughing. Her joy was contagious. The electric tang from her flesh faded and now he could smell the sweet perfume of honey in her hair and on her neck. He buried his fingers into her thick red curls and inhaled deep, losing himself in her touch, her scent, and the rousing sound of her musical laughter. In the nine-hundred years he'd been alive, nothing felt more exhilarating than her.

That's when Jack's eyes sprung open.

Oh, shit.

She was slipping under his skin. Jack wasn't too sure he wanted her there. Quickly but carefully, he put Adelle back down on her feet and stepped away, rubbing the back of his neck. He let out an awkward laugh then gave a thumbs up.

"Ha! Good for you. Um… yeah," he said.

Luckily Adelle was too wrapped up in her victory to notice that Jack had had a moment of twiterpated weakness. Oblivious, she grabbed his arm .The scales beneath his skin tingled deliciously at her touch. Every logical thought screamed at him to recoil, told him this was just another slippery slope to getting attached.

Mayday! Mayday! Back it up, Jack!

"Hey, I hate to be a killjoy, but I got to get back to open the gym," Jack said. A loud cough disguised the crack in his voice.

"That's fine," Adelle said. "Hell, I don't think I could repeat that trick today anyways." She snagged her purse and started back down the dirt path towards the car, still barefoot, waving her arms around in a frenzy. "Wow, I can't believe I did that! I want to run a mile now! Or dance for hours! Or maybe just lie on the couch and pass out. I'm not sure yet. But, wow!"

Jack bent down, scooping up her forgotten boots and socks. "You did good, Buttercup," he murmured, grinning despite himself. "You did good."

The overwhelming feelings of affection for her hovered in the back of his mind as they walked back to the car. They prodded him with sharp needles as he unlocked the passenger door. After sliding behind the wheel he glanced to Adelle. She looked tired and sated, eyes half closed and a small contented smile on her pink lips. He could still scent the delicate trace of honey on her flesh.

Don't get attached.

Jack didn't want to feel love for her.

Did I just think the word love?

No, he didn't. Love wasn't the word he meant. It was just lust he was feeling. That had to be it. Adelle was gorgeous. Her luscious body was pressed against every inch of him, and God above, she smelt so good. Yup, Lust. That's all it was. Adelle was just another smoking hot female. So what if she had an enchanting laugh, sharp wit, and a smile that made his knees week.

It was just lust. A lust that affected his brain before his pants.

Pantless lust.

Pantless lust?

Jack put his key in the ignition, intent on driving Adelle home as fast as possible. His wrist stopped mid turn when she pressed her fingers on top of his hand.

"Wait," she said.

He winced, jaw tensing with a click of his teeth. "What?" he asked, putting on his best indifferent expression.

Adelle chewed on her lower lip a moment. "You're going to think this is dumb."

"Try me."

"I got you something. A thank you gift."

Jack's shoulders relaxed when he realized he wouldn't have to explain what pantless lust was to her. Hell, *he* didn't even know what that meant. Relief aside, he arched a brow high, tilting his head. A gift wasn't what he expected. When was the last time anyone had gotten him a gift? Well, Wendy once had bought him some ridiculous outfits from one of those designer stores for Christmas. It was definitely nothing he wanted. Maybe Adelle did the same. Human females had a thing for buying clothes.

Adelle reached down for her purse and pulled out something wrapped in a brown paper bag. "I was going to wrap it and give it to you later today but your wakeup call changed my plans. It's not much."

"Look, you don't have to do this-" Jack was cut off when Adelle shook her head.

"Just open it, okay?" she said.

Jack reached into the bag, fingers touching cool, smooth glass. His eyes widened and the bag rustled as he pulled out a shimmering St. Germaine's bottle. It was the same one from Jolene's. He knew it was the same one; it had a nick on the side by its label.

When the bartender had tossed it into the trash bin, Jack had let out a whimper of want. There were plans of shuffling through Jolene's dumpster later to rescue it but he had never had a chance to get there. Jack figured the prize was long gone to the dumps. Yet there it was, resting clean and gleaming in his hands.

Jack stared at the cut glass as he rotated the twinkling bottle. Its crystalline surface glimmered in the threads of sunlight that peeked through the clouds. A lump the size of a boulder sat down in his throat, and his eyes started to sting for some reason. For the first time in his life, the dragon was speechless.

"I cleaned it out for you and um... Well, I know it's the one you wanted so the bartender put it aside for me," Adelle said. "I just wanted to thank you for, well, for everything. The room, the lessons, for knocking the crap out of that drunk guy. Everything you've done for me." Adelle rubbed the palms of her hands together as she watched him. Uncertainty drenched her voice as she babbled. "I mean, if it's not the one you want I can always..."

Jack continued to gape at the bottle. His eyes blurred, haloing the light refracting through the glass. The first gift he had received in centuries. A bottle. A beautiful glass bottle for his precious collection. This one was going on the top shelf in his living room. He wanted to look at it every day. To remind himself someone out there actually gave a damn about him.

"Oh God, don't do that," Adelle said.

Jack looked up. "Don't do what?"

"Do not cry. I don't think I can handle that right now."

"What? I'm not crying! What the hell makes you think-"

Jack reached up and touched his cheek, feeling moisture. A few more swipes of his face and he discovered tears were dripping down his jaw line.

"Shit!" He blotted his eyes with the sleeve of his jacket. "I was not crying! With all that siren crap you were doing, my eyes got all crazy. That's all!"

Jack wiped at his face, cheeks burning scarlet. He peered over to see Adelle smiling in amusement. The same way she did when she knew she was right.

"I wasn't crying," he growled.

Yes, he was crying.

Jack hadn't cried in over a hundred years. Nothing these days made him weep. He had seen too much in his centuries. He had lived through too many dark times to bother with tears. Tears were beneath him. Yet here he was, mewling like a hatchling because some female gave him a goddamned bottle.

"Okay, you weren't crying," Adelle said. She pressed a gentle hand over his. "But do you like it?"

Jack lowered his arm from his face and looked back to the beautiful prize still resting in his hands. "Yeah, I like it." Adelle's green eyes lit up and his heart leapt. "I love it actually," he quickly added. "Thank you."

Yes, Jack cried over a bottle. But it was Adelle's bottle. That glorious creature went to the trouble to replace one of his broken treasures. Someone cared about the old dragon. That seemed like a good enough excuse for tears.

World be damned, he'd shed more if she did it again.

Chapter 9

Adelle stepped into her room, fresh out of the shower, rubbing a towel against her long ropes of wet red curls. She grinned, still riding her high from the morning practice. All her life she had felt the swelling current of power that resided in the earth but whenever it entered her, it only created chaos and destruction. Control always floated just beyond her fingertips. This time, she harnessed it. Adelle had called to that magic and when it came, she wrapped herself around it, riding it into the ground like a bucking bronco, and bending it to her will. For a glorious few minutes, she was in control.

When the power was gone, she was left gasping for breath, exhausted. She wasn't ready to sing a full song yet, but there was a good chance she would be soon. The idea alone made Adelle walk on air all the way home. The memory of Jack's proud expression only heightened her joy.

She knew that Jack loved their morning practices. The twinkle in his amber eyes, the way his strong mouth would spread into a wide grin when they'd enter their sacred place. When she asked him why he was so jovial, Jack told her that it brought back old memories of being a young dragon in Scotland.

"I don't get many opportunities to go full form," he had said. "Too many humans looking on, too many folks to scare. Watching you makes me remember what I am."

Adelle lift her chin a little higher. Hell, if an old banged up dragon liked her siren's blood, she may grow to like it as well.

Usually, practice was followed by breakfast. This time, Jack just plopped her at the foot of the stairs. He waved a hand and rushed into the gym, keys rattling hard as he unlocked the front doors. Adelle barely got out a "See ya" before he slammed the door behind him. He was probably embarrassed. She assumed he was the type who only cried if something heavy fell on him. This was actual, honest to God, emotional crying. It was touching he loved his gift so much.

Adelle's cell phone rang with delicate musical chimes. She secured a towel, tucking it around her torso and snagged her phone off the nightstand.

"Hello?"

"Two months," an all too familiar female voice growled. "Two months, Dell. Two months of playing phone tag with you. You could be alive, you could be dead, or you could be a zombie by now."

"I miss you too, Val," Adelle said, flopping backwards onto her bed.

They had been missing each other's calls since she moved into Jack's place. Some were on accident; others were because she didn't want Valerie to know her new living situation. Valerie had a tendency to overreact. And lying was not an option. Her sister knew how to yank the truth right out of her. The only key was avoidance.

"I would like to point out that I returned every single one of your messages. It's not my fault you were too busy to answer," Adelle said.

"Two months!" Valerie snapped again. After a moment of silence long enough to make Adelle nervous, Valerie let out a crack of distinct laughter.

Adelle giggled, shaking her head. "You always make me nervous, you know that?"

"Yeah, yeah. I'm your big sister and you should be. Not me. Where's that little sister servitude?"

"That's what Phoebe is for."

"She's too squirrely. You were always more compliant. Easier to mold in my image."

Adelle smirked. "And that worked out so well in your favor."

The sound of her rousing laughter made the Valerie shaped void in Adelle's heart grow. Her heart ached at the sound of Valerie's voice. She missed her jokes, her hugs, and her ogling half naked men on Tumblr while screaming, "Freakzoid! You have *got* to look at this one!" Yes, her sister was crazy, loud, and on occasion overbearing, but that's what one would expect from a half Valkyrie.

"I miss you," Adelle said

"I miss you too, Delly," Valerie answered, her voice tender.

Before Adelle fell further into maudlin territory, she changed the subject. "Are you and Pheebs holding up all right?"

"It's been slow. A relief, somewhat boring, but it's better than the alternative. Still, it's a little daunting with just me doing all the work."

Adelle sat up like a shot. "Wait. Are you telling me you haven't told Phoebe yet about her powers?"

Valerie sighed dramatically. "She hasn't manifested yet, Dell. Besides, you know you're better at those things than I am."

"It doesn't matter. She needs to know."

"I know. And you should be the one to tell her all about it."

Adelle rubbed her temples. "So, you're waiting for me to come back home and break it to her?"

"No!"

Adelle pursed her lips, waiting for it.

"A phone call would work, too," Valerie finished.

"Val!"

"You know how sensitive Phoebe is. Remember how I broke it to you, Dell? Remember how well you took that?"

Oh, Adelle remembered. She had nightmares about it. It was her eighteenth birthday. Her, Cybil, Phoebe, and Valerie all gathered around her cake, the birthday song sung had been in the kitchen, and Valerie suddenly blurted, "Don't blow those candles out too hard, Freakzoid! You might make the house explode!"

That was followed by Cybil cuffing Valerie upside the head so hard, her face fell into the cake. Cybil then spent the next four hours explaining to Adelle how she really wasn't a human while she sat dumbstruck on the living room couch, the pointy party hat still sitting askew on her head. Luckily, only in her dreams did the house caved in on her. In reality, it ended with Adelle trying not to sob into her pillow. It was worse than when she first got her period.

"You have a point," Adelle conceded.

"Yes I do. I'll get to it if I can. Right now..." Valerie said before a long pregnant pause. When she spoke again, her tone was somber. "I don't know Dell, but I get the feeling that something big is coming our way. Big as in big and bad."

Valerie had a good sense for bad things. Amazing, actually. Her sense for trouble was as sharp as a bloodhound's nose. She called it her battle instinct. When Valerie said she had a feeling, Adelle got justifiably nervous.

"Val, the last time you said you had a feeling, Ethan was under my bed."

Her heart sped up. Valerie couldn't fight alone. Adelle had control now, even if it was fleeting. With Phoebe not even knowing she was a Dryad yet, Adelle was needed now more than ever. The problem was she didn't want to leave Whitmore. She had grown attached to her job, her new friends at Jolene's, even

Wendy had become less grating. And maybe, just maybe, she didn't want to leave Jack.

She swallowed hard then asked, "Do you need me home?"

"Nah, not yet. Might be nothing." Valerie's voice flipped to its usual jovial tones. Soon, another one of her epic laughs pierced Adelle's ear drums. "Don't worry about it. It's probably just me. I need to get laid and I'm getting antsy."

The change of subject helped push aside the cold feeling in Adelle's gut. "Oh wow, I bet it's been a whole three days since your last conquest. Poor baby."

"Shut up. It's been at least a couple weeks."

Valerie was a lustful woman. Back when they went out drinking, Valerie always came home with a hot guy - or four- after last call. Adelle always came home with a hangover. Those were two things Valerie could do that Adelle couldn't; hold her liquor and charm men right out of their pants. Adelle envied that. Taking home a random man for sex would have release a little of her pent up emotions. But she was too cautious and sentimental. Who knew what would happen if she lost herself in the throes of passion. Would she melt the poor guy? After she discovered her powers, she always kept sex on the tepid side, just in case.

"My sex drive is an important part of who I am and how I work!" Valerie said, "Do not taunt the Valkyrie!"

"Half Valkyrie," Adelle added.

"Details, details!"

The two laughed again. That feeling of sisterhood warmed Adelle from the inside. She clutched her towel against her chest, spreading her wet hair across the bed to dry.

"So, what gives with you lately?" Valerie said. "I even tried getting a hold of Wendy, but she wasn't answering her phone either. Are you two plotting something?"

Adelle laughed loud, ruffling her fingers through her sopping curls. "Oh, yeah. Because you know Wendy is such a team player."

Valerie's laugh overpowered Adelle's phone and she yanked it away from her ear. If anyone was in the living room, they would have heard the powerful guffaws.

"She's a giver. Our delightful cousin is treating you fair, right? You two getting along as roomies or is it the Odd Couple in Hell?"

Adelle pursed her lips. "Yeah, about that." This was not going to be easy to explain to her overprotective sister.

"Oh, shit. Is Wendy trying to use you in one of her weird schemes for popularity?"

"No. She's got herself a new boyfriend for that. A vampire half-breed."

"Seriously? What happened to that dragon she was seeing last time we visited?"

"She dumped him."

Valerie chuckled again. "Well, vampires are the more popular species these days. Dragons haven't been the hot ticket for years."

That sounded about right for Wendy. She was a flavor of the month gal and vampires were currently wetting her pallet. God love all those teen vampire movies coming out. God help Wendy if zombies became all the rage.

"Steven is only half vampire, though," Adelle said.

"A halfie? Poor guy. He doesn't stand a chance against Wendy's mind games. No hypno powers to protect him. I wonder what happened to that dragon. He was kind of a sourpuss but a fine piece in human form. Do you remember his ass? You could bounce quarters off those cheeks."

Adelle remembered it all right. She thought about it maybe half a dozen times in the last few hours. It was hard not to. "He's about." She swallowed hard.

"He's still around?"

All the time. In my dreams, sometimes.

The last dream Adelle had about Jack involved her, him, and the whirlpool bath he had down in the gym. The smell of sandalwood swirled in her nostrils and the heavy touch of his calloused hands skimmed up the inside of her bare thighs just as her alarm clock went off. Boy, was she was pissed when she woke up. The sweet taste of wood smoke haunted her lips all morning.

Dammit Adelle! Get your head together!

"More or less," Adelle said.

Valerie clicked her tongue in approval. "You bumped into him, I'm guessing?"

Adelle took a breath. "Kind of. So, about that..."

Valerie laughed again. "What, did he ask you out? Did you say yes?"

"Uh, about that, Val."

"Delly, did you go on a date?"

"Not really. Um... about that..."

The silence on the other line was deafening. Adelle held her breath, counted to ten, waiting for it. As predicted, Valerie slowly but firmly asked, "What are you not telling me, Adelle?"

She had the mom voice on. The same one Cybil used on them when they would try to sneak cookies out of the pantry or hid a broken dish under the couch. Adelle smacked her forehead with the heel of her hand repeatedly. Valerie was going to flip her top when she told her. Why *was* she telling her this? Because Adelle was a horrible liar, that's why. Valerie would get it out of her eventually.

Just say it. It will be like ripping off a Band-Aid.

"I'm kind of living with the dragon," Adelle blurted out.

As predicted, Valerie exploded with a thunderous, "You're what?!"

Adelle almost dropped the phone from the force of her shout. "Calm down, calm down." She clutched her towel close to her chest, putting on her best neutral tones.

Adelle was known as the voice of reason in her family. She had talked Phoebe down from devouring her sorrows in two gallons of ice cream after she was dumped at the prom. She once managed to change Valerie's mind about strangling the jackass who took up two parking spots at the Mall during Christmas. Her calm was proven to work on Valerie at least ninety percent of the time. Despite the hot temper, Valerie cooled down quick if you talked some reason into her. There was a good chance she could talk her off the ledge. Or there was a chance the Valkyrie would take the next plane up to Washington to come put the smack down on a nine-hundred year old dragon.

"Calm down?! "Valerie said. "I sent you up to Washington to hide with family! I sent you up there for your safety and you're shacking up with a strange dragon?! And you didn't tell me?!"

"You should have known Wendy would have found a way to ditch me eventually." Adelle kept her voice steady, knowing that Valerie could smell fear, even over the phone. "She's not the most reliable cousin, just the furthest. You said so yourself. Jack had a good rep and a spare room so, I took it."

"But you're-"

It's not shacking up!" Adelle cut her off. If she didn't, Valerie would have steamrollered over her with her rage. "We're not dating or getting married or anything like that. I pay him rent and live in the guest room. I'm safe here, and he's watching my back. Besides, it's better than cleaning Wendy's blood out of my fingernails. You know how well Wendy and I get along, Val."

Yet another long silence rang through the cell phone. Adelle bit her lower lip, keeping her breath slow and even.

Show no fear. Show no fear.

Hopefully Valerie didn't detect that Adelle wanted more than just friendship with Jack. She winced and shook the thought out of her head.

"So, he's cool?" Valerie grumbled. "He's not the grump I remember?"

More than likely he is. Adelle thought. Instead she answered, "He's been a good host."

Valerie sighed. "Fine then. But if I hear one thing about him doing a douchebag act-"

"You will have first dibs on his balls. I promise," Adelle finished.

"Good."

Adelle took a deep breath. That went better and faster than expected. Of course, Adelle left out a few details like the vow Jack had to make, the drunk he saved her from, and the fact that she would sell her left foot for a crack at him in bed.

"Actually, you having a dragon around may be a good thing," Valerie said. "Once again, this could be nothing. But word from Reina is that Ethan skipped town."

The hairs on the back of Adelle's neck stood up. "What?"

"Most of the crew that fed off you is dead or missing. Ethan and another guy are unaccounted for. Chances are he's in hiding. That would be my guess. Still, he might have made it up towards Washington looking for you. He did know that Wendy lives there and if he figured out you're gone, he could put two and two together."

Adelle pressed a hand against the side of her neck, feeling the scars left behind from Ethan's fangs. She shivered. Great, just what she needed, Ethan showing up on her doorstep for another hit. She swallowed down the fear, thinking back on her practice session that morning. Remembering the ease with her power soothed her anxiety. The fear of losing control was fast becoming a thing of the past. Not to mention having a dragon fighting on your side worked wonders for one's confidence. If Ethan got too close, she would blast him this time. She'd fight back. Her jaw set as new found confidence warmed her skin, pressing a smirk to her lips.

Bring it, Ethan.

"Thanks for the heads up. I'll keep an eye out," Adelle said. A cocky sense of overconfidence enveloped her. She even threw in some extra bravado for Valerie's sake. "Though, I think I can handle him now."

"Oh? Why?" Valerie asked. The curiosity in her voice practically dripped through the phone's earpiece.

"Well, I started practicing with my power."

A loud whoop cracked through the air. "For real? All right, Dell! That's my girl!"

Despite the bravado, modesty always won out in the end with Adelle. "Don't get too excited. I'm still in the learning phase."

"Either way. I'm proud of you," Valerie said.

Adelle's heart swelled as her mouth curled into a giddy smile. Her sister was never one to pass on praise like that. Considering she spent most of her time chastised for never using her powers, Adelle reveled in the moment.

"So," Valerie said, hiding her sudden onslaught of sisterly pride. "Back to the dragon's ass."

And just like that, Adelle's moment of glory ended. It was fun while it lasted.

Adelle rolled her eyes. "Val!"

"Okay, okay," Valerie said. Adelle could hear the snicker under her sister's voice. After five seconds of giggles, she added, "I'd look."

"You always look, Val."

"And that is why I have gotten some in the last month and you haven't gotten laid in almost two years."

Adelle snorted, flipping some wet hair from her eyes. "I'm picky!" she shouted.

"Border lining on desperate," Valerie muttered. "Now, unless he has dramatically changed in the last year I saw him, woman you better ride that dragon, now."

Adelle sighed, lying back down on her bed. God, she would if she could. It was getting ridiculous. Wanting that sexy dragon gave her nightly headaches. If she was the type, she'd just dive right into bed with Jack, have herself a good tumble, and get it done with. But there was that whole messy business of getting attached. Hell, she was already getting feelings for him and they never even kissed. Jack was a self-proclaimed happy bachelor. He had mentioned this to her many times. He didn't want a relationship. He wanted a quick lay. Something Adelle didn't want to be ever again.

"What?" Valerie said, hearing Adelle's heavy sigh. "Are you waiting for an engraved invitation to his sex farm?"

"No. I just want to avoid awkwardness."

"Adelle, how awkward is it to seduce a dragon? Wait. Don't answer that. I've seen you try to pick up guys. It's tragic."

Adelle made a sour face, hoping Valerie could hear it over the phone. "You know how I get when I get involved with a guy. We get friendly. We get intimate. Then the next thing you know, I want commitment."

"So? Just get over that little hurdle and do him!"

"It's not that easy for me Val! I'm not you! If I was, I'd cover that poor bastard in whipped cream and not let him out of the house until he couldn't walk straight."

A thud echoed from the hallway right outside her room. Adelle shot back up, clutching her towel closed, heart leaping into her throat. Someone was in the house. She turned towards the door, ready to find a weapon to defend herself.

Instead of Ethan or a burglar, Jack stood in the hallway, staring at her. His amber eyes were wide as saucers and his face was a lovely shade of cherry red as he ogled her, jaw open. His gym bag had slipped from his fingers and hit the floor.

Adelle felt her hands grow cold as all the blood rushed up into her face, turning the same color Jack was currently sporting. One look into his burning eyes and she could tell it wasn't embarrassment he was feeling.

His hands flexed into tight fists as he closed his jaw with an audible click of his teeth. When he wet his lips, gaze raking over her from top to bottom, trembles danced across her. For a moment, Adelle was certain Jack would barge into her room, rip the towel from her body, and take her right then. God help her, Adelle hoped he would.

Wait. Towel?

Adelle stumbled to her feet, throwing the phone down on the bed and reached for her robe hanging on the wall. Her arm swung at the cloth but missed, the momentum throwing her onto the floor in a graceful belly flop. Hair in her face, arms over her head, Adelle rolled like a turtle on its back before she finally snagged the fluffy blue robe and pulled it off the hook. Without much more fanfare, she threw it on over her head.

"Hello? Dell?" Valerie's tinny voice called from the abandoned phone. "You there?"

Adelle clutched the robe, trying to pull it around and down to cover her half naked body. It only succeeded in making her look like a fluffy nun. Jack's already arched brow raised even higher. How was she going to explain this one?

Lying.

Lying seemed like a good idea.

"Umm, It's my sister Val on the phone," Adelle said. "She was asking for advice."

"Advice?" Jack looked at Adelle on the floor, then to the phone, then back to Adelle. Her ridiculous pose seemed to ease Jack's lust and he nodded. "That was some impressive advice."

Jack reached down, picked up his bag and started walking away, eyes still fixed on her. Adelle continued to turn red and gave him a sheepish smile as he craned his neck to keep an eye on her.

Before she could shout, "Watch out!" Jack turned his head forward just in time to run into his open bedroom door face first. There was a manly cacophony of curse words as he clutched his nose. An angry growl rumbled the hallway, followed by the door slamming.

Well, at least you know there's a mutual attraction, now.

Adelle slapped a hand over her face.

"Dell? I can hear you breathing," Valerie shouted over the phone. "Pick up!"

Adelle scrambled to her feet, snatching the phone off the bed. With a glance over her shoulder to the hallway, she winced then pressed the phone up to her ear.

"I'm here," Adelle said. "Thank you Val. I think you just settled things becoming awkward in this house."

"What?"

"Never mind."

Jack sat in his usual booth at Jolene's, scarfing down one of their famous pub burgers. Whether it deserved that title or not, Jack didn't notice. He didn't even remember tasting it. One tended to sacrifice things like tasting food when they're hungry enough to eat their left foot. Three bites and a fist full of fries later, he was sated. Not even a drop of ketchup hit the plate. It was no wonder he was ravenous. Jack skipped lunch to attend to certain matters alone in his bedroom. Matters that human males attended to often and dragons attended to every once in a blue moon when desperate. And boy, was he desperate.

Well, what was he supposed to do? That glorious creature was naked, wet, and talking about using a dessert topping in a very un-ladylike manner. He saw the hunger in her eyes. His keen dragon's nose scented her honey sweet arousal when she caught him listening in.

It wasn't his intention to eavesdrop on her phone conversation. All Jack had in mind was a quick shower and lunch before he walked her to Jolene's. Work had managed to get all those mushy feeling out of his head and he was ready to face Adelle again, armor intact. But when he heard her talking to her sister, he found himself hovering just out of sight in the hallway, wondering if he was going to be mentioned. Well, he was, just not in the way he expected. It threw Jack off his game all over again.

His defenses were destroyed by Reddi-Whip.

Jack didn't come back out for air until Adelle had to leave for work. The looks they exchanged when he left his bedroom were awkward, to say the least. Adelle couldn't even make eye contact. Conversation was mostly comprised of clipped one word answers.

"So, how's your sister?"

"Fine."

"How was the rest of your day?"

"Fine."

"What did you do?"

"Nap."

"How's that whipped cream idea going?"

"Shut up, Jack."

As soon as they arrived at Jolene's, Adelle disappeared to the kitchen to fetch her apron and Jack slipped off to his usual booth to keep watch. That was when his stomach started to rage at its emptiness and the great inhaling of the pub burger began. It was Friday night -fifty cents wing night- making it busy for the wait staff. That only made it easier for Adelle to avoid him.

Advice for her sister, his ass. Adelle was a terrible liar. Jack knew she was talking about him. There it was, solid evidence that she was sexually attracted to him. He saw it, smelled it, could feel it pulsing off her body. That temptation alone was maddening. It was akin to putting a steak dinner in front of a starving man and daring him not to lunge at it. The will power Jack used to keep from pushing his way inside of Adelle's room, throwing her on her bed, and ravishing her was astronomical. A guy had to be dead to not want to.

Jack didn't want to get attached to Adelle but dammit, he did he want her, and in as many positions as possible. Maybe, if they just got all that sexual tension out of the way, he'd feel less compelled to care. It was a theory he was willing to test. For science, of course. He hated science but this was a special experiment Jack would make a noble sacrifice for.

After an hour of avoiding him, Adelle finally went over to his booth to refill his water. Her hand was shaking as she tilted the pitcher, her stare fixed on her work.

"Oh for God's sake, I'm not going to eat you," Jack grumbled, then paused, and smirked. "Unless you want me to."

"Don't start," Adelle said, keeping her eyes on her pitcher.

"Then don't talk about whipped cream in a provocative manner."

"Oh for God's sake, I was giving advice to Val," Adelle pulled away from the table but Jack reached forward and snagged her wrist before she got too far.

"Look me in the eye and tell me that," he said.

Adelle paused, catching his eyes with hers. It was only a second later when her gaze darted up to the ceiling. "I got a lot of tables," she muttered.

Jack leaned back in his seat, a grin splitting his face. "Admit it. You want me."

"*So* many tables to wait on, Jack. You're only one of many."

"You want me so bad."

"Not when you're acting like a douchebag. I don't screw douchebags as a general rule and you're ruining your chances."

"So, you're saying there's a chance." The glare Adelle gave him made Jack bust out laughing. He turned to her with a toothy smile, putting his hands behind his head as he reclined in the booth. "Yup. We should just get it over with. We both know the tension is great. You, me, a bottle of wine." He thickened his accent on his last word. "Wrastlin'."

That's when Adelle slammed the pitcher down on the table, droplets of water splashing onto the wood in a crescent. It was so damn cute when she got flustered. He wanted to reach forward and run his thumb across her pouting lower lip and then run his tongue over the spot where his thumb once was.

Adelle took a deep breath then finally looked him in the eyes. Her pink lips turned up into a smirk and she leaned in, whispering in his ear, "Wendy did a complete mind dump on me before we were introduced."

The smug smile dropped from Jack's face to the floor as the information sucker punched him. A mind dump. Wendy performed a mind dump on Adelle. Meaning, Wendy put every single memory she had of Jack into Adelle's head, including all the bedroom antics. Wendy wasn't much for editing those things out.

Jack had no problems boasting about his prowess but having every single detail revealed to a possible conquest from Wendy's perspective? Not cool. Or was it? Wendy was satisfied, right?

Of course she was. Why wouldn't she be? ...Right?

He turned to Adelle, who managed to pick up Jack's smug smile and wear it rather well.

"You're bluffing," he said. She only replied by batting her eyelashes oh so innocently. Jack's stomach lurched and he sunk down in his seat with a scowl on his face. "You're totally bluffing."

"So," Adelle said. "You really like it when a woman touches the back of your neck?"

Jack face grew hot. She wasn't bluffing. "Don't you have a lot of tables?" he asked.

"That's really all it takes, huh?"

"So many tables, Adelle?"

"Because if that's true, damn you're easy!"

"All right, all right! I get it! I was being a douchebag!" Jack shouted. He rubbed the bridge of his nose then muttered, "I'm sorry."

When the delightful sound of Adelle's laugh hit his ears, the corners of his mouth turned up. She leaned her forearms on the table, tucking some hair behind an ear. With a smart little smile on her face, she reached forward, taking a firm hold of his hand.

"Dude, let's just cool down, okay? Both of us. No whipped cream or using the word moist too much, got it?"

Jack pursed his lips then shrugged, putting on his best devil may care expression.

"Whatever you want, Buttercup."

He tried to smirk, but it came out a little more genuine than he intended as soon as he met her shimmering green eyes. Adelle ruffled his hair. She pushed away from the table to leave but then slipped her hand down the back of his jacket, brushing the nape of his neck with the tips of her warm soft fingers.

The sensation sent him bolting upright as tingling electricity shot down right to his groin. He slapped his palms down on the table hard. Adelle giggled and walked off with her water pitcher, leaving Jack sitting rigid in his seat, with something very rigid in his jeans.

"Dirty pool!" he called after her then sighed as he slumped down again.

Damn mind dump, now she knows all my secrets!

Jack's brain bemoaned. Despite the exposure, he couldn't hide the satisfied smile on his mouth.

Still, she totally wants me.

Adelle returned to flitting from table to table, filling orders and dropping off food. Unfortunately, that left Jack alone with the memory of her soft fingertips on the back of his neck. His mind told him to cool it with her but whenever Adelle came near, he'd start flirting all over again.

Even now he watched her run around the dining room floor, charming the hell out of everyone without even knowing it. She'd flip her magnificent mane and her laughter would fill the room, wrapping around him like silk. Of course, the male customers tipped her big. She was an alluring beacon that they couldn't keep their eyes off of. He couldn't keep his eyes off her, either.

"Hello, Jack. I thought I'd find you here."

Jack looked up to see Wendy standing beside his table. She was smiling, golden hair long down her back, blue eyes twinkling.

Her presence filled the room with a warm glow and soon everyone was glancing in her direction.

Jack blinked then rubbed his head with a little grumble. "Oh, Wendy. I didn't know you came here," he said.

For a moment, he was disappointed that Wendy's ethereal beauty distracted him from the force of nature that was Adelle. His mind would have rather focused on his quirky redhead.

"I don't," Wendy said. "But I heard you and Adelle have been around here and I felt it was a good place to find you." After another smile that stole his breath, she took the seat across from him. "How are things?"

"Good. Things are-" His eyes glanced over to Adelle. She was currently filling her tray with pints of beer and laughing with the bartender. Her warm grounded chuckle brought him out of his Wendy trance. "Very good," he finished. "Where's Steven?"

"Steven? Oh, he's out with his friends. I thought it would be good for him. You know, boys will be boys and all." She laughed, tucking some of her glossy locks behind an ear.

Wendy's laugh used to enchant him with its soft feminine chime. Now, it felt hollow compared to Adelle's robust chuckle. Jack shook his head clear and looked back to Wendy. Her eyes didn't shine as bright as they used to.

"What do you need, Wendy?" he asked.

Wendy pressed a slender hand against her chest. "What would make you say that?"

"Because you only come around when you need something."

"You're being hurtful, Jack."

"No, I'm not being hurtful, I'm being realistic. What do you need?"

Wendy opened her mouth to speak when Adelle placed a water glass in front of her. It hit the table with a sharp clack.

"Oh hey, Wendy," Adelle said. "Long time no see. Slumming it tonight?"

The smile on Adelle's mouth said happy to see you, but her eyes said "I want to hit you in the face with a shovel".

Wendy jumped to her feet and embraced Adelle, which only made her irritated expression intensify. "Dell! You look good! Small town life seems to agree with you."

Adelle gently pushed Wendy away, still wearing the forced smile. "It's not bad. Jack's been a good host."

"Oh, he is. I know that for a fact. Jack is good at many things." She put her hand on one of Jack's biceps as a knowing giggle trilled from her lips. A move like that usually gave him shivers. Not even a goose bump this time. That was odd.

Wendy leaned closer to Jack, close enough for him to catch the sweet scent of honeysuckle on her skin. "Adelle, could you be a lamb and fetch me a glass of the house Chardonnay? I need to talk with Jack a moment."

The annoyance in Adelle's eyes turned murderous and her jaw tightened. The grinding of her teeth cut through the din of the pub.

"Sure," she said in a clenched voice. Adelle turned on her heels and stormed towards the bar.

Jack drummed his fingers on the table and looked to Wendy, eyes narrowed. "Now who's being hurtful?"

"I was asking for some Chardonnay and it's her job," Wendy sighed, sitting back down. "Besides, I need to talk to you in private."

"Then talk."

Wendy pursed her lips together a moment. "I was feeling bad. About tricking you into taking that vow."

That was not something Jack expected to hear. He arched a brow, looking her up and down as if she were an alien.

Wendy continued, rubbing her hands together. "So, I am going to release you of your promise. You are free from your vow."

A sudden chill touched Jack's skin and the weight of the vow he made months ago lifted from his shoulders. He blinked, mouth hanging half open. The vow was lifted? Was this really Wendy? It looked like Wendy and smelled like Wendy, but this was not her style at all.

"Just like that?" Jack said.

"Just like that." Wendy folded her delicate hands on the tabletop and gazed into his eyes. Jack gasped at the sight of the cornflower blue. He had forgotten how beautiful they were.

"I'm sorry to put you through that in the first place," Wendy said. "I kept hearing stories about how you've had to follow my cousin around like a watch dog and I felt just awful."

"It really isn't that bad," Jack said. And it wasn't. Adelle had proven to be one of the highlights of the year for him. Though, it was kind of nice to see Wendy again.

"Now, now, don't pretend it wasn't," Wendy said.

"No really it..."

He trailed off as the words sunk in. Wendy did have a point. He was giving up his evenings for Adelle. It's not like he had anything going on but yes, he could have been doing other things.

"I know Adelle," Wendy said. "She can be stubborn and prideful. She always expects to get what she wants. I'm worried, Jack. She seems to be controlling you."

Jack swallowed hard as his brow furrowed. He *did* have to follow Adelle around. Why did she want to go all over the place, anyway? She could have stayed hidden and not made a peep until all of this blew over. But she didn't. First, she had to get a job then she had to drag him out every morning to practice her damn powers. Adelle didn't even know how to use her powers. What a friggin' waste of time.

"I guess." His jaw clenched and his temples began to throb.

"Look," Wendy said. "If you want, I can ask Adelle to move back in with me. I can get her out of your hair. It was awful of me to just force someone like that on you."

Jack jerked his head up to Wendy. Having Adelle move out was ludicrous. He'd grown so accustomed to her.

"You don't have to-"

But at the same time, it seemed to be the only solution to his growing anger.

"Please. I need to make this up to you, Jack."

Wendy took his hand, fingers tracing over his knuckles in lazy circles. Her skin was soft and her touch was tender. He almost forgot about how amazing Wendy felt. His gaze traveled up the length of her arm to her divine face. Memories of tumbling her in his bed, the velvety touch of her flesh against his, and her whispered sighs in his ears cascaded over him like warm water. Soon, all he saw was Wendy's shimmering blue eyes.

Then his face grew hot with rage when he remembered that Adelle broke three of his most prized bottles. She broke those bottles right after she stared him down and made him feel castrated in his own home. Right after she blatantly ran off, not caring about his damn vow. Right after she forced him to teach her how to use her powers. She'd probably use them against him when the time was right. Adelle had been laughing at him the entire time. That devious witch enjoyed playing tricks on him.

Who the fuck does she think she is?!

A splash of ice cold liquid hit him in the face, dousing his rage. With a vehement grunt, he slapped a hand over his eyes, the other groping frantically for a napkin to blot the fire out under his eyelids. The liquid dripped onto his lips, tasting like iced fermented grapes.

Chardonnay?

"What on earth were you thinking?!" Wendy screeched.

His mind was a mess of clouded thoughts and images, as if he woke from a deep sleep. Jack wiped his eyes off with the sleeve of his jacket. The hazy figure of Adelle stood by the table, an empty wine glass held in her left hand. The last few drops of wine dribbled from the rim of the glass, pooling onto the table. A frown etched across her mouth. Jack was ready to bellow obscenities that would make a sailor blush. Instead, he snapped "What the hell?!"

Adelle swallowed. "Sorry. It's just that you looked... *glazed*." Her voice hit her last word, hard.

When her eyes flicked over to Wendy in warning, his tongue stilled. That shot of cold wine in the face put his thoughts into razor sharp focus and the revelation hit him like a freight train.

She mind fucked me, he thought. *That crazy blonde bitch mind fucked me.*

"Adelle!" Her manager's voice cut in. "What is the meaning of this!?"

Adelle fled before she could say anything more, empty glass still in hand.

Wendy wrung her hands, brow furrowed in irritation. "I have no idea what got into her. Now do you see what I'm talking about?"

Jack's lip curled up into a snarl. "You are so full of shit Wendy, I'm surprised your eyes aren't brown."

Wendy paled. "I don't know what you're talking about."

She put her hands on the table to push herself out of her seat and retreat but Jack pinned one of her hands down with a violent thud against the table. The glower he cast on her was hair-raising and she cringed. Wendy swallowed, looking around the room for a distraction. None were to be found.

"I expected more from you," Jack said. "I didn't think you'd stoop to fucking with my mind like that."

"I wasn't-"

"I trusted you. You know how hard it is to gain my trust?" Jack's fingers tightened around her hand, pressing it harder into the wood, "You know how angry I get when someone betrays my trust?"

"I'm sorry!"

"Sorry isn't going to cut it. You know, if you were anyone else, I would tear you in half."

Wendy lowered her eyes, her cheeks red.

"Why did you do it?" he asked then looked away, not able to look at Wendy without disgust choking him.

"She doesn't deserve you." Wendy sunk back down in her seat with a scowl. "She's unruly and fat and she'll bore you."

Jack's mouth fell wide open. "What?"

"She isn't worthy of you!"

"Are you... jealous?" The scowl that screwed up Wendy's otherwise perfect face told him yes, she was. Jack rubbed his forehead as he throbbed from Wendy's mind spell. "So you were just going to string me along? Your cousin shows up and suddenly you need to prove you're the alpha?" When Wendy sunk further into her seat, Jack laughed out loud. "Oh, this is great. I finally found what threatens you the most. A relative."

"It's not like that!" Wendy cried. "I am just looking out for your wellbeing!"

"Bullshit. You can't take the idea that an ex doesn't think you fart unicorns."

Wendy glared ice daggers at Jack. "I don't need this." She tried to pull away but his grip on her hand was too strong.

Jack waggled a finger at her. "Oh, no you don't. You make a vow to me, right now, that you will not screw around in my head ever again."

Wendy looked disgusted at his request. "Jack, you're being ridiculous." Her voice trailed off when she felt the pressure of his large hand increase over hers.

He bared his teeth and growled. "Make your vow or sit here until you do. I can stay here all night, sweetheart."

Wendy turned her lips up into a furious pout. After a moment of tense silence, she finally whispered, "I vow to never get into your head again."

The prickly touch of magic that ran up her arm made her wince. Satisfied, Jack let her lose.

Wendy tore her hand away. "So, that's it then." She smoothed her hair back, trying to regain her poise.

"That's it," Jack replied. It only made Wendy scowl deeper. He couldn't recall the last time she looked so furious. The sight of it filled him with delight.

"Fine." Wendy lifted her head and looked down her nose at him. "Just so you know, Steven and I are getting engaged." She spat the words out, trying to hit him with their acidic sting.

Jack's eyebrows rose. "Engaged?" Funny, months before, that news would have sent him into a rampage. Tonight, it had no effect. "Ah, good for you two."

Wendy eyed him a moment, then rephrased her statement. "He asked me to marry him. I'm going to say yes. You and Adelle are invited to the engagement party." She folded her arms and waited for a reaction. There was none. "If you actually want to come, that is."

Jack nodded then waved a hand in dismissal. "We'll see."

She grew more chafed with every non reaction he gave to her big news. Her eyes burned with a steaming fury as she turned towards the exit. "Well, good luck with your decision, Jack. You'll need it."

"I like a challenge. I dated you, didn't I?" Jack said.

Wendy snorted then shook her head. "She's still fat."

"I prefer the term voluptuous. I like a gal with meat on her bones. Now, I suggest you head on out before I consider your insults to your cousin rude and I have to act on them."

He gave her a serene smile and wiggled his fingers in a dainty little wave. Wendy narrowed her eyes at the dragon then turned and bee-lined right out the door.

Damn, that felt good.

Chapter 10

Adelle was too wrapped up in her text to notice Jack approaching. She sat on the back door stoop of Jolene's, wrapped up in her thick polar fleece sweatshirt. Her smart phone was clutched in her hands. Jack hmmed as she scowled; her eyes squinting at the glowing blue screen.

"So, did they fire you?" he asked.

With a start, Adelle looked up at the sound of Jack's voice, her thumb sailing across random keys. He noticed the name Valerie with a half written text message typed out clumsily.

Wendy is up to her olf tricks agi-@3#.

"Huh? Oh. No." Adelle shook her head, hit save and slipped her phone back into her pocket.

"So, you're good then?" Jack rubbed the back of his neck, guilt nudging him. It was kind of his fault she got into trouble, after all.

"I got written up but its procedure." She shrugged, a little smile touching her lips. "Thanks for talking to my boss. Though he did find it hard to believe that you requested I throw the glass of wine in your face as part of your order."

"You've had weirder requests."

"Yeah, but not many." She ran a hand through her curls. "I was encouraged to sit out here and cool off for the rest of the night."

Adelle had to sit in time out. She was one of the most composed beings he ever had met. A time out never seemed like anything she needed. Jack couldn't help but snicker at that.

"Well, shifts up. Let's head home." He offered his open hand to help her up. Adelle chuckled as her slender fingers slipped into his palm, their touch raising goose flesh on his arm and widening his smile.

“Gladly,” she said. “Between getting written up, Wendy, and the many attempts guys took to pinch my ass, I’m done for the night. Remind me to soak my feet when I get back."

"Not to mention soaking your butt from all the pinches."

"My butt is harder than it looks." She paused in mid step and her eyes widened. “I mean... Shit." Her face turned fuchsia and she groaned.

Jack grinned. "Now, that's ridiculous. Your butt is firmer, maybe, but not harder."

Adelle looked at him, face stone serious. “Jack, we agreed not to talk about that type of stuff.”

“You told me not to use the word moist. You never said anything about talking about your butt.”

Adelle groaned again as her steps quickened. “You’re impossible, you know this, right?”

“Just like my mother hatched me, Buttercup.”

It was a quiet night. Street lights pooled yellow across the asphalt every block. There was a sharp chill in the air. One that said snow and frosts were on the horizon soon. Jack took a deep breath, lungs filling with the frigid breeze, leaving a brisk tang on his tongue. The coolness calmed him after his heated discussion with Wendy. While others were bundled up in overcoats and scarves, the dragon didn’t need much more than his leather jacket out in this weather. It paid to have fire constantly burning in your belly.

“So, what happened back there?” Adelle asked, blowing onto her fingertips.

“I had a burger and wings. The burger was slightly overcooked in my opinion.”

Adelle rolled her eyes in response, just like he expected her to. "That's not what I meant and you know it. What the hell was Wendy doing, pulling that mind mojo on you?"

Jack shuddered. If Wendy was gutsy enough to enchant his mind right out there in public, she had probably done it the entire time they were together. He must have looked like a complete idiot following Wendy around like a beaten dog. God, he might even have looked as stupid as Steven did. Outrage began to simmer.

As if sensing his distress Adelle said, "It's hard to spot if you don't know what to look for. I know the signs. I was trained in this type of thing."

Her words quenched his temper. He ruffled his hair then looked to Adelle again. "Yeah. I've been meaning to ask you about this training thing."

She smiled. "Answer my question first and all my secrets will be revealed, oh mystic dragon."

Jack snorted and shook his head. He was about to tell her how Wendy released him from his vow but the words stalled on the tip of his tongue. A part of him didn't want to her know yet. No more vow would change a living situation he had grown rather accustomed to. Maybe he'd tell her later on, but a couple days without telling her wouldn't hurt anyone. Would it?

"She's jealous that I'm not giving her attention anymore." Jack said. It took him three steps before he noticed Adelle wasn't walking beside him. Jack stopped, turned, and caught her stalled on the sidewalk, staring at him as if he were covered in lizards.

"Are you serious?" Adelle asked.

"As a hernia."

Adelle blinked slowly at him then snorted out a laugh. "She was jealous?"

"Look, sorry to break this to you but your cousin-"

"Is a manipulative, self-centered bitch that thrives off all men paying attention at her at all times?" A few long strides and Adelle caught up with him again. "Yeah, I've known that since I was eight."

It warmed Jack's heart to hear Adelle tear into her cousin. Most of Whitmore considered Wendy the town sweetheart. She must have planted that concept into the mind of everyone she encountered, himself included.

"She and Steve are getting engaged," Jack added casually.

Adelle rubbed her hands together to warm them. "And you didn't throw her out a window at that news? I'm shocked."

"Nope. I considered it, evaluated the situation, and decided it wasn't prudent. See? I'm growing."

Adelle laughed, filling his heart with her music. He grinned. Yes, her laugh was indeed ten times better than Wendy's.

"I just assumed that you'd be more upset. You two were pretty intense, huh?" she said.

"You asking, or just confirming what you already know?"

"I don't know. A little of both I guess."

"Yeah, well, I'm not carrying a torch for her, if that's what you mean."

Adelle eyed him. "I don't think I believe you on the torch thing, no offence."

Jack pursed his lips, lifting his eyes to the cloudy evening sky. He was crushed after Wendy left him. He couldn't eat. He couldn't sleep. All that time he had assumed his true mate had rejected him. But after tonight, he was reevaluating that. How much of his love sick feelings were genuine and how much had Wendy planted into his brain? His gaze slid back down to Adelle, who was keeping stride beside him. She chewed on her lower lip, her expression pensive. It was comforting, seeing her concern. No false smiles. No masks of serenity.

"Maybe I was. Things change." A ghost of a smile touched his mouth. "I answered your questions. Now you answer mine."

"Sure. Sounds like fair play."

Jack stopped to lean against the brick wall of a convenience store, slipping his hands into the pockets of his leather jacket. "What exactly do you and your sisters do?"

Adelle looked amused as she took a place on the wall beside him. "You've been chomping at the bit to find out since you met me, haven't you?"

"You're half siren. You sister is half Valkyrie. I'm not even sure what the hell your youngest sister is. You bring up the word training a lot when you talk about your childhood." He reached over, tucking an unruly curl behind her ear. "Color me curious."

Adelle took a deep breath then looked up to Jack. "Val, Phoebe, and I were adopted because we were all half-bloods. My mom, Cybil took it upon herself to train us to fight monsters."

Jack arched a brow. "Monsters like me?"

Her answer was in the form of a cute smirk. "No. Not Wyrd creatures. Monsters. Rogues. Dark mages. Things that decide to go on rampages or want to take out all the humans in a five mile radius. In theory, there are others who do this but my sisters and I are the only ones I know about."

"So you're the Wyrd police?" Jack heard rumors about this before but never met anyone who did such things.

Adelle gave him a nod." Pretty much. Mom used to be a nun. She saw some crazy things when she was a novice. Things that the Catholic Church didn't talk about at mass. Some good. Some bad. She left the veil and decided to start hunting down the baddies."

Jack snickered. "Your mom sounds like a badass."

"In her heyday, she was hard core," Adelle said with a giggle. "When she got older, mom started looking for replacements. So she adopted Val, then me, and eventually Phoebe knowing we were all half-blood. All of us girls have a foot in each world. So-"

"You're not bound to Wyrd rules or human skepticism, letting you police the bad guys," Jack finished for her.

It was a hard rule in their world. Full bloods never got involved in the business of humans. It was all right to know them and even befriend them. Hell, some even mated with them. But to fight their wars, deal in their politics, or protect them as a whole was forbidden in most cases. It was obey the rules or else. The "or else" part varied from species to species. In a dragon's case, it was punishable by the karmic waves that controlled the magic.

Adelle had both human and Wyrd blood. Like mages, she and her sisters could interfere all they wanted with no cosmic force crushing down on them. Cybil was smart.

"So you, your mom, and your sisters hit the town putting things back in line?" Jack said.

Adelle shrugged as she blew onto her fingers again, her breath puffing out a white cloud of steam in the frosty air. "Well, Mom and Val were the ones that would do that. I was more research and development."

"And they're fighting evil as we speak, huh?"

Adelle's pink mouth turned down into a sad frown. She was quiet for a while before looking down to her hands. "Mom was murdered a few years ago," she murmured.

Jack felt the pit of his stomach grow cold and he chastised himself under his breath. Knowing what it's like to lose a parent was not foreign to him. He had lost both. It was centuries ago, but it still stung.

"I'm... I'm sorry," he said. Jack could see the pain in Adelle's luminous green eyes. Tears shimmered there for a moment before her face slipped into a neutral expression, hiding everything deep down inside.

"You didn't know. It's all right," she said. "She was out on a mission with Val. There was a mage we knew. Tony. We grew up with him. Hell, he and his family used to have Christmas with us. When he got older, Tony started to dabble in dark magic. Val and mom went over to try to talk sense into him. He killed mom during the argument then disappeared." She fell silent a moment, holding her breath. After a long sigh, she continued. "I was away at college up in San Francisco. I moved back to San Diego after that and finished school there. For years I was angry at myself for not being there but eventually came to terms with it. Though sometimes... Well, sometimes I wonder if it would have been different if I was there."

They stood in silence. She said she was over the ordeal but something in her somber expression said otherwise. He regarded Adelle, not sure if he should say something, touch her, hold her, or just keep his distance. His instinct told him to put his arms around her but he held back, not trusting them. Instead, he decided to keep the conversation moving.

"What did you tell your baby sister?" he asked.

"We told Phoebe mom was in a car accident. She doesn't know about us yet."

"So Phoebe has no clue about magic? The Wyrd? Nothing?"

Adelle ran her fingers through her hair with a frustrated groan. "Yeah. Mom made us promise to not to tell Phoebe about any of it before her powers manifested. She was really adamant about giving us a normal a childhood. Val and I developed in our teens and found out then, but Phoebe is twenty five now and still hasn't manifested. It has me worried. What if she never turns?" After a beat, she snorted in amusement. "Phoebe thinks I'm up here to help Wendy start a hairdressing business."

Jack's lip twisted and he let out a guffaw. "Hairdressing?"

"I don't even know what Wendy does for a living, do you?"

Jack blinked as he realized that he didn't. He furrowed his brow then shook his head. "Well, that's going to be messy when she's fully operational, don't you think?"

She squeezed her eyes shut. "Don't remind me. I'll probably be the one who has to break it to her. Val's people skills are lacking, to be generous about it, and Phoebe is high strung. I'm expecting a full out panic meltdown from her."

"What is she?"

"A Dryad."

"A fucking fairy? Oh yeah, meltdown city."

The two had a good cackle together which appeared to lighten Adelle's mood. She rubbed her hands together again, shivering. Without much thought, Jack reached forward and took her trembling hands into his, pressing them between his warm palms. Her fingers were like icicles against his skin but since Jack was a walking heater, he'd have her warmed up in no time.

Adelle paused, her eyes fixed on his strong hands. When Jack cleared his throat, her gaze snapped back up to his. She gave him a sheepish grin and shrugged. The flush of her cheeks made his heart stutter, and he couldn't help but he charmed by her sudden awkwardness.

"So," Jack said. "What was your part in all this guardian angel stuff?"

"I was more along for moral support. Back up cross bow or something along those lines," Adelle said.

"Because you hated your powers."

"Exactly."

The corners of Jack's mouth tugged upward. "What about now?"

"Now?" Adelle cocked her head to the side.

"Do you hate your powers now?"

Adelle's teeth sunk into her lower lip as she mulled the question over. Soon, a little grin crept across her pink lips. "Now, I can honestly say I like them a lot more."

Jack was pleased with her answer. He even preened. After all, he was the catalyst for her new found confidence.

A tiny flicker of white caught his eye, then another, and another. A light flurry of snowflakes fell from the dark grey skies, settling onto Adelle's fire kissed curls as they twinkled in the amber streetlights like tiny little diamonds. Jack felt her hands tremble again despite them already being warm. He held them tighter.

"You better get yourself a good winter coat, Buttercup. You'll freeze in another day or two in these parts."

"What? And give up the best pair of gloves I ever had?" she teased. He felt his mouth twitch into another smile.

Just holding Adelle's hands filled him with a heat that rivaled the one that burned inside his gut. Jack reached up to dust the collecting snowflakes from her hair, the curls soft and smooth against his palm. He took a deep inhalation, the sweet scent of honey filling his nostrils, and stepped closer to her. He could hear the beat of her heart speed up when he grew near. Her eyes grew heavy lidded and dreamy which only encouraged him.

"One more question," he said.

Adelle smiled. "All right, shoot."

Jack lowered his face right next to her ear and in a heated whisper said, "Why don't we go to my bed tonight?"

There was that beautiful blush again. Jack wondered if she blushed that color all over. He'd spend every cent of his hoard to find out.

Adelle stared at him, mouth wide open. "Well, you're just going to lay it right out on the table, aren't you?"

"I'm not one to mince words." Jack leaned in even closer, able to catch her hot quivering breath against his skin. "I know I'm not the only one here who wants to."

Adelle looked down at his hands encasing hers. "True," she said.

Jack pulled a hand away, tucking it under Adelle's chin to lift her face towards him. His thumb padded over the softness of her bottom lip, and he tingled at the sound of her trembling sigh. He bowed toward her, longing to slant his mouth over hers and break this tension once and for all.

"Then what the hell are we waiting for, Adelle?" he whispered.

"You want the truth?" Adelle asked.

"I don't ask for much."

His lust filled trance was broken when she took a generous step back. "Jack, I'm one of those women who get attached to men afterwards. You strike me as the type who doesn't want attachments."

Jack felt his jaw clench. His spine straightened in an instant as her words sunk in.

She gets attached. She wants a mate. The very last thing I want, right now.

"You told me that you're not interested in that," Adelle said. After swallowing hard, she looked up at him, her gaze heavy. "That's still true, right?"

Jack's head swam with confusion. Of course he didn't want a mate. Not after the way Wendy had played with him. Jack was his own dragon and no one else's. Unfortunately, Adelle had wedged herself under his scales. If he took her to bed, it would only get worse. Where would he be when she left him to return to San Diego? He didn't need that. Best to not tempt the fates and end up with yet another broken heart. A real one, this time.

Jack cleared his throat, squirming under Adelle's watchful eyes. "Yeah. It's still true," he said with a snort.

It could have been his imagination, but Adelle seemed to deflate, shoulders slumping, and her eyes lowering to her feet. Then after a quick breath, she pulled her shoulders back and looked him dead on. "Well, I'm not going to put myself into that situation then." Her voice was firm. "I'll end up hurt. You'll end up resentful. And that will be it."

She slipped her hands out from between his and they disappeared into her sweatshirt pockets. Suddenly things felt very chilly.

Jack heard Adelle's teeth grinding as she waited for his reaction. He opened his mouth, to speak, afraid that the words "I take it back. Let's make this work" would come spilling out from his lips. What good would that be to him? Falling for a female that he couldn't hang on to, getting another round of emotional pain he wasn't willing to take on.

Fuck that.

"I can respect that," was his only response.

"Good," Adelle said. "Because I'm not going to budge on it. Hell, I already went two years without sex so-"

"You've gone two years without sex?!"

Jack's roar of shock echoed down the empty streets of Whitmore, rattling windows and making dogs bark. Adelle went crimson and glared at him.

"Really, Jack?" she said, clipped and irritated

"Sorry. I was just surprised is all." He pushed himself from the wall trying to keep his cool demeanor intact. He went to take her hands again but noticed that they still remained tucked away in her sweatshirt. With a gruff snort, he turned on his heels. "Keep your hands in your pockets. We're only a block from home."

Adelle did just that. She walked beside him in silence, hands shoved deep into her sweatshirt. Jack kept his hands locked to his sides, making no more effort for physical contact. It was for the best. Now that he knew where she stood with him, this whole ridiculous infatuation can be buried. They would go back to being roommates and things wouldn't be strained anymore. It was for the best.

So why do I feel awful?

Adelle's thoughtful visage soon melted into a natural mask. He hadn't seen that bearing on her before. Even if she couldn't fully express her emotions, Adelle usually had a twinkle in her eyes and passion in her smile. Now, she was calm and stoic. Impenetrable as a fortress. As they walked the rest of the way in silence, Jack rubbed his hand against his aching chest. The pang made him realize she was shutting him out. She was protecting her heart from him.

And God, it hurt.

Chapter 11

Day seven in the countdown to their oblivion. Ethan and Brett huddled in San Diego State University's library, basking in a computer monitor's blue glow. The college was the only library Ethan knew of that kept late hours. Too much time was wasted breaking into public libraries to gain internet access. They'd been pouring through Wendy after Wendy on Facebook for hours. If Anthony wanted them to find Adelle in a timely manner, he should have at least hooked them up with a goddamned laptop.

Ethan had seen Wendy once before when Adelle happened to show him a photo of her. That was a hard face to forget. Wendy was beautiful in the way poets described golden goddesses, even in a picture taken with a crappy phone camera. Unfortunately, Adelle never told him Wendy's last name. Much to his dismay, there were at least seven-thousand Wendy's living in Washington State. So many social networks with so many Wendys. Some profiles had photos but none were the breath taking blonde that Ethan remembered. Neither Adelle nor her sisters had an internet presence so he couldn't track Wendy through them.

It was hopeless. The magical time bomb Anthony had planted in his chest was ticking away. Ethan could hear it echoing in his ears. That masochistic bastard added that extra auditory detail to remind them they were on borrowed time.

"This is fucking useless," Brett grumbled from his chair. He rubbed a hand over the stubble on his chin. Brett hadn't shaved the day he was turned and was cursed for all eternity with a patchy five o'clock shadow.

Ethan let out a shuddering sigh, tossing the stringy brown hair from his eyes. It was starting to dreadlock from the weeks of no hygiene. He knew he was disgusting. His clothes reeked of sewer sludge and decay. The once new blue jeans he wore were now brown with filth. His button down shirt - which was a light blue at some point- was a muddled mess of blood and mud. When he was still a human, Ethan was rather meticulous over his appearance. Hair always combed and neat, every button buttoned, every shoelace tied. Now, he didn't even *have* shoes.

The withdrawals from Adelle's blood were getting worse. Ethan's hands shook. His stomach knotted in anguish and he itched as if thousands of ants were racing over his flesh. He dragged his fingernails down his neck until the pale skin grew purple with scratch marks. Scratching the invisible bugs away didn't make him feel any better.

"She has to be on the internet somewhere," Ethan said in a hushed voice. "Adelle said she was a narcissist. Those types always have Facebook pages."

Brett slammed his hands on the arm rests of his chair. Ethan hissed a "shh" at him, not wanting to call any attention to themselves. Vampires did have the power to make themselves less noticeable in a crowd but Ethan didn't want to risk anything further.

"Then you find her!" Brett said. He thrust a dirty finger under Ethan's nose. "I found you a thousand Wendys so far! None of them are her! I didn't want any part of this, man. *You* got me into this!"

Ethan grumbled as he shut his eyes.

It was Adelle's fault. That bitch started it. She's your ruin. She's your downfall. Kill her for this!

He turned the voices in his head off and pushed Brett from the keyboard. "Shit happens," he said as if that would explain all of Brett's worries away.

Brett's chair wheeled away with a high pitched squeak as Ethan started typing. He pursed his lips then let out a manic giggle. Why didn't he think of this before? Ethan gritted his teeth and typed in the last name Constance and hit search.

Nothing.

"Fuck!" he shouted, slamming his hands down on the computer desk.

Students jumped, finally noticing the two dirty, twitching vampires. Brett waved a hand and the gawkers turned their eyes away as if they never heard a thing. Ethan leaned on the backspace button, deleting the last name when a new crop of names popped up in the browser window.

Wendy Con…

Wendy Cona.

Wendy Conles.

Wendy Connelly.

Ethan scrolled to the final name on the list and clicked.

There she was.

That beautiful face, the cornflower blue eyes, and that ethereal smile. It was Wendy Connelly, from Washington, Adelle's cousin. If Ethan had a beating heart, it would have stopped. "Oh, God. Oh, sweet God, we found her!"

He clicked on the link next to the small thumbnail of Wendy's photo and went to her profile. For the most part, it was set to private. He couldn't see her status updates or other photos. Luckily, it wasn't a complete lockdown. Some of her information was visible.

Wendy Connelly
Occupation: n/a
Studied at: University of Washington
Status: Engaged
Lives in: Whitmore, Washington.

When he searched Whitmore, he noticed how small the town was. More relief flooded him. They had a fighting chance now. He just hoped to God that Adelle was there. Ethan squealed in delight, banging his fists on the desk in a rapid fire bang, bang, bang.

"What? What did you find?" Brett jumped out of his chair to look over Ethan's shoulder.

With a smug smile, Ethan tapped the monitor with his dirt encrusted fingernail. "Whitmore, Washington. Population nine-hundred. In a place that small someone has got to know Wendy and definitely knows if her cousin is in town. We're golden!"

As relieved as he was to know they had a fighting chance to live, what excited him more was the inevitable taste of Adelle's blood on his lips. He ran his tongue across his upper lip in anticipation.

Oh God, let me hold on for two more weeks.

"Great. Whitmore. How do we get there?" Brett ran a hand across his smooth scalp and started to pace. "I don't have any cash, do you?"

Ethan's glee hit the pause button. The cash Anthony paid him to kidnap Adelle the first time was long gone. They sure as hell couldn't walk to Washington. Were they supposed to flap their arms and fly? Ethan wished that turning into a bat cliché was true.

He turned to answer Brett when a metallic jingle hit the computer desk. A pile of quarters were stacked up neatly beside the keyboard as bills floated down from thin air to join the stack of change.

The two vampires exchanged a puzzled look before hearing Anthony's voice say, "Bus fare".

They spun with a start to find Anthony standing behind them in his well pressed suit, leaning on his sleek ivory cane. "Bus fair and lodgings," he said. "Well, go on. You seemed to have found her. Go clean yourselves up and buy a Greyhound ticket. Not much time now." He raised a finger, twitching his hand side to side, singing, "Tick Tock, Tick Tock.".

"We're doing our best, okay?" Ethan muttered, running a hand through his greasy hair. The grit he shook loose fell to the carpet in black and grey flecks. "This affects you too, so cut us some fucking slack!"

Anthony rolled his eyes. He turned and strolled into the stacks of shelves, his cane clicking softly on the floor as he went. Ethan vaulted out of his chair, fangs bared. He wanted to tear that smug little bastard apart with his teeth and bite that smile right off his face. When he turned the corner into the stacks, the mage was gone. The ticking in his head grew louder with the relentless beat of a snare drum. Ethan balled his hands into tight fists as his skin crawled with prickles and itches.

"Dude? What's going on?" Brett called after him. "Did you catch him?"

"No," Ethan grumbled.

"So, now what?"

"We do what he told us. Get cleaned up and head to Whitmore." Ethan set his jaw and headed to the exit.

"I swear man. I will kill that bitch when we find her."

Ethan waved Brett and his own murderous tendencies aside. "Yeah, well killing her will kill us too, so curb that idea."

Two weeks were all they had left. Two weeks to find Adelle, take her back, and remove the curse. Two weeks for Ethan to save his hide. Two weeks to adjust to the fact he was going to kill his ex-girlfriend.

I'm so sorry Adelle. But it's you or me.

And he was going to be the one that survived.

Chapter 12

The phone rang in the kitchen. Adelle was just about to run out from her on campus apartment and off to class. She looked to the phone a moment, hovering halfway out the door. If it was Valerie, she'd keep her on the phone forever, making her late yet again.

"You going to get that?" Her roommate Alma shouted from her bedroom.

Adelle pursed her lips then sighed, turning on her heels. "I got it!" she called back and yanked the receiver off the cradle, pressing it against her ear. "Hello?"

"Dell," It was Valerie. Here we go with the long conversations about her latest patrol findings.

"Val," Adelle looked to the door again. "Can I call you back? I'm running late."

"No, you can't." Valerie sounded strained. She always hated when Adelle gave her the brush off.

Adelle groaned, rubbing the bridge of her nose. "I will call you back right after class I promise."

"No, Dell," Valerie insisted.

"Seriously, Val, I-"

"Mom is dead."

Adelle froze. The phone almost slipped out of her hand but her fingers tightened around it before it slid too far. She swallowed hard, throat dry as the perimeter of her vision grew dark.

A nervous laugh shook from her parched throat. "That's not funny, Val."

"I know it's not funny! Do you think I'd say that trying to be funny?!"

Adelle's limbs turned to ice. The sound of Phoebe's horrified wailing echoed in the background.

"Sorry, I'm shaken," Valerie said, voice softer.

Her brain went spinning out of control, trying to process everything. Valerie just said. Mom is dead? That can't be right. Mom was always there. She was a healthy woman, and a smart, strong fighter. How could she be dead? Adelle's belly grew cold and her knees felt weak. She pressed her back against the wall, forcing herself to stay standing.

"How...?" was all she could stammer.

The sound of her baby's sister's crying faded and Adelle heard a door close before Valerie answered with, "Tony," her voice covered in ice.

"Tony? What does Tony have to do with this?" Thick silence greeted her on the other side. She waited, hearing Valerie sniffling across the other line. "Val, answer me. Please." Tears pushed against Adelle's eyes, and she fiercely wiped them away with her sleeve. When they returned, she slammed her eyes shut, holding them captive, still begging for her sister to continue. "Please, talk to me Val."

"Tony was practicing dark magic. His parents asked us to talk to him. To get him to stop. So, we did. And he... He killed her, Dell." Valerie's voice shook with pain. "He killed her."

"Why? Christ, Val, it's Tony! He's like a…"

Adelle gagged on her words. She couldn't say the word brother. Even if he and Adelle fought more than talked, Tony still stood by her and her sisters. Before this moment, she'd call Tony her brother in a heartbeat. He was a brother of the heart. Now the word tasted too bitter.

"What does Phoebe know?" Adelle asked.

"I told her it was a car accident... It was the only thing I... could...."

Adelle sunk her teeth into her lower lip as she listened to Valerie collapse into sobs, fighting the need to join her. Her hand pressed over her mouth hard and she inhaled deep through her nose.

Just stay calm, *she heard Cybil's voice tell her.* Just stay calm, Adelle.

But composure continued to slip out of her grasp.

"I'm on the next flight out," Adelle whispered. She cleared her throat to push down the trembling in her voice. She had to be calm.

Be calm or else. You can do this Dell. You can handle this.

"Why couldn't you have been here?" Valerie snapped. "We could have used you! Why weren't you here?! Maybe we could have stopped him if you weren't off doing your own fucking thing!"

Adelle's stomach twisted. She bit down hard on her lower lip as her sister's words stabbed her in the heart. The metallic tang of blood filled her mouth.

You were miles away, pretending to be normal, that's why. You turned your back on family. She is dead because of you.

"I'm sorry." Adelle fingers clutched at her chest, keeping her heart from cracking through her ribcage. The acidic taste of bile hung in the back of her throat as she grew close to vomiting on the kitchen floor.

After a long pause, Valerie said, "I'm sorry. That wasn't fair of me." The apology didn't help and Adelle bit her clenched fist, fighting tooth and nail to keep from screaming. "Just, call me when you get your flight. I'll come get you."

"All right," Adelle said.

Valerie didn't even say good bye. There was just a heavy click, followed by the hollow sound of a dial tone.

Somehow, Adelle managed to get the phone back on the hook. She stood up, still propped up against the wall, not able to move, and barely able to breathe. Her jelly knees were locked, making her legs throb. She pinched her arm, twisting her flesh until it purpled, praying that the pain would wake her. But this wasn't one of Adelle's nightmares.

Cybil was gone. Adelle would never hear her mother's laugh, or feel her arms around her again. She would never again delight in the phone calls home, or cry on her shoulder and hear her voice sooth, "Just keep calm and everything will be fine". Nothing was going to be fine ever again. Mom was never coming back. All because Adelle wasn't there.

Her knees gave out on her and she slid down the kitchen wall, landing into a clumsy sit on the linoleum floor. Hot tears burned her cheeks. Not able to contain it anymore, Adelle threw her head back and let out an anguished cry. The walls of the apartment shook with a violent fury, and she slapped her hands over her mouth.

"Did you feel that? Was that an earthquake?" Alma called from the bedroom.

Adelle's fingers dug into her cheeks, clutching at her mouth as anguished squeaks leaked from between her closed lips. Feet kicked at the floor. Teeth sunk into the inside of her mouth. She banged the back of her head against the wall over and over. Anything to lessen the sorrow.

Nothing eased the suffering.

Hand still clasped over her mouth, Adelle scrambled to her feet and dashed out the front door. She sprinted across campus, needing to get as far away as she could. She had to find a place to scream, any place to pound her fists and wail out her grief in safety. She ran until her legs ached, until blisters swelled on her feet. But no matter how far she ran, crowds found her. Soon, she fell to her knees, too terrified to remove the hands from her lips. Tears stained the collar of her t-shirt, her breath in short heavy pants as the world closed in on her.

Hours later; the campus police found Adelle curled up like a fetus on the steps of the library. She was shaking, her hands clasped so tight over her mouth, purple finger shaped bruises covered her cheeks. They pried her hands from her face, finding her lips bloodied from her teeth tearing through the tender flesh.

When an officer asked what happened, all Adelle could whisper was, "My mom died… And I have to keep calm for her."

Adelle had lied to Jack about her mother's death. She wasn't over it. Since the day she talked about Cybil, the memories of her death gave her nightmares. She hadn't had a decent night's sleep in four days due to the constricting sense of not being able to scream. Naps throughout the day only made her groggier, so she didn't bother with them. Besides, sleep brought back memories she didn't want to encounter anymore.

Every morning she jolted awake, covered in sweat, and helpless to take a breath until she forced herself to. By the time her heart beat slowed to a normal rate, she would have to get up for a practice with Jack. Practices became tedious. She couldn't focus her powers, which resulted in Jack hauling out the fire extinguisher from the trunk of his Impala.

This morning, Adelle skipped practice all together. When Jack came in to wake her, she groaned how she wasn't feeling well and she just needed to rest. That lie lead to Jack constantly questioning her health which was getting more than aggravating.

"You sure you're all right?" Jack asked from the living room couch. He watched Adelle tie her sneakers on as she readied herself for work. "You've been looking pale the last couple of days."

"I'm fine. Stop mother henning me," Adelle grumbled.

Jack folded his arms and smirked at her. "Then stop doing things that make me believe you're getting sick."

Adelle looked at his smug expression, let out an irritated snort, and finished putting her shoes on. The nightmares weren't the only thing bothering her. They were accented by an angry pain brought on by Jack's rejection. Adelle didn't expect the reality to hurt so much but it stung like a deep paper cut. Jack was the only one who truly understood her, yet he had no interest in wanting her like she wanted him. And God, did she want him. Adelle wanted to call him hers like no one else. But he made it perfectly clear that he was only interested in a brief bedroom romp.

The pain in her heart was hard to ignore but with time she'd either get over it, or move back to San Diego. Until then, they were still stuck together like glue due to Wendy's vow. So, Adelle did what she did best; shut down, step away, and keep her distance. What made it all worse was that the scaly bastard acted even nicer than usual to her afterwards.

The day after their talk, Jack bought a new coat for her, suitable for the oncoming winter. Adelle found it on her bed. A wool, navy blue peacoat with brass buttons, the lining a colorful green and blue paisley. Adelle loved paisley. She didn't even know that Jack noticed that. Either he was trying to woo her into bed or curb any guilt he had for leading her on.

"Hello? Earth to Adelle. Come on, Buttercup, answer me." Jack leaned forward on the couch towards her, peering at her with those piercing amber eyes. He pressed a hand to her forehead. "You're sick. I can tell."

Adelle bristled at the once endearing nickname and jerked her head away from his touch. "I'm not sick! Just haven't been getting much sleep lately is all."

"Why not?"

"Lumpy mattress, I guess. I don't know." Adelle chewed on her lower lip, realizing that she tied her thumb into her shoe laces. She let out an exhausted sigh and started over.

"Then stay home from work," Jack insisted. "Come on, Buttercup-"

Adelle turned on him, eyes blazing. "Stop it! Just stop calling me Buttercup, okay? It's stupid!"

Jack leaned back as if slapped. When she saw his wounded expression, Adelle almost took back her outburst. She finished tying her shoes instead. "If I'm working, it takes my mind off things," she said.

"Things." Jack narrowed his eyes. "Things like our discussion four days ago?"

Adelle jumped to her feet to find her purse. "No," she replied curtly.

Jack groaned loud as he stood up. A few quick strides and he blocked her path to the kitchen, arms folded across his broad chest. "Bullshit. Tell me the truth."

"The truth is that I'm going to be late for work." She tried to go around him but he snagged her by the arm and pulled her back into place.

"I told you I was fine with your decision," he said. "I thought we were good. Now, you don't say more than five words to me in a day if I'm lucky."

Adelle yanked her arm free of his grip and raised her stubborn chin to him. "So? I'm not your girlfriend. Why should you care?"

She regretted the words as soon as she saw the pang of hurt behind Jack's eyes. Her heart shuddered. She wanted to hug him tight, to press her cheek against his chest and inhale his comforting scent. She wanted to cry.

"It's not you, it's me," Adelle said, then blinked as she heard the words leave her mouth. "Oh hell, did I actually say that?"

Jack pointed an accusing finger and her and bellowed, "Stop using your girl logic!"

Adelle threw up her hands and side stepped him, zipping around him to get to the kitchen. Jack's hurt ego swiftly turned into anger as his eyebrows lowered over his stormy glare.

"You're acting like a petulant child!" he called after her.

"I am not!" Adelle shot back.

Jack smirked. "Oh, I'm sorry. I meant to say you're acting like a crazy bitch. My mistake."

Adelle wanted to scream. She wanted to scream so loud that she'd blast him through the wall of his own kitchen. Instead, she kicked over a chair, sending it sailing across the room. It landed to the floor with a crash, one of the legs cracking off and rolling across the tile. She turned to glare at him, keeping her voice trapped in her clenched jaw.

Jack was unmoved by the tantrum. He scanned the mess and looked back at her, eyes cold. "I call them like I see them. Thanks for breaking my chair."

"You know what? I don't need this today. I don't need this or your attitude or any of this crap!" Adelle threw her smartphone and a set of keys in her purse. Her bitter laugh left a horrible taste in her mouth. "But I guess that doesn't matter does it? Because you're still going to be there, reminding me that you don't give a fuck. Trailing after me like my smart mouthed shadow because of your stupid vow!"

"No, I'm not." The resentment on his face was crystal clear.

"What are you talking about?"

Jack hovered at his bedroom, fingers clutching the door frame with white knuckle intensity. "The vow. Wendy took it back four days ago."

Adelle stared at him, slack jawed at the news. That must have been what Wendy needed to talk to him about. Whatever twisted motives she may have had, Jack was free of her. He had been for four days.

"And you didn't tell me?"

"I'm telling you now," Jack snarled. "And I'm taking a night off tonight. I fucking earned it. Enjoy work and enjoy martyrdom." He stormed into his bedroom, slamming the door behind him.

Adelle gaped at his closed bedroom door, dumbfounded. A long moment of silent staring passed before she snapped, "You should have told me that you big... lizard!"

She threw her hands up then slung her purse over her shoulder. Her loud footsteps stomped to the door as she grumbled under her breath.

"The vow was broken and you don't tell me? Why am I even angry? Why do I even care, anymore? This is ridiculous!"

She should just pack up and head home to San Diego. Might as well do both of them a favor. Even Valerie's wrath was better than this. Adelle's hand grasped the front door knob and she froze, hesitant to storm out like she originally planned.

Jack had been free of his vow for four days, and yet he stayed close to her, all on his own free will. That wasn't the behavior of someone who didn't care. A glimmer of hope twinkled inside her. Could Jack have been lying about his feelings? Maybe he needed to feel safe as much as she did. Adelle sighed, her hand slipping from the knob and she slunk over to Jack's bedroom, pride tucked between her legs. He was right. She was acting like a crazy bitch.

Adelle hovered outside his door a long moment. His name caught in her throat before she could call it, so she raised her hand, knuckles about to knock. That too was halted. With a long ragged sigh, she pressed her forehead against the door.

"I can hear you breathing, Adelle," Jack's muffled voice called. "Just go to work."

Adelle shut her eyes, pressing her palm flat against the door. "Jack-"

"Get out."

All the words she wanted to say withered in her mouth. Adelle's teeth sunk into her lower lip hard, and she turned without a word. She reached up to snag her new peacoat off the hook by the door. The soft blue wool ran through her fingers and tears pressed against the back of her eyes.

I blew it.

She bypassed her new coat and grabbed her ratty fleece sweatshirt, instead. Adelle threw it over her head, and walked out the door to the snow dusted streets, alone.

Chapter 13

Adelle's plan to get her mind off her problems didn't come to fruition. In fact, work only made it worse. It was a busy night at the pub, full of drunken jackasses and whining customers. They were short staffed, so Adelle had to work double duty and the tips were getting smaller and smaller the later the night went. When Adelle had a rough shift, Jack's warm grin would pick up her spirits, putting a spring back into her step. Tonight, his booth was populated by a group of obnoxious sorority girls complaining about not getting enough vodka in their gin martinis. The contradiction made Adelle's left eyelid twitch.

Jack's absence only reminded her of what a jerk she had been. And that only reminded her of the other mistakes she'd made in her life, including Cybil's death. Adelle slogged through work, fighting the tears that threatened to pour down her cheeks. No wonder she was getting rotten tips. No one tips a Debbie Downer.

It was only a few minutes before closing time. The bartender had made last call thirty minutes ago and Leah, the hostess, was politely shooing the last of the customers out the door. Adelle was back near the kitchen, ready to grab her purse and clock out from her hellish night when Leah poked her head around the doorway.

"Hey, Adelle," she smiled. "Someone is asking for you. Can you go see him before you clock out?"

Adelle's dark mood lifted. Jack must have come by to check on her. He wasn't the type to just abandon her, even after a fight.

Not that I didn't deserve it.

Her heart skipped. If Jack was waiting in the dining room, Adelle could apologize for her awful behavior. Things could go back to quasi-normal. Maybe their friendship could be salvaged.

"No problem," she told Leah. "I'll be out in a sec."

As soon as Leah left, Adelle wiped her fingers under her eyes then fluffed her hair. After she determined it was as good as it was going to get, she hurried out to the dining room, heart racing.

I can fix this. I can fix this, Jack.

Her sneakers came to a screeching halt as soon as her eyes hit the table Leah had seated. There sat Ethan, tall, pale, and jittery. His shaggy brown hair was longer than before and his red eyes were looking a little less bloodshot than she remembered. Overall, he looked almost normal.

Ethan was clean and well dressed in his white button down shirt and skinny jeans with his pale hands folded on the tabletop, fingers trembling. She would have suspected him being detoxed from her blood if he wasn't shaking so much. Their gazes locked. He gave her a nervous closed mouth smile, hiding his fangs then lifted a hand in a gentle wave. He greeted her just like he did the first time they met.

Adelle felt her throat close as she went ice cold. The last time she laid eyes on Ethan, she was zip tied to a dirty bed and he was tearing one of her arteries open with his teeth.

Breathe Adelle, her brain screamed and she gasped hard, taking in mouthfuls of air.

Her gaze darted around the dining room for reinforcements. There was only her, Ethan, and a couple of bussers cleaning the glasses from the tables. Ethan would be a fool to start anything with humans about. But he was never very smart about staying incognito. He had made scenes before when they were together. He made worse scenes when he was withdrawing.

Memories of her capture hit her in a rush, melting her terror into a white hot fury. She bit the inside of her cheek to keep from screaming and stormed towards Ethan, her teeth churning and grinding. Ethan's soft brows furrowed in reply.

"What the fuck are you doing here?" Adelle hissed in a low voice. "Why are you here and when are you leaving? The answer to the third question better be right now."

"I can explain," Ethan said.

Adelle looked over her shoulder to make sure no one was listening in, and then fixed him with a black look. "I don't want an explanation. I want you gone."

Ethan put up his hands in surrender. "I came to apologize."

She narrowed her eyes at his explanation. "How did you find me?" she asked.

He shook his head, casting a pained expression her way. "I did some research. Look, Adelle. What I did was awful-"

"Awful?" She leaned down almost nose to nose with Ethan. Adelle wanted to kill him. She wanted to belt out a note so powerful, he would turn to ash. Yet she held back, wanting to hear what he had to say. Goddammit, part of her still felt bad for the bastard. "You tortured me for five days. You almost killed me. Awful is only the tip of the iceberg, Ethan."

"I know. God, please." Ethan swallowed hard, running his trembling fingers through his hair. "I just need your forgiveness. I don't want your blood. I don't want-" he twitched when the word blood left his mouth. "I just want you to forgive me. Please."

Adelle watched him, mulling over his words. Maybe he was sincere with his apology. Ethan wasn't horrible until his addiction took hold. When they first met, he hadn't had the nerve to hurt a fly. But after he took her blood, he changed. Whatever he craved in Adelle turned his hunger into rage and obsession. Every hit made him lose more of his mind.

Ethan's red eyes fluttered closed and he slid to the edge of his chair. With a long inhale through his nose, he whispered, "I missed you, Adelle," moaning her name.

Adelle shivered. "Stop that. Stop smelling me."

Ethan snapped out of his euphoric trance. "I wasn't."

He wetted his lips and peered at her throat, losing track of his words. His lecherous stare made Adelle slap her hand against the side of her neck. The raised scars from his fangs were rough on her palm, reminding her of what he had done.

"Yes you were," she said. "And you came here to make me believe you wanted to apologize?"

Ethan wrung his shaking hands. "Adelle, I'm in trouble. You're the only one I can go to for this."

"What?" Adelle leaned back, peering down at the pathetic, shivering vampire.

Ethan clenched his jaw and his shaking grew worse. He screwed up his face, clutching one of his ears, as if something loud was pounding in his head. "You're the only one who can save me."

"You seriously think that I give a rat's ass about you now? After what you did? You're lucky I'm even talking to you and not finding a sharpened stake!"

"Please. I need you." Ethan reached for her but she pulled away, his fingernails grazing her wrist.

"Get a therapist or go take a long morning walk. Both will solve your problems," she said.

Adelle turned to leave but Ethan growled and swiped at her. His strong fingers snatched her wrist and clamped down, yanking her back. She stumbled, falling onto the table. Bent over the table and helpless, her eyes darted around the dining room. The bussers had already vanished into the back with their collected dishes, leaving the two alone.

"You will come back to San Diego with me now." Ethan's pupils dilated as his hard stare burned through her skin. "I will die if you don't."

Adelle swallowed. Despite her fear, her defiant nature dominated. She raised her chin in the face of his unstable rage and said, "Screw you and screw your addiction."

She tried pulling her arm away, but his vampire strength was more than she could fight. He must have fed recently. The thought made her insides curdle.

"I'm trying to ask nicely, Adelle. I apologized and everything. I don't want to hurt you again, so don't *make* me hurt you again." His eyes grew frenzied, the pitch of his voice lifting higher and higher.

The last time she saw that crazy look in his eyes was the night she told him it was over. He threw a chair through a bookstore window and sent her running. Ethan's grip on her wrist tightened with a slow painful twist. Adelle hissed as her delicate bones strained and crackled. Her frantic heartbeat crashed in her ears. She gritted her teeth, pushing the dread into the pit of her stomach.

"Go home, Ethan." Her voice cracked, betraying the brave mask she wore.

"I will. And so will you." Ethan's eyes flickered with a yellow light, irises swirling in hypnotic patterns of red and gold. Adelle tried to look away but she wasn't fast enough. She fell in, tangled in his gaze like a fly in a spider's web.

"You are coming back with me," Ethan said.

Adelle went slack, slipping into a warm bath of paralysis. Her head bobbed up and down in compliance, despite every inch of her screeching *No!* When he kidnapped her, he had done this to coax her into peaceful numbness. A stare to calm her and venom from his fangs to incapacitate her while he and his friends fed.

The more she stared into Ethan's eyes, the further into his trance she fell. Her mind screamed at her to fight but the fight was completely drained from her. Her will was his.

"The lady said go away," a voice, deep and fierce, rumbled from behind her. Jack's huge shadow cast itself across the two of them.

He came! Oh, thank God!

As soon as Ethan broke the stare, Adelle could feel her skin tingle with the prickling pain of forced sleep. She yanked her wrist free, stumbling back into strong hands. Jack pushed her behind him. A sob of joy caught in her throat and she pressed her cheek against his broad back, clutching the soft cotton of his red t-shirt. The warm balm of wood smoke wrapped around her like a security blanket. Jack was an imposing fortress. Every roped muscle tensed, amber eyes burning with rage, his hands white knuckle fisted. His ferocious power gave Adelle the strength to straighten up and steel herself to the vampire.

"We're having a conversation right now. Get lost," Ethan said.

Jack leaned back, giving Ethan his best *oh, please* face, a smirk twisting his upper lip.

The flippant response made Ethan scowl. He opened his mouth wide and flashed his fangs at him. The razor canines grew long, gleaming white and dripping with saliva. He let out a hiss before finishing with, "You don't know what you're dealing with."

Jack's rolling laugh practically shook the building. "That's cute. That's really cute," he replied, scraping his black fingernails across his chin. "Vampire, huh? Immortal, super strong, hypnotic powers?"

Jack eyed Ethan as he continued to bare his fangs. With a swift arch of his arm, he slammed his hand onto Ethan's table. The sudden slap of flesh against wood made Adelle jolt in surprise.

"Well lemme tell ye somethin, *laddy.*" Jack's brogue slipped out, thick with anger. "I'm older, wiser, and a whole lot meaner than a wee vampire." Ethan shut his jaws with a loud click as Jack's mouth curled into a sinister grin.

A spine tingling scrape made both Ethan and Adelle look down at Jack's hand. Long black talons dug groves into the table, curling strings of wood in their wake. The red and gold tattoo on Jack forearm rippled, each scale lifting and tearing from his flesh, forming into solid plates. His fingers swelled, changing his human hand into a dragon's gnarled claw. Adelle watched the partial transformation, pressing her mouth up against his shoulder.

The vampire flashed his hypnotic gaze at Jack but it deflected off the dragon, useless. Jack's smile fell as he glowered at Ethan. Then his lips parted, revealing a mouth full of long, dagger sharp teeth.

"Now, go away," Jack snarled. Curls of black smoke swirled from his nostrils, haloing his head.

Ethan sprung to his feet, his chair crashing to the floor. He stumbled back, failing to keep the fear off his face, His horror filled gaze snapped Adelle into its sights. "You just killed me. Do you know that, Adelle?"

"Good," she replied without missing a beat.

Ethan flinched as she spat the word at him. He looked between the two in disgust then raised a finger to Adelle. His eyes burned as he screamed, "I'll make you pay for this, you bitch! I'll make you suffer!"

Jack snarled and lunged for him but Ethan was out the door in a blur before Jack could even take a swing. Vampires were the cheetahs of the Wyrd. Once they took off, it would take a herculean effort to catch up.

Adelle's adrenaline left her in a rush, leaving her cold and trembling. She grabbed the back of the nearest chair and leaned all her weight on it to stay up. All consuming panic devoured her insides, making her skin clammy and her head pulse with a splitting agony. She closed her eyes, trying to mend the cracks in her emotional walls.

"Your ex-boyfriend is a douche bag," she heard Jack say. His deep voice splashed over her like a bucket of ice water, sobering her mind out of spinning hysteria.

"You came back. You're here," Adelle said.

Her heavy wool peacoat was placed onto her shoulders.

"...You forgot your coat. It's cold out," he said.

The gentleness almost made Adelle sob.

Almost.

Keep Calm, Adelle!

"I-I need to get out of here."

Her voice was cracking along with her walls. If she didn't find a safe haven soon, she would cry and crumble Jolene's down around their ears. Her hands clamped tight over her mouth, holding any sound back.

The secure strength of Jack's arms slipped around her shoulders and he pulled her tight against him. On instinct, she buried her face into his chest, inhaling that wonderful musk of wood smoke and sandalwood.

Jack's scent.

Sanctuary.

He didn't say another word, only walked her out the door.

Chapter 14

She needed to get to their practice circle. Someplace she could scream and no one would get hurt. All Jack had to do was dump her off on the side of the road and she could handle the rest. Adelle's legs shook and she stumbled like a drunken toddler, hands still tight over her mouth. With every step, her heart raced and her breath grew shallow. Jack watched her as they hurried down the street, amber eyes glued to the fingers clutching her mouth. She ached to tell him, just to whisper her plans into his ear, but she was too far gone. If she even tried, all Hell would break loose.

Adelle found herself at the foot of the long staircase to Jack's front door. He walked her home. Was he insane? She stared up its length wild eyed, and shook her head hard, sweat dripping down her face. Jack pressed a hand against the small of her back, urging her to move forward.

"It's all right, Buttercup," he whispered to her. "It's all right. We're home."

Things were as far from all right as they could get. She couldn't go up there; his home was right in the middle of town. Adelle whipped her head side to side in protest, eyes slamming shut. Her feet were swept out from under her as Jack cradled her in his arms, carrying her up the stairs, boots crunching in the snow. She squeaked, pressing her palms harder against her lips. Every struggle was surrendered to the strength of Jack's arms and eventually she curled up against his chest, like a tightly coiled spring.

With one hand, Jack wrestled the keys out of his pocket and unlocked the door, then carried Adelle over the threshold and into the kitchen, setting her down on her feet by the sink. Adelle was light headed from her panic, legs wobbling beneath her. The faucet turned on, the sudden sound of rushing water making her jolt.

Jack soaked a kitchen towel in the cold stream, then dabbed it carefully over Adelle's forehead. The chill stung her wind nipped skin but did calm her heart to a steadier pace. Just when she thought she could regain herself, she felt Jack's iron fingers pry under her hands, pulling them away from her mouth. Dread wrapped its barbed tendrils around her body.

"No!" Adelle shouted. The window's rattled. She wanted to slap her hands back over her mouth and stifle her cries but Jack held her wrists.

"Easy," he said. "Easy, Dell. You're safe."

He had no idea how wrong he was.

With a wild flail, she slipped out of Jack's hold and tumbled onto the floor. Her body hit with a slap, the back of her head smacking the white tiles so hard, she saw stars. One yelp made the floor shake. Jack reached to pick her up but Adelle ripped her arm from his grip. She scooted back on her rump, across the floor and away from him. Her back hit the cabinet and its metal handle slammed against her spine making her gasp, almost forcing out a scream.

"Keep calm! Keep calm, Adelle! Keep calm!" she repeated in a frantic whisper.

The more she spoke, the worse the urge to cry grew. Adelle ran her hands up her face clenching fists full of hair to yank.

She was going to lose her cool.

She was going to scream.

She was going to kill Jack.

"Adelle," Jack said.

The sharpness of his tone snapped her gaze up. Jack kneeled down in front of her, gripping her arms. He looked into her eyes.

"Just let it out."

Tears pooled in the corners of her eyes. Images of Jack's flesh melting from his bones, flashed before her. "I can't," she whispered, "I'll kill you. Don't you see, I can't? "

"Yes, you can." Jack pressed his large hands on either side of her face. The pads of this thumbs brushed away the tears that rolled down her cheeks. "Nothing will happen to me. You won't let it. You know why? Because you control it now. It doesn't control you."

Her breath came in short strangled gasps. She could hear her own wheezes echoing through the kitchen. Her fingers curled into his T-shirt, gripping the fabric so tight, she feared she'd tear it apart. Jack kept his gaze as steady as his warm, gentle voice.

"Just do it," he said. "Let it out."

Jack leaned in and pressed his forehead against hers. Over and over he murmured how she was in control; that it was all right to let go. All the while he stroked his strong fingers against her tear drenched cheeks. God help her, she was starting to believe him.

Her mouth opened, yet no sound came out. Adelle shook her head, wanting to tell him that she didn't know what to say or do. Not a sound. After ten years of holding in her tears, she didn't know how to set them free.

Jack sat down on the floor beside her. He pulled Adelle into his lap and wrapped his arms around her trembling form. The strong beat of his heart muted Adelle's terror, and she went limp against him. Lifting her chin, Jack pressed her mouth against his shoulder, burying his fingers into her thick red curls to secure her there.

"Go on," he whispered into her ear. "I got you."

Adelle shook her head. "I can't."

"Yes, you can."

"I'll hurt you."

Jack stroked her hair, rocking her fragile body back and forth. "You won't."

His warmth and his touch made her feel safe, so very safe. For that moment, everything was going to be all right, just like he said. It only took a couple strokes of her hair before she buried her face into his shoulder and let out a long grief stricken scream of pain.

Hot tears poured down her face in endless rivers as sob after sob bolted from her body. There was no turning back now, the dam had broken and she couldn't stop the long overdue flood if she wanted. Adelle wrapped her arms around the dragon, tight, to keep from drowning in her sorrow. There were so many tears to catch up on. So many feelings buried deep inside her, clawing their way out. Adelle cried for her kidnapping, for the fear of seeing Ethan again, for treating Jack so horrible. But mostly, she cried for her mother.

"Why wasn't I there, Jack?" she cried. "Why wasn't I there? I should have been there! I should have saved her! I miss her so much!" She soaked his neck with her sadness, voice strangled and harsh. "I'm so sorry, Mom. Oh God, I'm so sorry." More tears choked the remaining words from her lips, and she fell into non-verbal sobs.

It felt like eternity on that kitchen floor, keening into Jack's shoulder. The release was crippling. Jack tensed as she cried out ten years of repressed grief. He rocked her in his arms, telling her that it was going to be all right. Soon, the years of heartsick began to fade and her violent wails softened. Adelle slumped against Jack, pressing her cheek on his shoulder. She felt hard scales against her face. Her fingers reached up to confirm the solid plates as well as the burnt edges of his T-shirt.

"I'm sorry," Adelle whimpered.

"I'm not, "Jack said. He tightened his embrace. The soft touch of his lips brushed the top of her head. "So don't you be, either."

Adelle lay in his arms, staring at the gleaming white tiles of the kitchen floor. Jack continued to stroke her hair as her breathing slowed, keeping her bundled in a protective cocoon. Her eyes burned and her limbs hung like wet sand bags. Everything else was blissfully numb. The memories she had relived were horrid. That was all they were now. Just memories. For the first time in her adult life, she had found a safe place. That place was Jack's arms.

The warmth of his body and the strong sound of his heart lead her deeper and deeper into still waters. Jack gave her a gentle nudge then leaned over to see if she was asleep. When her bloodshot eyes met his, he smiled and brushed her hair away from her damp face. He managed to stand, still holding her. Adelle laid her head on his chest as he carted her down the hallway. Her eyes cracked to see Jack pushing her bedroom door open with his hip. In protest, her hand tightened its grip on his shirt. Now that she had found this sanctuary, she would do just about anything to keep it.

Jack looked down at her, brows raised in surprise. "You sure?" he asked, reading her signals. A ghost of a smile touched the dragon's lips.

Adelle nodded again before she buried her face against his chest. Jack walked to his room, pushing the door open with his hip and headed to the bed. With a gentleness that almost made Adelle weep all over again, he laid her out.

The moment her face touched the pillow, she hugged and nuzzled it's softness with a long exhausted sigh. His sheets smelled like him; smoky and strong. She snuggled down, wrapping herself in his essence. Jack unlaced her shoes, removing those, her socks, then eventually pulled her work clothes off and slipped her pajamas onto her prone body, showing no other motives than to make her comfortable. She didn't protest as he tucked her in.

The mattress dipped as Jack settled on the other side, springs creaking. After he slid under the blankets beside her, she felt his arm wrap around her waist. Adelle turned right into him, tucking her head under his chin, spooning his length. Another long sigh escaped her lips as she drifted off into a dreamless sleep.

After ten years, she finally felt true peace.

Chapter 15

The morning sun streamed through his window. Jack pressed a hand against Adelle's shoulder and whispered, "Hey, Buttercup. It's morning." To which Adelle replied with an incoherent mumble, possibly about chicken sandwiches, then rolled over and fell right back to sleep. He chuckled and left her slumbering under the mountains of blankets piled on his bed as he readied for work.

Jack headed into the bathroom for a quick shower, peeling off his shirt. When he caught a glimpse of himself in the mirror, he noticed a large red splotch covering his shoulder. The same shoulder that Adelle had cried into. He prodded at it with his fingers, hissing as the burn stung.

"That girl packs a punch," he muttered.

Last night, he'd had the presence of mind to raise the scales before Adelle let her floodgates open. Dragons' healed quickly, so a superficial wound like a burn would be a distant memory come nightfall. Just a tiny burn. Nothing more. He couldn't help but feel pride at how she controlled her powers, even if she couldn't control herself. The damage could have been cataclysmic.

Jack stripped down and stepped into the shower. The hot water sluiced over his weary muscles and he bent his head down, letting it beat onto the back of his neck. His thoughts circled back to the fight they had, Adelle's breakdown, and how she had cried. Oh God, how she had cried. Her sobs tied his stomach in knots. They tore at his chest. Jack couldn't even fathom how much grief she had buried for so long. Adelle was so together, so in control of herself. Sometimes, it made her a little uptight but he never would have thought that underneath there was so much pain. Never mourning the loss of your mother? When his own parents died, he had raged for weeks on end until all the sadness was out. Adelle had never cried a single tear. She couldn't, no matter how much she wanted to. His heart ached for her, feeling guilty about making things worse. First he brought up her mother, and then lied to her about his feelings. Ethan had only brought things to a head.

Ethan.

The name alone sent Jack's fury into overdrive. His growl echoed off the shower tiles as his claws dug into his white bar of soap, crumbling it into flakes.

How dare that blood sucking son of a bitch touch her!

He had every intention of letting her stew last night. After all, Adelle had been a stone cold bitch to him for four days. Yet, when he had left his bedroom and saw her new coat hanging there, the anger subsided. Jack couldn't bear the idea of her shivering all the way home, lips blue, hair covered in snowflakes. He was glad that his concern for Adelle was stronger than his stubborn nature.

Jack had walked in on Ethan pulling that damn vampire hypno bullshit on her, where they hypnotized their prey into obeying their will. It didn't work on dragons but boy, did it work gangbusters on anyone with a drop of human blood in them. The helpless look in Adelle's beautiful green eyes, how she had tried to fight Ethan's gaze. The sight made Jack's temper flair to violence. But the plan to snap that little fucker over his knee had been cut short when Ethan dashed out the door. A vampire's speed was the only thing that had kept Ethan alive last night.

Jack spent the morning in his office. After the overwhelming events of last night, he needed to get his head back in order. On a regular day, Jack would have sat in his hoard cave -a gigantic cavern down in the sub-basement of the gym- for solace. But that would take him too far from Adelle for his liking. A crazy vampire was still about and there was no way he wasn't going to abandon his post now, vow or no vow. Instincts urged him to run up the stairs again, to wrap his arms around Adelle, stroke her hair, and tell her he would never leave her.

Maybe Jack had deserved her silent treatment. He had lied to her. He had made it clear that he only wanted sex, nothing else. The truth was he couldn't imagine a day without Adelle. At least, he didn't want to. The realization hit him when she had tucked her small body tight against his as she slept, warm and soft. Jack buried his face in her fire kissed curls, breathing in her sweet honeyed perfume.

I want this every night, he had thought. *I want her every night. My beautiful, brave siren.*

Sure, at first he had wanted just her body. Now, he wanted her completely. He wanted her laugh, her kindness, and her courage. He wanted to share everyday with that magnificent creature, both good and bad.

Love.

That was what he felt.

Jack honest and truly loved that glorious female more than any before her. This feeling was entirely new to him. Wendy's love was nothing more than a mage's glamour. But Adelle was someone who could love him back. And that scared the holy hell out of him when he thought about her returning to California.

Jack let out a sigh and noticed he'd been sharpening the same pencil for the last thirty seconds. It was now just a nub with an eraser. All his pencils were tiny little nubs, scattered across his desk. He groaned, got up, and told his staff that he was taking the rest of the day off.

When he made it upstairs, Adelle was in his kitchen, still in her pajamas. A grin teased his mouth at the sight of her. She was sitting on the floor, brow furrowed in concentration as she wrestled with the broken chair, a roll of duct tape, and bottle of wood glue. The minute she heard the door open, she looked up, cheeks flushing in guilt, duct tape clutched in her hands. Jack folded his arms and leaned against the door frame with an amused smile. His gaze slid over to her handy work.

The chair leg was at a cockeyed angle, wadded over with strip after strip of duct tape. Wood glue cascaded down the spindles in thick yellow drops and onto the newspaper she had spread beneath her work space. Adelle shouldn't give up her day job for carpentry, that was for sure

"Hey," she said, before her teeth bit her lower lip. "I fixed your chair."

"You... did something to my chair," Jack said.

Adelle rubbed the back of her neck, pushing the mess away with a bare foot. "I sort of fixed your chair."

"I wouldn't go as far as to call it fixing, Buttercup."

"I'll buy you a new chair."

The two stared at each other a long silent moment. Adelle broke first, eyes still puffy and red, darting to the ceiling. She rubbed the palms of her hands together. "About last night. I was such a bitch. I-"

"As far as I'm concerned, it's just a memory." He could already see her eyes welling with residual tears. The idea of her crying again cracked his usually ironclad heart.

"I really am sorry," Adelle finished.

Jack shook his head with a sigh. "You already apologized last night, and you know what I said."

"Yeah but this time I meant for the chair." Her lips quirked up into a little smile.

Jack laughed, ruffling his hair through his fingers. "Would you feel better if we went chair shopping?"

"Yes. Chair shopping is the only thing that will fill the empty void in me."

Adelle's lips twitched. A snort escaped, she wrinkled her nose, and then she burst into laughter. The sweet sound made Jack's face split into a wide grin and soon he joined her.

"Get showered and dressed," he said.

"Yeah, about that," she looked down at the pajamas she wore. "I'm pretty sure I didn't fall asleep in these."

"You didn't. I put them on you." He glanced over to Adelle, whose eyes grew wide like they always did when she was embarrassed. "Oh, don't get all touchy. I didn't do anything. You smelled like beer and cigarettes, and I couldn't sleep with that smell on your clothes."

"Uh huh," Adelle smirked at him.

"I only looked once."

"Jack."

"Maybe twice."

"Jack!"

Jack gave her a grin. "Just kidding." He was relieved to see she was smiling at the exchange instead of glowering. "Seriously though, get dressed. We need to practice."

"This late in the day?" Adelle pulled herself to her feet. She was overwhelmingly cute in her pajamas. The light green cotton capris and camisole hugged that voluptuous figure in ways that made his lust go into overdrive. The fact that the pajamas were dotted over in teeny tiny skull and crossbones only made the picture more perfect. He shook his head at the thought and poured a glass of water.

“You had four days of crummy practice. Actually, three. You slept through the last one. If your ex-boyfriend is in the neighborhood, getting a handle on your powers will make you feel better.” He handed the glass of water to Adelle. “That and you smell bad so a shower will do you wonders.”

“I can’t fight that logic.” She took a quick sip of the water and leaned against the table with a sigh. "I’m not sure if I’m up to snuff anymore.”

We’ll get you back there,” Jack said. “This is about your safety now. And you know how serious I am about your safety.” He chucked her under the chin, and she let out a shy giggle. It made his heart flutter like a trapped butterfly in his ribcage.

“You sure you don’t want to try out the chair?” she asked.

“I also take my own safety very seriously.” He winked then headed over to his room to change into his non gym attire.

“Jack?”

He turned around, greeted by those fantastic eyes. Jack’s stomach twirled as he fell into her emerald gaze. He held his breath taking all her loveliness in. Adelle brushed some of her messy curls from her face as she shuffled from barefoot to barefoot.

“You’re a good guy,” she said. “And I know I can be difficult. Thanks for putting up with me.”

There she was, pajama clad, sleep tousled, and smiling in his kitchen. Nothing was more beautiful than she was at that very moment. Jack took in every visual ounce of her, not wanting to forget a single thing.

Yes, I love her.

“You’re never difficult,” he said in a soft voice and then slipped into his bedroom.

Jack pulled his shirt off, and leaned his back against the closed door. He considered going back out there and spilling everything to Adelle. In the dragon world, confessions of love meant claiming a mate for life. Never did the need to claim a female consume him like this. This was a huge step, one he never thought he would take.

Was she ready?

Was *he* ready?

Just lay it all on the table, he thought. *Stake your claim, Jack.*

He remembered how she felt in his arms last night. Her warm skin, the sweet, rasping sound of her breath. It haunted him. He didn't want to sleep for fear of never feeling her that close again.

You love her. Tell her.

Jack turned, hand on the door to make his way back out but he paused. Granted, she was feeling a bit more up to snuff but Adelle had been through the ringer last night. Did she really need another emotional bombshell dropped on her head?

"Not yet," he muttered to himself. "Wait for the right moment."

That's what women wanted, right? The right moment? Jack hoped to God he'd know what the right moment was when it came. Until then, well, he'd just have to wait.

After a quick shower and a change of clothes, Adelle slipped into the passenger seat of the Impala, reluctantly ready for another practice session. Amazing what a night's sleep could do. She was feeling a lot more like herself. That was a relief. She hated being grumpy. She especially hated being grumpy, tired, and terrified of her ex-boyfriend. It was total luck that Jack had happened in when he did last night. All on account that she was being spiteful and not taking the coat he bought her with her to work. That was the first time being passive aggressive turned out in her favor.

Of course, the night turned into an explosive evening of emotion followed by a healthy dose of vulnerability. Hell, she couldn't even stand afterwards. With anyone else, Adelle would have been humiliated. She already felt humiliated after her encounter with Ethan. All that bravado, all that confidence she had in her powers, and she couldn't even squeak out a note. She had turned into her old self, timid little Adelle, too scared to evaporate a bastard like Ethan. She felt so weak.

Jack parked the car over to the side of the forest road as usual. Despite it being three in the afternoon, the woods were still quiet and uninhabited. Snow dappled the trees and was piled up knee high along either sides of the blacktop, signs that the rangers had done a little plowing that morning.

The air was frosty, puffing out in solid breaths that hung in the air for a moment, before evaporating into the sky. Adelle was never more grateful to have that new coat than now. She was rather toasty wrapped up in that, plus the plaid scarf and black gloves Jack loaned her. Both were gifts to him from Wendy. The mage never really grasped that Jack didn't need heavy clothing to keep the heat in. The gloves swallowed her hands in fur lined leather and the scarf practically hung down to her knees, but both were snuggly warm so she didn't knock them.

The flurries they had experienced over the last day had encrusted their dirt path in fine powder, and it had proved a bit tricky for Adelle to maneuver in. Being a Southern California girl, snow was something she only saw on Christmas cards. A few steps in and she would get stuck, almost losing her boots as she sloshed through the frozen muck. Jack kept by her side, taking her hand and helping her step into the banks the right way. Eventually, she got the hang of it, picking up speed as she imitated his steps.

The blackened earth of their practice circle was blanketed in white. Delicate icicles dripped from the tree branches, dappling the ground with the afternoon sunlight. The soft whisper of wind rustled through the trees. It was as if Adelle and her powers had never been there. So peaceful. So lovely. She sighed, pressing a hand against her chest, inhaling the cold scent of green. It filled her with serenity.

Jack stepped aside, shoving his hands into the pockets of his leather jacket. "All right then. Here we are. You ready to roll?"

Regardless of her meditations on the cool winter air, she still felt shaken. Ethan's confrontation, the nightmares about Cybil, and the fuzziness in her head made it that much harder to focus. A distraction could lead to disaster. Adelle sunk her teeth into her lower lip.

Back to square one. Shit.

One bad moment and Adelle was a frightened lamb yet again. Her hands shook and she tucked them behind her back, tangling her fingers together.

"I'm not sure if I'm up to this yet," she said.

"Yeah, you are," Jack replied. He walked to her, a little swagger in his step, and a roguish grin on his mouth. "Last night you were a wreck. But you still managed to not hurt me or bring the roof down on us."

He reached a hand into the purse that was still slung over her shoulder. After a little rummaging, he pulled out her iPod and ear buds. Adelle arched a brow, looking at him curiously.

"Today you're just a little fuzzy headed so this will be a piece of cake," Jack said.

He stepped close to her, a white round ear bud in each hand. Heat radiated off him, warming Adelle right through her coat. She wet her lips as she took in the corded muscles under his shirt and strength in his large hands. He towered over her, the top of her head just barely brushing his shoulder.

"I guess I'm just scared," she said with a shake of her head.

Jack smiled down at her, one filled with tenderness, not sarcasm. "I really don't know how many times I have to tell you that you know what you're doing."

Ever so carefully, Jack placed the ear buds into her ears, taking a moment to tuck a lock of her hair away from her face. His fingertips caressed her jaw with a whisper of a touch. Adelle held her breath as his gentle gesture sent an electric shiver through her entire body. She closed her eyes, using all her willpower to keep from leaning into his fingertips.

"When I was a kid, my father taught me a few things about breathing fire." Jack's deep rolling voice poured over her like warm chocolate. One of his large hands skimmed over her hair. Adelle let out a wistful little sigh, trembling from his touch "I was all power, blazing things up and setting more sheep on fire than I should have. I had a lot of rage behind my flames, but it wasn't enough. Father told me; Lad, it takes passion tae get the power. But it needs compassion tae control it." He slipped a finger under her chin, raising her face to his. Adelle found herself swimming in the golden galaxy that was his eyes. He grinned at her, giving a wink. "And I'm damn sure you have both in spades, Buttercup."

The pad of his thumb brushed her lower lip, and their gazes locked. Adelle took in the powerful features of his face, offset by the soft, affectionate light in those amazing eyes. She felt every little detail about him; the powerful beat of his heart throbbing in his broad chest, the warm breath that escaped his lips and tickled her cheek. The intoxicating scent of smoke and sandalwood filled her nostrils and gave her comfort and peace. Jack leaned down, pressing his forehead against hers. Adelle's eyes fluttered shut as she reveled in his closeness. For a long moment, they stood as snow flickered down from the grey clouds overhead.

God, if only you would kiss me, Jack.

But instead of a kiss, Adelle felt him slip her iPod into the palm her hand, closing her fingers around it.

"Now, make me proud, "Jack whispered to her. Before Adelle could protest, he stepped away, giving her room.

Adelle shook her head, trying to sober herself. Her heart was pounding and her stomach filled with a heat that spread through her entire body; hands, toes, and between her legs. Everywhere. While fumbling with her iPod, she expected to hear a chuckle from the peanut gallery but Jack was eerily silent. She couldn't bring herself to look at him.

After peeling off her gloves and scarf, her thumb ran over the selection wheel to choose a song. Adelle bent down to remove her boots. As soon as her bare feet stepped into the snow, Jack opened his mouth to object but he was silenced when Adelle said, "Just trust me." Jack backed off with a nod of his head, gesturing to her to continue.

The icy frost between her toes hit her with a stinging jolt which brought everything into a razor sharp focus. She gasped at the sensation, closed her eyes, and hit play on her iPod. The soft tinkling of a piano intro whispered through her ear buds and she lost herself in the music. Adelle held her breath, thinking on Cybil's death, Ethan's threats, all the grief and anger she was harboring for ten long years, and then on Jack and his uncanny ability to make it all better. Her lips parted and the song flowed from her.

The snow around her feet began to melt. The pulsating power from the earth thundered under her toes. Another breath and it began to flow into the soles of her feet, through her legs, and into her heart. A warm, white light swirled and vibrated through her, connecting her with the magical currents that flowed through this world. Currents that wanted to follow the sound of her voice.

It all came back to her now; the power racing through her veins, the heat that touched her fingertips and toes, all threatening to overwhelm her and explode, destroying everything in its path. Adelle's heart raced as the power almost slipped from her gasp. Then her thoughts returned to Jack's arms and the peace it brought her. His embrace stilled her mind and filled her with a pure sense of happiness.

She belonged there.

She was safe.

The unwieldy power yielded, pulsing inside her, waiting for command. It wasn't just energy, it was an entity. One that flowed through her, reacted to her emotions, and was harnessed by that wonderful memory. When Adelle felt peace, so did it. With her song, Adelle drew that humming energy into her body. It pushed against her eyes and haloed her vision in white. It seeped up from the dirt, the trees, and rocks, through and into her, becoming part of her. They were one now, she and the power of the world.

Her flesh blazed, and Adelle burned patterns into the snow with a bright blue fire that radiated from her body. She rolled her fingers in the air to the languid rhythm of the music, creating swirls, curls, and angles in the white powder, all the while singing her song.

Shimmering clouds of blue and white swirled in a cyclone around her. It kicked up snow and leaves. Debris moved as if it were under water, flowing in a languid tornado, Adelle was the eye of the storm. She focused her glowing eyes on the tree in front of her, using her sapphire fire to scrape the bark from its trunk until one side was smooth and pale from its tall top to its roots.

Sparkling air flowed under her, and her bare feet parted with the melting slush. Her body lifted five feet, six feet, climbing and climbing until the tops of the trees brushed her toes. She glanced down at Jack on the ground far below. He stared, wide eyed and mouth open, in complete awe of her majesty, pride beaming from him.

Adelle's heart swelled and a geyser of energy exploded from the earth, rising up and slamming into her. She felt the power crash through her spine, slipping between each vertebra and flowing into her entire being. Adelle shut her eyes and threw back her head, belting out her final note.

Light exploded from her chest and into the sky above. The beam arched, and then slammed down onto a tree, smashing it down with a thunderous percussion of sapphire flame. As soon as it ignited, the flames blew out, letting the tree slowly crumble to a pile of ash, grey flakes fluttering down with the snow.

Adelle began to descend back to earth at a lazy pace, her feet delicately touching down as her song ended. Her limbs were heavy and her body weak as a child's. Exhaustion was overpowered with elation.

I did it.

For the first time in her life, raw energy worked in harmony with her mind and soul. The heat rushed from her, and she shook as the winter chill tore through her weary body. Adelle's cheeks burned, and her toes stung from the biting frost. Before she could fall to her knees, strong hands caught her and hauled her to her feet. Jack wrapped his arms around her waist and pulled her close to him, lifting her up to get her feet out of the snow. She pressed her cheek against his shoulder, clinging to him.

"You're freezing," Jack whispered.

Adelle laughed. "Yeah. That kind of happens when you fly, I guess." She snuggled herself close to Jack, using his body heat to get the feeling back into her limbs. That same peace enveloped her once again, and she smiled against his shoulder. "I'm going to safely assume that I made you proud."

Jack's chest rumbled with deep laughter as he tightened his embrace. "Yes. You definitely made me proud."

"I think to mark this achievement; you should take me out for pizza and beer."

He chuckled again as he put her down on a tree stump. "I will take you out for pizza and beer."

"And a foot massage."

"I will give you a foot massage."

"And a million dollars."

"Now you're pushing it."

Adelle grinned as she rubbed her hands together. She watched as Jack gathered her gloves, socks, and boots, and handed them over to her.

"Now, put these back on before you get so cold we have to amputate," Jack said.

She took her things and sat herself down, slipping her socks and boots back on. "Thank you, Jack," she said.

Jack shoved his hands into his pockets again, cocking a brow. "Thanks for what? I just stood here. You've been thanking me way too much lately."

Adelle tucked some hair away from her face and behind an ear. "For helping me. For believing in me."

Jack shook his head. "You did that yourself."

"I used a good memory to help me control my power," Adelle said. "It was of you." Jack's cheeks turned red as he stared at her. His lips parted as if to say something but no words came out. "So, thank you," she finished, looking back to her boots and lacing them fast.

Adelle clenched her jaw as the tension between them grew thick in the cold air. She remained locked on her boots until Jack's hand rested on her head, his palm running down the length of her hair. His fingers tangled in her wind swept curls and her eyes closed, reveling in his touch.

"I'm honored," he said.

Her eyes opened just in time to see his genuine smile before he pulled away. Soon, Jack was striding towards the path back to the car as fast as he could.

"Come on, Buttercup. Pizza awaits! Mushrooms, right?" he called over his shoulder.

Adelle grinned as she watched him walk off. "Right."

Chapter 16

Valerie heard Phoebe running across the house yelling, "I got it I got it I got it!" She had no clue that Valerie was standing in the kitchen, right next to the ringing phone. Valerie reached over and plucked the cordless receiver off the cradle, just as Phoebe skidded into the room. Her mouth turned up into a pout, and she put her hands on her hips.

"I was going to get that," she said.

"Expecting a call?" Valerie asked.

Phoebe smiled. "No. But I like the thrill of answering the phone."

Valerie held the phone up to her ear then stopped, staring at Phoebe with an arched brow. Was that pink she spied? "Hold on," she said into the phone then turned on Phoebe. "What did you do to your head?"

Phoebe touched her short blonde hair; the tips now dyed a bright pink. "I got bored," she replied with a shrug of her delicate shoulders.

"You're pink."

Pink usually made Valerie want to gag. But she had to admit, it looked fantastic on her baby sister. Still, it was pink.

"Just the tips," Phoebe said.

"But, you're pink."

Phoebe lifted her chin. "I'm expressing myself as an individual, Val. You shouldn't stifle me. I will grow resentful of our relationship."

Valerie raised her brow even higher. "Dell told you to tell me that if I bitched about your hair, didn't she?"

"...Maybe?"

Valerie snorted and removed her hand from mouthpiece of the phone. "Constance residence, Valerie speaking." She had answered the phone like that since she was six. Old habits die hard.

"Val, Its Reina," a sultry feminine voice said on the other line.

Reina was a dear family friend. She was also a fierce warrior, a centuries old vampire, and didn't take anyone's shit. Reina was the head of all the clans on the west coast, which made her as busy as a one legged man in an ass kicking contest. Vampires were an unruly bunch, their numbers growing ever since those teenage romance books became the rage. Luckily, Reina was never too busy for the Constance girls. After Cybil had saved her from a beheading, Reina had indebted herself to her family from that moment on.

"Reina! Good to hear back from you!" Valerie smiled.

"Is that Reina?" Phoebe asked. She got up on her toes, leaning over toward Valerie. "Hi Reina!" she shouted into the phone.

Valerie winced and shoved Phoebe's head away. This only resulted in Phoebe struggling with her face pressed up against her outstretched hand, swinging her arms in the air like a psychotic windmill.

"Child abuse!" she yelled.

"You're twenty five!" Valerie yelled back.

"I'm a child in spirit!"

Valerie sighed and snagged Phoebe's arm in a firm grip. With a quick twist, she spun her into a headlock, tucking her under her left arm. Phoebe struggled against Valerie's grip, grunting and panting like an over active Sharpei.

"Uh, am I interrupting something?" Reina asked.

Valerie "oofed" as a flailing limb hit her back. "No. It's just the usual chaos here. What's up?"

"I'm invincible, Val!" Phoebe cheered.

Valerie tightened her grip on Phoebe's neck and she let out a loud, hacking cough.

"Just following up with you," Reina said. "About that Ethan guy."

"Yup. Lay it on me."

When the struggling stopped and the pathetic wheezing for air began, Valerie released Phoebe from her iron grip. Phoebe stumbled back, smoothed her hair out, and attempted to regain her dignity. Then she stuck her tongue out at Valerie, losing her dignity once again.

"So, I did some deeper digging. My eyes out there said three months after this Ethan disappeared, he was seen outside a downtown club attacking a normal."

Eyes. Reina's informants. She had them everywhere. It paid to have the head of the vampires as a gal pal. "Charming," Valerie said.

"Oh!" Phoebe interrupted. Valerie sighed and rolled her eyes. She looked to Phoebe, brows jutting over her hazel eyes in an irritated V. "Tell Reina that the hair dye she told me about worked great and thank you."

Valerie glared at Phoebe, expression flat; wondering if that was worth the third interruption. "Phoebe's pink now and she thanks you," she said into the phone.

"Hair dye?" Reina said.

"Yup."

Reina's velvety laugh tickled the phone. "Tell her you're welcome and not to wash her hair for a day so the color sets."

Valerie looked to Phoebe with the same dull expression. "She says you're welcome. Don't bathe." She turned her back to Phoebe, hoping that was the end of it. "Anyways, information?"

"He attacked a human," Reina said. "I sent some enforcers out to bring him to me but apparently he was intercepted."

"Intercepted? By who?"

Out of the corner of her eye, Valerie caught Phoebe peeking over her shoulder. She took a deep breath and counted to ten before considering another headlock, adding a choke hold to knock her out.

"Are you two talking about work or something cool?" she asked.

Valerie had convinced Phoebe that she and Reina worked as night-time security guards. It helped explain where Valerie was, and why she only saw Reina at night. When Phoebe learned the truth, it would blow her poor little mind. Dryads were so volatile. Valerie winced at the thought. She'd make Adelle handle that when she got home. Their middle sister was always better at those types of things. Until then, Phoebe was going to be curious and Valerie would have to keep on spinning tales.

"Yes," Valerie said. "We're talking work. Boring, mind numbing work."

"Done!" Phoebe announced. She put her hands in the air, turned on her heels, and walked out of the kitchen.

Valerie sighed in relief. "Sorry about that. Intercepted, you were saying?"

"Yeah," Reina said. "He and about four other vampires were abducted right after Adelle's rescue. At first, I thought it was you guys dishing out some home grown justice."

"It definitely wasn't us." Valerie pulled a chair out and sat herself down. "I mean, I did kill one of them when I went to get Dell back but I told you about that. Besides, he started it."

"No loss. Bill was a dick," Reina confirmed.

Valerie chuckled with a shake of her head. "So, any clues who our vampire kidnapper could be?"

"Word has it that a mage may be in on it."

"Mages?" Valerie snorted as she twirled a pen from the phone caddy between her fingers then lowered her voice incase Phoebe was in earshot still. "The mages haven't caused a ruckus in years. Mom and I ran out the dark mages. The ones in town now mind their own business."

Reina let out a long sigh. "I didn't say mages. I said a mage. One."

A tingle of dread jabbed at Valerie. She swallowed hard, spine going rigid. "Did they give you a description?"

"Hold on." There was a rustling sound of papers moving about before she said, "Yeah. Short black hair, dark hazel eyes. Tall and pale with high cheek bones. Was impeccably dressed. Oh, and carried an ivory cane with him."

Valerie's stomach dropped. There was only one mage she knew who carried an ivory cane. *No. It couldn't be him. He wouldn't dare come back here.*

"Oh shit," Valerie whispered.

"Oh shit, what? Do you know this guy?" Reina's voice went taught as a bow string.

Valerie's fingers curled into tight fists. Her face burned in rage, teeth clenched. "Knew him. It sounds like Tony." She spit the name out from between her teeth.

Reina was quiet a moment then asked, "Tony? As in your old neighbor, Tony?"

"Yeah." Valerie got to her feet, hackles raised. She padded back and forth across the kitchen, springing on the balls of her feet like a caged tiger. There was more to Adelle's kidnapping then some junkie vampires needing a hit. They were in deep trouble. The whole city was in deep trouble. She let out a string of curse words under her breath.

"Reina, I got to call Dell and warn her. Send some eyes out around the city and see if you find out any more."

"I'm on it," Reina said. The call ended with a sharp click.

Valerie sat back down in her chair, fists tight as her heart slammed against her chest. Tony was back. The evil son of a bitch that took Cybil's life was back in San Diego. Chances were he wasn't here to apologize, either. She took a deep breath, willing herself calm. It didn't work. The mere thought of Tony's face sent her into a shaking rage. Her face reddened as her anger burned deep in her gut.

"Val, are you all right?"

Valerie looked up from the table to see Phoebe hovering in the kitchen doorway, delicate brows knitted in worry. Valerie let out a breath as her mind raced to find a story to explain her rage.

"Yeah. I'm fine," she said. "I...I was just thinking about Mom, is all."

Phoebe gave her a sad little smile and walked over to her sister. "I miss her too, Val." She put her arms around Valerie and gave her a squeeze.

Valerie reached up, holding Phoebe a moment as she collected her thoughts.

He won't hurt my sisters again. He won't hurt me again.

She would find Tony. Find him and kill him.

"I'm going to call Dell. I'll be right back." Valerie marched off to her bedroom, the cordless phone still in her hand.

"Tell her I said hi and I love her!" Phoebe called after her.

"Will do!" Valerie replied as she shut herself up in her bedroom. As soon as Phoebe's footsteps clomped off down the hallway, Valerie hit speed dial.

She waited, pacing across the floor as the other line rang.

And rang.

That dark feeling of dread crept over Valerie's body, the one she would get when she knew something disastrous was going to happen. It started in the pit of her stomach and grew into creeping chills across her flesh, knotting her gut into a tangle mess.

"Come on. Come on, Dell. Pick up," she muttered as the phone rang. Adelle's phone rolled over to her voice mail. "Dammit!"

She re-dialed, waited, and got the same result. Valerie clutched the phone in both her hands and shook it, teeth bared. On the fifth try, she finally left a message:

"Dell, its Val. Tony's back in town. I think he's looking for you. If you get this, don't leave the house and call me back immediately!"

Chapter 17

Jack stood in the bathroom, in just his jeans, staring into the mirror. He ran a hand across his rough jaw, black nails scratching his chin. Maybe not shaving for that stupid engagement party would send the message that Wendy was well into the past. Besides, his stubble grew back way too fast to keep track of it. If he shaved now, it would grow back by the end of the night.

"Hey, pretty, pretty princess." Jack caught the reflection of Adelle poking her head through the door. "You know, if you keep primping, we'll be late," she said.

"One has to look one's best when going to an ex-girlfriend's engagement party," he said with a smirk.

Adelle stepped into view and his breath stopped. There she was, a vision in a green and blue paisley wrap dress that fit her like a glove. He had never noticed how small her waist was. Her fiery hair was long and free down her back and a pair of twinkling, large earrings of blue and green stones, framed her stunning oval face.

Adelle gave a quick spin, her skirt lifting just enough to give him a peek of her firm thighs. The colors she wore made her come alive and the smile she gave him was jaw dropping. When she tossed her curls over her shoulder, he longed to bury his mouth against her slender neck and suckle her until she moaned.

"Do I look all right?" she asked.

Jack gave her a lingering look up and then down. Her hips were luscious, and her dress was cut just low enough to give him a little peek of the top of her full breasts. Oh, cleavage was a wondrous thing. He shut his eyes tight.

Think unsexy thoughts! Think unsexy thoughts!

"You look presentable," he said.

Presentable. What an understatement. The only thing that could beat this vision would be her completely naked and spread out before him. He shut his eyes again.

Think unsexy thoughts, dammit!

"I'll take it." She smiled, folding her arms across her chest. Adelle didn't seem to notice how overwhelmed with lust Jack was. He finally tore his eyes away and turned back to the mirror. Talking to her reflection kept his groin well hidden behind the sink.

"You also look like you're going to freeze your ass off," Jack said. "That's a short skirt and short sleeves."

Adelle wagged a finger at him. "Oh, yes. I have a plan. Bundle up in the car. Take off my coat when I'm indoors where it's warm, then bundle back up back to the car."

Jack let out a little snort, running his fingers through his hair. "And freeze your ass off in the process." He picked up his razor again and looked at it, trying to keep his mind off of the gorgeous creature taunting him from the doorway.

She tilted her head as she examined his tense reflection. "You sure you want to go?"

"Yeah, I'm sure. I think it would be a good laugh."

"Because if you want to stay in-"

"Adelle, this is the third time you asked. We're going." Jack looked back up at her reflection and smiled. "It's fine. At worst, it'll make Wendy uncomfortable and that is always a plus for me."

Adelle laughed and shook her head. "Oh, but you're a spiteful, old thing, aren't you?"

"Nine-hundred years in the making." Again, he looked down at the razor pinched between his fingers. "Think I should shave?"

Jack furrowed his brow. When did he start asking for opinions on his facial hair? For the matter, when he start caring about his appearance?

"Eh. We're going to a place fancier than Jolene's. Might as well." She leaned her shoulder up against the door frame and gave him a sly grin. "Besides, I like clean shaven men." She winked, then turned and slipped back out of sight. As soon as she vanished, he snagged his mug soap and got to work lathering up his jaw.

Jack shaved and put on the only button down shirt he owned, a nice deep red one that looked like it was just taken out of the box -because it was just taken out of the box. Of course, that meant he also had to put on the only pair of black slacks he owned. Both items were gifts from Wendy. She had a habit of buying him clothing he would never wear. There was an entire drawer full with the tags still on. Jack hated dressing up. Until now, that is. He liked how Adelle looked at him tonight and caught her more than once gazing up the length of him, eyes twinkling with heated interest. That alone was worth the itchy dress shirt.

Wendy's engagement party was at the rather swanky *Empire Grill*, just on the outskirts of town. It was a nice place that locals went to for special occasions. Wendy and Steve were taking over for their party, which was unheard of. No one had the money for that. Jack guessed Wendy used her mind juju once again to get what she wanted, with a discount, no less.

They pulled into a parking space along the sidewalk. When Adelle bundled herself up in her new coat, she opened her door and stepped out. A gust of chilled air whisked in and she shivered, almost losing her footing. Jack chuckled as he leapt out of the driver's seat and to her rescue. With three long strides, he was there, tucking her against his side. His heat would keep her comfy. Besides, having her that close to him wasn't necessarily a bad thing either.

"I told you you'd freeze," he said.

Adelle's teeth chattered as she doubled her pace to get to the entrance. "I'll suffer in the name of fashion. I love this dress." She suddenly gasped and slapped her forehead. "Oh, crap!"

"What?"

"I forgot my phone on the kitchen table."

"Eh, you probably won't need it."

Adelle pursed her lips, then after a beat she nodded. "True."

Jack glanced down to her as they approached the entrance. For days he had been pondering when to finally confess his feelings to her. His dragon's claim sat hot on his lips but it never seemed like the right moment.

Is this what could be considered the right moment? he pondered. *She's dressed up. I'm dressed up.*

Jack was clueless about these female type things. He took a deep breath.

"Adelle?" He clenched his jaw as she looked up at him with a smile.

"Yeah? What's up?" she said in a cheerful voice.

Jack opened his mouth to at last say the words he needed to say. "Do I look like an idiot in this shirt?" He blinked as the question escaped his lips.

"You look fine," Adelle reassured him. "Red's your color." She gave him a smile then pushed the door open and slipped inside, leaving Jack staring dumbfounded on the stoop.

"My shirt," he grumbled to himself. "I asked her about my shirt. Goddammit!"

The bar was larger than expected, decorated in a sleek contemporary look. Simple, angular, and unadorned, in eye searing yellows and whites. All the things Jack despised in modern architecture. He was a lover of the complicated gobbledygook of the old days. There was a small buffet set up to the right of the bar complete with roast beef and carver. To the left, there was a three piece band set up to play in front of a small temporary dance floor. He'd bet there was an open bar available, too.

"So, want to sit down at the bright yellow bar, or the bright yellow booth in the corner?" Jack asked, scanning the crowded room with a squint. "Why the hell is everything in here white and yellow? It's killing my eyes."

Adelle shook her head. "I'm guessing the decorator really liked eggs sunny side up."

Jack snickered before he caught eyes with his ex-girlfriend and her ever silent blood sucking fiancé. Wendy waved a hand and dragged Steven behind her, setting a course straight for them. The smile dropped from Jack's lips.

"In coming," he muttered to Adelle through the side of his mouth.

"Oh, I see them," Adelle said through the teeth of a rather fake smile. She slipped her arm though the crook of his elbow. Its touch brought his smile back and he lifted his chin with swagger.

"You both made it, how nice," Wendy said. She leaned in giving Adelle a weak hug then turned to Jack to do the same. With a little snarl, Jack's hands went up in warning. Wendy wasn't so stupid to know when to back off. She hugged Steven's arm as the half vampire just stared with vacant eyes. Jack shuddered, wondering if he had worn that same glazed over look when he and Wendy were together.

"Thanks for the invite, Wendy," Adelle said as she looked about. "Really nice place you chose."

"Isn't it? It's where Steven and I had our first date. Isn't that right?" Wendy looked to Steven who just nodded with all the enthusiasm of a cadaver. Her gaze darted back to Jack and she gasped then giggled, pressing a hand against her chest. "Oh, Jack. You're wearing that shirt I bought you. You look fantastic in red."

"Yeah," was all Jack said.

When Adelle said that, he smiled. With Wendy, he only wanted to kick her in the shins. The awkward silence that followed made it clear that he still wasn't amused with her.

"Oh, well," Wendy stammered. "It's an open bar."

"Of course it is."

Adelle's hand patted his forearm and his temper simmered down.

"And the food is ready to eat. Enjoy your evening, you two." She slipped her hand into Steven's and hauled him far across the bar to harass other guests.

Adelle raised her eyes to Jack with an amused grin on her face "Another unused gift?"

She was well aware of the Wendy drawer.

Jack snorted in reply, rolling his eyes.

"Come on Mr. Grumpypants. Let's go sit at the brain exploding yellow bar."

"I'm not grumpy," Jack growled as he plopped himself down in the most uncomfortable bar stool he had ever sat in.

Adelle pulled out one of the strange cup shaped stools, and perched herself as dainty as a bird. "Really? The growling threw me off. My mistake."

All right, so maybe he was being a tiny bit grumpy. Jack rubbed his face, forcing himself to lighten up. It wasn't all bad. After all, it was his idea to come to the stupid party. It wasn't often he was out at a fancy restaurant with a beautiful redhead, all on his ex-girlfriend's dime, even.

Adelle looked around the room. "Is it me, or are a lot of guys here wearing red shirts?"

Jack lifted his head and glanced around. She was right. It seemed like every other man in the bar was wearing a red button down dress shirt, practically identical to his own. On closer inspection of who was wearing them, Jack groaned. His face burned in humiliation.

"Oh, you are fucking kidding me." He reached up to rub his straining eyes.

Adelle perked up. "What?" She twitched her head around like a meerkat.

After a moment of trying to rub away the aggravation headache that throbbed behind his eyes, Jack muttered, "They're all her ex-boyfriends."

Adelle gaped at him a moment. She gasped, slapping a hand over her mouth to keep a giggle from escaping. "You're kidding, right?"

"I wish I was." Jack waved for the bartender to come over and ordered four shots of tequila for them, just in case Adelle felt the need to drown any frustrations as well. If not, well four shots wouldn't do much to him.

Adelle's lips moved as she counted the amount of red shirts in the bar. When Jack heard her giggle, he turned his head, glaring at the redhead next to him. Adelle had her hand clamped over her mouth as she tried to mute her snickering. They only grew into guffaws. She looked at him, eyes watering, cheeks puffed and red. Jack rolled his eyes as she threw her head back, cackling. She slapped the bar top with her hand, pressing her forehead against the bar.

"What?" Jack said.

"Oh God," she gasped out between chortles. "Oh God, they're all wearing red shirts!" She slapped her hand on the bar again, other arm wrapped tight around her belly. "Is she marking her territory? Why doesn't she just pee on them instead?" Adelle sat up, wiping the tears from her cheeks. She almost teetered out of her bar stool as another wave of hysterics overtook her. "Oh lord, I can't! I can't even!"

Jack felt his mouth start to twitch. He shook his head trying to fight it, wanting to be furious, wanting to brood like he always did. But soon he joined her, grin spread wide with mirth. Adelle sat herself upright, looking to Jack with eyes aglow. Warmth coiled in the depths of his stomach and he let out a long deep belly laugh.

"Did you ever watch Star Trek before?" Adelle asked.

"No," Jack said. He rested his chin on his fist, eyebrows raised in amusement.

"Then you wouldn't get the reference. But trust me when I say that it's hilarious!" Adelle managed to get her laughter under control, blotting the side of her eyes with a cocktail napkin.

"Here." Jack pushed two of the tequila shots across to her, wondering exactly how alcohol would play into this.

She looked down at them, teeth nibbling on her lower lip. "I'm not much of a drinker."

Jack's mouth spread into a devilish grin. "Live a little."

Adelle smiled, and picked up the shot glass, eyeing it a long moment, then shrugged and kicked it back. After the golden liquid coursed down her throat, she choked out a hacking cough. "Sweet God! It burns!"

Jack gave her a gentle slap on the back. "Puts hair on your chest."

"Why on earth would I want that?" she croaked.

Jack only laughed and waved the bartender over again. "I'll take your shots and order you something that won't destroy your perfect vocal cords."

"I'm warning you Jack, I'm not a drinker." Adelle cleared her throat of the tequila, rubbing her chest. "Sheesh, it burns the whole way, doesn't it?"

"Yes, it does. And don't worry. I promise I won't let you get so tipsy you make an ass out of yourself." He chucked her under the chin. "And we all know how serious I am about my promises."

Two margaritas later, Adelle was feeling no pain. Jack assumed that she would have partaken in alcohol often in college. That is, unless she was one of those students that actually studied. After taking a long look at her flushed cheeks and swimming squint, Jack deduced that yes, she was one of those students that actually studied.

"Oh my God, you totally got me buzzed." Adelle teetered on her stool, looking at the pale green liquid in her glass. "Seriously. This is your entire fault."

Jack chuckled with a shake of his head. Adelle was adorable when tipsy. Her cheeks and nose were pink and she moved with what could only be described as... drunken grace.

He reached over, plucking the glass from her hand. "Okay, I'm cutting you off. Two is obviously your limit."

Adelle's fingers chased after the glass, pawing at it. "Naaaaah! I'll be fine! I'll just pace myself." She plucked the glass from Jack's grip and took a long drink, emptying the vessel.

"Yeah, and you're doing such a great job so far."

"We should go dance. Let's go dance!"

The band was in full swing and filling the bar with hopping music. Jack looked over to the crowded dance floor, mostly populated by Wendy's gal pals and their boyfriends -who were all wearing red dress shirts. He shuddered at the view. Jack's courage hit its limit when it came to dancing.

"I'm not much for dancing," he said.

"And I'm not for drinking, but I humored you." She slipped out of her seat to her feet, hanging from his arm, feet shuffling across the floor. "Come oooooon! It'll be fun!"

He patted her head. "Why don't you head over and I'll catch up later."

"Chicken."

"Yes. I'm cowardly poultry." He nudged her away. "Go work off the booze, Buttercup. And I'll catch up."

Adelle put her hands on her hips. "You are absolutely no fun. You're the fun sucker."

She stuck her tongue out at him then giggled and turned on her heels, heading over to the dance floor. Jack bust out a rumbling laugh, rubbing his face. He ordered himself a couple more shots, killing them quick as he watched Adelle dance all by herself.

She had absolutely no coordination whatsoever. Arms over head, hips going every which way as she gyrated wildly in a circle. Yet he found her erratic dance moves extremely charming. She was so fearless out there. The courage probably came from the margaritas she had guzzled down earlier.

After a few rounds of her doing the running man, Jack decided it was time to haul her back to the bar. Adelle was bad dancing right on the line between adorable and complete loss of dignity. Discreetly, he slipped onto the dance floor with the intentions of tugging her way from the crowd of bumping women and crimson shirted men.

Adelle turned and flung her arms around his neck. "You promised me one dance," she said.

As if on cue, the song ended, and after a brief pause, a much slower song took its place.

"No, I didn't. I promised to keep you from making an ass out of yourself," Jack replied.

"I was just dancing."

Jack tapped the tip of her nose. "Hence why I had to step in."

Adelle laughed that contagious laugh of hers and laid her head down against his chest. "Just one dance. I'll even settle for half of one. It's a slow song so no one will know you're uncoordinated."

"Me, uncoordinated?" Jack stood there helpless as Adelle continued to cling to him. The other couples had already submitted to the dreamy tune, arms entwined, bodies pressed together. He pursed his lips then looked down to her. "Ten seconds."

"I'll take it."

His arms slipped around her waist and they swayed to the intoxicating music. He rested his chin on the top of her head, eyes closed, and he pressed her warm soft body even closer to him. The sounds of Adelle's sweet sighs brushed over his skin, smoothing out his ruffled scales.

Maybe this is the right moment?

Adelle jolted as she let out a loud hiccup. The smell of tequila filled his nostrils as she let out a drunken titter.

Maybe not.

Jack pulled away, taking Adelle by the arm and leading her off the dance floor. "Come on."

He was answered by a long drawn out "Aawwwwww!" but she complied, laughing the entire way. Either the margaritas were very strong or she was a light weight. Probably both. Adelle threw her head back and let out a loud cackle, her feet slipping sideways. Jack caught her before she went sprawling. What he needed to do was sit her down and get some water in her. He looked towards the bar, only finding himself face to face with Wendy. Her arms were folded across her chest as she looked down to Adelle, pink mouth scribbled into a scowl.

"Hello, cousin!" Adelle waved a hand to Wendy.

That didn't change the look on Wendy's face. If anything, her frown deepened. "Everything all right here?" she asked, unamused.

"Yep," Jack said. He started to sidestep her when Wendy snagged a hold of Adelle's arm and pulled them both to a stop.

"Dell, you are completely embarrassing me!" Wendy said.

"She'd not that bad." Jack reached up and grabbed the finger Adelle was trying to stick into his ear while he defended her. "There are other folks drunker."

"None of them are related to me!'

Before he could say more, Adelle swung around, getting nose to nose with her cousin. She tapped a finger against Wendy chest so hard, she stumbled backwards a step.

"Congrats to you, Wendy. Really," Adelle said. "You finally found someone who can put up with your shit. Good for you! Though I don't have any idea why you would even choose the iceberg over there over this guy." She gave Jack's broad chest a good smack.

Wendy's cornflower blue eyes went huge with either anger or complete bafflement. Jack tried to hold back the laughter, but a few snorts escaped. He pinched his nose.

"Also, also, also." Her hand waved like a spastic butterfly. "Let me tell you something, missy. You can only have one! One! Just one! Got it? Pick one! Apparently, you did! He's over there... somewhere." She made a broad gesture to the entire bar, sweeping her hand so full; she hit a passing waitress in the boob on accident. The squeal from the waitress didn't stop the drunken tirade. "So, this one?" Adelle smacked Jack's chest again, which made him oof. "Off limits. Got it? I am so sick of you hogging all the good ones!"

Wendy looked to Jack in astonishment. She tapped her foot on the floor in a rapid beat. "Are you going to let her talk to me like that?"

"Yes," Jack only replied, keeping Adelle up on her noodle legs. "I'm going to take her home now so you can get on with whatever this is all about."

Wendy threw her arms up in the air. "You both disgust me!" she snarled. "I should bend both your minds for what you're doing tonight! Both of you are ruining my-"

"Shut up, Wendy," a foreign voice cut in.

All three turned their heads to see Steven glowering at them, his fists balled. Jack had never heard him say a word but there he was, talking. His voice was soft and rather raspy. Not something he expected from tall, dark, and comatose.

"We need to talk about how you treat your guests, my love." His words were clipped and heavy. He turned his dark gaze onto Jack. "And Jack, I'm done tolerating your presence. I think it's time for you to head home."

"Agreed," Jack said.

Well, Steven spoke, Adelle was drunk, and Jack was the one being an adult about it all. The world was just full of surprises tonight.

Wendy batted her eyes at her fiancé. "Honey, don't be mad," she cooed, slipping her arm into his.

The anger in Steven's eyes started to melt away as Wendy worked her magic on him. The perfect distraction. Without another word, Jack snagged their coats and dragged Adelle out the door, keeping his hands on her shoulders to make sure she didn't slip in the snow. He poured her into the front seat of his car, then got in.

She snickered. “I totally told off Wendy.”

“Yes, you did,” Jack said, his tone the one you’d use when praising a small child.

“It was totally sexy!”

His lips curled into a devilish grin. “Yes, it was.”

It was too short of a drive for Adelle to doze off into a drunken stupor. Soon, Jack was scooping her up out of her seat. He slung her arm around his shoulders and started the trek to his front door, dreading the idea of that long stairway. The two paused in front of it, staring at each step in dread. Jack’s gaze slid over to Adelle, who was now hanging limp off his shoulders and cackling like a mad woman.

“Hey, Buttercup. Can you make it up these?”

She swung her head around and looked at him blurry eyed. That did not bode well.

Adelle blew air through her lips in a loud ptttffft. “Oh, yeah,” she assured him. “I climb these every day!” She looked back to the stairs again, eyes growing huge. “They seem a lot taller than I remember.”

Jack hoisted her up again. “Come on. Foot up.”

He nudged her leg with his boot, urging her to step up. Adelle managed to get one foot up before her knee wobbled like jelly. Rousing laughter escaped her throat, tumbling snow off a nearby tree, right down onto Jack’s head. He yelped as the ice-cold frost slipped down the back of his shirt collar.

“Nope. Not making it.” Adelle turned to him, her face in a melodramatic frown as she clutched his shirt. “It’s too dangerous! Go on without me!”

After a long-suffering sigh, Jack said, “Fine, we’ll do it my way.” He snagged Adelle by the waist and threw her over his shoulder. Her squeak of surprise melted into yet another peal of laughter.

My God, you're tall!" she said in a deep voice.

Jack felt it best not to answer. Adelle was being distracting enough with all the giggling and now the drumming on his rump with her hands.

Is she making bongo noises?

A jingle of keys, a little juggling of his cargo, and Jack managed to unlock the door without hurting anyone. He plopped her on her feet, propping her against the wall. As soon as he turned to lock to door, Adelle slowly slid down the plaster and to the floor. Jack spun and snagged a grip on her before she hit the hardwood, kicking the door closed with a mighty slam.

Oh, come on!" he whined. "Really? Only after two margaritas?"

"Three margaritas," Adelle corrected.

Jack's jaw fell open. "Three?"

"And a shot of tequila."

"What?"

"And that glass of wine Wendy's friend, Deirdre, handed me on the dance floor."

Jack stared at Adelle, slack jawed as she listed off the many alcoholic beverages she consumed throughout the night. "Anything else?" he asked.

Adelle pursed her lips then her already flushed cheeks turned even pinker in guilt. "Half a cosmo," she added.

Jack grinded the heel of his hand into his eye socket. "Where did you get all of these drinks?"

"You."

"I meant the other ones."

"You weren't supervising me while dancing." Adelle grinned then lifted a finger and pressed it against the tip of his nose while letting out a high pitched, yet soft, "Beeeeeeep."

Drunken people were never amongst his favorites to deal with. That two year stint as a club bouncer back in the 1970s did it. He had never witnessed more vomit than in the seventies. Jack wrinkled his nose with a scowl, still keeping her vertical with his hand pinned to her shoulder. Adelle smiled right back, her eyes glazed over with the fog of booze. Well, it didn't look like she was going to vomit. That sent relief coursing through his veins. Jack felt a smile curl around his mouth and he laughed at the entire situation.

"Buttercup, you are going to be wrecked tomorrow."

"Oh, I know." Sober Adelle peeked through the alcohol haze, trying to regain some sense of composure and dignity. There wasn't much left of either by Jack's judgment. She lifted a hand, shoving her messy curls out of her line of vision. They only fell right back. "Warning you now. I'm a huge baby when it comes to hangovers."

"Why am I not surprised?"

He reached up and smoothed her hair back from her face, the strands silken against his palms. Those dancing green eyes were alight, sparkling in the golden street light that cascaded through the window. She stared at him with such heat; he could feel it against his flesh. Jack's heart quickened. He couldn't stop himself from running his thumb across her lower lip. A tiny gasp of air sucked between her soft pink lips. Jack dared himself to taste them. Instead he leaned in and rested his forehead against Adelle's. Her honeyed essence cocooned him, and he wished she wasn't so damn drunk tonight. It took an act of strong will to get him to finally pull away.

"Come on, let's get some coffee in you," he said.

Jack stepped back only to be stopped by Adelle's fingers entwining the front of his shirt. The last time she had clutched him like that was the night she cried. The same night Jack had held her in his arms for the first time. She pulled him closer.

"You all right, Buttercup?" His voice was rough as his throat turned dry.

Thud, thud, thud.

Jack's heart almost burst through his ribs when she let out a long shuddering sigh. A sigh of want. She was so close. The feel of her breath on his neck was hot and her breasts were pressed against his chest, caressing him as they rose and fell. Jack swallowed hard. Their eyes locked for a long agonizing minute.

"Adelle," Jack whispered.

Adelle replied by leaning in and feathering her mouth over his. Her silken lips set him ablaze, skin hot, belly on fire. That brief connection was pure heaven. It made him ravenous for more of her. All of her. But before Jack could fully act, she pulled her kiss away. The sudden absence of her mouth sobered him up quick. He forced his lust back, about to lose his mind.

Dammit. Control yourself Jack!

"Sorry," Adelle murmured. "I'm sorry."

"No harm, no foul," Jack said, mouth still tingling from the delicate kiss.

Adelle shut her eyes and leaned her head back against the wall with a frustrated groan. His involuntary hand slid down to her waist as she leaned forward again to nuzzle his chin. All the lust he forced away came rushing right back.

"Oh God, I want you so much, Jack," she whispered.

Too much. It was all too much to hold back anymore.

"Oh, fuck it," Jack groaned.

His hand slipped around the small of Adelle's back and he pulled her body tight against his, claiming her mouth. Adelle kissed him greedily; tiny, breathy moans escaping her as she did. She slid her arms around his shoulders, fingers running up the back of his neck and into his hair. Jack stiffened when her velvet fingertips danced up his nape. With a fierce snarl, he pushed her up against the wall, devouring her yielding mouth. The fire in his belly urged him on, begged him to fall further into Adelle's abyss.

Jack took a firm hold of her round backside and crushed her hips against his. Adelle hooked her leg around his hip, grinding hard as her teeth nipped his throat. His hand palmed her breasts, kneading the warm flesh. Her nipples stiffened against the smooth fabric, welcoming him. Her intoxicating scent filled his nostrils as heat swelled up in what little space was between them. The sensations made him instantly erect. Sweet God, it was pure agony to be blocked by so much clothing.

Jack ran his hand up the length of her thigh, his fingers slipping under her skirt and under the waistband of her panties. When he touched the wet curls between her legs, Adelle gave a sharp, excited gasp. As a reward, she kissed him harder. Jack wanted more of that. More of the breathless sounds of her pleasure, the hot, wet feel of her wanton mouth. His fingers ran up her slick sex, exploring, demanding the sweet, sensual sounds she keened.

Adelle shuddered and moaned, "Jack," clouding his mind with insanity. After that moan, Jack wasn't going to be satisfied until he was plunged deep inside her and she was screaming his name. She continued to ravage his lips, her hands fumbling with his belt buckle, tugging as if that would magically loosen it. Her breath came in short and hurried gasps.

"Yes. Please, Jack. This. All of this," Adelle moaned against his mouth.

That was when Jack caught the faint smell of tequila on her. His eyes popped opened as he remembered how many drinks Adelle had consumed that night.

Shit.

Gently, he removed his hand from her panties and pulled his mouth away from hers. He wanted her more than anything. But not like this.

"Adelle," he said.

Adelle didn't answer. Her hands were still tangled in his belt. She finally pulled it free, her mouth in a tight line of concentration. Jack grabbed both of her wrists, holding them fast before she could undo the fly of his pants. He'd be lost if she got that far.

"Adelle, honey. Stop."

Adelle raised her blurry eyes and stared at him through a haze of tequila and lust. "Huh?" she eloquently stated.

"We're stopping," Jack said.

Adelle's brows creased over her narrowed lids as a frown twisted her mouth. "What?" she said through her clenched teeth.

Jack winced as he heard the words, "We need to stop," come out of his mouth.

"Don't do this to me, Jack," she snarled.

"You're drunk off your ass, Adelle."

"Two years, Jack."

"You need to sober up first."

"Two *long* years, Jack!"

"Look!" Jack untangled himself from her limbs in annoyance. "I didn't say forever! I'm saying sober up and see how you feel!"

The frown Adelle wore melted into a desperate, pleading guise. "Oh, come on! I'm a little drunk, yes, but tequila is more of a truth serum for me!"

For a moment, Jack almost fell for it. Or at least he wanted to. But his common decency won out. "Adelle, we're not doing this if you're not in control of your decision making skills!"

Jack ran a hand through his hair as his crotch screamed at him to reconsider. What an inconvenient time to grow a conscience. The way she stared at him with her mouth half open made him extremely uncomfortable as well. He sighed and shook his head, knowing he was making the right choice, despite what the raging hard-on that was straining against his slacks told him.

"You deserve better," Jack said. "A lot better than a quick drunken fuck against my living room wall."

Adelle chewed on her lower lip, silent as she mulled Jack's words over. Her mouth, still beautifully swollen from his kisses, turned into a sad frown. "Are you not attracted to me?" she whimpered.

Jack's expression was somewhere between complete amusement and utter astonishment. "Were you asleep during the last ten minutes?"

"I'm serious!" Adelle snapped.

Jack rolled his eyes. Instead of justifying that ridiculous question with an answer, he took her by the wrist and placed her hand over the huge, throbbing bulge in his pants. Adelle hesitated a moment, then that wide eyed expression he loved so much spread across her face.

"Ah. Well that question is answered," she said.

"Indeed," Jack grumbled.

When Adelle's hand started to caress his aching shaft, he leapt away from her. If she started in on that, there would be no stopping him the second time around.

"Go get a glass of water. I'll put a pot of coffee on and..." *I'll spend the rest of the evening trying to work off the blue balls after you pass out on the couch.* "We'll go from there."

Adelle sighed. She pushed back the tangled hair from her face, banging the back of her head against the wall one, two, three times.

"All right," she said.

His heart was glad that he wasn't the only one feeling massive disappointment. After the initial shock wore off, he had to admit, it was all pretty hilarious, even if painful for his groin. Jack let out a little chuckle and moved towards her again.

"Hey, Buttercup," he said.

Adelle looked at him, mouth turned into a pathetic little frown. Her lower lip quivered. She appeared to be sobering up, the fog lifting ever so slightly. Jack took a gentle hold of her chin and angled her face towards his. A ghost of a smile finally graced her lips when their eyes met. That was enough to entice him to give her another kiss, one that was delicate and tender. Her eyes fluttered closed as she leaned toward him, a hand resting on his chest. When he pulled away, Jack gave her a cocky smile.

"Try to sober up quick, all right?"

Adelle let out a low chuckle and nodded. "I'll do my best."

She pulled away and dragged herself to the kitchen. When she was a safe distance, Jack rubbed his temples and gave himself a good shake. Cold showers were going to be in order for at least a week.

"For what it's worth," Adelle said as she trudged to the kitchen table. "I probably wouldn't hate you in the morning."

"I'm not taking that chance, Buttercup."

"You'd be breaking me out of a two-year dry period, after all. You'd get laid and a medal after that."

Jack tried to think of a snappy comeback. But when he opened his mouth to reply, the only words that came out were, "I'm falling in love with you, Adelle."

Adelle stopped in her tracks and Jack winced at his horrible timing. Utter astonishment blanketed her features as she stared at him.

So much for waiting for the right moment.

It was out there now. No turning back. Jack straightened his spine, looked his female dead in the eye and staked his claim.

"I love you," he said.

Chapter 18

It was true. The most honest three words he had ever spoken. Jack's claim for his mate slipped from his lips as natural as a breath.

So why do I feel so goddamned nervous?

He clenched his hands, praying that Adelle would say the same. Right now, she just stared mute at him, eyes round and wide, lips slightly parted. That was not encouraging. The words hung in the air, frozen as he waited for a response.

Adelle opened her mouth to speak when her cell phone started to ring. She let out a few curse words under her breath and the distracted tipsy cloud she was floating in and out of shrouded her once again.

"Go on and get it," he told her. "I think I need to recover from that bomb shell, too."

"Right," Adelle said, voice dazed. She snatched up her cell phone. "Hello? ...What?" Adelle pulled the phone away from her ear to look at the screen, blinked, and then went back to speaking. "Twenty-three missed calls, Val? Really? Hold on, hold on, I need to take my boots off." After hitting the speaker button, she slumped into a chair and tossed her phone on the kitchen table. "All right. Proceed."

"Dell!" Valerie's echoed from her phone. "I've been calling you all night!"

"Really? Whoops."

"Woops?! I called you twenty-three times and all you say is whoops?!"

Adelle leaned her head back and giggled. "Whoooooops!"

"Where have you been?"

"Out doing stuff... That may or may not involve alcohol."

Stuff. Jack wished they were doing "stuff" right now. He ran a hand through his hair. It was damn hard getting the memory of her body writhing against him out of his mind. And there he went, cock at full salute all over again. Instead of wallowing in sexual frustration, he just listened in on the sisterly banter.

"You went drinking?" Valerie asked in disbelief.

"It's my only defense against Wendy's social gatherings," Adelle said.

Jack leaned his shoulder up against the kitchen door frame, watching Adelle bend down to unzip her boots. "That your sister?" he asked.

"Yup."

"Who's there with you?" Valerie's disembodied voice demanded.

"Just Jack," Adelle answered as she yanked her boots from her feet.

"Jack? Who the hell is Jack?!"

"The dragon I just tried to drunkenly seduce. He turned me down." She looked up from her boot long enough to shoot him a smirk. "It wasn't very nice of him."

Jack snorted out a little laugh. The angry grunt from the phone said that Valerie was not as amused.

"You spent this whole time getting drunk and having sex while I worried my ass off?!"

"Getting drunk? Yes. Having sex? No. The sex part would have been nice but noooooo. He had to turn around and be a gentleman." Adelle kicked her boots aside and wiggled her toes free.

Jack raised a brow. *She's right. Tequila is her truth serum.*

"He told me he loved me, though. That was pretty amazing." The corners of her mouth turned up into a giddy smile. That gave Jack some hope that his claim wouldn't be rejected. Her twinkling eyes caught his and the smile grew, cheeks glowing with delight. "I think I might-"

"Look, you two can have all the sex you want as long as you stay indoors," Valerie said.

"Well, I sure as hell wasn't planning on rolling around naked in the snow." Adelle got up and went to the sink, groping for a clean glass in the drying rack. "But mark my words. There *will* be sex."

"Do I have any say in this?" Jack called out.

A thunderous, simultaneous, "No!" from both sisters made him put up his hands in casual surrender. Instead of arguing, he worked on brewing a fresh pot of coffee for his drunken siren.

"Dell, focus for two seconds," Valerie urged on. The uneasiness that strangled her voice made Jack's ears perk. "There's more to your kidnapping than just Ethan. I think he's working for someone worse."

The name alone made Jack's stomach drop into his boots. Ethan was just a lackey? That would explain why the vampire trudged all the way up to Washington, ready to challenge a dragon. Junkies were never that desperate for a hit. Adelle had gone pale as she stared at her phone. Hackles raised, he turned towards the table, teeth bared.

"What do you mean? Who is he working for?" he demanded.

Valerie either didn't hear Jack or was ignoring him. "Dell, just stay put and let that dragon be your watchdog because-"

Shards of glass exploded across the kitchen sink, scattering everywhere with a shrieking tinkle as the window exploded. Adelle managed to turn and throw her hands over her head, sharp splinters slicing red lines across her arms. A figure sat perched on his countertop, straddling the sink, shoulders hunched, fingers curled into claws.

Ethan.

He looked up to Jack, his eyes red from pupil to whites, fangs bared. Smoke hissed from his flesh as it bubbled open with gruesome pops of thick, yellow pus. The vampire dared to enter a home uninvited and the laws of magic were seeing he was punished for his crime. Ethan's gore covered arm snared around Adelle's waist. She opened her mouth to scream but his hand caught her throat and squeezed the voice right out of her. Jack dashed to the broken window, the pebbles of glass crunching under his boots. He reached forward to snag Ethan, but his fingers curled around nothing but air as the vampire carried Adelle into the night. Within a breath, they were gone.

Jack stared out the window, his keen eyes trying to catch sight of them. Nothing. His fist slammed into the counter, webbing the granite with cracks. A sick panic rose in his gut, erupting into an infuriated roar.

"No! Fuck!"

Valerie's voice screamed from the phone sitting on the table. "Dell! What happened? What's happening over there?!"

"He took her," Jack shouted back to the phone. Various curses answered him. He climbed up onto the counter, taking a deep inhale. Ethan may have been fast, but Jack had one hell of a sense of smell. He caught her sent in his nostrils as well as the rotting decaying stench of the vampire. It was strong but fading. "And I'm going after her." He leapt out his window before Valerie could reply.

Jack's boots hit the snow with a thump, leaving deep divots in the soft white. The scent was fading faster and faster. He turned around, looking for footprints or any traces that Ethan left behind. There was none, other than a few shattered pieces of window pane sticking up in the snow like tortured icicles. Jack cursed under his breath. It would only be a matter of minutes before Adelle was too far to scent. She'd be lost to him forever.

No, no, no! I won't let that happen!

A glint of red caught the corner of his site. Spatters of crimson dotted the white powder. Peering forward, he spotted another cluster of bloody specks, and then another before the blood trail in the snow disappeared at the foot of a neighboring building. Adelle's blood. It had to be. Ethan must have leapt to the next rooftop and took off running from there.

She was hurt.

Now, it was time to kill.

Jack bared his teeth. He began to follow the trail when someone tackled him from behind with tremendous force. He slammed into the ground hard, skidding through the icy cold frost. With a swipe of his hand, Jack wiped the snow from his vision to see a pale bald man clutching his shirt. Eyes blood red, the man opened his mouth and hissed, his canines long and sharp. Another vampire. The display only raised Jack's fury.

"Two of ye?" His accent slipped in his rage. "Two of ye arseholes?! Doona ye know what I am!?" He reached up and grabbed the vampire's neck squeezing hard. One mighty swing and Jack threw him off like he was made of paper.

The vampire crashed into a pile of snow as Jack jumped to his feet. Though Jack may have had stamina, the vampire had speed. He was on his feet and rushed at Jack again, hitting him low in the knees. Jack's head hit with a crack. His vision swam in waves of white before snapping into place with boiling hot rage.

The vampire didn't notice his anger and continued his attack, swiping his claws across Jack's cheek and drawing blood. When he reached back to strike again, Jack snagged his wrist. A sharp twist and the vampire's bones snapped like toothpicks. Before he could even yelp in pain, Jack pushed the bloodsucker off him, rolled to his knees, and landed a powerful blow into his adversary's gut, then another. He wasn't going to stop until the vampire was pulverized into raw meat.

The vampire squirmed away and instead of flesh, Jack punched the pavement. A gaping hole swallowed his knuckles, cement cracking in grey, jagged peaks around his fist. He looked up to see the vampire staring in terror, curled in agony. Then he was off, becoming nothing more than a pale blur as he scaled the wall of the far building. With a growl, Jack wiped the blood from his cheek with the back of his hand. Ethan had a friend. A friend who made a decent distraction.

As the scent of Adelle grew faint, dread churned in his stomach. Jack clenched his fists as his burning hatred grew inside him, threatening to erupt into a trail of fire. Those bastards weren't going to take her from him. And if they did, they would spend the rest of their eternity paying for it.

Jack's flesh began to ripple. Scales tore through his skin, peeling back from his body and hardening into golden-red plates. He shut his eyes and ground his teeth, as they grew long, sharp. An inhuman howl rolled through the streets and Jack fell onto his hands and knees, clothes ripping to shreds as he grew. Limbs swelled, bones creaked, and his spine broke with a sharp crackle. It reformed into the back of a huge beast.

Enormous black wings tore from his shoulder blades and flared open with a whoosh of air, flurrying the snow around him. The great red dragon threw his huge horned head back with a roar. He was whole again. Whole and ravenous for vengeance. With a swipe of his wings, the creature took off into the night to bring back his female.

Chapter 19

Adelle's drunk, fuzzy mind snapped into razor sharp focus as soon as Ethan took hold. He squeezed her throat so tight it crushed the scream right out of her. Then she was flying, falling, legs bashing into the window's jagged glass remains. Ethan dashed across the rooftops at an uncanny speed. Adelle was tucked under his arm like an oversized football, arms pinned to her sides. His free hand was vice clamped over her mouth and she jerked and bumped against him. He leapt to the next building, ran, and then leapt again, each time landing so hard that it made her nauseous. The further from Jack they grew, the more terror Adelle felt.

A sharp relentless pain throbbed from her thigh. Adelle manage to twist around to discover a six inch shard of glass wedged into her flesh. Blood trickled down her leg, spreading a stain of scarlet along her skirt and marking their path on the snow below with little red droplets. A clear trail for Jack to follow. He was a good enough hunter to pick it up, but how fast could he catch up was the question.

Her panic grew frenzied. If Jack couldn't get to her in time, Adelle had to get loose on her own. She wiggled, trying to break out of Ethan's grip but his strength was too much for her to struggle out of. There was only one other option. Without another thought, Adelle took a deep breath and let out a scream. The hand clutched over her lips began to sizzle and the putrid smell of baking flesh hit her nostrils.

After leaping onto the Greyhound station rooftop, Ethan screamed and stumbled. He came to a skidding halt, swung Adelle out of his grip, and slammed her down onto her back. Spasms webbed through her and she let out a shout of pain, not sure if her voice made the building shake or if her body was shuddering from the blow.

The iron weight of Ethan's left hand pressed her down on her chest as he hauled back and rammed his fist into her throat. Adelle choked, her head falling back hard against the roof as hot tears clawed at her eyes. The blow wasn't hard enough to crush her windpipe but it had enough force to silence her. She was just about to comprehend recovery when Ethan kicked her in the gut; knocking whatever wind she regained right back out of her.

"You know I hate it when you use that voice shit!" Ethan screamed.

Adelle tried to wrap her arms around her stomach to soothe herself but Ethan slung her over his shoulder and took off again. Pain, nausea, and dizziness all swirled together in a gruesome cocktail. Sickly green stars danced before her eyes. Her eyes rolled back and all went black.

When Adelle's eyes fluttered open, she found herself staring up at a dingy white ceiling. A raspy groan escaped her lips, vision fuzzy and doubled. She rocked her head from side to side, trying to regain focus.

Come on, Adelle. Recover. Get your game back. Where are you? Who's here? Can you speak? Can you take them on?

A hand was clutched around her throbbing throat, forcing her up on shaking legs against a wall. Adelle opened her mouth to speak but only coughed, throat raw.

"Shit, you're a mess!" a strange voice said.

Adelle slid her focus towards the voice. First she saw Ethan. His skin was blistered, flowing with gore in bubbled patches across his face and hands. Blood red eyes narrowed, his fangs bared and dripping with saliva. Under all that boiled flesh were sunken eyes, shrouded by blue shadows, and cheeks so gaunt that he looked more like a skull than a man. That was his hungry face. The scent of the bleeding cut on her leg deepened his frenzy. A hungry vampire was an unreasonable vampire, and a vampire withdrawing from siren's blood added crazy into the mix.

Behind him stood one of the vampires from her kidnapping. The twitchy bald one that paced all the time. Brett was his name. She only remembered that because the other vampires had screamed at him over and over to stop pacing. He scratched his neck with a spastic hand, walking in a tight circle behind Ethan. Brett also looked drawn and thin but not half as bad as Ethan. But then, Brett had only had that one night of her blood. Ethan had had weeks. The bitter taste of bile touched the back of her throat. Her hands shook. Her heart slammed.

Keep calm, Adelle, she told herself. *Figure out where you are.*

She inhaled deep, pushed back the fear, and flicked her eyes across her surroundings.

The room they were in was small. Two double beds sat across from them to the left, separated by a chipped and worn wooden night stand with a cheap lamp sitting atop it. She looked to the right to see the front door, a plastic do not disturb sign hanging from the knob. There was another door, probably a bathroom. It was a motel room. It had to be. She didn't know of any motels in Whitmore proper, only a couple bed and breakfast places and a quaint inn. The only motel she knew of was one she had passed when coming in from the airport. It was comprised of little one room cottages that had probably never been remodeled since 1962. Her heartbeat cranked up to maximum speed. Ethan had gotten her almost two hours out of town.

Brett peered over Ethan's shoulder at Adelle, hand clutched against his chest as if wounded. "I can't believe you actually broke into his house," he said.

Ethan kept his deadly gaze locked on Adelle, squeezing her bruised and swollen neck. She grabbed at his forearm, fingers weak as she tried to pry his steel grip away.

"You told me to go get her," Ethan said, red eyes pulsing. "You told me to wait outside the house. I got sick of waiting." He turned to Brett with a ghoulish smile. "Call me a pussy again, Brett. I dare you."

Brett went paler than he already was. He took a healthy step back from Ethan, shuddering. "Fine. You win. You're not a pussy. That guy is going to be on us in a few minutes. I tried to hold him off, and he kicked my ass. Now what? "

"We get out of here." Ethan ran his jagged thumb nail up the side of Adelle's throat, snagging her skin under its path. "We weaken her, steal a car, shove her in the trunk, and head home." He grinned at Adelle as red froth dripped from the corners of his mouth. "Still think you're going to see me die, Adelle? Nah, you're going to be first. I'm sure there's something far better waiting for you at home."

"Ethan." Adelle voice was a croaking whisper. "What are you talking about?"

She had to keep a conversation up. If she kept using her voice, she might be able to get some sound back. Hopefully Ethan was too distracted by his hunger madness to notice her scheme.

"The mage." He leaned in, taking a long inhale of her hair. "There's a mage that wants you more than I do. I'm sure he'll give you a slow and painful death." His tongue ran across her earlobe, making her shudder.

"A mage? What mage?" Adelle's whisper grew in volume. "What is his name?"

"Why should you care?"

"Ethan, what's his name?"

Ethan leaned in to nuzzle her neck, and Adelle winced at the slimy touch of his puss covered cheek. "Anthony. That's all you need to know."

There was only one mage she knew named Anthony. Adelle stomach dropped.

But it couldn't be him! It couldn't be!

"What did he look like?" Adelle said in a raspy murmur. Her strength was returning.

Ethan's hand tightened around her throat. "You're talking too much, Adelle."

"Ethan, if this is who I think it is, you-" She gagged as Ethan squeezed.

"Shut up!" He shook her by the neck and the back of her head bounced against the wall, sending a myriad of stars dancing across her vision. "Just shut up, bitch! You're talking too much!" Ethan turned to Brett. "Come on, help me drain her."

"Are you crazy?" Brett said.

"Not all the way! Just enough to keep her from moving!" Ethan lurched toward Adelle, fangs bared. When she flinched, he cackled loud.

"Don't do this," Adelle whispered. "Ethan, you're letting your addiction control you. You're not like this. You're not a killer."

"Don't do this? That's all you can say?" His tongue ran across a fang, the sharp edge puncturing the tip. Blood dripped down his lower lip, staining his teeth scarlet. "Oh yes, I'm a killer now. You made me one. You think I'm going to let you walk away? Go on, Adelle. Beg for your life. Tell me you take it all back." He leaned in and whispered, "If you beg, maybe I'll ask the mage to spare your sisters and your fuck buddy." Ethan was gone now, completely taken over by the madness.

Everything inside Adelle stilled. Calm washed over her as white light burned at the edge of her eyes. Her siren's fury began to churn in her gut. *Kill him. Burn him. Turn him to ash for what he did to you,* it whispered. She willed her voice to come back, begging for the chance to consume the vampire in her rage.

"No, Ethan," she growled. "I promise you, you're going to die in my fire." She took a quick intake of breath. Voice ready or not, she would unleash hell upon him.

The scratchy scream Adelle released shook the ground. Ethan slammed a hand against her mouth but her power seared his muscles, burning his palm down to the bone. With a cry, Ethan reared his head back then plunged his fangs into her neck, tearing her open. The venom paralyzed the scream from her throat. Her knees buckled and she fell into a sit onto the worn grey carpet below. Ethan rode her the entire way down, lapping the warm ribbons of crimson up like a hungry cat. His tongue ran up the length of her neck before he clamped his mouth over the punctures and drank hard and deep.

"Stop," Adelle tried to say but the venom had rendered her helpless. Someone grabbed a hold of her arm. Brett. It must have been Brett. Two sharp pin pricks of pain and a second mouth sealed itself over her wrist. Her body grew ice cold as the two sucked her dry.

This was how it would end. Her life drained away, replaced with a cold, lonely despair that pulled the fight out of her. She couldn't move. She couldn't speak. Adelle was trapped, collapsed on the floor of a crappy motel room with two vampires who couldn't cease drinking before her heart stopped. The only solace she had was that Jack would kill them both after she died.

Jack.

Her mind returned to her dragon.

I never told him I loved him back.

Her vision grew tunneled as she felt the last of her will slip into the dark.

The thunderous crash wracked Adelle's ears. Huge black claws tore a hole through the drywall as if it were cardboard and the head of a scaly red dragon burst into the room. Two black horns curled back from its brow ridges like a ram's, the rest of its long face framed by translucent webbed ears. A pair of enormous amber eyes glared as the beast snarled, bearing long white teeth under its curled lips. It shook the rubble off its head as black smoke snorted through its nostrils, filling the room with the scent of smoke and sandalwood.

The vampires pulled their mouths away long enough to make Adelle's body tingle back to life. Brett dropped Adelle's arm and jumped to his feet with high pitched scream of, "Her boyfriend is a fucking dragon!"

He tried to dash away, but Jack snapped his jaws, snagging him between his sharp fangs. Terrified screams echoed through the dilapidated room as the dragon shook his head from side to side, its jaws tearing through Brett's middle. He was tossed against door, landing in a pile of mangled flesh. His torso clung to his legs by a few torn sinews of muscle, drenched in the bright scarlet blood that once filled his belly. Brett screamed again, clawing his wrecked remains across the carpet. Jack's scaled lips curled back and a stream of blistering orange fire roared from his mouth. The flames tangled around Brett's torn body and he writhed in a pathetic attempt to escape the blaze that danced his flesh away. With one final screech, he collapsed into a burning heap.

Adelle felt an arm coil around her waist. The world spun like a top when Ethan hoisted her to her feet, dragging her through the wreckage to the snow blanketed parking lot. Jack swung his head towards the sudden movement, his glare teeming with violence. Black talons grazed Ethan's jeans and sent them toppling into the snow. The cold slush on her skin snapped her out of her stupor and Adelle started to crawl away to freedom. Ethan snagged her leg, yanking her back under him. Adelle clawed and bit, bursts of little screams shaking the ground. Jack frenzied at the sight of his female being manhandled. Leathery wings flared like black sails and he reared up on his hind legs, ready to blow fire again.

"Stop!" Ethan shouted. He pulled Adelle against his chest, claws grabbing her chin and the back of her head. "Back off or I break her neck!"

Adelle had no doubt that he would snap her neck and deal with Tony's consequences later. Ethan's muscles twitched as he started to twist and she went still, clamping her mouth shut. Ragged, foaming breaths rattled in her chest as her heart raced. With an echoing snap of his teeth, Jack slammed his mouth shut. Black smoke billowed from his nostrils, mouth curled into an angry jeer. He lowered himself to all fours in submission.

Pink saliva spattered Adelle's cheek as Ethan's mad cackle curled in the air. "So, the big badass does have a weakness after all."

He squeezed his hands harder against Adelle's head. Jack snapped his jaws again with a fierce bark of protest. As her every muscle went rigid, the glass embedded in her thigh lit up with an excruciating stab of pain. In the adrenaline rush, Adelle had forgotten it was even there. She held her breath. It wasn't much, but it was a weapon. That is, if she could get it out of her.

"You want the bitch to live, you let me and her run," Ethan continued. Steam blew from the corners of Jack's mouth. He dug his claws into the pavement, long white fangs gnashing with loud scrapes. It only made Ethan laugh harder. "Yeah. You're going to be a good boy, aren't you?"

Adelle worked the six inches of glass back and forth with her thumb and pointer finger, biting back cries. Shredded nerves sizzled in agony as wet flesh curled up with every pull. Blood drenched her hand, making the glass too slick to keep ahold of. Those little wiggles weren't going to get it free. She'd have to yank it. Jagged edges bit through her palm as she wrapped her hand around the glass. Sensing the movement, Ethan stiffened, hands pressing tighter. She stopped before he caught on. Adelle needed a distraction while she freed her makeshift weapon. Jack was crouched down on his haunches, shoulders raised. Every inch of him was taut, ready to kill. But as long as Ethan had her, Jack remained motionless.

Look at me, Jack. Look at me. I need you.

As if hearing her thoughts, Jack cocked his head and locked his sights on her. He saw her torn dress, the bloodied hand on her thigh, and the crimson trails gushing down her leg. His brows knitted and his vicious face grew frightened, tortured. Amber eyes flared and worry melted into wrath as Jack lost control. A roar cracked the atmosphere, blowing both her and Ethan's hair back. Ethan's iron grip faltered, giving her the opening she needed.

Without hesitation, Adelle yanked the glass free and swung her arm back behind her, plunging it into Ethan's neck. A curtain of blood showered down his front as she dragged the shard across his throat. He clawed at the glass, stumbling backwards, gargled screams bubbling from his mouth. Adelle stumbled away way just as Jack slammed his hand down over the vampire, pinning him to the blacktop under his claws. A long, low growl vibrated from his long throat, shaking the ground and the corners of his maw curled up into a vicious smile. He leaned close to his prey, snorting steam into his face. Ethan thrashed like an animal in a snare under Jack's grip. Curses spilled from torn lips in wet, garbled snarls. When the vampire caught sight of Adelle, he grabbed at her, clawing the air, eyes red with crazed bloodlust.

Adelle watched the frenzy with her fists balled and bloody. In flash after flash, every image of pain Ethan had caused her whirled through her mind. Adelle remembered how she was tied to that bed and tortured. She remembered the threats sent to her sisters. And now she remembered that he was working with the man who had killed her mother.

A burning surge of outrage boiled in the pit of her belly. White light haloed her vision and her fury turned to ice in her veins. There was no passion anymore. No anger. Just a cold need to kill the one who had wronged her.

Rage blinding her, she raised her eyes to Jack. She expected him to stop her, to tell her to keep calm. Someone had always told her to keep calm. Instead, Jack nodded and leaned back, giving her a clear shot of the bastard.

Adelle hands crept over her ears and she took a deep breath. Pink lips parted and a long ragged scream ripped the black night. The force blew Adelle off her feet, holding her body in the air. White lines of power scurried through the snow and shot up into her, jolting her, keeping her aloft. Pulsing blue veins crawled up her neck and face. The faint outline of feathered wings enveloped her in crackling light.

The scream continued as flurries of white snowflakes and blue light swirled up in a tornado. The magic was bright, turning her vision white, and setting her blood on fire. Yet the pleasure it filled her with was heady; whispering, *Release me.*

Power exploded from her mouth and split into two blazing arcs, dodging between Jack's fingers. It slammed into Ethan with a burst of sapphire flames. Ethan howled as the flames consumed him, peeling the meat from his bones, dissolving him into grey ash. All that was left was a pile of soot and dirty clothes.

Exhaustion hit her as her feet touched down on the ground again, the cold snow biting her toes. The delicious anger that fueled her drained away, leaving her with a throbbing numbness.

Adelle felt weak but before she could fall, Jack slid his large head under her arm, propping her up. He snorted a bit of steam and then nudged her hip with his snout. Beautiful amber eyes peered up at her under heavy furrowed brows. A weary laugh squeaked from Adelle's dry mouth and she fell to her knees, wrapping her arms around his long neck. Her hands stroked his red scales, their warmth pushing the chill from her bones.

"I'm all right," she whispered. "I'm safe."

Strong, human skinned arms wrapped around her shoulders, and Jack gathered her against his chest. His large hand stroked her hair as he rocked her back and forth. Adelle's eyelids grew heavy and soon she fell limp in his arms.

"Oh my God! Fire!" a man's frantic voice shouted in the distance. "Is anyone over there?"

Adelle was curled up in Jack's heat, too tired to answer. He answered for her. "Over here! We're good! Not sure what happened, everything just exploded!"

"Good to hear, mister. She okay? I can call 911."

Adelle pressed her face against Jack's shoulder, letting out a soft groan. The calloused palm of his hand brushed her cheek and she calmed.

"She's breathing and conscious. Must have gotten caught in the blast," Jack said. "I'm taking her to the hospital right now."

"Sure you don't want me to call 911?" The stranger was perplexed. "Because... Well I'm not sure if you noticed son, but... You're naked."

“Fully aware, pal. Have a good night.”

Adelle felt Jack scoop her up before she slipped into peaceful blackness.

Chapter 20

Adelle didn't want to wake up. Something soft cushioned her body and she was lying next to what could be a radiator, it generated so much heat. It was like being burrowed under a million fuzzy blankets on a cold winter morning, tucked away from the grey gloom in a safe, peaceful haven. Everything felt so warm and comfortable; she probably could have coaxed herself back to sleep if she tried.

But where the hell am I?

Uncertainty nagged at her so much that there was no turning back towards dreamland. Slowly, Adelle took a breath, and opened her eyes. The room she was in was dim, shrouded in a halo of flickering, gold fire light. It was a cave lit only by torches bolted into the craggy stone walls. Her breath caught as she took in the piles and piles of glittering treasures heaped around her.

Either I'm having a pirate dream, or I'm in Jack's hoard room.

All dragons had a hoard room, somewhere. They needed gold as much as a fish needed water. It fueled their fire, energized them. Essentially, gold kept them alive and healthy. So, dragons collected shiny objects from the day they were hatched until the day they died. The bigger the hoard, the stronger the dragon. And Jack's collection was immense.

There were countless amounts of gold coins, shimmering gold plates and cups accented with deep colored jewels, and wooden chests overflowing with strings of pearls, rubies, emeralds, and other precious stones. The gold and jewels were plentiful, but the colored glass outnumbered the currency. All the vases, bottles, and apothecary jars Jack couldn't fit in his home were here, twinkling in the guttering torch light, casting colorful shadows across the stone floor.

Hard scales pressed up against Adelle's back and she realized she wasn't sleeping next to a radiator. She craned her neck and looked up at the magnificent beast curled around her. That's exactly what Jack was in true form. His black wings were folded close against his back, showing off the tall spiked ridges that traced his spine from his head to his long, spayed tail. Vapors of steam wafted from his nostrils as he slept, his great chest rising and falling with a low rumble of air. He had arched his claws protectively over Adelle; just enough to shield her but not so much that she couldn't slip away if she wanted. The sight filled her with tenderness, making her smile.

Adelle pushed herself up and a combo of worn blankets, pillow stuffing, and soft straw yielded under her fingers. It carried Jack's masculine scent of smoke and sandalwood.

A nest? How adorable.

As Adelle moved, Jack snorted, pulling his black claws gently away from her. "Adelle?" Jack said. It was his voice, but deeper, echoing from his tremendous body.

"Yeah. I'm here."

He stirred, tail and arms slipping out of site. She began to turn over when Jack's human hand press against her shoulder. "Hold up, hold up. Don't turn around yet."

Adelle tensed. "What is it? Are you all right?"

"Yeah I..." His voice sounded normal now. Normal and embarrassed. "I'm just buck naked."

That woke her up. Jack's gorgeous naked body was mere inches away. She had dreams that started like this. The rustling sound of him wrestling into a pair of pants came from behind her.

"Seriously? *Now* you're modest?"

"Just hold on."

"You chased me down the street in your underwear. Suddenly you're shy?"

"I don't want to scare you off with my colossal wang."

He zipped up his fly. Adelle wouldn't be surprised in the least at the size of his cock. Everything else about him was huge so, of course, that would follow suit. She swallowed hard.

"Okay, you can turn around now."

Adelle rolled over onto her side to face him. He was still magnificent. All she wanted at that moment was to touch him, run her mouth across those pale scars to make sure he was real. She wet her lips, thinking of the heat of his skin against them.

Jack sat up, studying her, his brow furrowed in concern. "How are you feeling?"

Adelle shook off the sudden bout of lust the best she could with a nod. "Human, at least. Not as awful as I thought I would feel. How long was I out?"

"Almost twelve hours, Buttercup. I was getting worried." Jack helped her sit up. "Easy now."

As soon as she was vertical, he took a gentle hold of her chin, tilting her head back. He examined her neck for bruises and cuts. Adelle shivered when the pads of his fingertips slid down her throat.

"Where are we?" Adelle asked.

"The basement."

She arched a brow, tilting her head to the side. "The basement? Your basement is a cave?"

"More like a sub-basement. We're pretty far under the gym. I dug this place out when I first came to Washington. There's an entrance tunnel just outside of town that can fit my true form and a false door in the gym's real basement."

"So, we're in your hoard room."

"Pretty much." He looked at her, somber. "You're safe. I swear that to you."

Though she was sure of her safety, hearing him say it put Adelle's heart at ease. She felt good after her sleep, even if her head felt like a bubble of air on a stick. After a fight like last night's, she should have felt like fifty shades of ass.

Jack pulled his hands away, making Adelle touch the spot he just examined. Ethan's bite was gone. Brett's bite had vanished too, her wrist just smooth flesh. No cuts, no scabs, not a sign that she was hurt. She lifted the hem of her dress to examine the wound on her thigh. A thin pink scar was all she found. It looked like it had been healing for days. This was fast, even for her siren's blood.

"Jack, are you sure I was only asleep for twelve hours and not twelve days?"

"Oh, you mean the cuts? Yeah." Jack cleared his throat. "I did that." He gave no more explanation.

Adelle's raised her eyebrows. "You healed my cuts?"

"More or less. You sure you don't need any more sleep? Or a glass of water?" He leaned in to look into her eyes, checking if her pupils were dilating properly.

"How?" Adelle asked.

"How what?"

"How did you heal wounds in a night that would probably need stitches?"

Jack coughed and muttered something under his breath. He wiped his mouth with his fingers and then went back to looking at her throat by lifting her chin again.

Adelle pushed his hand away. "What did you say?"

Jack's rolled his eyes up to the ceiling, cheeks burning bright red. "Oh, don't make me say it."

"Jack, say it."

With a sigh, Jack sat back on his haunches. "I... licked you."

A laugh boiled out of Adelle before she could help herself, earning her a hard glare. "You licked me?"

Jack growled. "It's not funny! Dragons have healing properties in their saliva, so I licked you and you healed. I don't like doing it! It's weird and we don't like making it public that we can do that!"

The pouting began.

Adelle tried to push the laughter back in by clasping her hands over her mouth. "Well, thank you," she said, voice muffled. "For licking me." The giggles started all over again.

"Fine. Laugh it up."

"So, when you kissed me, does that count as a flu shot?"

"Drop the subject, Buttercup."

Complying, Adelle grinned at him. "All right, all right. Consider it dropped." Soon, Jack was back at his examinations, tilting her head to study her throat. Adelle reached up, taking his hands. "Jack, I'm fine."

"Let me finish. I want to make sure the bruises are gone."

"Jack, I promise you, you won't have to do anymore unauthorized licking."

"Dammit Adelle, just let me finish!" he snapped.

The sudden outburst made Adelle fall silent and she let go of his hands immediately. Jaw ticking, Jack finished giving her a look over, brushing his hand over the place where Ethan had bitten her. He pulled away satisfied, blotting his wet eyes with the heel of his hand.

"I'm not hurt," Adelle said. A lump formed in her throat.

Jack stared at her, eyes glassy, the cords of his neck taut. It was the same pained expression he had worn when Ethan had her hostage. Adelle's heart had almost broken at her dragon's wilted visage. On his human guise, it was so much worse. Without warning, Jack yanked her close and buried his face her neck, breathing her in.

"I thought I'd lost you." His deep voice was thick with emotion. "I don't know what I'd do if I lost you."

Adelle sniffed a little laugh. "You'll have to try harder than that to get rid of me."

Her laugh faded when Jack only shuddered, his warm tears dampening her neck. The words hit her like a truck. *I don't know what I'd do if I lost you*. Jack, the most fearless creature she ever knew, was afraid of losing her?

Adelle's heart stumbled as she slipped her arms around his waist. She stroked his back, trying to comfort him. "Jack. It's all right. I'm-"

The tightening grasp on her shoulders cut her words short. He clung like he was afraid she'd vanish, pulling back to look upon her, tears welling in the corners of those wonderful eyes. Eyes the warm color of whiskey, and just as intoxicating. For a long moment, Jack stared, mouth half open, lower lip quivering with words that wouldn't come out. There was a little shake of his head before he grabbed her by the nape and slanted his mouth over hers.

A spike of unfathomable desire shot through her, fatigue washed away by his needful kiss. Her body formed to his contours, wanting to get closer. She shivered and ran her hands across Jack's chest, clutching, clawing. Wanting. Adelle was his, mind, body and soul.

Jack moved his lips against her throat, trailing his way down to her collarbone in desperate nips. When his teeth grazed her flesh, a delicious shiver shot down her spine. Gasping, Adelle tilted her head to welcome him. Strong hands slid down her back, getting a substantial hold of her behind through the fabric of her tattered dress. He crushed her against him, letting out a wanton groan as he did. That groan tensed her muscles and made her sex ache. She felt his hard shaft pressing through his jeans as he slipped between her legs.

For months she had dreamed of this; how his tongue would slip into her mouth, the possessive clutch of his arms, but she was always too afraid to take the blind leap. Not anymore. Today, she'd have him. All of him. Adelle grabbed the hem of her dress and pulled it over her head, tossing it over her shoulder.

Clad only in the delicate pink lace of her bra and panties, she knelt before him, exposed, vulnerable, yet feeling so safe. Jack gasped. His amber eyes burned as they traced every inch of her, caressing her skin with fire. Adelle pressed her hands against his face. She studied his chiseled jaw dusted with stubble, his strong mouth that made her melt when it curled into its crooked grin. When her thumb brushed across the small scar that ran under his eye, she was treated to that very grin.

So handsome. So mine.

She nibbled his lower lip before diving back in to devour his mouth. Their tongues danced together again. As they kissed, Jack's hands grasped a hold of the strap across her back and tugged one, two, three times. With a grunt of frustration, he started to pull at her bra, giving her the giggles.

"Hold on, hold on," she whispered.

Without much thought, Adelle reached behind her and with a quick flick of her wrist, she undid the hooks. Jack gawked as if she were the supreme sorceress of ladies' underwear, and a low chuckle rolled from his throat. Before long, his eager fingers slipped the straps down her shoulders. Lace smoothed over her nipples, puckering them as her bra was peeled away. His large hands cupped her breasts, palms rough and calloused. Yet his coarse skin only enhanced the bliss of his gentle touch.

The pads of his thumbs circled around her nipples and Jack leaned close, pressing his lips under her ear, hot breath tickling her skin. His movements were achingly slow as he explored her body; sweeping from her breasts to her belly, and caressing across her hips. It was nothing short of sweet torture. His fingers played in the waistband of her panties, teasing her into thinking he would pull them away before he moved back to savoring her breasts again. Adelle throbbed. The scorching gleam in his eyes told her that he was as well. When she went to embrace him, he held her back, shaking his head.

"Just, give me a minute," he said. His accent peeked out from behind his words, making his usual deep gravel scratched voice even more lustful. "I need… I need tae..."

A stern cast of concentration set Jack's face as he poured over her in worship. Through his eyes, Adelle felt like perfection. He marveled at her large, pale breasts, her soft belly, even at the two tiny brown moles that sat just above her hip. Awed words in Gaelic slipped from his lips and never before had Adelle wished she spoke a different language. Jack lowered his head. He took one of her hardened nipples into his mouth, brushing its top with his tongue, eliciting another cry.

"Jack!"

The dragon stiffened at his name then growled in approval. He continued to suckle her breast murmuring against her, "Ye taste so sweet, love. Like I dreamed ye would."

Her other breast was lavished with the same sensual attentions, hands stroking her backside, overloading her senses. It took Adelle a moment to realize that she was tugging the fly of his jeans open. As Jack concentrated, her hand crept beneath the soft denim, grazing the smooth, taut skin of his cock. He moaned at her touch.

Encouraged, Adelle wrapped her hand around him, sliding her fingers up and down his length. His shaft pulsed, jerking with the pleasure her hand gifted. With a harsh cry, he pitched forward and slammed his eyes shut. Strong fingers dug into her skin.

"Ye doona know what ye do to me, Adelle!" he strained through clenched teeth.

The control she had over him was exhilarating. It only took three strokes of her hand until Jack pushed Adelle down onto her back. He was carnal, a beast possessed. Heart pounding, she watched him tear her panties from her hips. When he found the red curls between her legs glittering with moisture, Jack pulled his jeans down, unleashing his iron-hard cock. It stood proudly as he pushed her knees apart. Adelle spread them willingly, hungering for him to fill her.

"Tell me ye love me," he demanded, shaking with longing. "Tell me ye want this."

Jack hovered over her, hands braced on either side of her head, a chiseled figure carved in the glow of the torch light. His heady scent swathed her tingling skin. Adelle reached up, and ran her fingers down the nape of his neck. His eyes rolled back and he arched.

"I love you, Jack. Please. I need you." Her anticipation exploded into euphoria as Jack clutched her hips and buried his shaft inside her.

He thrust slow then pulled back just a bit before venturing forth again. Each time he delved deeper, his body rasping against her clitoris as he moved. The ecstatic tingle of pleasure shot through her body and into her fingertips. Soon, Adelle was curved against him, wanting him rooted inside her as deep as possible. With every turn of her hips, Jack showered her mouth with kisses, tongued her neck, and suckled her breasts.

Another hard thrust and Adelle screamed. The deep rumble of shaking walls echoed in her ears. She didn't care. The cave could fall down completely and it wouldn't even matter. Nothing mattered but him as he rolled his beautiful body against her. She wrapped her legs tight around his hips in defiance to her loss of control.

"Yes! Oh God, Jack!" The more she cried his name, the harder it spurred him on.

Beads of sweat formed across Jack's shoulders and neck, trickling down his muscled chest. Flickering torchlight made the faint hint of red and gold scales glisten under his skin, outlining his well sculpted muscles. Heat radiated off him like the blazing sun on a summer's day. Adelle's skin grew slick. The feel of their hot, wet bodies sliding together was the most erotic experience of her life. The smell of smoke and sex filled her nostrils and the sound of his growls vibrating from his throat only led her further into the fire.

On and on it went, Jack pushing her into paradise. When she didn't think she could get any higher, a twist of his hips or a roll of his tongue would send her rocketing closer towards oblivion. God, he was amazing. She never wanted this to end.

"You're gonna make me lose control." Jack swallowed hard, leaning in close to her ear to whisper, "But no' before you."

Determined, he laced his fingers with Adelle's and pinned her hands over her head. Her breasts bounced in rhythm as his hips pistoned. Their eyes locked. Love, hunger, and unwavering need flashed across Jack's face. Adelle couldn't look away. Instead, her mouth fell open with a low, passionate moan.

"Don't stop." She curled her fingers around his. "Oh God, Jack, please don't stop."

The pleasure grew too wild to contain and Adelle threw her head back, letting out a scream of release as she climaxed. The cavern thundered with a mighty quake, accented with the delicate sound of falling coins and shattering glass. Wave after wave of ecstasy crashed through her as her howls continued to make the cave tremble.

A look of wonder melted across Jack's face as he watched her come. With one final thrust, he erupted, his entire body shaking with a fury. Jack's voice rose up to join hers in an inhuman roar. He pulsed inside her, hands tight around hers, legs quivering as Adelle's sex wrung every last drop from him.

The echoes of their cries faded and they collapsed in a tangle of arms and legs. Adelle trembled beneath him, panting. Jack laid his head on her shoulder, struggling for breath and he whispered a few more astonished words in Gaelic. His fingers gave hers a tender squeeze before he finally released her. He wiped the damp red curls from her face and kissed her lips over and over until their bodies slowed.

After their tremors stopped, Jack tucked Adelle against his side; protective arms curled around her, shielding her from the chill. She felt his hand stroke her hair as the beat of his heart soothed her tired body.

"Hey," she said. Jack glanced down at her, a lazy smile tracing his lips. She rubbed the palm of her hand through the golden hair on his chest. "I love you."

Jack smiled, running a tender hand along her cheek. After a moment, he answered her with a cocky, "Yeah, I figured."

She laughed, gave him a swat on the chest, and then placed a delicate kiss over his heart.

He rubbed the spot her lips just caressed and asked, "How are you feeling now?"

Adelle pursed her lips, giving the question some thought. After a moment, her arms encircled his waist and she pressed herself up against his side with a grin.

"Calm."

Chapter 21

It was hours after sunset when Jack's heartbeat finally slowed to normal. All was quiet down in the hoard room, just the flickering sounds of torches and the occasional jangle of coins settling. He sprawled in his nest, sated and sore with his arms wrapped around Adelle. She was draped over him like a blanket, body still flushed and damp from their lovemaking. Fire-red curls spread wide across his chest as she nuzzled him, smiling. If she were a cat, she'd be purring.

This was not a place Jack was expecting to be.

Not that he was complaining.

No way, no how.

He ran his hand though her soft hair that rested on top of him. How could anyone complain after last night? This beautiful, smart mouthed, siren had ruined him. Jack kind of liked being ruined.

After making love to Adelle, he knew he'd want no one else. Jack craved her kiss, her moan, and the feel of her tightening around his shaft as she came. When she arched against him and screamed until the walls shook, he fell into oblivion right after her. Knowing he could elicit such explosive reactions out of her made him preen. Jack especially loved hearing her cry his name. No one had ever spoken his name with such possession, such adoration. Every time it slipped from her quivering lips, he fell in love with her even more. Jack would never get enough.

"You speak Gaelic." Adelle said, tracing a finger around his nipple.

He grinned, brows raised as he watched that languid finger make lazy circles. "I'm nine-hundred years old and Scottish. Sometimes it slips out."

Yeah, it slipped out. Only when he was so thrown he forgot he was speaking it. Jack fell into his old tongue more than once when with her.

Adelle peered up at him with a mischievous grin. "So, what did you say?"

"That's personal, Buttercup," Jack said, brushing his fingers through her hair again.

Her musical laugh enchanted his ears in reply. She he sat up and folded her arms across her chest. The gesture only pushed her amazing breasts up for a better view. Jack started aching for her all over again.

"Personal? And what did we just do for the last couple of hours, hmm? Come on. What did you say?"

The side of Adelle's mouth quirked into a cute smirk as she waited for his answer. Jack's cheeks grew hot. He was not sure if he wanted to tell her what he said. The truth hurt. Hurt him, actually

While Adelle had slept her wounds away, Jack had obsessed about all the time he had wasted not telling her he loved her. So many words he hadn't said because he was bitter. So many times he had turned away because he was terrified to get attached. Last night was a wakeup call. Adelle could have disappeared forever. She still could. After all, she was half human and her life wouldn't be nearly as long as his. Time wasn't going to wait for Jack to get his act together.

Never again. From now on she'll always know how I feel about her.

After smoothing his mussed hair back, Jack took a deep breath. "I said, how could I have been so stupid." His face turned redder as he added, "Then I said, thank God, for you."

The smirk melted from Adelle's face and her expression softened. "Oh, Jack." The way she said his name consoled his aching conscience. She pressed her hands against the side of his face and kissed him. Jack shivered at the feather light touch of her lips.

When Adelle was ready to get back up to the house, Jack reluctantly helped her get dressed. The snow was still thick on the ground and Adelle's dress was no better than a dish rag. Of course, stubborn as always, Adelle refused to be carried up the stairs despite her lack of shoes. So instead, Jack pulled her against his side and they hurried up to their home. It would be warmer inside but with that broken window, he'd have to make sure his siren kept warm. That wasn't such a bad idea, really.

As soon as they walked through the door, Adelle's cell phone started ringing. Chances were it had rung all night. Adelle groaned, rubbing her arms to shake off the last of the chill.

"I bet that's Val. She's probably had a stroke by now." But instead of going to her phone, Adelle bee lined it to the bathroom. "Could you answer it? Sorry. This can't wait."

Before he could even say yes, Adelle had shut the bathroom door, leaving Jack staring at her phone as it vibrated across the kitchen table. Valerie seemed like a woman who didn't like being kept in suspense. And since no one had contacted her immediately after Adelle's rescue, she was probably a wreck. Jack shuddered then snatched up the phone and hit answer.

"Oh my God, Dell!" Valerie started talking before Jack could even say hello. "Thank God. Are you all right? What happened?"

"It's not Adelle," Jack said. There was a deafening silence on the other end. That definitely wasn't the best way to start the conversation. "I mean, Adelle Constance's phone, how may I help you?"

Valerie snarled. "I don't know who you are asshole, but if you hurt my sister I will find you and-"

"Calm down, calm down lady," Jack cut her off. "She's fine."

"Then put her on the phone!"

"I would put her on the phone, but she's in the bathroom." Jack paused again then added, "Doing... bathroom things. All right, that sounds like a lame cover-"

"Who the hell is this?"

"It's Jack."

Another long silence answered him.

"Jack, the dragon."

Yet more silence.

Jack sighed and rubbed his forehead. "The guy your sister almost screwed last night."

He could hear an audible growl on the other end. Well, he couldn't knock her suspicion. Valerie seemed just as willing to kill for Adelle as he was. It was admirable, despite how exasperating it was.

"How do I know you're who you say you are?" Valerie said.

Jack rolled his eyes. "You came up here two years ago to help Wendy move and you wouldn't stop looking at my ass."

"Oh! *That* Jack the dragon!" The ice in her voice melted and suddenly it was like they were lifelong friends. "Look Jack, I'm at the airport now. I'm buying the next ticket to Washington."

Jack's jaw dropped open. *The Valkyrie is heading up here? Ah, crap.*

"Whoa, whoa! Save your money," he said. "She's all right. There was a fight, but we handled it."

"What about Ethan?" Valerie asked.

"He and his cronies are dead."

"Are you sure?"

"Can vampires survive being set on fire?"

"No."

"Then trust me, they're dead."

Valerie let out a long sigh of relief.

Jack echoed the sentiments then continued. "Adelle's a little banged up, tired, and possibly hung over, but fine. You should have seen her. She was badass out there. You'd be proud." That earned a little laugh from Valerie but Jack could still sense her unease. He drummed his fingers on the table. "I know you don't know me, Valerie but believe me when I say your sister means more to me than anything in the world. And I've been around this world a long time. I'll do whatever it takes to keep her safe."

There was a long silence over the phone before Valerie finally said, "That makes two of us. Thanks Jack, for taking care of her."

The door to the bathroom opened and Adelle returned.

Saved by the siren!

"All right! She's back, here you go, Valerie!" Jack shoved the phone into Adelle's puzzled hands and busied himself with cleaning up the glass scattered around his kitchen floor. It was one thing to get touchy feely with his mate, it was another matter completely when it was with her sister.

Adelle placed the phone to her ear, a pinched gaze tight on Jack. "Hey, Val. Yeah... Yeah I'm all right... They're dead, both of them... Yes... I'll tell him... Yes, I did look at his ass." Jack snickered as he swept the debris into a dustpan. "No," Adelle continued. "No, Val you don't... Val... Val! Seriously you don't... Okay fine. Fine, fine, fine... Call me when you get here... I love you too... Oh and Val? I totally nailed him."

The sound of Valerie's piercing laughter echoed from Adelle's phone, abruptly cut off by her hanging up.

"Valerie's showing up on our doorstep anyways," Adelle said. "She'll be here tomorrow night."

Jack chuffed at the news. "Should I be worried?"

"Yeah, probably." A ghost of a smile touched Adelle's mouth then flittered away. The sudden change of expression caught Jack's attention.

"What is it?" he asked. Jack held his breath, half afraid that she would express regrets over their time in his hoard room.

"It's just..." Adelle bit her lower lip. "When Ethan had me, he said something that was really upsetting."

Jack let out a long sigh, relieved that the problem wasn't him, but disturbed that Ethan still haunted her. "What did he say?"

Adelle rubbed the back of her neck, hands shaking. "He said that he was taking me to Tony."

"The mage who..." Jack trailed off when he saw the pain in her eyes. She turned away, shoulders curling as she paled. His anger flared, making him want to tear this Tony character limb from limb. With two quick strides, he was in front of her, hands grasping her shoulders. "Adelle, look at me." She did as he asked. The minute he looked into her big green eyes, Jack knew he would do anything to keep her fear away. "If he ever touches you, he will pay."

Adelle cracked a tiny smile as tension drained from her shoulders. Her hand rested against his face, fingers stroking his cheek with a tender touch. "Thank you," she said.

Jack sighed, his own hand engulfing hers. Let the mage come. He would make him suffer for what he did to his woman and her family. "Let's get this mess cleaned up."

In a short amount of time they had the kitchen swept and the window boarded up. Jack put away the tools, looking over their handy work. They made a good team. He had never seen himself as a team player but with someone like Adelle, he could learn to play well with others.

"Much better. It's already starting to warm up in here," Adelle said. She looked down at herself, cringing at the state of her favorite dress. What a shame. Jack loved her in that dress. Another look at her disappointed visage and he vowed to buy her many more like it if she asked. From this point on, his beautiful siren would never go wanting.

"God, I need a shower." Adelle pushed back her wild hair then glanced over to Jack, raising her chin with an expectant smile.

Jack cocked an eyebrow at her with a laugh. "What are you implying, Buttercup?"

In reply, she slipped her arms around his shoulders and pressed her warm mouth against his. After a slow, lingering kiss, he knew exactly what she was implying. Mischief spread across her face.

"Didn't I satisfy you already?" he asked, astonished.

"Two years, Jack," Adelle said.

"No, really. You were just complaining how you couldn't walk straight on our way up here."

"Two *long* years, Jack."

"You were attacked by two vampires."

"And I was asleep for twelve hours after you licked me back to health."

Jack shuddered at the mention of his reluctant healing technique. "Could you never mention that ever again, please?"

"Fine. But do you think you're only allowed one shot, tonight?" Her finger tips danced up the nape of his neck. A deep shuddering gasp sputtered from his tight lips as a stirring thrill shot right to his groin. His cock sprang to full salute yet again.

"There's a very large shower in there calling to us," Adelle said, still stroking her hand along his electrified skin. "And we really should answer it."

A lustful growl escaped his lips. Adelle hung from his shoulders. Her playful grin, the warm feel of her full breasts, and her fingers dancing on the nape of his neck were making it impossible for him to say no. Not that he was planning to say no.

Jack smirked, hooking his arms around her lower back. "You still sore?"

"Oh God, yes. Be gentle."

Jack nodded then bent down and snagged her by the waist. Adelle let out a peal of laughter as he slung her over his shoulder, her curls tickling his cheek as she passed. "Oh, I don't think so," he said and marched her to the bathroom.

If Adelle was fantastic in his hoard room, she was Heaven in his shower. Jack took great delight in bathing her smooth skin and lathering those luscious red curls both on her head and between her legs. He was enchanted by how she yielded so eagerly, each time with a smile that made him spoil her with affection. The washing went forgotten and turned to exploring, panting, and running their mouths over each other's bodies. Soon, Jack scooped Adelle up, pressed her back against the dark blue tiles, and plunged inside her. Her harsh cry of pleasure set him on fire and he gritted his teeth, struggling to keep from coming right then and there.

Tiles cracked from both her howls and his claws. A few thrusts and Adelle's yells grew too loud for the walls to handle so Jack leaned in, stifling her cries with deep kisses. She straddled his hips and once again they made love, water cascading over them until it ran cold. It all ended in sweet oblivion, staring deep into her adoring eyes. Heaven. That was definitely the best word to describe her.

It was hours later in his bed when Jack pulled Adelle, sweat covered and satisfied, into his lap. He curled his arms about her waist, both of them working to catch their breath. Not only was she a piece of Heaven, she was insatiable as well. Jack had taken her numerous times and still Adelle begged for more. Well, who was he to turn her down? Especially when she ran her fingertips down the back of his neck and whispered a heated "Please" into his ear. Just that little word made him wrap his strong arms around her until his seed was spent, long and hard.

Adelle let out a breathy little chuckle as she laid her head against his chest, looking up at him. "You're going to kill me," she said.

"You'll die happy," he replied with a smug grin on his lips. He was feeling pretty proud of their marathon. After all, he had made a siren sing for hours.

"You sir, are getting full of yourself."

"Give me one good reason I shouldn't. I believe you gave me a few. Like, 'Oh God, Oh God,' and 'Don't stop.' Think those are good reasons?"

Adelle cackled and elbowed Jack delicately in the ribs. "Jerk."

"But I'm your jerk. That counts for something." Jack leaned down and pressed an affectionate kiss to the side of her face, tasting the salt on her skin. He whispered in her ear, "We got about ten hours before your sister is in town."

Adelle giggled as she pressed a hand against his thigh, making him shiver in delight. "Are you intending to keep me hostage in this bed until then?"

"Yup."

After a brief moment of thought, Adelle said, "Huh, I could live with that."

She nuzzled him, her mane spilling over his arms. He loved the feel of her hair against his skin, so soft and smooth, like spun glass. With a lover like Adelle, he could definitely get used to being a claimed dragon. Having her close every night, curling up together on those cold winter evenings, maybe the occasional night out of dinner and dancing. Adelle seemed to like dancing, even if she was God awful at it.

"So, why a gym?" Adelle asked.

Jack jolted out of his meditations on monogamy. "What?"

"For your cover. You own a gym. Why a gym? I mean you could just have a house, or own a coffee shop or something."

Jack shrugged in a noncommittal manner. "Seems like a good cover. I mean, look at me. I look like a guy who would own a gym."

"Okay, I'll give you that. But with as much gold you have stashed away, you could be living just fine without a job for decades."

Jack laughed. "It's called a hoard for a reason. I don't spend the hoard unless I have to. Besides, when you live for centuries, you need things to pass the time. I own the gym because it keeps me busy. When I get bored of this job, I'll move to another."

He felt Adelle grin against his chest. "Then what kind of jobs occupied your time for the last nine-hundred years?"

Jack hmmed. "Let's see, I was a farmer for a while, soldier, blacksmith -that was fun- bouncer -that was not." He took a breath as the list flowed. "Security guard, sword for hire, cattle driver, garbage man, carpenter, truck driver. I *did* own a coffee shop in the nineties and it bored the hell out of me, umm..." His amber eyes looked towards the ceiling as he tried to recall his other jobs. There we so many, he was having difficulty remembering them all.

"Okay, I get it," she said, laughing.

"I'm a dragon of many hats."

Adelle ran a hand across his belly, making the muscles contract in anticipation. "And along those many hats, did you ever have someone special?"

"Nope."

The quick reply made Adelle sit up in his lap to get a good clear look at his face. Her hair cascaded down her shoulders, curling around her breasts, the shocks of red a startling contrast with her creamy complexion. His mouth watered. Jack always loved the taste of cream.

"Really?" she said.

"Yup," he answered, now full out staring at one lock of hair that curled around her nipple. She didn't seem to notice how it started to grow stiff as the curl swayed over it. Oh, but Jack sure did. He grinned then brought his attentions back to her words.

"Nine-hundred years and you never had a girlfriend?" she asked.

"I didn't say that. I had plenty of girlfriends." He tucked that unruly lock behind her shoulder. "I just didn't have anyone special."

She smiled then nestled herself against his chest again. "Arguing semantics."

"What? It's true. Dragons mate for life. So even if I was planning on finding a mate -which I wasn't- I was going to be picky about it. I had women who felt the need to stick around for a few weeks maybe even a month or two. Nothing serious. It was more like a mutual, fleeting attraction. When they realized I wasn't interested in commitment, they moved on. No harm, no foul. No one I wanted to claim."

Adelle arched a brow at him. "Claim?"

"Mate with for life."

"And how does a dragon claim a mate? Wild monkey sex?"

Jack smirked at her remark. “If that was it, I’d have a fuck ton of mates. Nah, it’s through confession.”

Now, she seemed very interested. Adelle cocked an eyebrow and asked, “Confession of what?”

Jack ran his thumb down the side of her face, tracing her cheek bone. “Love. That’s the first part. After the mate claims back I would say ‘You are mine and I am yours’ then vow my protection and tah-dah. Claimed.”

She giggled. “How very National Geographic.”

“I’m a Wyrd beast. Not a Wyrd being. It’s how we roll.” He tapped the tip of her nose. “Don’t forget, you got a beast in you too. Admit it. The idea turns you on.”

After a moment of laughter, Adelle leaned back with a tilt of her head. Despite the puzzled expression she wore, Jack couldn’t stop ogling those full rosy peaked breasts and freckle dusted shoulders. There wasn’t a doubt in Jack’s mind that she was the one he wanted forever.

“How would I go about claiming you back?” Adelle asked.

Jack pursed his lips. That was a good question. Adelle was halfblooded. There was a good chance that she would never claim him in the Wyrd sense. If she was more human than beast, there wouldn’t be a claim from her at all. Unfortunately, the words couldn’t be said without a return claim and those words meant everything to a dragon when finding a mate. Claiming was true, unchallenged love. The doubt ruffled Jack more than he wanted to admit.

“Don’t know,” Jack said. “Every creature claims differently. And I guess it would depend on if your human or your siren’s side is more dominant.”

“So if my siren’s side is the dominant one, how would we know I claimed you?”

Jack gave her a shifty eyed grin. "Guess we're just going to have to keep trying to find out, huh?" He lunged forward and tackled her down against the mattress.

Laughter pealed from Adelle as he pinned her arms over her head. "Hey now! Give me at least a few more minutes for recovery!"

"Sorry, you talked your recovery time away." Jack pressed his mouth against the side of her throat and she squealed. Once again, he grew hard at the sound of her delight.

"Aren't you worried about creating a bunch of little dragons after these shenanigans?" Adelle half giggled, half moaned.

"Got to get you to claim me first, Buttercup, before I can get you pregnant. And even then, it might be a bit of time." He ran his tongue up her neck to behind her ear. "Dragons like to take things slow." He growled and her body relented. Elated by her squirms, he kissed her nipples until they stood hard and stiff.

"You'll chafe me at this rate," Adelle whimpered.

"Yup. Chafing." Jack flicked his tongue against her. "So much chafing."

She sighed, almost completely under his seduction. With one last half assed effort she said, "Jack, are you sure-"

"I'll use the accent."

Adelle's eyes grew wide. "That's dirty pool."

Jack leaned down and whispered, "Aye, lass. That's whatta dragon is all about," with a brogue as thick as paste. Adelle's eyes rolled back and she let out a tiny moan of promise. "Ye gonna be a good lass now and let me have my way with ye?"

"Goddammit, Jack." Adelle tilted her head up and kissed him fiercely.

Chapter 22

That must be the infamous Valerie.

Jack peered out the window to see a leggy, dark haired woman step out of a sexy, little red Mustang. Adelle's older sister had arrived. Valerie must have driven like a maniac. The trek from the nearest airport was a good two and half hours and it had only been one hour since she had texted that she landed. It must have been quite a site for the neighbors to see yet another attractive woman show up at his home with a suitcase, a rep he'd be willing to live with. Valerie stopped and eyed Jack's Impala a moment, hands on her hips.

Don't touch the baby. Don't touch the baby.

When she ran a finger across its hood in a lecherous manner, Jack's jaw ticked. He reminded himself that she was the sister of his beloved and sometimes you just had to put up with things. That is unless Valerie continued to molest his car. Then he'd have to have a talk with her.

"I think she's here," Jack said.

"Then let her in," Adelle called. "I'll be there in a minute."

Car fondling forgotten, a smile curled around Jack's lips. Adelle was still in the bedroom, attempting to get herself dressed. She had trouble walking after round seven. It was like watching a dizzy cat fall out of a spinning desk chair. The curses she threw at him were epic but so worth it.

Jack looked back out the window to watch Valerie climb the stairs, dragging her wheeled suitcase behind her with a dramatic thump, thump, thump. He could have sworn the woman was already smirking.

When he opened the door, the tall beauty stuck her thumb over her shoulder and asked, "Is that your Impala in the parking lot?"

Jack scowled. "Yeah."

"Nice ride." Valerie gave a nod of approval and slipped passed him, suitcase rattling across the floor as she entered. "I always wanted an Impala. You should see the Firebird I have at home. The rental I got though isn't too bad. But man, the things I'd do behind the wheel of an Impala. I should take yours out for a test drive."

Jack's temples throbbed. *She's her sister. Don't set her on fire.*

Valerie stood almost as tall as Jack and like Adelle, she was gorgeous. Her face was heart shaped, with well-defined cheekbones and sharp hazel eyes surrounded by dark lashes. A thick mane of jet black hair hung down past her shoulders in a loose ponytail.

There was a stark contrast between the two. Valerie was a stark pillar of strength and well defined muscle, a complete hundred and eighty degrees to Adelle's earthy color filled curves and shorter stature. Also, unlike his lady love, Valerie appeared to know how to dress for winter weather. Her toned body was clad in jeans, a heavy black wool coat, and tall fur lined boots to keep the chill away.

Even though they weren't sisters in blood, there was still a resemblance between Adelle and Valerie. Both struck a dramatic cord when they walked into a room. It had to be the Wyrd blood in them. That special something humans wouldn't recognize as anything more than charm and an "it" factor.

"Are you harassing my dragon, Valerie?" Adelle walked out of the bedroom, wearing a pair of jeans and one of her big baggy grey sweatshirts, the letters SFSU emblazoned across the front. One look at her and a smug sense of satisfaction filled him. That was his woman, his mate, and God was she beautiful. Adelle was beaming as she stepped over to her sister, giving the taller woman a warm embrace. Valerie let out a laugh and squeezed her sister tight, making Adelle grunt from the force.

"Harassing?" Valerie said, "I wasn't harassing. I was complimenting him on his sweet ride. Hell, I didn't even know dragons liked to drive."

Jack snorted. "After centuries of walking and flying, sometimes it's nice to have something do it for you, babe."

"Oh, and he nicknames too? Adorable." Valerie cackled, the sound ringing the dragon's ears. It was even louder in person. "What's yours, Dell? Shortcake? Red?"

"Buttercup," Adelle said.

Valerie turned to Jack, placing her hands on her hips. "Buttercup? How unexpected and old school."

Jack rolled his eyes. "Hey Buttercup, didn't you tell your sister to stop harassing me?"

The dark haired beauty grinned. "I told you I am not harassing! Now this?" Valerie pulled her arm back and slapped Jack's behind hard. He jolted at the blow, surprised by her strength. "*This* is harassing."

"Gah! Jeeze lady!" Jack rubbed his throbbing behind and growled under his breath. By now, Adelle had clasped her hands over her mouth to keep from laughing out loud. Tears glazed over her eyes. "You said I should be worried if your sister showed up," he said. "Consider me worried."

"Oh please," Valerie laughed. "I have no plans on encroaching on my sister's territory."

"Like I'd let you." Adelle gave Valerie a wave of her finger. "I would kick your ass."

Valerie raised a single dark eyebrow at her sister, cocking a hip to the side. "Oh yeah? Since when?"

"Since I set fire to a forest and evaporated my ex." Adelle shrugged her shoulders then gave Valerie an innocent bat of her eyes. Valerie threw her head back and cackled again, leaving Jack to ponder how many ear drums she had burst in the past.

After finishing her gale of laughter, Valerie turned to Jack and offered him a hand to shake. "Let's start over. I'm Valerie. Go ahead and call me Val instead of babe. I promise not to spank you again."

Jack's ire melted away. It was hard to be mad at a woman who laughed like that. He grasped her hand. She had a grip like steel.

"I'm Jack. A pleasure. I'm never one to turn down a good ass grabbing but that's Adelle's job, now."

"Oh, good answer! I like this one, Dell." Valerie smiled as she unbuttoned her heavy wool coat, slipping it from her shoulders.

"Yup, I'm a keeper." Keeping up the gentleman's facade, Jack took Valerie's coat and hung it on a hook by the door. "I can even change a tire and break a man in half over my knee. Ideal traits women look for."

Valerie looked to Adelle with a devilish cast. "Manly, hot, and a smartass. Wow, he is so different than your usual type, Dell."

"Her usual type?" Jack looked over his shoulder at Adelle with an expression that begged for more information.

She had her hand covering her eyes, cheeks stained crimson. "Can you not go there, Val?" Adelle was downright adorable when she blushed. It only made him want to tease her more, just to see that wonderful hue paint her cheeks. Valerie had that part covered though.

"You see, Jack. My sister here used to be a lover of the sensitive poet types. You know, the skinny dark brooders that teenage nerd girls fawn over?'

Adelle groaned. "Shut up, Val."

"Seriously. She dated an actor once, you know."

"Val!"

"An actor? Was he a whiney actor?" Jack rubbed his hands together as the ammunition began to flow. *Thank God for older siblings!* That's what Adelle got for giggling at his healing saliva techniques.

Adelle gave him a mean glare which only made her look even sexier than when she blushed. "Oh don't you start in, Jack!"

"Oh yeah, the whiniest!" Valerie said. "That was, what, two years ago?"

Jack turned his head to look at Adelle, a vainglorious grin wrapped about his mouth. "Two years, eh?" he asked.

Adelle would have burned holes through him if siren powers included laser death glare. Luckily for Jack, it wasn't part of the package. Her jaw clenched. "Don't. Don't you even-"

Valerie turned to Jack and pressed a hand against his shoulder. "Oh God, *please* tell me you broke her two-year streak!" she begged.

"Val!" Adelle shouted, stomping her foot on the floor.

Valerie tapped her lower lip with a slender finger in mock contemplation. "Todd struck me as the type who cried after sex. Did he cry after sex, Dell?"

"I don't cry after sex," Jack said. "Right, Dell?"

Adelle threw up her hands. "That's it! I'm done!" She turned on her heels and marched into the kitchen. "My worst nightmare has come true now! Thank you, both!"

Jack chuckled at her little tantrum and called after her, "Revenge is sweet, Buttercup!"

The embarrassment of "sisterly teasing" passed and Adelle eventually returned to their company with beers in hand. The three sat on the couch, exchanging funny stories like when Valerie punched her first date through a wall when he tried to grope her. Or when Adelle and Valerie invaded Phoebe's prom night and introduced the safety dance to all the disenchanted high school juniors.

For Adelle, it was home again. All that was missing was Phoebe running through the room and saying something nonsensical. With Jack there, it was perfect. Adelle hadn't felt like her family was whole since their mother had died. She sighed in contentment and laid her head on her dragon's shoulder.

"What is it?" Jack asked, looking down at her.

"Nothing," Adelle said. "Just happy."

Jack smiled and turned back to the conversation, slipping a hand over hers. He and Valerie were getting along well, swapping battle stories and telling dirty jokes. It wouldn't be long before they'd be thick as thieves.

Soon, the chaos of the last two days caught up with Adelle and the beer didn't help much either. Her eyes began to droop and she yawned into her hand, sinking back into the couch. Jack noticed her exhaustion and he sat up, turning back into a mother hen. After years of needy boyfriends, it was nice to be fussed over for a change.

"Tired?" Jack asked.

Adelle gave him a reassuring smile. "Yeah. It's been a long couple of days."

"Eh, I should head to bed anyways," Valerie said. She raised her arms over her head, stretching with a robust yawn. "Flying always wears me out. Dell, come say goodnight before you crash."

Valerie started her way down the hall, snagging her suitcase on the way. When Adelle rose, Jack was beside her in a blink, hand on her elbow. He inspected her in concern, still on high alert.

"I'm fine, I promise," she told him.

"I worry, you know," he said, then pressed a kiss to her temple and added in a quieter voice, "I'll see you in bed."

Adelle giggled. "For sleep this time? I'm sore enough."

"Tonight, yes. I make no promises about the morning." Jack grinned.

He leaned down for a real kiss, only to be stopped by Valerie shouting, "Hey Jack! You know the name of a good tattoo place around here?"

Both Jack and Adelle turn to the hallway, eyebrows raised in suspicion. "What?" they asked in unison.

Valerie poked her head back into the living room. "A tattoo parlor? You look like the type who'd know."

"Why?" Adelle asked, her Valerie senses tingling.

"Steel Church on Main Street," Jack answered. "It's the only tat and piercing place in town. And I concur. Why?"

"Just some sisterly bonding is all. Nothing to worry about. Come on Dell, girl talk time." Valerie disappeared down the hall again, slipping into Adelle's old room.

Adelle let out a long exasperated sigh looking to Jack. "Ah, family."

Valerie made herself at home, unpacking her suitcase and rumpling up the bedding in the process. Rumpling bedding while doing nothing in particular was Valerie's hidden talent. It drove their mother to madness on many occasions. Adelle slipped through the door as Valerie finished shoving her things into the top drawer of the dresser. She turned around and grinned.

"He is cuuuuuuute!" she said. "Seriously. Cute, tight ass, manly grumble. I approve!"

"I appreciate that," Adelle said. "So, what's this tattoo thing about?"

She folded her arms across her chest and fixed her sister with a stern glare. It wouldn't work. The stern glare never worked on Valerie but it was worth a shot. When Valerie answered that glare with a devilish smile, Adelle knew she was shot down again.

"It's about time you found a man who appreciates you," she said. "You can see it in his eyes. That is complete devotion in there."

"Thank you for the reassurance. Tattoos, Val. What are you aiming at?"

"Did I mention his ass?"

"Valerie Marie Constance, I will strangle you in your sleep if you do not answer my question."

"Tracking runes," Valerie finally answered. "I was going through Mom's old journal. She was researching runes for tracking us. I think she was considering trying them out before..." She trailed off and her eyes grew dark. Valerie had never fully gotten over Cybil's death and was damn good at hiding her dark moods but Adelle could spot them in an instant. Before Adelle could say anything to comfort her, Valerie shrugged it off. "Anyways, I am following through on this."

"So, you're going to get a tattoo so we can find you easier?" Adelle asked.

"No. *You* are getting a tattoo," Valerie said.

"Wait, What?"

Adelle was not morally against tattoos. It was rare to run into a girl without one these days. Valerie already had a couple; one of angel wings on her shoulder blade, and Cybil's name scripted on her ankle. Even Phoebe had a little heart tattooed on her wrist.

Adelle enjoyed the novelty that she was the one sister that still had "virgin" skin. Now, Valerie wanted her to get one. Adelle wasn't too keen on needles.

Valerie rummaged through her suitcase and pulled out an old leather journal, held together with a few rubber bands. It was Cybil's journal. Adelle remembered it as a child. Cybil used to sit at the kitchen table in the morning, scribbling absently on its pages while Adelle, Valerie, and Phoebe ate their oatmeal. Sometimes she'd find an article in the paper, clip it out, and fold it neatly into the book, saving its knowledge for future use. One thing about Mom, she was thorough and did her research like a pro. Now the pages were crinkled and the soft binding was giving way.

"One of Mom's journals?" Adelle said. "What are you-?"

"I found it in her room. She'd let me read through them when we were patrolling together." Valerie's shook her head before the heartbreaking thoughts consumed her, then waved a hand. "Spells, descriptions of creatures, names, locations, rune combos she was putting together; she wrote everything down. According to this one, she was planning to put tracking runes on all of us so we could always find each other. In case, you know, one of us gets kidnapped by vampires."

Adelle's face went hot and she rolled her eyes. "Oh hardy har-har."

Valerie grinned back. "Anyways, look here." She sat down on the bed, pulling the rubber band off of the journal with careful fingers. Adelle took a seat beside her, peering over at the strange symbols written in Cybil's handwriting. Adelle had avoided advanced studies of magic, spells, and charms as a young adult. Back then, knowing magic meant she was one step further away from normalcy. But considering the current state of her love life, she was willing to relearn.

"If you take this series of runes and put them near a pulse point like your wrist or throat, it makes a mighty fine tracking device," Valerie continued. She pointed to each symbol as she spoke. "Raidho for travel, Algiz for protection, then a rune that represents each of us, which she had picked out already. Just etch it onto the skin and Bim-Bam-Boom, we can track each other."

"So, why a tattoo?" Adelle asked. "Why not just draw them on with a Sharpie pen?"

"Because it needs blood," Valerie said. "Our Wyrd blood is the catalyst to making this whole thing work. I mean, I could stab you with a Sharpie then-"

"Pass." Adelle shook her head, as she absorbed the information. "So, my options are getting a tattoo or getting stabbed by office supplies. Got it. And you're sure this will work?"

Valerie nodded as she wrapped up the journal. "It worked with Phoebe when I tested it."

Adelle waved her hands in the air as if to stop this roller coaster of a conversation. "Whoa, wait. You managed to get Phoebe tattooed with something she didn't understand? How the hell did you do that?"

Valerie snorted "A bottle of wine and a sister bonding trip to that tattoo parlor. It didn't take much. I told her we'd be like the actors from *The Lord of the Rings* movies. She thought it was some sort of Tolkien thing." Adelle's expression must have been unconvincing because Valerie sighed and added, "What? It worked!"

"How do you know it worked?"

"It was fucking cool! Phoebe went off to the movies a few days back and didn't tell me. All I had to do was think about her and her location popped right into my mind. Like I was seeing things through her eyes. When she got home and I asked her where she went, I was right. Mom knew her runes, that's for sure."

Adelle chewed on her bottom lip a moment. Tracking would save them a lot of trouble. Especially if Phoebe's involvement grew. Knowing exactly where each other was with a single thought? Brilliant.

She slid a tight eyed look to Valerie. "You won't abuse this, will you? Like when Jack gets naked around me, right?"

Valerie only batted her eyes. She pressed a finger against her lips as if she had no idea what Adelle was talking about. Adelle laughed then snagged a pillow from the bed, and smacked her sister in the head with it.

"You are insatiable!" Adelle said, giving Valerie another smack.

In return, Valerie let out another trademark cackle, yanking the pillow from Adelle's hands. "I swear on Cybil's journal, I will not use the runes to look at your hot dragon boyfriend naked," she said "My intentions are completely practical. If things get bad, we can find each other if we're separated."

Adelle let out a little sigh then smiled. "You sound convincing enough," she said. "So, where's your tattoo?"

"Well it has to be near a pulse point on the body, so..." Valerie smiled again, as if holding in a delicious secret.

Adelle regard her with a deadpan expression. "You did not get it on your crotch. Please tell me you did not get a crotch tattoo."

It wasn't the fact that the wild Valerie may have gotten a tattoo on her delicate lady bits. She could get one wherever she wanted. It was the fact that if Valerie did indeed get a tattoo on her delicate lady bits, she would try to convince Adelle to get one there too, for safety reasons and possibly a good laugh as well.

"Relax, I got it on my hip." Valerie reassured her. "It's close enough to the femoral artery for it to work." She rose to her feet, hooked a finger around the belt loop of her jeans, and pulled the waistband down, revealing a tiny string of runes etched onto her skin in a delicate script. It sat low on her right hip. "Phoebe got one on her ankle, by the posterior tibial artery."

Adelle looked at the tattoo and sighed in relief. It was tiny and discreet. She could probably get one on her wrist or forearm and no one would even notice

"So," Adelle said "Sisterly bonding time at the tattoo parlor tomorrow?"

Valerie grinned again. "Exactly."

Adelle laughed, running a hand through her wild hair. "After all these years Val; you still have an uncanny knack of talking me into things I don't want to do. Is it a pheromone?"

Valerie giggled and leaned back on the bed. "It's the magical power of being the eldest. You and Pheebs always think I know what I'm talking about. Luckily for you, this time I *do* know what I'm talking about."

Adelle leaned her elbows on her knees, still sitting at the edge of the bed. "So, how's the Pheebs?"

Valerie sunk her teeth into her lower lip a moment, inhaling with a long hiss. "She, may be manifesting now."

Every muscle in Adelle's body went taut as her posture straightened. "What?"

"Don't get too excited yet. I'm not sure. I've just been noticing things. Like the potted spider plant we had on the porch for the last couple of years."

"The half dead one?"

"Yeah. Phoebe went out to water it a couple nights ago. I was pretty sure I was going to have to toss the thing. It was all brown and crunchy. The next morning, I walked out to grab the mail and it was completely green like the day we bought it from the store." She shook her head. "And our yard is a lot lusher than it has been. More squirrels too. I'm thinking she's going to manifest something big soon."

Adelle fell silent, mulling over the new information in her thoughts. Phoebe was starting to manifest. Hopefully it wouldn't be in a violent manner like with her. She shuddered at the memory.

"You tell her anything yet?" she asked.

"Not yet. Not until I'm sure." Valerie stopped then lowered her brows hard over her dark hazel eyes. "What? You're frowning. What is the problem?"

"Nothing," Adelle sighed in frustration. "I'm just dreading the day we have to come clean to her. We're talking decades of lies we have to undo, Val."

"She's strong, she can take it."

"And what about Tony? What if he comes poking around her?"

Valerie went silent, turning her back on Adelle and unpacking as if she never said anything.

Adelle rubbed her temples. "I know it was Tony that Ethan was working for. He told me."

She watched her sister stiffen as she slammed the drawer to the dresser shut. Every inch of her was tense as she stood, fists clenched.

"Don't mention that name," Valerie said in quiet warning. "Please, Dell."

"I told Jack." The news made Valerie tense even more. She liked to keep things in the family, especially anything dealing with Tony. Valerie could view Adelle telling Jack as a betrayal. Adelle shook it off. She had to tell him. He had a right to know the truth. "I know what Tony meant to you. And he'll use that-"

"Dell, please!"

Adelle held her tongue, not wanting to push the subject any further. "Phoebe is our sister and she trusts us. What do you think she's going to do when she finds out we've been hiding all this from her for years?"

Valerie pursed her lips into a sour expression. "I'm picking up where mom left off," she said, her voice curt. "We promised Mom that we would not tell her anything. Besides. When you come home, you can handle it."

Adelle blinked at her sister. "When I come home? "

Valerie just laughed. She opened her mouth to speak then paused as she caught the distressed look in Adelle's eyes. "You... are coming home right? I mean come on! You wouldn't dump us like that, would you?"

Silence was Adelle's answer. For so long she assumed that after Ethan was dealt with she'd return to San Diego and continue her life as usual. Now, things were different. She had found herself a little niche in Whitmore. Adelle had made friends with the other Wyrd in the town, she had a job she loved, most of all, now she had Jack. The thought of leaving him made tears well in her eyes. She turned her eyes away from Valerie, hoping she wouldn't catch them. But she did.

"Dell, are you crying?" Valerie asked.

"No," Adelle said far too quick to be believed.

She closed her eyes, waiting for Valerie to lose her temper, to scream at her for wanting to abandon her family once again. The phone call from so many years ago replayed over and over in her head. She hunched over, burying her face in her hands, preparing for the tirade.

"Dell," Valerie's tone was low and cautious. "Do you love him?"

That was not a question she expected. Adelle shut her eyes, nodding her head, her face still covered with her hands. She clenched her jaw tight, grinding her teeth so hard she feared they may crack. The mattress shifted as Valerie crawled over to sit beside her.

"Dell, you're freaking me out, honey," she said.

Adelle took a deep breath, gathering the strength to look at her sister. Hot tears spilt down Adelle's face. "Do you remember what you said when you told me mom died?" Valerie shook her head, confused. "You told me that if I was there she wouldn't have died. Please don't do that to me again, Val. Please. I carried that with me for so long."

Valerie paled and she was up in an instant, pacing away from her. Adelle held her breath, unable to read what her sister was thinking. Those angry words echoed over and over. *Why weren't you here? Why weren't you here*?

After walking in a tight circle for a minute, Valerie faced her, shoulders back, chin raised. Adelle braced herself for the oncoming words.

"I'm sorry," Valerie said.

Adelle's jaw dropped. She couldn't remember the last time she had heard her sister apologize. On reflex Adelle began to say "It's all right," but Valerie trampled over her words.

"I am so sorry. I didn't mean any of that. Oh God, I don't even remember exactly what I said. Was it that bad?" When Adelle nodded, Valerie started pacing again like a cornered tiger, hands clenched, shoulders raised.

The silence went on long enough to make Adelle nervous. She lifted her eyes to the ceiling and kept talking in hopes Valerie would understand. "Val, you're my sister and I love you. I will never turn my back on you and Phoebe, ever. When there is trouble I will come home. I will come home the minute you call me, I promise. I won't ever let you down. But I love him, Val. I just want some time with him. That's all. Just time."

"I never meant to hurt you," Valerie said her voice drenched in regret. Tears began to roll and Adelle winced at the sight.

"I know, Val," Adelle said. "Don't cry. I don't think I can handle that."

"You can't handle anyone crying, Dell. Not even yourself."

The two ladies looked at each other and shared a soft laugh between them.

Soon Valerie's pacing slowed and she was sitting back beside Adelle on the bed. She pursed her red lips in thought. "I'll call you if and when things start to go south. Until then, Reina and I can handle the wheels until Phoebe is ready. Though I still may have you call her if she suddenly explodes with power while you're gone."

"I can handle that one."

Valerie's hand tightened around hers. "I want you to be happy, Dell. He makes you happy, right?"

Adelle felt her mouth curve into a smile. "Extremely happy."

"And he treats you well?"

"Better than any man I ever met."

"Good. Because if he doesn't, I'll break his kneecaps, dragon or no dragon," Valerie said.

Adelle didn't doubt that Valerie could. She was stronger than she looked and meaner than she came across. Valerie slung an arm around her shoulder, giving Adelle an affectionate squeeze. Soon they were wiping each other's tears dry, and smiling once again.

"Go on, get to bed," Valerie said. "We'll head out tomorrow. Then after lunch you can show me Jack's ass."

"Nice try, Val." Adelle smirked as she rose to her feet.

"You can't blame a girl for trying." Her sister gave her a wink then waved her off. "Don't keep your dragon waiting."

Chapter 23

True to his word, Jack let Adelle sleep through the night. She drifted off to the low roll of his breath and his warm arms enveloping her body. Peace. Pure peace. In the morning, she woke to the feel of his mouth suckling on her neck and his fingers caressing her belly. She giggled as he slipped his hand between her legs.

"It's morning," Jack whispered against her ear. She gasped in bliss as his fingers slipped into her sex.

"I can see that," Adelle whispered back. Her heart sped up as his fingers caressed her.

"And I made no promises," Jack added.

He wrapped an arm around Adelle's waist and rolled onto his back, pulling her on top of him. When her legs slipped around his hips, she felt his rock hard erection through his boxers. The sensation made her shiver. Jack's fingers tangled themselves into the waves of fiery curls and he pulled her head down to ravage her mouth with a long passionate kiss. It was too arousing of an invitation to resist and Adelle relented. The two made love with slow, quiet ease until the sun came pouring through their bedroom window to announce the beginning of the day.

By the time they got out of bed, Valerie had breakfast ready. The look she gave Adelle made her blush all over again. After some coffee and a few hidden lusty glances, Jack rose from the table.

"I better head down to work," he said.

As he passed, Jack ran his hand down the length of her hair with a content grumble under his breath. She began to notice the growing infatuation the dragon had with her hair. Jack couldn't go an hour without sinking his fingers into it. Maybe it was the color. Dragons did have a love of fire and you couldn't get much fierier than Adelle's curls. She grinned into her coffee cup.

"I know it's pointless to say this," Jack said. "But you two at least attempt to be good. I don't want to dip into the hoard to pay your bail."

"Valerie is here," Adelle said. "I can't promise you anything."

As if on cue, Valerie raised her head from her newspaper and gave Jack a toothy grin. Adelle couldn't help but follow suit, putting on one of her more pristine smiles and widening her eyes to puppy dog proportions.

Jack started at the two for a long moment, snorted, and shook his head. "God help me. There are two of you."

The tattoo parlor was easy to find. It was the only place on Main Street that had tribal designs painted on its windows and a sign in rusted iron reading *Steel Church* in bold, block letters. Huge rivets accented the vowels. The front door was painted fire engine red while the rest of the facade was gun metal grey. Not the typical design choice you'd see in a small town that based its aesthetic around the word, quaint. Still Whitmore's population was at least eighty percent Wyrd and that percentage liked their alternative lifestyle choices.

Steel Church was run by a man named Floyd, who probably had more metal in his face than in his shop's sign. His arms were covered with colorful tattoos and his tongue was forked, pierced with a huge iron ball and rod. He wore thick gage earrings that stretched his lobes to the top of his shoulders.

Floyd walked over to Adelle and Valerie, giving a smile, the rings on his lower and upper lips clinking together as he did.

"Welcome to *Steel Church*. Name's Floyd. Looking for some ink? Piercings maybe?"

The idea of a metal rod being rammed through other parts of her body made Adelle's stomach knot up. She considered turning around and walking out but Valerie placed herself right behind her, blocking any hasty exits she had planned.

All right, she thought. So *you're a wimp when it comes to this stuff. Just admit it and move on. You took on two vampires and won. What's a little tattoo going to do?*

"Yeah," Adelle said, her voice pitching a bit higher than expected. She cleared her throat before continuing. "I'm looking to get this on my forearm." She handed Floyd a piece of paper with the string of runes scribbled onto it. "Nothing big or fancy, just a little line here." She rolled up her sleeve, pointing to the inside of her forearm, high up towards her elbow.

Floyd took the paper and studied it a moment before he lifted his eyes to Adelle. They were a startling deep purple with a dark blue ring around the edge. Contacts maybe, but she could tell he wasn't wearing any. At closer inspection, that forked tongue was not man made and his wicked sleeve tats were covering up a strange texture under his flesh. There was a light green undertone to his skin, not to mention his eye color wasn't found in nature. He was definitely of the Wyrd.

"It's a personal thing," she added before Floyd could ask any questions.

Floyd looked back down at the paper then nodded. "Sure. I can do this. Won't take long. Go ahead and have a seat, we'll discuss details." Floyd then raised a ring encased brow ridge. "Are you... Are you Jack's lady?"

Adelle's eyes widened. She had never been referred to as Jack's lady before. The title filled her with pride. "Yeah." She smiled at Floyd.

"Cool," Floyd replied with another metal clinking smile. "Jack's good people. Kind of an ass sometimes but a fun one. I'll be right back. Go ahead and have a seat."

As soon as Floyd was out of earshot, Valerie twitched her chin in his direction. "Oh, he is *so* not human."

Adelle watched Floyd as he leaned over his drawing table, sketching out the runes in a larger size. Adelle nodded. "Definitely not human. What do you think? Reptile or Mer?"

"I'm going to guess Mer on shore leave. Reptile folks hate cold weather." Valerie took Adelle by the arm and walked her over to the chairs in the back of the parlor.

"This is not how I planned to spend my Sunday afternoon," Adelle said with a long suffering sigh.

"Oh, don't be such a whiney baby," Valerie said. "It will take only two seconds to get a tattoo that size done and it won't hurt a bit."

Valerie was a dirty liar.

Her pants would have been a blaze if the schoolyard rhyme were true.

When the needles bit into her sensitive flesh, Adelle almost brought down the roof. Another church she almost destroyed. How ironic. Of course screaming, "Oh Fuck Me Running!" at the top of her lungs would do that. Not only did the quake take Valerie by surprise but it scared the crap out of poor Floyd the merman.

"Wouldn't hurt a bit, my ass! I swear I am going to kill you, Val!" Adelle roared.

"Easy now, Dell," Valerie laughed. She placed a hand on her shoulder as the windows rattled. "It will get easier. I promise."

"Bullshit!"

The mirror opposite them steamed then cracked and Floyd rolled his chair away, purple eyes huge with fright. The tattoo gun was still buzzing in his hand. Adelle bit her lower lip hard in an attempt to calm herself.

"Sorry, I will pay for that," she said through clenched teeth.

"Damn, lady! What the hell are you?!" He caught on rather quickly that Adelle wasn't all human. Luckily, no one else was in the shop other than them and a couple of Floyd's employees. They kept their distance from the crazy lady with good reason.

"She's a siren," Valerie said, keeping her voice level.

"I'm a half siren!" Adelle corrected with a groan.

"Fine, half siren."

"I'm a pissed off and in pain half siren!"

"Look," Floyd said, "I can't do this if you're going to scream and tear down my shop, okay?"

Adelle took a deep breath, trying to calm her nerves. "I'm fine." she said, mostly for her own sake than for Floyd's. Her ire began to fade even if the sharp stings from the tattoo gun didn't. "Sorry. It took me off guard. My dear sister assured me it wouldn't hurt that much and she is a liar."

"It didn't hurt *me* that much," Valerie interjected, earning her a sharp glare from Adelle. "Come on. You got one rune down. We only have three more to go. Don't be a chicken."

Adelle bit back the need to punch her. She took a deep breath then attempted to give Floyd a smile that didn't look angry, manic, or crazed.

"I'm fine now, I promise. No more screaming."

With her free hand clamped over her mouth and tears streaming down her cheeks, Adelle held herself still in the chair. Floyd frantically finished the tattoo. It was the fastest job he had ever done in his life.

"So, let's see it," Jack said with a gleeful grin.

He was waiting on the couch, beer in hand as the ladies walked in. Word traveled fast in Whitmore and it wasn't long before a friend of a friend came into the gym telling a story about the wailing crazy woman in the tattoo shop. Adelle got herself a tattoo which was the most uncharacteristic thing he could think of her doing. So she must have been under the influence of Valerie. Her older sister definitely had sway over his lady. Luckily, it was a positive sway, albeit a sometimes embarrassing one. He liked the woman for that. Valerie was crass, loud, and fearless. They might have been drinking buddies if they had met in another century. So he'd cut her some slack if she persuaded Adelle into getting a tattoo. And knowing Adelle, she would have stonewalled her until she turned blue in the face if she truly didn't want one.

Adelle blinked at Jack. "What are you talking about?" she asked, trying to feign innocence. The way she nursed her left arm as she removed her coat spoke volumes.

"Come on. My Buttercup got some ink. I think I'm entitled to see it."

Valerie cackled as she followed inside. "Ah, so you found out," she said. "I figured you heard the screams from Main Street."

Adelle rolled her eyes at her. "It hurt, okay!?"

"Wimp. Stop sulking. It wasn't that bad, you big baby."

"I react badly when there are needles being stabbed into my skin in a repetitive motion."

"Aww, Buttercup," Jack laughed, putting down his beer. "Come here, you rebel, and let me see."

Adelle walked over to the couch, rolling up the sleeve of her orange paisley blouse. Outlined in pink swollen skin, was string of runes in small, elegant black script.

"It's not that impressive," she said.

Jack studied the simple design on her arm, cocking an eyebrow. "Are those runes?"

"Yeah." Adelle lowered herself to the coffee table, stealing Jack's beer to take a quick sip.

"Why the runes?"

"Tracking spell," Valerie said as she appeared behind her sister. "Helps us all keep an eye on each other if we're separated. In our line of work, it's vital."

Jack rubbed his chin. "Huh. Not a bad idea."

Actually, it was a brilliant idea. If Adelle ever went back to San Diego, he'd rest a little easier knowing her sisters could find her if she was in danger.

San Diego? Shit.

Jack went cold. She couldn't be considering heading back so soon could she? Adelle had become so ingrained in his everyday world that it seemed impossible to not wake up to the sound of her laughter or the scent of her sweet honeyed skin. In the few months she had been here, Jack's life was turned completely upside down, and he didn't want it to end. The thought of losing her left a burning hole in his heart and he swallowed hard to quench it. But it didn't help. He smiled to the two ladies before they saw the dismay on his face.

"And to think, I could have gotten you a tattoo all these months instead of following you around," he said.

"What? And miss weeks of my sparkling personality?" Adelle grinned as she messed up his hair. Jack dodged the attempt to dishevel him, grabbed a hold of her good arm, and pulled her into his lap. If she *was* considering heading back to San Diego, he would convince her otherwise every second of every day. He planted a loud slobbery kiss on her cheek, reveling in Adelle's laughter as she pushed his face away.

"Down, Simba, my arm still stings," Adelle said.

"Cry baby," Valerie replied as she crept up beside them.

Shaking the dark thoughts from his head, Jack held her wrist and stretched out her arm examining the tattoo. After a brief moment of exaggerated contemplation, complete with pursed lips and chin rubbing, he declared, "You're right. It's not that impressive."

"And she screamed like she was being-" Valerie doubled over with an oof as Adelle's elbow slammed into her gut.

"I think you should spice it up a bit," Jack said. "Get a dragon beside it."

He was treated to another one of Adelle's irresistible smirks as she shook her head. "As adorable as I think it would be to have my boyfriend etched into my skin, I can't add to the design. It ruins the integrity of the rune spell."

Jack's face screwed up into a disgusted frown. "Lame," he said then planted another kiss on the side of her neck. "It would be sexy if you had me tattooed on you," he murmured, looking up just in time to see Valerie roll her eyes and turn away.

"Gross," she said, strolling towards the kitchen.

"It's my house, Valkyrie," Jack said. "If I want to ravage to your sister on my couch, I can."

"And I'm out of here." Adelle wiggled out of his lap to escape. "There is no way I am doing the horizontal bop on the couch with my sister in the room."

"I'm in the kitchen now, actually!" Valerie yelled from a distance. "Go at it!"

Adelle out an exasperated giggle as she stumbled to her feet. She smoothed her hair back from her face. "You're both disgusting animals," she said, a ghost of a smile on her lips. "I should serve dinner in a trough to both of you."

The hours ticked on, dinner was eaten –not out of a trough- and Valerie soon retired to the guest room, muttering something about forgetting her ear plugs back home.

Alone, at last. Jack thought.

Unfortunately, Adelle was wearing her "Not tonight honey, I have a stinging tattoo on my arm" face, so any hanky-panky would have to wait. Besides, he wanted to discuss this whole returning to San Diego scenario that was causing his gut to churn. He'd ease into that conversion… somehow.

"So, she talked you into a tattoo," he said, pulling the bedding down for them. Jack peered over his shoulder to watch Adelle peel her shirt off over head, gazing at that smooth creamy flesh wrapped in a black and white polka dot bra. The vision made him grin from ear to ear. "I didn't think you could be talked into anything."

"She had a good point and already proved to me that it worked. I figured, why not? I've had my fill of being kidnapped for one year." Adelle unbuttoned her fly and shimmied herself pantless.

Oh lord, she's wearing matching panties.

Why a matching bra and panty set made Jack's cock jump to the bar was beyond him, but there it was. Black and white polka dots hugging that glorious behind and curving around her luscious breasts. It made his mouth water. Maybe he could hold her arm out of the way if she was willing to try.

No. Stay on target, Jack.

"Besides, she's my older sister. I'm supposed to listen to her," Adelle finished.

Jack rubbed his forehead as if trying to push the lust filled thoughts out with his fingers. "Is that how it works with humans?" He turned away from the buxom beauty and pulled his own shirt off as he readied himself for bed.

Was it getting hot in here?

Control yourself, Jack. For God's sake, you're nine-hundred years old. Show some damn discipline!

"Some of them," Adelle said. "Val is my older sister. She took care of us when mom died, and she hasn't steered me wrong yet."

After getting into her pajamas, Adelle sat down on the bed, running a brush through her hair. Jack flopped down beside her and watched, memorizing every movement, every curve of her body. Dread overtook him as he gazed at her. This may be one of the last nights he'd have her in his bed. It could be who knows how long before he could touch her again, hold her. No. It was way too soon. They had just started this life together.

Jack reached over and pulled her into a gentle snuggle against his side. In response, Adelle giggled. When she turned to him, her smile dropped as she caught his pensive expression.

"Jack, what's wrong?" she asked.

He buried his face against her hair like a hiding child. "I don't want you to leave."

"Leave? I thought we were going to bed?"

"I mean to San Diego."

Adelle pulled away, confused. "You think I'm going home with Val this week?"

Jack pursed his lips. Now he was feeling like a jackass, especially with how Adelle was looking at him. "...Maybe?" he said.

Adelle's perplexed expression melted into a little smile. "Val wanted me to come home with her. I won't lie to you." She pressed a finger against his mouth before he could protest. "But I told her no. I'm staying here."

Jack let out a sigh of relief. "Good."

"But..."

But? There's a but to this conversation? Oh, Hell.

Jack tensed right back up again. "Go on."

"I promised her I would come back if things began to go south. Even though I'd rather be up here, Jack I still have a job to. I can't leave Val to do it on her own."

Jack nodded, trying to remain calm though his heart was twisting into a knot. "I can move down with you, then."

Adelle regarded him with a flat look. "You want to move down to San Diego... Really?"

Okay so, she caught him in a lie. He didn't want to move. Moving a dragon was akin to moving the Statue of Liberty back to France. Hell, when he came to the New World, it was a long drawn out affair involving months and months of sailing ships. Then moving from coast to coast was even worse and he was still considered a youngling back then. That was when he was adventurous and *wanted* to move. Now, the hoard alone would take years to relocate. He doubted Adelle's family home had a basement big enough. If they even had a basement, that is. And then there was the God forsaken hot Mediterranean weather all year round.

"It would take some logistics," he said.

"Logistics my ass," Adelle said. "Jack, I'm not going to ask you to uproot your life after centuries of living here."

"Not centuries! Only maybe… a century or two."

"Semantics, Jack."

"Fine!" He folded his arms across his chest. Already he wanted to head outside and smash his fists through a few trees.

"Jack." Adelle pressed a hand against his cheek. "You know what I do down there. If you come down, you'll want to get involved. If you do, you'll screw up the balance and fate will want payback. You could die."

It wasn't the idea of *him* dying that bothered him. Adelle almost lost her life once. He'd need to be close to her, to keep her safe from that mage, and smash any of those bastards that would dare lay a hand on her. But it was more than that. A deep sense of need tore through him whenever he thought of Adelle. A need that would destroy him if she was taken away forever. He would break if he lost her.

"I'll find a loophole!" he snapped.

"What if you don't? I want you safe just as much as you want me safe."

"So, I wait and hope you eventually you don't get killed and show back up? How long do you expect to be away?"

Adelle shrugged. "However long it takes. But as soon as we get things wrapped up? I'm here. For good. I promise."

"As long as it takes?! How long would that be? And what about that mage who's after you? What if he comes back?" Fury burned behind his eyes. He wanted to give her a good shake, tell her she had to choose; here or there, him or her sisters!

Adelle ran her hands through her thick curls, exasperated. "I don't know!"

"Well, fucking find out! I'm not losing you!"

"I made a vow, Jack!'

Jack felt his skin grow hot with resentment. He shut his eyes tight and bellowed, "Break your goddamned vow!"

Adelle cringed back at his anger for the first time and the sight cut him in two.

What the fuck is wrong with you, Jack?

Jack clutched hunks of his hair, sitting back against the headboard. Now that he had Adelle, all he wanted to do was keep her close. But he didn't want to steamroller over her like some dominating jerk wad. Adelle was his mate, his equal, not his pet.

"I'm sorry," he said. "Just thinking of losing you and I go completely berserk. I..." He swallowed hard and confessed, "I've never felt this way before."

Adelle pressed her forehead against his, soothing his raging temper. "Let's just cross that bridge when we get to it," she soothed. "Val and I used to go for months without anything cropping up. Hell, I could be here for years before that phone call ever happens."

Jack nodded, shoulders slumped in defeat. "All right."

"I'm never going to leave you, Jack. That's not a promise. It's a fact." The words smoothed Jack's ruffed scales and he kissed her in apology.

Tempers calmed and the two snuggled in bed, Adelle's head tucked securely against the crook of his shoulder. It wasn't long before she was in a deep slumber but Jack laid awake, eyes fixed on the ceiling. Adelle had duty to her family, one he needed to respect, no matter how he felt. If she returned to San Diego, he had to let her. He just hoped that she could claim him before that day came.

He still had yet to see if she was even capable of the deed. What if she left him before he could ever say the words? What if she never came back? What if she found a human male that was much less complicated than he was? Jack shook his head. That was ridiculous. Adelle was a woman of her word. If she said she'd come back, she'd come back.

He snorted and rolled over, forcing himself into a fitful sleep. Just like she said, they'd cross that bridge when they came to it.

Chapter 24

It was turning out to be a wonderful day for Phoebe. The sun was shining, the birds were singing, and that cute guy in her statistics class smiled at her when she walked in for her finals. The magnificent power of cute gave her the confidence to push through that last test, and she was convinced she aced that sucker. This would have been celebrated with beef tacos and wine in the living room with Reina.

At least, that was the plan until Phoebe found a bear in the back yard.

Curious that, considering there has never been a bear sighting in her neighborhood in the last century. Yet there it was, a humongous, mountain of brown fur and teeth, sprawled out on the back patio, sunning itself.

At first, she had thought it was one of Valerie's old fur blankets. Her older sister had a thing for fur blankets, even in the warm San Diegan weather. Usually, Valerie would haul them out from winter storage and leave them on the back patio to air out. Chances were she had been in the middle of that process before she had to fly up for an emergency intervention. Apparently Wendy and Adelle were not getting along and Adelle had called threatening blood shed on the horizon. It seemed like bullshit, considering Adelle's infinite patience with everything but then most of the things Valerie told her sounded like bullshit.

At the wise age of twenty-five, Phoebe was convinced that her older sisters had been hiding something from her for years. The question was, what? By the time Phoebe started to think on this, like she had many times before, she spotted the furry mass outside through the living room's French doors.

"Sheesh, Val," Phoebe muttered. "Clean up much? Or ever?"

The mornings had been dewy, soaking anything outside. If Valerie had left that blanket out a couple days ago, chances were mildew was already building up. Ugh, there was a smell Phoebe would be happy to forget, especially after the one and only time she had left her wet clothes in the washer for a couple of days. As punishment, her sisters had made her wear them as is until it was her turn to do the laundry again. The acrid smell of body odor and rotting fabric was definitely not a guy magnet.

Phoebe pushed the doors open and trudged to the wooden patio. The usually dormant grass was growing like crazy. Adelle and Valerie must have been using new fertilizer. With a long suffering sigh, she reached down and snagged a corner of the brown fur blanket.

She didn't expect it to have claws.

Big claws.

Big, long, black claws that could probably slice her into itty bitty chunks.

The sleepy head of a bear rose up, its tiny ears twitching, beady black eyes narrowed to contemplate her. Phoebe's jaw dropped open to scream, only to release a pathetic wispy squeal of terror.

"Bear," Phoebe whispered to no one. "Bear? Bear! Val! Dell!"

She turned to run back to the house, forgetting that her sisters were not even in the same state as she was. Eventually, she found her voice and screamed, "Bear! Oh my God! Bear! Bear! Bear!"

She only ran a few feet before the furry paws of doom wrapped around her middle and yanked her down. Tears scalded her eyes and she let out a quivering cry of sheer horror.

The bear reared up, then pushed her to the ground. As soon as her back hit the soft grass, Phoebe curled up into a ball, covering her head with her arms.

Everyone always said play dead when confronted by a bear. Well, everyone on sitcoms. There were really no bears in the urban part of San Diego unless you counted the zoo. The number of bear attack survivors she knew was a big zero.

"Oh God, Mr. Bear!" Phoebe cried. "Please don't eat me! I'm so stringy!"

Maybe the bear would listen to reason. Maybe he would see how gamey she was and go eat that fat kid across the street. The one that peed on their front lawn and tormented the neighbor's poor tabby cat.

That little bastard deserves it!

The bear nudged her back with his cold wet nose, rocking her onto her side. There was some gruff growling as she felt the weight of the bear flop over behind her. Its clammy nose poked against her ear again, sniffing and snorting dusty air into her canal, then a long purple tongue flicked its slimy surface against her cheek.

"Ew! Just get it over with and stop tasting me!" she screamed.

It didn't eat her. It didn't even take a nibble of her. Instead, the bear curled up on the ground, spooning its gigantic furry body against Phoebe's back. It let out quivering rumble that was deafening.

Phoebe opened her eyes. Her heart pounded hard and fast as she waited for the final killing blow. Any minute she'd feel those razor sharp teeth tear into her neck and those long talons pull open her gut. It would feast on her entrails, drink her blood, and suck the flesh from her bones.

It would kill her.

Any minute now.

Five minutes had passed when the bear started snoring.

No, she wasn't a meal. She was a cuddly teddy-human to snuggle with. Five more minutes passed and Phoebe realized she was not going anywhere. It was winter time in San Diego.

Don't bears hibernate in the winter? Shit!

Phoebe wiggled slowly, as to not to arouse her new friend but a giant paw had her right arm pinned down securely and her other was stuck under her own body. This was going to take some time.

After some straining, twisting, and a wiggle, wiggle, wiggle, Phoebe managed to pull her cell phone out of her front jeans' pocket. She unlocked the screen, using her nose to put in the key code, then hit speed dial for the first person on her list.

Adelle had a warm gooey masterpiece of a hamburger lifted to her mouth. She was starving and had waited all day for dinner, now she, Jack, and Valerie had finally made it to that new much awaited burger place on Main Street. In her hands sat the *Peanut Butter and Jelly Fantasy* burger, an amazing concoction topped with peanut butter, jelly, bacon, Swiss cheese, and probably fairy dust and a child's laughter. Her teeth were ready to sink into the sticky sweetness when her smart phone rang.

She almost ignored the call, thinking it was a telemarketer or worse, a much scorned Wendy. When she saw Phoebe's name pop up on the screen, Adelle sighed. Phoebe usually called Valerie when she wanted to chatter. She called Adelle when she needed advice.

Must be boy trouble.

The Peanut Butter and Jelly Fantasy was reluctantly placed back onto the plate and Adelle held up a finger to Valerie, pausing one of her carousing stories to hit the answer button.

"Hey Pheebs! How are you? I miss you!"

"Dell! There's a bear in my ear!" her little sister cried into the phone.

She was struck silent at that one. Valerie was staring, her dark hazel eyes showing just enough concern to make her swallow hard.

"I'm sorry, what did you say?" Adelle asked.

"I'm being attacked by a bear!" Phoebe said in a raspy panic.

Adelle looked back to Valerie, whose concern was deepening into full blown panic. She would have to be delicate. When it came to Phoebe, Valerie's mama mode had a hair trigger. Any hint that Phoebe was in trouble and she would be in a frenzy of shouts and violence.

"Phoebe," Adelle said making sure she appeared calm. "Have you been drinking?"

"No, I haven't been drinking!" Phoebe snapped. "There is a bear in our backyard!"

Valerie scooted to the edge of her chair and leaned across the table, her palms pressed down onto it. Adelle took a deep breath and turned her eyes to Jack, who had devoured half of his second burger. He stopped and looked at her, cheeks filled like a chipmunk storing up for winter. Bacon grease dribbled down his chin.

"What?" he asked between mouthfuls of meat.

Adelle gave him a brief scowl, knowing he wasn't going to be any help. She turned away, cupping her hand around the phone. "When you say bear," Adelle said in a low voice. "You mean bear as in the gay, hairy man persuasion, right?"

"No! I mean a real bear, Dell!" Phoebe screamed into the phone, loud enough for everyone to hear.

Valerie jumped to her feet, the legs of her chair screeching across the stone tile floor. She was in full big sister mode now and nothing would calm her down. Jack on the other hand was coughing hard, as a lump of his burger drifted down the wrong pipe. Adelle waved her hand at them both as if she were battling a swarm of mosquitoes. She wasn't sure what the gesture meant, but she hoped it would get Valerie back into her chair. Instead, it made her hold out a firm hand and mouth the words, "Phone. Now."

To which Adelle mouthed back, "No!" then went back to verbal speech with Phoebe. "So," she said, trying to sound casual. "A real bear, huh? With... fur? And teeth?"

"I just said a real bear, Dell!" The loud growl of a bear rumbled behind her little sister's voice which confirmed the story. "What do I do?"

Panic's sharp talons seized Adelle's heart and gave it a tight squeeze. How the hell did bear get into their backyard? "Well, get inside the house, for God's sake!"

"I can't!" Phoebe said.

"Why not?"

"Because it's spooning with me!"

"It's *what?*"

"It pulled me on the ground and it's cuddling with me on the lawn, Dell! It won't let go and my legs are cramping up and I got an ant up my nose!"

Adelle covered the mouth piece of her smartphone, took a deep breath, and allowed her heart to slow back to a normal pace. Then, in the calmest voice she could manage, she turned to her older sister and said, "Val, I think Phoebe just manifested."

"What?!" Valerie screamed. Conversations in the restaurant stopped at the sound of her raging screech.

"Val," Adelle hissed through her teeth. "Sit down!"

She looked back to Jack who had managed to stop choking on his food. He had a hand over his eyes and his mouth hung open with wheezing squeals of laughter.

Note to self, don't have sex with Jack tonight as form of punishment.

"Jack, tell my sister to sit down," Adelle said.

Jack put his hands up, his amber eyes now bloodshot from mirth filled tears. "You actually think she'll listen to me?" He laughed even harder.

Ignoring them both, Adelle went back to her phone. "Phoebe, honey. It's s sunset now, right?"

Phoebe gave a pathetic little sniffle. "Yeah."

"Dell, tell Phoebe she's manifesting!" Valerie demanded.

"Right now?" Adelle gaped. She pressed her hand over the phone again. "Are you insane? What am I supposed to say? Phoebe, you're a magical fairy! Congrats and don't let the bear hump you?!"

"Dell?" Phoebe's panic soaked voice cried. "Are you still there?"

"I'm here Pheebs. I'm here. If its sunset, get off the phone with me and call Reina. She'll come over and pry the bear off you."

Valerie held her hand out with all the authority that could only be expected from an older sister. "Give me the phone, Dell!"

"What, Val? Are *you* going to tell her she manifested?"

"Well since you chickened out, I just might!"

Jack had his face down on the table. One arm covered the back of his head and the other pounded a fist on table top, rattling the place settings. His laughter echoed up through the vaulted ceiling. Adelle frowned at him.

Note to self, don't have sex with Jack tomorrow night, either.

"Pheebs? I'm going to hand the phone over to Val, okay?" Adelle said.

"All right," Phoebe whimpered.

Before she could say more, Valerie had snatched her smartphone. "Phoebe, baby? You all right?"

Jack raised his head to look at Adelle, tears streaming down his cheeks as he coughed up another strangled giggle. When she narrowed her eyes at him and shook her head, he knew he wasn't getting any that night.

"Good," Valerie continued. "Look Phoebe, I… Um..." Her voice trailed off and she looked to Adelle, begging for help. Adelle put her hands on her hips, staring daggers. She wasn't about to give her any.

"Go on, tell her," she said. "Man up, oh mighty warrior."

Valerie gave her sister a fierce frown. "Phoebe, do what Adelle says. Call Reina. Then call us right back when you're in the house. You'll be fine." She punched the end call button and tossed the phone on the table.

"Ah," Adelle said. "Good job there, Val. So, Phoebe took it well? You delivered the news to her very smoothly."

"Oh, shut up," Valerie grumbled.

Jack managed to sit up, drying his eyes with the cloth napkin on his lap. He raised a hand to the nearest server. "We're going to need some to-go boxes here," he said.

Chapter 25

"She's a little shaken, but all right," Reina had said when she called. "All she needs is a hug, a glass of wine, and to never watch a *Yogi Bear* cartoon ever again."

Reina managed to get Phoebe free and had used her vampire hypnosis to slip Phoebe from the bear's grasp. It lumbered off from whence it came, wherever that was. Thank God that power worked on creatures not of the Wyrd. From that moment on, Phoebe was convinced Reina worked as a security guard for the San Diego Zoo. How else would she have had such control over an animal like that? Reina just went along with it.

What should have been a weeklong visit turned into just a three-day excursion, after that incident. Phoebe manifesting her Dryad powers had Valerie packing her bags and booking a flight home for the next morning. Not that Adelle blamed her. Today a bear, tomorrow, maybe a herd of deer or a beanstalk growing in their front yard.

The morning went fast; Valerie had a quick breakfast and said her goodbyes to Jack and Adelle and Adelle tried not to make it a tear filled one. After all, she was just a plane ride away. Still, emotion clogged up her throat and she found herself trying to cough away the sadness.

"So," Valerie said. "I'm not going to change your mind and have you tag along, am I?"

Adelle shook her head. "I can always tell Phoebe about her powers over the phone if you still don't want-"

Valerie cut her off. “No, I should tell her. Really. I mean, I’m the head of this family, right? It should be my job.”

Adelle pursed her lips a moment. “Yeah, but I do handle these things better than you.”

“Well, now I got to prove you wrong then.” Valerie let out a laugh, turning to Jack. “Take good care of my sister, all right?” She gave him a punch in the shoulder. Other men practically fell over from one of her hits, Jack didn’t even flinch.

“Trust me,” he said. “There is no place safer for her than with me.”

After several affectionate hugs, Valerie climbed into her rental car and drove off. Adelle stood at the door, watching the Mustang turn out of the gym’s parking lot. It headed down the road, and faded into tiny scarlet dot on the snowy horizon. Adelle let out a quivering sigh as she watched her sister vanish.

Jack wrapped his arms around Adelle’s shoulders, pressing a kiss against her temple. “You’ll see her again,” he said.

“I know.” Adelle’s eyes fluttered closed at the feel of his warm lips upon her face. The sadness from watching Valerie leave wasn’t gone but the weight on her heart lessened at his touch. “I’m more worried about what the circumstances will be when I see her again.”

Her gruff dragon squeezed her against his broad chest. Adelle could feel his heart beating, the warm breath on the back of her neck. It comforted her like a warm blanket on a dark, chilly night.

“Whatever the circumstances are, Buttercup,” he said. “You can handle them.”

Months of calm and clear days passed which Jack welcomed with opened arms. Routine consisted of waking up, breakfast with Adelle, work- but really thinking about getting home to Adelle-, then rushing up the stairs to see his ravishing redhead and perhaps ravish her, which was often. Very often.

Jack woke every morning, eager to feel Adelle's lips on his cheek and to hear the soft whisper of, "Good morning, sunshine". While getting up in the morning was a treat, going to bed at night and curling up against the voluptuous curves of his siren was indulgent.

Sex with Adelle was like a drug. Not a day went by when he didn't crave her hands on him or her skin pressed against his. He memorized every inch of her; the two moles that sat on her hip, the way her lower back dipped into her round plump behind, he even memorized the runes on the inside of her arm. At night, he would trace his fingers against the black ink until he fell asleep. Being in love made him loopy eyed and the dizziness was invigorating.

The winter months faded into spring and the little town of Whitmore began to thaw. There was just enough cold in the air to keep a body awake, but no more than that. Now that the sun was shining, Adelle could take off her shoes and bury her feet into the earth without having to worry about frostbite. Her toes were safe, but he missed the days of carrying her back to the car over his shoulder.

Jack sat on the overturned tree in their practice circle as Adelle touched down. It wasn't often that she levitated during practice. The amount of concentration and energy it took to get her airborne was astronomical. When he asked, she claimed it was to get the feel of her full powers but Jack could tell she was showing off for him. After an eye popping show of light spiraling about her, she hauled herself up above the trees. Ear fobs stuck in, eyes closed, she sang with every ounce of joy, sorrow, and fear inside her then she landed as dainty as a pixie on a rose petal, grey smoke and the acrid smell of sulfur rising around her.

She wore a bragging smile as she padded towards him. Jack saw this routine hundreds of times and yet it still astounded him. Before Adelle could bend down to put her boots back on, Jack curled an arm around her waist and buried his face against her hair. He was rewarded with one of her musical laughs, slipping onto his lap with ease.

"It's too early to go home yet," Jack said.

Adelle let out a sigh, leaning her head against his chest. "True."

That enchanting smell of honey wafted from her hair and wrapped around him. "What do you say to hanging out here a little longer?"

"Ten more minutes, then." Adelle closed her eyes. She tilted her head to absorb the sunlight, grinning.

Jack gave her a scrutinizing gaze. "Only ten minutes? You insult me."

Adelle swung her head towards him, one delicate light brow arched. "Are you saying what I think you're saying?"

"What? You're here. I'm here. It just... happened."

As if he hadn't been thinking about taking her on that fallen tree. It was a constant thought, even before the first time they made love.

"Seriously?" Adelle laughed.

"Yup," Jack said.

"Right here?"

"Right here."

"In... nature?"

Jack threw his head back with a loud laugh. The trees shook as the birds that braved Adelle's powers, scattered. "Oh, come on! You've been digging your bare toes in the dirt and snow around here for months now!"

"Toes, yes," Adelle replied. "But dirt on my delicate lady bits I do not approve of."

He tucked her curls behind her ear and whispered, "You know you want to. Don't pretend."

Adelle ran her hand across the coarse brown crackling skin of the downed tree. "I'm more worried about bark chafing."

Well, she had a point. Her skin was far more delicate than his. Damn her point. Jack dipped her backwards and planted a long hot kiss against her wanting mouth. Her body softened against him.

"How about we come back with a blanket, then?" Jack grinned, waggling his eyebrows.

The corners of her mouth lifted into a smile and she gave him a firm nod. "You're on."

"Good. Ten more minutes then, while I kiss you until you can't feel your toes."

Her green eyes widened as she fluttered her eyelashes. "Only ten?"

True to his word, Jack mercilessly kissed Adelle into submission. That was no easy feat either. Adelle's stubborn streak was hard to conquer and she counteracted his kisses with her own fierce, passionate ones. But conquer it he did and eventually she was reduced to a pile of quivering jelly as he ravaged her mouth. It had been years since he had a good old fashioned make out session.

Adelle's lips quivered against his as she swung her legs around his hips, straddling him. Her nipples grew hard beneath her blouse as his strong fingers kneaded the soft flesh of her breasts. She ground her warm, clothed body against his until he was rock hard. It took a mountain of willpower to not lose all resolve, rip her clothes off, and bend her over that fallen tree but she *had* asked him not to. Well, not yet. For now, this was excellent. Later they would come back. He'd find that blanket. Then he'd slowly peel her clothes off under the clear, darkening skies. God, he couldn't wait.

The two stumbled back home, lips swollen red with kisses and limbs tingling in anticipation. "What sounds good for dinner tonight?" Adelle asked as she pulled off her jean jacket. "Want to eat out?" She turned to him just in time to see a sinister grin peel across his face. She smirked in return. "Oh, very mature."

Jack only put up his hands in defense, his chuckle anything but innocent.

Adelle laughed and shook her head. "Food first. I'm not being a tease. I'm hungry." She clicked on the television in the living room, the five o'clock news murmuring under their conversation. "Food, shower, then…"

That wink told him exactly what came next. His jeans suddenly felt two sizes too small. Adelle flopped on the couch and kicked her feet up on the coffee table, careful to avoid spilling any of his bowls of glass.

"Then I'm calling for pizza." Jack strolled into the kitchen. "They're a fast delivery and obviously I have things to tend to tonight." He punched in the number on the phone and listened to the metallic ring over the receiver. "You want your usual, Buttercup? Mushrooms?" Jack drummed his onyx fingernails against the phone as he waited for her reply.

She didn't.

"Baby?" he called again.

Still no answer.

Cold dread punched his gut and the rhythm of his heart became very loud and very fast. He hung up the phone and rushed into the living room shouting, "Adelle!?" Thank God, she was still there sitting on the couch. A rush of air escaped his lungs as he walked over. "Jeeze, you scared the hell out of..."

Her rigid posture halted his words. That cold sensation in the pit of his stomach returned and began to spread. The words *what's wrong* were on the tip of his teeth when Adelle sprung to her feet and turned up the volume on the television, despite the remote sitting right next to her.

"-three San Diego Catholic churches consumed in flames in the same evening." The slicked haired newscaster's words snapped Jack's attention to the screen. "*St. Joseph's Cathedral*, *Our Lady of the Sacred Heart*, and *Our Lady of Angels*."

Images of the burning churches flashed across the screen in a hellish montage of orange, yellow, and black. The serene voice continued. "*The Immaculate Conception*, a church in the Old Town San Diego, Historical Park appears to have been threatened but was rescued by their Pastor, Father Matthew DeAngelis. He and other members of his parish managed to fight the flames until firefighters arrived on the scene."

Jack looked to Adelle who now sat on her knees in front of the flat screen. All the color drained from her face as she stared slack jawed.

"Authorities suspect the nature of the fires to be arson. No signs of arson have been found as of yet. Investigators are currently-"

"That's not arson," Adelle whispered. "Three, almost four churches. All of them in flames. All at the same time."

The ring of her smartphone was like crashing glass to Jack's ears. They turned to the sound coming from her purse. Jack dashed over and yanked out the phone reading the screen. He shuddered the moment he saw the name.

"It's Val," he said.

Of course it was Valerie. Three churches simultaneously up in flame? No sign of arson? That was magic. Mage magic. The moment he dreaded for months was here. He went numb as he placed the phone in Adelle's hand. Her fingers curled around it then she hit the answer call button and pressed the phone to her ear.

Jack did his best to swallow down the rocks in his throat.

"Val," Adelle said, voice tight.

"Remember that bad feeling I had?" Valerie said.

Her entire body ached with anxiety. She had to remind herself to breathe, to keep her head but she knew what this meant. She knew this was it.

"I just saw the news. What the hell is going on down there?"

"I don't know. There's no evidence, but it is arson. Just not mundane arson. These were magical fires."

"A fluke?" Adelle shut her eyes tight. Her hand grew clammy.

Valerie let out a long sigh. "I don't think so. This was too precise. My guess is Tony is starting shit."

"Fuck." Adelle sat back on her haunches. Tony needed her for some reason. And now, he and his other dark mage pals were burning down churches. A cabal of mages worked in mysterious ways. This had a meaning. Lord only knew what it was.

Valerie was silent for a long while. Then after a reluctant minute she said, "I'm going to have to ask-"

"I'll book a flight and be home by the end of the week." Adelle's voice was hollow. She turned to look at Jack who was crestfallen, brows knitted, mouth screwed into a frown. Her heart cracked.

"Thanks Dell," Valerie said. "I'm sorry. I really am. I am so very sorry."

"It's all right, Val. I promised I wouldn't let you down. I won't." She lowered her phone, touching the end call button with her thumb. It slid from her fingers, hitting the floor with a soft thunk. The sting of tears pressed against the back of her eyes as she looked back to Jack.

"Jack..." The rest of the words caught her throat. She wheezed in a deep breath and shook her head.

He stared at her silently a long moment, the crease between his brows deepening. "Booking a flight tomorrow?" Jack said.

"I..." Adelle shut her mouth into a tight line. She closed her eyes, trying to calm the panic down before it threatened to burst from her mouth with a sob. When she opened them, Jack had turned his back to her, leaning a heavy shoulder against the kitchen doorway.

"Jack," Adelle said. "Jack, I'm so sorry."

"Don't be sorry, Buttercup." There was a tremor to his voice.

"I'll call her back," Adelle said, wanting to fix this, wanting to do anything to make him smile again. "I'll tell her I'm sorry. That I have to stay here."

Jack's muscular back rippled at her words. For a moment, she thought he'd agree. Instead he spun on his heels to face her, the gold in his eyes blazing. "Don't even think about it."

"But I-"

"You made a vow to your sister," he said. "Don't let this emotion; don't let *me* make you go back on your word." Jack strode over and grabbed her by the arms. "Dell, there is nothing I want more than for you to stay here with me. If there was a possibility, I would set this world ablaze for you." He swallowed as the next words seemed to be the hardest he ever uttered. "But you need to go home." Tears rolled down her cheeks when Jack cracked a sad smile. "You know how serious I am about vows."

Adelle sunk her teeth into her lower lip then nodded in reply. He was right. Damn him for it. She let out a choked little cry then slipped her arms around his shoulders, hugging him tight.

Jack's office held the only working computer in his domain. It was an old model but could still do the basics like email, internet, and spreadsheets. Adelle thanked God he wasn't so archaic as to only have dial up.

"Okay," Adelle said into her phone. Valerie sat on the other line as she reported in her progress. "*American* and *Southwest* are all booked up too." Finding a flight out was easier said than done. It was spring break and just about every flight to San Diego was booked. She rubbed her forehead with a sigh. "All the college kids are heading out to party. I can't even find a flight with a layover."

"Fucking college kids," Valerie grumbled.

Adelle rolled her eyes. "The earliest I can get home without us having to sell the house to pay for it is in four more days."

"I think that's doable," Valerie said. "Not ideal but doable. What about your dragon?"

"He'll manage," she said.

She tried to numb herself. Adelle wanted return to that controlled state she was locked in before Jack. But there was no going back. He'd opened the floodgates.

"That does not sound like the Adelle I know. You sure he can't come with?"

"Val, he needs his hoard to survive. And he sure can't move it to our place."

"Then just a little bit of his hoard? Won't that keep him going?"

"He can't come down here and get mixed up in this mess. He's full blood. If he takes sides, he'll die. And knowing Jack, he'll get involved. I can't risk his safety like that."

Valerie was quiet on the phone for a while before she admitted, "Point taken."

"Yeah," Adelle only answered. "I'll book for Friday and email you the itinerary."

After getting her flight, she slipped out of Jack's office. Jack was waiting at the front of the gym, staring out the picture window. His arms were folded across his massive chest, body ready to snap like a rubber band. As soon as he heard Adelle close the door, his gaze jerked right to her.

"So?" he asked.

"I'm not flying out until Friday." Adelle said. Jack's shoulder deflated and he let out a long sigh.

"Well, I got you for a few more days then." His voice was hopeful which only made Adelle cringe more.

"Yes. But only four."

"I'll take what I can get." Jack strode over to her and she fell against him, snaking her arms around his waist. "Four days," Jack murmured, "I'll make them count. I'll close the gym for the week. It will be just you and me for the next four days." His large hand swept across her hair.

"You don't have to go to any trouble Jack," Adelle said. "I mean closing the gym-"

"I have an entire staff that can run this place blindfolded. I'm taking the days off. Period." There was no convincing him otherwise and Adelle was glad of it. Four days left with her dragon. She was going to make them count.

Chapter 26

"You done fucked up, boy."

Anthony spun around with an arm thrust out, ready to cast a killing hex at the trespasser. An older woman with unkempt mottled brown hair smiled as she lifted a lit cigarette to her lips, inhaling long and deep until the tip glowed orange. Her shoulder was pressed against the door frame as if waiting for a bus. She wore a rather out of date black pantsuit, something you'd find during the peak of *The X-Files* popularity.

He scowled and lowered his arm. Hexing a superior mage wouldn't score him any favors, even if she was a horrible bitch. Lucy Drake was one of the few people who could sink right under his skin. She was like a rash, a scary, irritating rash that nothing could relieve.

"How did you get past my wards, Drake?" he demanded.

Lucy shrugged her shoulders with a smirk on her thin pale lips. "I'm better than you?" she said, as if that would answer all his questions.

Anthony felt his hands tremble in rage. He smoothed the front of his crisp white shirt, trying to regain some of his pristine image. At least he kept his shoes on. That gave him a little feeling of power in front of her.

Guests were never on his agenda so his usual sharp attire was reduced to an untucked shirt and black slacks. His house was well warded, out in the middle of nowhere in the rocky hills of Jamul. Desolate, secluded, and not even detectable by the main road, which was an unkempt one lane dirt path. Most people who approached the threshold felt the sudden urge to turn away with dread and never return. Those who pushed past it were subject to a flesh melting curse for their persistence.

Anthony straightened his posture, feigning indifference to her sudden appearance. “Drake. What brings your charming presence here today?”

Curls of grey smoke wafted from Lucy’s mouth. “Just came here to tell you what a fuck up you are.”

Her eyes darted around his office. Simple furniture, every surface uncluttered, every item placed just so. Even the ancient tomes that lined his bookshelves were dusted and stacked perfect. It was neat, tidy, and sleek. Just the way he liked it. Just the way he dressed. The slovenly woman standing there was a complete juxtaposition to his decor. It made Anthony’s eyelid twitch.

“Niiiice place,” Lucy continued. “You could really use a big screen T.V though. Oh, wait!” She slapped her forehead in a mock sense of urgency. “You’re above watching television! Silly me. I forgot what a pretentious little prick you are.”

“Are you trying to intimidate me, Drake, or merely irritate me?” he said.

“Lil’ of column a, lil’ of column b.” She took another long drag on her death stick and blew a lung full in Anthony’s direction. He waved it away with annoyance. “Shadow wants to talk to you.”

Anthony went stiff. Shadow was the key to getting inducted into the cabal. Induction meant access to knowledge and power beyond anything he could comprehend. He hungered for it. His body ached for it. And he was so close.

Obtaining a siren’s song was Anthony’s first task towards entrance into Shadow’s cabal. The other mages may have had the skill to extract a siren’s voice but *he* knew where to get a siren. Even a half-blood like Adelle would do. But getting her was more difficult that he predicted. Shadow was probably furious at him for losing Adelle a second time. He wasn't a forgiving soul. When something went wrong, Shadow sent Lucy, his she-bitch messenger girl, as the harbinger. Lucy hated everyone, making her the perfect candidate to inform people of their screw ups.

Anthony smoothed his dark hair and looked Lucy in the eye. "Tell him my back-up plan is in effect," he said then turned away from her. He had full intentions of showing Lucy the front door and how to use it.

Lucy snorted. "You tell him. He wants to talk to you. Hell, he talks to me every damn day."

"My current plan is to both find a siren's song and to obtain the Spear of Long-'"

"Oh, yeah. The church burning thing. Yes, very subtle."

He was grateful his back was to her so she couldn't see the frustration on his face. Lucy was uncouth, slovenly, and apathetic, but she was also a killer. One of Shadow's best due to the fact that she truly did not give a fuck about life; hers or others. Just a misplaced word or weak expression would give her an excuse. He closed his eyes and took a deep breath to calm himself.

Show no fear. Show this cow you are her equal.

"I can force both things out in the open." The words ground through his teeth. "After the fires, the spear will be moved for safety."

The cabal's other agent, Adam Steig, tortured a local priest for three days to find out the spear was hidden in San Diego. By the end of the ordeal, the priest's body was a twisted wreck, begging for death. Adam made Lucy look compassionate. Anthony was convinced he was devoid of emotion, a shark eyed husk that carried out any and all of Shadow's orders.

"And the siren?" Lucy asked.

"I know the Constance sisters. An incident like that will bring them together and into the open, the siren included."

"Yeah, see, bringing them together is the problem," Lucy said taping still smoldering ash onto the white carpet. Anthony seethed. "Those cunts are a pain in the ass separately. As a pair, they're worse. And once the third one joins them-"

"I know how to handle them," Anthony snapped.

"Just because you fucked one of them in the past-"

The loud bang of his fist hitting the wall silenced her. Anthony didn't lose his temper often, but after his botched plan of using the vampires to find Adelle and Lucy's uncanny talent for pushing buttons, keeping his cool was not in the cards.

How the hell Lucy had found out about his past with one of the Constance sisters was beyond him. That was a part of history he longed to forget. But after what he did to those women, he knew it would haunt him for the rest of his life.

Forget. Forget!

He only heard the sound of Lucy blowing more smoke from her pursed lips, nothing more. The acidic stench of cigarette tobacco burned his nostrils and he could feel it already sinking into the clothes he wore, the pores of his skin, making him want to retch.

After a long silence, Lucy spoke. "Fine and dandy, Tony the Tiger. But you still have to tell the boss this in person. He has his reservations about the vulgar use of magic."

"Oh please, spare me," Anthony spat. "An average human could barely comprehend the forces of magic. Half the time they just ignore it and explain it away."

"True. Still, Shadow is a stickler. He likes things being done his way."

Shadow's way usually consisted of subtle magic, collecting souls, and raising the dead. He was a death mage, and they were not to be trifled with. After a suppressed shiver, Anthony curled his fingers into tight fists. He turned his back to her, his face a blank slate.

"Fine then. When and where?"

Lucy reached into her jacket pocket and pulled out a business card. She laid it on her palm, then pursed her lips and puffed a breath of air onto its surface, as if blowing a kiss. It twirled and floated towards Anthony in a delicate dance, landing in his outstretched fingers. The bitch also loved parlor tricks.

"Memorize it. It will catch fire in a few minutes." Lucy tapped her cigarette with her ring finger leaving left a swirling trail of ash from his office to the living room as she followed him. Anthony frowned but said nothing. "He wants to discuss your plan, when the siren will be delivered, as well as future parts you will play in our end game."

The cold terror finally loosened. If Shadow wanted Anthony in his end game, he was getting a second chance. His life was still worth something to that arrogant bastard. Access into the cabal was still in reach. He nodded in reply to Lucy, looking down at the address and date written on the card. Lucy turned to leave, grey tentacles of smoke pouring from her mouth.

"Oh, and buy a rug doctor while you're out," she said with a wink of her eye. "Good luck, tiger. "You'll need it."

Chapter 27

The sun's golden beams streaked through the parted curtains and across the bed. It touched Jack's closed eyelids, and he let out an agitated groan.

Day four, he thought.

Tomorrow morning, he'd drive Adelle to the airport and say goodbye for who knows how long. Jack was spooned against Adelle, her back molded to him as she slept. He reached up and combed his fingers through the few stray red curls that grazed his bare shoulder, then propped himself up on an elbow to watch her sleep, taking her all in before she was gone.

Adelle had made Jack promise not to brood during their last four days together. "I don't want the last memory I have of you being your moping face," she had said. That was a fair enough deal. Jack, being a dragon of his word, managed to remain upbeat. He focused on the time they had and not on the moment she'd board that plane. Yet here, at the end of the four-day stretch, he was starting to brood. Jack smoothed a hand down her shoulder then took in the scent of her hair. Adelle stirred at the touch. He shook off the dark mood and pressed a kiss to the side of her face.

"Go back to sleep, Buttercup. It's still early," he whispered.

Stubborn as usual, Adelle blinked her eyes open anyway. Her breasts strained against the flimsy green tank top she slept in as she arched her back into a stretch. Jack swallowed hard. That was definitely a sight he would miss. She rubbed the back of her hand against her cheek and gave him a lazy smile.

"I don't wanna," she said, in a sleepy low growl.

A grin curled around his lips. "Far be it from me to tell you what to do."

If his siren didn't want to sleep in, she damn well was not going to sleep in. She deserved a little spoiling on her final day in Whitmore. Jack leaned over and kissed her forehead, then scrubbed a hand over his face as another bout of lust slapped him. Just watching her stretch in his bed stirred his blood. Unfortunately, chances were she was still pretty worn out from their vigorous rounds last night, which were her idea. Well, partially her idea.

After returning home, Adelle had tackled him to the floor and wrestled the jeans from his legs. That was when he discovered she hadn't worn panties to dinner. Jack wasn't sure what turned him on more; the idea that Adelle had had this tryst planned all night; or watching her pull her skirt up, straddle his bare hips, and slide down the length of his shaft. The memory of her riding him, head thrown back as she moaned his name, made Jack groan. They never made it to the bedroom. Hell, he never even got her naked before the first orgasm. With that memory in hand, Jack slipped out of bed to grab a cold shower before instinct took over.

"I'll get some breakfast started in a bit," Jack said as he tossed the sheets aside. "Then we'll hang out for a few hours before we head out."

Adelle padded after him on her bare feet. Before he could get to the bathroom, she had snagged him around the waist, pressing kisses up the length of his back. His skin tingled wherever those soft lips touched and he stumbled a couple steps, expecting another ninja sex attack.

"Head out? Where are we going?" Adelle asked.

"I got plans."

The corners of her mouth turned up into a smart little smirk. "Plans, eh?"

"Surprise plans. As in, I'm not telling you until we get there, plans." He pried her hands from his middle. "So calm yourself, Buttercup and be sure to wear a jacket tonight."

She giggled. "Adelle go walkies?"

He patted her head. "Yes. Adelle go walkies."

Near dusk, the two piled into his Impala and drove out of town and into the woods. The sun began its descent, turning the sky a deep, burnt orange. Purple tinted clouds slashed across the horizon and soon the moon was greeting the world with its silvery glow. Jack glanced over to Adelle who was gazing out the window, chin resting on her hand. Her brow was furrowed as the moonlight reflected in her shimmering eyes.

"What's on your mind?" Jack asked.

"Your mysterious plans. Are you planning to propose to me?"

Jack let out a rolling chuckle as he shook his head. "Dragons don't get married. That's strictly a human thing."

"Well, then how do you expect me to hang on to you, huh?" she teased.

"Easy. They just need to look into my eyes to know I'm taken." Jack gave her a toothy grin. "Technically, I proposed when I said I wanted you for my mate."

"And I accepted."

Jack clenched his jaw. There was still no return claim from Adelle. Maybe her human side was the dominant one. Maybe a verbal yes was all she could give. If that was the case, Jack would have to find a way to fight nine-hundred years of instinct and accept it. Tight lipped, he nodded.

"Yeah," was all he said.

They pulled up to their usual spot off the road. With a tilt of her head, Adelle acknowledged the dirt path that lead to their practice circle and frowned at him. "Do not tell me that our final night together is going to be spent practicing."

Jack pretended he didn't hear her. "Stay in the car until I call you." He said then popped open the door to scoot out.

"Wait. What? Jack, wha-"

He closed the car door on her.

Before she could roll down the window to shout at him, Jack rounded the car, opened the trunk, and pulled out two plastic bins that he packed earlier that morning.

"Hey!" Adelle stuck her head out the window. "What do you mean, stay in the car?"

Jack slammed the trunk closed. "I mean, stay in the car. I got stuff to set up." He headed down the dirt path with the bins tucked under his arms.

"Set up what?"

Jack's reply was to keep on walking.

"Jack. You're really starting to irritate me," Adelle called after him.

"Good," Jack said over his shoulder. "That means you'll be happier to see everything when I'm done. Big win for me. Now, stay in the car!"

The exasperated growl she let out made him grin.

It took Jack a little longer than he expected to get everything set up. Granted, he had packed about two-hundred and fifty candles. Finding places to put them where they wouldn't start a forest fire was the tricky part. Under the branches? No. In the trees? Definitely not. He managed to scatter them around the clear circle of scorched earth.

Getting his glass lanterns hung was an even bigger pain in the ass. Valuable time was wasted shimmying up trees to hang them, then falling out of the trees while cursing a blue streak, then climbing back up again because he forgot to put the candles inside. He had just picked himself up from his third fall, grumbling and cursing, when he heard Adelle creeping up on him fast.

"So, it's been an hour," she called.

Dammit!

It was stupid to think she'd actually listen and stay put. The sound of her footsteps crunching on the leaves cut his prep time down to zero point zero seconds. He scanned the circle to make sure things were in place. The candles were set, the blanket and pillows were spread, and the lanterns, after many bruises later, were hung.

Well, good enough, he thought to himself.

In a few quick strides, Jack met Adelle out on the path, moving in front of her. Adelle raised herself up onto her toes, trying to peer over his shoulder, a curious smile plastered her face as she swayed from side to side, attempting to look into the circle. Jack weaved and bobbed with her, blocking her view with his clumsy dance at every pass.

"I thought I told you to wait in the car," he said.

"It's been an hour. I'm cold, and it's creepy out there." Adelle hinged at the waist, trying to peek between his legs. He quickly stepped them together.

"Creepy? Like you couldn't handle what is out here on your own?" He grabbed a hold of her before she could slip around him.

"Spiders, Jack. There could be spiders out there."

"You're not afraid of spiders."

"I could develop one after being neglected in the car for so long." Her eyebrow quirked as she rested her hands on her hips. "What are you doing over there? Building a house?"

Jack took Adelle by the wrists. "Close your eyes."

Adelle giggled as she continued to gibe. "Ah, you *are* building a house! A quaint cottage in the woods for us. How thoughtful."

The frown that threatened to conquer his mouth was tenacious. Jack never made sweeping romantic gestures, this one being his first and the teasing was beginning to batter his ego.

"You know, we could go back home," Jack snorted.

Adelle teases turned into heartfelt smiles. She freed a hand from his grip and soothed his bruised ego with a gentle caress of his cheek. His frown lost the battle and Jack grinned.

"I'll be good. Promise," Adelle said.

"Good. Now close your eyes."

Finally, she listened to him. Adelle lowered her eyelids, her lashes forming light crescents on her cheeks. He led her into their practice circle, careful to guide her feet around the bumps and brush until she stood by the fallen tree. Adelle took a deep breath, perking up.

"Do I smell... pizza?" she asked.

"All right, you can look now."

When Adelle opened her eyes, Jack waved a hand in the air. All the candles took flame in a shimmering flash. It was the only magic spell he knew and it was impressive looking. Candles of every shape and size surrounded them, bathing the clearing in a golden circle of light. The lanterns overhead cast colorful shadows of blue, purple, and green, their glass twinkling like the stars that swarmed above them. At their feet was a small nest made from an old worn comforter and all the pillows he could stuff into those bins. He turned to look at her, eager for her reaction.

"So, what do you think?" he asked.

Adelle's mouth fell open as the candle light danced in her eyes. She didn't say anything but the tears told him all he wanted to hear. It was enough encouragement to make him aggrandize some of the other details she might have missed in her shock.

"Aaaaaand..." He strode to the makeshift nest and lifted up the pizza box he had placed on the blanket. The lid popped up, revealing a steaming, extra-large mushroom with cheese. "Eh? Eeeeh?" He gave her an opened mouth smile, holding the pizza up by his face like a spokes model on a game show. Adelle burst out laughing, clasping her hands at her chest.

"Wait, there's more!" Jack continued. He reached down to pick up the bottle of champagne that he placed by the pizza, then grabbed the bottle in both hands, pressing his thumbs against the cork until it let out a merry pop. "Am I the best mate a woman could ever have or what, huh?"

Adelle's cheeks flushed, eyes twinkling. She bent down, snagging the two red solo cups by her feet. "You're not bad," she replied with an impish grin.

"Not bad? This is the first meal we had together. See, I remembered that. I just added the champagne for effect. Let's see one of your human guys have a memory like that." He poured the bubbly liquid into their cups, then lifted one and scrutinized it. "Okay, maybe I should have invested in glassware for the whole nine yards."

Adelle's scanned their glowing nest, her lips still curled up into that elated smile. Jack's heart felt light, her joy filled face warming him from fingertips to toes.

"I wanted to make tonight something that stuck with you." He offered her the red solo cup. Adelle took it then slipped her hand into his, her fingers warm yet trembling.

"This is the nicest thing a guy has ever done for me," Adelle confessed as she gazed up to the colorful lanterns overhead. Tears trickled down her cheeks as her mouth spread wide into another large opened mouth smile.

"Your old boyfriends were dicks," he said.

Adelle stepped onto the blanket and threw her arms over his shoulders, champagne splashing against the back of his neck.

He encircled her in his firm embrace and smiled. She felt perfect in his arms. So perfect.

Half a pizza and two big cups of champagne later, they laid back on the old comforter, gazing at the glimmering silver that spattered the black sky. Most of the candles were burned down to shriveled wicks and melted wax nubs. Adelle leaned her head against Jack's shoulder, her fiery hair tickling his neck.

"Nice, huh?" Jack asked.

"Better than a movie." Adelle craned her neck so she could take the final sip of champagne from her plastic cup. Then she set her drink down and rolled onto her side to face him. "I really couldn't think of a better way to end the week."

A dark cold heaviness pressed against his heart. He reached over, rubbing the rough pad of his thumb across her lips. They were quiet as Jack committed every detail of her lovely face to memory; her vivid green eyes that hid nothing from him, that wide expressive mouth that covered him with kisses, the ghosts of golden freckles that graced her nose and cheeks. His brave, beautiful siren.

"God, I'm going to miss you," he said. "I know I said I wouldn't grieve until you left but... Dammit." He lowered his face. "This isn't a promise I can keep. I tried."

A sad laugh escaped Adelle's lips. "It's all right. Because I'm not doing much better over here. I will call every day. I promise. As soon as it all clears up, I'm back. And I'm here. And I'm yours." A trail of tears spilt from her lower lids and pooled beneath his fingers. Jack felt his heart crack from their warm touch. "I'll always be yours."

"Hey now. No crying." He pulled her into his arms.

"No fair, Jack. You can cry but not me?" Adelle sniffed.

"I'm not crying. I'm the man in this relationship. I only cry if something hits me in the crotch." The mood lightened when Adelle let out a squeak of a laugh.

"Crap," Adelle muttered against his shoulder. "I was keeping it together so well, too."

"We both know what happens when you try to keep things in." Jack nuzzled his way through her soft curls. He pressed a kiss to the top of her head. "For now we're going to be in the moment, all right?"

Adelle let out a sigh then nodded. She kicked off her boots and lay against him for a while, wiggling her toes. Jack stroked her hair, brow furrowed. His muscles tightened waiting for her to say more. He could sense something was on her mind. But what? When Adelle pulled away and sat up, his palms started sweating. Adelle only wiped her eyes with the heels of her hands then nodded. After a lingering moment, she gave him a tender smile and pulled herself to her feet.

"Everything all right?" He couldn't hide the crack in his voice.

She peeled off her denim jacket. "Everything is perfect."

"Then where are you-"

His words stalled when Adelle pulled her shirt up over her head. She tossed it to the side of the blanket and looked down at him with need. Jack's mouth watered. A tiny smile touched Adelle's pink lips as she undid her jeans, pale fingers plucking at the button and zipper. She slipped them over her full hips in a smooth languid movement, the denim sliding down the length of her legs. She wore that sexy polka-dotted bra and panties set he adored. The tops of her full breasts peeped out of the top of her bra, creamy white tinged silver in the moonlight.

"What are you doing, Buttercup?" he asked, as if he didn't know.

Adelle smiled as she kicked her jeans aside. “I’m going to make love to you,” she simply said.

Those few words sent a scalding demand through him. The corner of his mouth turned up into a crooked grin. “I thought you said the dirt and chafing out here isn't your thing?”

“What? You brought a blanket. That’s all I needed.” Adelle laughed. The stunning combination of music, joy, and honey seeped into his ears blanketing him in warmth.

Jack sat up and reached for her, arms stretched out in wanting. But she held out a hand to stop him.

“Hold on,” she told him with a wag of her finger. Reaching behind her back, she unhooked her bra, slipping one strap down a pale shoulder, then the other.

Jack groaned, eyes locked on her breasts as the cups of her bra slipped a few more centimeters down her pale, freckle-dusted skin. The edge of her soft pink areola peeked from out the top.

So close. So close!

Jack’s jaw ticked, every ounce of self-control locked down tight as he sat stone still before her. His cock grew hard, pulsing for release against the fly of his jeans as his beautiful siren stripped for him. The sway of her hips was intoxicating. The heavy sound of her breath quickened his own. Adelle’s smile brightened as his expression grew more strained.

“Don’t tease me like this, Adelle,” he said roughly.

“What? I thought you said be in the moment.”

“Yeah well, the moment is going on a bit long and I’m ready for the next moment.”

Adelle bent down towards him, her hands still holding the cups of her bra against her chest. Her sweet scent filled his nostrils as tendrils of hair brushed his cheek. He let out a shuddering sigh, balling his hands into tight fists.

“You’ll thank me when I’m done,” she whispered.

Her sensual display was driving him mad with desire. Jack shut his eyes and let out another tight groan. When they reopened, she had peeled off her bra, baring her round, rosy peaked breasts for him. The site of her magnificent full curves never ceased to take the breath right out of his lungs. The cool spring breeze raised goose flesh on her skin and stiffened her nipples. He longed to take them into his mouth and suckle until she cried out his name. That's when he noticed his fingernails were biting into his palms.

Adelle crept her hands up her belly, finger caressing her body. They brushed past the curve of her breasts then up her neck. She let out a soft moan of anticipation for his touch and wet her lips with the tip of her tongue, eyelids heavy.

"Oh, God." Jack's whisper was ragged as she kept him on razor's edge.

Adelle stepped toward him, running her hands through his golden brown hair. The tips of her fingers were electric, sending shocks down his spine. The moment her warm fingertips touched the nape of his neck, he was done for.

Jack grabbed her hips, jerking her forward. Still on his knees, he pressed his cheek against her, breathing her in. His large hands skimmed up the back of her legs, black nails catching her skin until they clutched her backside. He pressed his mouth against the inside of her thigh. Adelle shivered when the stubble on his jaw prickled her flesh.

"No more teasing," Jack said, voice low and rumbling, heavy with promises.

Broad fingers peeled Adelle's panties down to her ankles. He nuzzled the thatch of fiery red curls between her thighs. Even there, she smelled like honey; sweet, sensual, longing to be tasted. The smell of melted candles mingled with her honey drenched scent. Adelle's fingers tightened in his hair in anticipation. She let out a sharp gasp as his lips brushed her sex.

"Jack," she whispered.

He growled through his teeth, "Want you."

Jack ran his tongue between her legs, tasting her, teasing her to arousal until her thighs parted, until she tilted her head back and moaned. His nails dug into her behind as Adelle's knees buckled. She was wet and slick against his mouth. Wet and wanting him. Her hips churned as he swiped his tongue across the warm silken folds, her trembling moans growing more urgent as she clutched the back of his head and pushed him against her harder. Steamy, breath-choked words demanded him not to stop but Jack pulled away before he sent her over the edge. Her frustrated groan made him grin like the devil.

Pulling Adelle to her knees before him, Jack sealed his mouth against hers. He closed his eyes, savoring the heat of her tongue and the essence of champagne still lingering on her lips. Jack yanked off his t-shirt, throwing it God knows where.

The feel of her silky, warm flesh against his bare chest quickened his pulse. Adelle shivered as she pressed delicate kisses along his shoulder and up his throat. Each one sent a pinprick of delight through his ragged nerves, making him lift his chin for more. He could feel her blood pulsing under his palms. His cock ached, wanting release, demanding to be buried inside his sweet siren. But tonight needed to be savored. Jack wrapped his arms around her, stroking her back as he reveled in the sensations.

Adelle pushed him down onto the blanket and unzipped his jeans. Dried leaves and earth crunched beneath the comforter as she pulled them down his hips, his long, hard, shaft springing forth. The chilled night air wrapped about his bare tingling flesh as she ran her fingers up the length of him. He almost spent right in her hand. Instead, he clenched his jaw and arched his back with a tortured grunt. Then her mouth was upon him. Adelle wrapped her lips around the crown of his shaft and dragged them up and down in a torturously languid pace. Jack grabbed tight fistfuls of the worn comforter as the touch of her heated tongue shot through him. He croaked out a groan as she continued licking and sucking.

Jack let out an angered growl when she pulled away, feeling the frustration she had felt only minutes ago. He looked up to delight in her sliding up his body to straddle him. Adelle hovered over him a brief moment, looking into his eyes. Those beautiful eyes, green as sea moss and ivy. Eyes that held complete love for him and only him. She lowered, welcoming his length into her with long, delicious, feminine noises. Every muscle within him shuddered. Strong hands dug into her hips, pushing her down further.

"Yes," she hissed through clenched teeth.

Adelle's hips began to rock, her sex sheathed tight around him, clenching his cock, teasing and caressing it. It was madness. Madness he didn't want to come back from. Jack gazed up at her in wonder; her hair shining crimson against the dark night, pale smooth curves bathed in silver moonlight. Adelle's radiant face was haloed by the twinkling stars in the inky sky above. She was Goddess. A force of nature. Jack lifted his hips to meet hers as she rolled against him, riding her dragon.

"I love you. Don't forget that," he whispered.

"Never," she said, strained and tight.

He loved her. That's all he wanted to say over and over.

I love you Adelle. I love you more than anything. I love you more than life. I'll love you forever.

Those words were reduced to primitive groans and heavy, wanton breaths. Despite the cool air, her skin was hot and shining with sweat. His own was on fire. The echoing sounds of crickets and birds' night songs filled Jack's ears along with the music of Adelle's moans. When he reached up to clasp one of her full, round breasts, he felt her heart pounding. He had to possess her mouth. It was a need he couldn't fight.

With a hungry grunt, Jack sat up, seized the nape of her neck, and yanked Adelle to him, devouring her lips. His hips thrust hard, making her gasp as they kissed. The need to make her come was overpowering, controlling every last inch of him. His singular goal was to hear her scream in ecstasy. Instincts made him push harder.

They rutted like common animals overcome by the need to breed. Adelle tore her mouth away to yell, thrashing. His eyes lowered to where they were joined. There was an erotic joy in watching the rivulets of sweat roll from their bodies and into each other, flesh against flesh, soul against soul. Adelle arched, the tips of her breasts jutting towards the sky. Her fingers curled into the muscles of his shoulders.

"I need ye tae scream for me, love," Jack growled. "I need tae hear it. Please."

Sparkling white veins of light webbed cross Adelle's skin. The more she writhed against Jack, the brighter she grew. She locked eyes with him as they continued to make furious love. Her heart ignited, illuminating her skin from the inside out until she was nothing but a white beacon of magic. Yet her eyes never changed. They remained the same sparkling green he loved. Jack's heart swelled.

"Jack! I love you!" Adelle threw her head back, and let out a powerful scream of ecstasy.

A tornado of blue and white light spun about their bodies, extinguishing the remaining candles. The air around them crackled with bright sparks. In that incredible climax, Adelle finally claimed him as her mate.

A mighty dragon's roar shook the trees above them. With one final thrust, Jack flooded her with his heat. He convulsed as his seed spent harder than ever before. All his love, his lust, and his passion for her flowed out from him. His heart slammed against his ribs as he thrust again and again, not wanting it to end. Adelle rolled her hips and clung to his body as her orgasm thundered through them both, by the force they created together.

The tornado of magic evaporated and the air went still. Adelle collapsed against him in a quivering ball. Jack fell back onto the blanket, clasping her to his slick chest. He was still hard inside her and even the slightest twitch sent electrical aftershocks through both of their bodies. After a breathless minute, Jack rolled them both to their sides. He laid her head on a pillow, stroking the sweat drenched hair from her face. She took in a shaky breath.

"What… What just happened to me?" she whispered.

Jack couldn't help but smile at her wide eyed expression of wonder. "I think you just claimed me." He ran his thumb across her lower lip, beaming with pride.

"Claimed." The word slipped from her lips with ease.

His mouth formed into a serious line as he continued to trace her features. Staring deep into her eyes, he said, "You are mine and I am yours. Nothing will ever happen to you as long as I'm alive. I promise you this."

Words never felt so good to say. After those words, Jack felt whole. Complete. In thanks, he kissed her forehead, then her eyes. Adelle's mouth curved into a smile as his lips met her skin. She tucked herself against him.

"You are mine. And I am yours," she repeated. After a long moment she nuzzled his chest and whispered, "Sucker."

Jack's laugh echoed up into the trees, frightening the birds above into flight.

Chapter 28

Saying goodbye was as hard as Adelle expected it to be. The drive to the airport was quiet and when they arrived; neither were willing to walk towards the security line. Jack placed a gentle hand to her lower back and nudged her forward, urging her not to miss her flight.

"I'll call you as soon as I'm home," Adelle said.

"Please." Jack rubbed the back of his neck. The muscles in his jaw tensed as he clenched his teeth. Then he looked at her and said, "It's only temporary."

Adelle wasn't sure if he said it for her sake or his own. While it was true, she still didn't know how long she would be away. How long *could* she stay away? They were mated now and being parted after claiming him made her heart ache.

"I know." Adelle gave him a reassuring smile. She took his large hands into hers, giving them a tender squeeze. "Besides, I'll bother you so much with phone calls you may not want me to come back."

Jack gave a little snort of a laugh. "Not going to happen."

Her dragon grinned then leaned down and kissed her goodbye. Adelle's eyes fluttered closed as she savored the taste of his warm, generous mouth one last time. When they parted, he rolled up the sleeve of her jean jacket and ran his thumb down the runes on her forearm. He opened his mouth to speak then seemed to think better of it and instead gave her a sad smile.

"I'll visit," he said.

"Best not to. I don't want you to risk getting..." She trailed off. His eyes were hard, determined, and glazed with the tears he forced back.

"I'll visit," he repeated with determination.

The corners of her mouth turned up into a little smile.

For a moment that felt altogether too short, they held each other until Adelle dragged herself away. When she looked back across the security stanchions, Jack held his thumb and forefinger up to the side of his head, mouthing the words "call me". A crooked grin ghosted across his mouth. The image stayed etched in her mind the entire flight home.

The spring air was unseasonably hot and sticky in San Diego. As soon as she stepped out to the Airport's curb, every curl went limp and humidity slathered itself over her. Already she was longing for the constant crisp chill of Whitmore on her skin.

True to her word, Adelle called Jack the minute she set foot in San Diego. After a promise that she'd call Jack back when she was settled, she spotted her sister's black Thunderbird, Freya, purring in the white zone. Adelle hung up and hurried her travel weary feet to the car. She tossed her bag into the trunk and slid into the passenger seat where Valerie's apologetic smile waited for her.

"How'd he take it?" she asked.

"Better than most," Adelle said.

"Really? I figured him to be a tantrum thrower."

"Well it's not like he wasn't upset. He was. But he understood I had to come home."

Valerie let out a sigh and nodded as Freya's engine roared back to life. Tires squealed and they took off towards the freeway.

Adelle ran a hand through her hair. "There's something else."

Valerie smirked. "You're pregnant."

Adelle rolled her eyes. "No. He claimed me." The screech of the breaks split Adelle's eardrums. She lurched forward, slamming a hand on the dash before her forehead did. "Jeeze, Val! What the hell?!"

"He claimed you? Are you serious?! You're mated to him now? "

"How come I'm the only one who had no idea about this claiming business?"

"Because you never did your homework when you were younger." Valerie bared her teeth. "Did he force you into it? Because if he did-"

Adelle waved a hand in her sister's face. "No! No one forced anyone into anything. I said I wanted it. He claimed me, then last night..." She rubbed the back of her neck and sunk into her seat, afraid of Valerie's reaction to her next confession. "I claimed him back." Valerie's astonished stare burrowed through her. Instead of more squirming, Adelle pulled her shoulders back and looked her straight in the eye. "What? I told you I loved him."

"I know I'm just shocked that out of the three of us, you were the one who was claimed by a dragon. I mean, well you seemed so adamant on ignoring the Wyrd that..." She finished her sentence with a noncommittal shrug, pulling Freya back onto the road. "You've changed. For the better, I think."

Those words mulled through her head. Adelle had changed. Before Whitmore, she was a scared little girl wrapped up in layers and layers of hard rock. A whole decade spent in denial, wishing she was just a plain human with a plain life. Now she was returning to San Diego having won the love of a fierce dragon and proud of her siren's blood. College aged Adelle would have had a coronary if she knew this was coming.

"I know," Adelle said.

Valerie gave her a warm smile. After a beat, she asked, "So, how does a siren claim its mate?"

Adelle felt her face flush. "I glow when making love."

A dark brow arched high as Valerie's eyes slid towards Adelle. "You glow?"

"Yup. Glow. White. Hot. Glowing. Swirling winds. The works." She grinned as Valerie looked suddenly uncomfortable.

Valerie gulped. "Damn. Jack must be epic in the sack."

Adelle's boot barely touched the porch when Phoebe barreled out the front door, the screen bouncing behind her with a loud thunk. She flung her arms around her neck and the two went toppling back into Valerie. Luckily, Valerie had the strength and consciousness to brace herself before the three of them tumbled down the steps.

"Dell! I missed you so much!" Phoebe said as she smashed her cheek against hers. The affection lightened Adelle's mood.

Phoebe buried Adelle in tons of questions as they walked through the door. What was Washington like? How was Wendy's business doing? What the hell did Wendy do for a living, anyway? Her bubbly voice continued to chatter about school as well as the bear incident. When Adelle asked if it happened again and she said no, Adelle sighed in relief. But that meant Valerie hadn't told her about her powers yet.

Oh, lordy.

"Val said you were totally into a guy up in Washington," Phoebe giggled. Adelle's face flushed a bright pink. "Is it true? And is he cute?"

She took a deep breath then nodded. "Kind of. Yeah"

"Kind of true or kind of cute?"

"Kind of true and he isn't cute as much as…" *Panty droppingly masculine? Epically sexy?* "Rugged."

A much better word than cute.

Phoebe cocked her head to the side. "So, why didn't he come back with you?"

Adelle pursed her lips. How was she going to explain that? Well, she could say that she had fallen in love with a nine-hundred-year-old dragon that couldn't follow her home due to being in danger of an epic karmic curse if he dabbled in their business. Since Phoebe didn't know that dragons even existed, she stuck with a standard, but vague answer.

"It's complicated," Adelle said.

Phoebe nodded in understanding. "Ah. So he dumped you." She replied in a sage voice.

"What? No!"

"You dumped him?"

"No! No one dumped anyone!"

"Then what do you mean? When someone says it's complicated it means someone is getting dumped." Phoebe wagged a finger at her. Adelle glanced over to Valerie who had been snickering from the couch the entire conversation.

Thanks for the support, sis. Adele rolled her eyes.

"He owns a business up there," Adelle said, "But he'll probably come and visit later on."

"Ah, okay. I see." Phoebe smiled then turned to head over to the kitchen. Adelle watched she cup a hand against her face and mouth the word "Dumped" to Valerie before slipping out of the room.

Days turned into weeks, then into months. Adelle called Jack every night, his low voice comforting her. Each call ended with Jack saying, "I love you, Buttercup. I'll see you soon," even though soon wasn't going to happen. Three months had already passed with no sign of resolution. But "I'll see you soon" did sound better than "Goodbye".

Afterwards, Adelle would bury herself under her quilt and pretend that sleep would come easy. It never did. She spent most of her nights with her eyes half closed, remembering Jack's protective body nestled beside her and his warm breath on her neck as he snored. She missed his calloused hand on her hip and his masculine smell of sandalwood and smoke. Now that he was gone, sleeping was a chore. On the outside, she was the usual Adelle; smiles and sharp words with both feet firmly grounded. She hid her longing under a thick façade of calm. Though she was aware of what would happen if she held in her emotions, it was vital to keep Valerie's moral up, especially after Tony's trail ran cold.

Every night Valerie would hit the streets, asking questions and looking for clues. She was pulling her hair out over Tony's sudden return and just as sudden disappearance. After the church fires, there were no sightings and no more chaos. Not a single peep. Valerie would return, enraged, taking it out on the punching bag hung that in the garage. Tony's betrayal tore them all to pieces but it was the hardest on her.

Valerie still didn't want Adelle out on patrol, fearing that she was at risk. So, Adelle stayed in and researched for answers. Cybil had books and journals that filled most of the three storied home and a good chunk of the attic. Plus, the internet helped fill in the blanks.

Books were fanned around the coffee table and couch, surrounding Adelle with pages and pages of Wyrd knowledge. It was enough to make her head spin with over saturation. Valerie dragged herself in through the front door, dark angry circles under her eyes and her ebony hair falling from its ponytail in wispy strands.

"Where's the Pheebs?" she asked.

"Out at the clubs with her girlfriends," Adelle said. "So, I spread out here for the night. Still nothing?"

Valerie threw her purse onto the dining room table. It skidded across its surface and onto the ground with an angry crash. "Still nothing!" With an aggravated sigh, she stormed to the couch and flopped down beside Adelle. "No sign of him. All these sightings, a big blow out, then nothing. I thought the church burnings were done to drive you out of hiding. I was sure of it. But now, I'm starting to think that maybe Tony was after something else. And that maybe he found it and took off." Valerie grunted a tangled thread of curse words, banging the back of her head against the couch.

"I think you're partially right," Adelle said. "I think Tony was looking for something else other than me. But I don't think he's found it yet." She thumbed through one of Cybil's leather bound journals. "Mom kept massive relic lists. And she updated it whenever anything was moved, added or destroyed."

Valerie groaned and rubbed her temples. "I've seen that list before, Dell."

"Yeah, but did you see the other lists she made after this one?"

Valerie sat up ramrod straight, anger forgotten. "How many?" she asked.

Adelle gestured to the books that covered the coffee table in front of them. "I found them buried at the bottom of her hope chest, under her habit."

Valerie stiffened. "You went into mom's hope chest?" Her voice quivered. That hope chest held Cybil's mementos from when she wore the veil. To Valerie, it was sacred.

"You know she wouldn't have minded," Adelle said.

Valerie let out a long breath between her clenched lips then nodded, regaining herself. She took the journal into careful hands. "So, what am I looking at?"

"The three churches that were torched, all three of them at one time possessed the same relic." Adelle reached over and tapped the page Valerie read. "This relic. And it's a doozy."

Valerie's hazel eyes grew wide and she clenched the journal in her fingers. "You are shitting me," she whispered.

"I don't think Mom was joking when she wrote that."

"The Holy Lance?!"

"The Spear of Destiny, yup."

Modern churches in the states secretly guarded powerful relics, like the Spear of Destiny. Considering most people assumed such things were kept in ancient cathedrals, no one searched a small town church for a holy relic. No one, until Tony. Cybil had tons of contacts within the San Diego churches and kept lists of each sacred item. Since her death, the lists went out of date but Adelle still found them useful.

Adelle scooted over to Valerie. "The spear hopped around for years between these three churches. *St. Joseph's Cathedral*, *Our Lady of the Sacred Heart*, and *Our Lady of Angels*. Then after going back and forth between Sacred Heart and St. Joseph's, it ended up at *The Immaculate Conception* for a while. That one almost caught fire like the others."

"So, you think it may still be there?" Valerie arched a dark brow as she rubbed her chin.

"Possibly. I think Tony was using process of elimination. But here's the thing." Adelle tapped a couple sentences written in the journal's margin. "Mom wrote this note. 'Spear given to A.R.'. After that, the spear isn't tracked anymore."

"Could A.R. be another church?" Valerie asked.

"Not likely. I can't think of any churches in the county that have the initials A and R in them."

"Then maybe A.R. is someone who works at *The Immaculate Conception*? A priest maybe."

"Could be. Guess I can do a search on the sta- Where are you going?"

Valerie had sprung her feet. "Going to go check out the church," she said as she slung her purse over her shoulder.

Adelle stared at her. "At almost two in the morning? Val, I'm pretty sure that no one is there."

"It's just a hunch," Valerie said. "Most of mom's connections weren't human. If the A.R. is in the Wyrd, then he or she might be awake. If not, no one will answer when I knock. Besides, aren't churches open twenty-four hours?"

"It's a church. Not a Taco Bell drive-thru."

Valerie waved an agitated hand in Adelle's direction, deliberately ignoring her remark. "I'm going."

"Can't it wait until morning? You're exhausted."

Valerie spun on her heels in a fury, her long ponytail swinging around her shoulders. "I am not letting Tony win!"

Adelle raised her hands in surrender as she rose to her feet. "Then you're not going alone."

"You're too much at risk, Dell."

"You're tired and when you're tired you don't think things through. Either we both go now, or I force you to stay here tonight and we go tomorrow." Valerie opened her mouth to protest when Adelle raised her chin and hardened her gaze. "Don't push me, Val," she said.

Valerie let out a long hiss of a breath then nodded. "Fine, get your shoes on."

The Immaculate Conception was the oldest church in the city, nestled right in the heart of the Old Town tourist area, not too far from the Constance home. It was a small church designed in the Spanish mission style that was prominent in San Diego.

The usually crowded streets of Old Town were deserted, occupied only by the buzz of the street lamps humming through the late night silence. Valerie cut Freya's roaring engine. As she pulled up in front of the church, Adelle pressed the white ear fobs of her iPod into her ears then turned her music on at a low level.

"What the hell," Valerie asked. "You planning on relaxing with your tunes while we're here?"

"I'm planning on being prepared. I need musical accompaniment," Adelle said. "Think I want to be caught off guard?"

Valerie considered a moment then nodded as if agreeing that it was a good decision. The two slipped out of the car. Their footsteps echoed in the empty streets as they approached the church, its white walls gleaming even in the dark of night. Valerie marched up to the large wooden doors, giving one a push and finding it was open. She looked over her shoulder to Adelle who still hovered by the car door.

"What I tell you?" She grinned and let herself in.

Adelle sighed with a shake of her head. "I can't believe that worked."

She was just about to start after her when the bright shine of headlights caught Adelle's figure. A car pulled up behind her, silhouetted in black by the glaring light. Adelle shielded her eyes as the petite shadow of the driver got out and slammed the car door.

"Phoebe?!"

Phoebe hesitated by her car a moment before scurrying onto the sidewalk. She was still dressed in her girls' night out attire, a black short skirt and a bright green V-neck sweater dotted with sequins. Her tall heels clicked with a fury as she stepped onto the sidewalk, teetered, and then stopped to regain her balance.

"What the hell are you doing out here?" Adelle demanded.

"What the hell are *you* doing out here?" Phoebe placed her hands on her hips. She teetered again then straightened, fixing

Adelle with a mean stare. "It's two in the morning! I was just pulling into the driveway when I saw you two driving off. What is going on?"

"Phoebe, now isn't a good time."

"It's never a good time, Dell! You two have been keeping things from me for years!"

"Phoebe-"

"Do you think I'm an idiot? That I just believe everything you and Val tell me? Because I don't! I just keep my mouth shut to keep the peace!"

Adelle clenched her jaw as Phoebe tapped her foot on the sidewalk. Each furious tap made Adelle's temples flinch.

Might as well come clean. It's now or never.

She began to speak but shut her mouth with an abrupt snap of her teeth when she saw movement over Phoebe's shoulder. Her sister's voice faded into white noise as three figures stalked towards them. Her eyes locked on the trio, her hands balling into fists.

"Dell! Are you even listening to me?" Phoebe cried.

Tony walked beside two others, his ivory cane clicking on the blacktop, echoing his steps. The man on the left was slender and lean with well combed blonde hair and glasses, clad in a conservative vest and khakis. The one in the middle was large and broad, in a long dark coat. A black fedora and scarf obscured his facial features.

"Get inside the church, Phoebe," Adelle said.

"What?" Phoebe looked over her shoulder, spotting the approaching men. Tony raised his cane high above his head. It surged bright with power, casting the three in blue shadows.

"Move!" Adelle shoved Phoebe away just as a crack of lightening arched from Tony's cane and smashed into the pavement where Phoebe once stood, scorching it black. Phoebe screamed.

"Run! Now!" Adelle shouted at her.

Phoebe dashed down the sidewalk, her heels twisting under her feet. She stumbled then picked herself up, kicking her shoes off and leaving them behind.

"Get Val!" Adelle shouted, not taking her eyes off the three men closing in on her. Her shout shook the ground, making the three stop in their tracks.

Adelle snagged her iPod out of her back pocket and slipped out of her flip flops, grounding her bare feet onto the pavement. The power she called tore through the street in jagged glowing lines, shooting through her, setting her eyes a flame.

Charged, ready to explode.

She took a deep breath, cranked the volume up on her iPod, and belted a song. Waves of blue and white power tidal waved over the trio. Tony and the blonde man tumbled backwards from the force, but the covered man leaned his shoulder into the storm. He stomped his feet down with a thunderous echo. His shoes cut grooves into the blacktop as her song pushed him back. Step after plodding step, he inched his way closer as if wading through waist deep mud. Adelle furrowed her brow, singing the second lyric, her eyes blazing.

Tony and the other man clung to a lamp post blocks away, struggling to stay alive in Adelle's violent storm. Through her haloed vision, she saw the covered man creep closer. His long coat began to spark and burn at the edges and his leather gloves crumbled away from his fingers. Yet he kept coming. Adelle heard Phoebe pounding at the church doors. She didn't know they were unlocked and Adelle couldn't stop singing to tell her.

"Val! Oh, God! Help!" Phoebe cried as her fists pummeled the hardwood over and over.

The mage was right before her now. Adelle gritted her teeth. She willed the power back to her. White veins of magic crackled through the pavement, lifting Adelle up from the street and into the air. She shot another chorus at the mage, raining swirling winds of light down upon him. Finally, he stumbled back, clutching his wrist with a low angry growl.

Got him!

She took a deep breath, preparing to finish him off. The mage fell to one knee, hat blowing off to reveal a thick mane of jet black hair. A grey scarf covered the rest of his face. He turned his hidden face to Adelle and she could have sworn she saw him grin beneath that scarf before he threw his hands toward her.

Clouds of ash swirled from the sleeves of his long coat. It wafted up into the air, dusting Adelle's jeans and catching in her eyelashes before landing in tall piles below her feet. She coughed, eyes burning as the grey flakes choked the song from her. Then she felt a violent tugging at her ankles. Adelle looked down to find hands reaching up out of the piles of ash, grabbing for her. The dust formed into decayed bodies. Adelle kicked one in the face. It exploded in a cloud of dust. She took a breath and screamed at another, crumbling it to ashes.

As Adelle fought, she saw another pile appear, then another, then another, all growing into lifeless bodies. Eyeless faces opened their mouths wide in silent screams. Countless hands reached for her with gnarled fingers, yellowed nails twisting into her hair. She screeched again, aiming her voice at anything that stumbled in her way. But with every ghoul she destroyed, two more came to take its place.

"Dell!" She heard Valerie scream.

But Adelle was unable to answer, buried deep under a sea of grey stinking flesh. She clawed through the mass, fighting her way towards the small sliver of sky that peeked through the haze of dead bodies. The whistling sound of metal could be heard and she saw her sister's hand reach for her own. Adelle stretched painfully for it, the ghouls yanking her down.

"Val!" Adelle bit the fingers off a ghoul's hand as it tried to cover her mouth. She spat out the ashes as it dissolved. "Val! I'm here!" A high pitched scream made Valerie's hand jerked away, their fingertips only brushing.

"No! Get away from her!" she heard Valerie shout.

Panic clutched Adelle's heart.

They're going after Phoebe.

Adelle struggled, trying to wrench herself from the pit of ghouls only to be pushed down further, smashed until her lungs couldn't hold any more air. She fought but hundreds of hands covered her face, smothering her. Her head slammed against the ground and sickly green stars swam around her eyes. With her last breath, her howl tore through hands, severing wrists and fingers into grey puffs before she fell. The screams of her sisters filled her ears, before her vision went black.

Chapter 29

The phone hadn't rung in days. Adelle was religious about calling Jack, though the times varied, but once a day his cell phone rang without fail. It was only the reason he used his cell phone now, to make sure he never missed a call. Jack was damn eager to contact Adelle. After doing a little research with the local witches and their countless amounts of ancient books, Jack had found a loophole. Being officially bonded as mates meant his vow of protection would override the forces that could backfire on him. As long as he protected just Adelle and did nothing to get involved with the sisters' work, they could be together. He was chomping at the bit for her phone call, ready to surprise her with the news.

But the phone never rang.

Jack's stomach was in knots. At first he chalked it up to being paranoid and over excited. The sunset on day two and still no phone call. He called her. It went straight to voicemail and that's when he started to worry. He left a few voicemails for her. One that morning:

"Buttercup it's me. Call me back, I have great news. Love you."

One four hours later:

"Baby, where are you? Call me as soon as you get this."

And one eight hours later:

"Dell... I'm worried."

Maybe she had caught the flu and was resting up. Perhaps her smartphone had finally busted and she couldn't get a new one right away. Then Jack wondered if he said something to upset her last time they spoke. That couldn't have been it. Their last conversation was one of their 'special' conversations that ended with orgasms on both sides of the phone. Heartfelt I love yous were exchanged before they hung up. No. She wasn't mad and Adelle wasn't the moody type who would ignore his call if she was. She'd lay right into him. Something was wrong. Very wrong.

On the third day, Jack tried calling Valerie. When her phone went straight to voicemail as well, an acidic, bubbling unease threatened to push bile up into his throat. Something bad had happened to the Constance sisters. Jack was sure of it. For all he knew, Adelle was dead or dying.

No! No, don't think like that. She's alive. She's stronger than that.

His first instinct was to get to San Diego and tear that city apart until he found her. But San Diego was ten times bigger than Whitmore. He would be searching for weeks, maybe even months. Lord only knew what could happen to her by then. He didn't even have her address. Adelle wanted to keep the temptation of getting involved as far away from him as possible so she never told him. Damn him for agreeing to that one. He should have put his foot down.

Why didn't I sneak a tracking spell-

His eyelid twitched. Adelle's rune tattoo. Jack had memorized it, spent so many times idly tracing over the black ink with his fingers. He could find her through her tattoo. Unfortunately, his rune knowledge was only the bare basics. He had to find the exact ones to work for his dragon's blood or he'd be back to square one. A mage would need to help him. He was afraid it would come to this, but Adelle's life was far more important than his bruised pride. Without a second thought, Jack yanked out his cell phone and dialed.

"Hello?" Wendy's sweet voice answered.

"It's me," Jack said. "I need a favor."

"Me? Who is this?" Her tone was soaked in sarcasm. "This couldn't be Jack, could it? He was so *very* rude to me the last time we spoke."

Jack's face flushed with anger. "You owe me after digging in my head instead of being honest. Now either you help me or I'm coming over to make you help me."

Wendy let out a sharp laugh. "I don't owe you anything."

"Then you owe your cousin after dumping her ass when she first got here."

"Adelle's a big girl who can take care of herself."

"She's missing, Wendy."

He expected Wendy to laugh and hang up. Instead, a tense silence rang in his ears until it was interrupted by Wendy's quivering intake of breath. "Missing?" she asked.

"Adelle is missing. Valerie is missing. I'm going to assume the youngest is gone too," Jack growled. "Do I have your attention now?"

"You do," Wendy said. "Do you know what happened to them?"

"You actually give a damn?"

Wendy's voice went cold when she replied, "Just because my cousins can irritate me doesn't mean they're not family. What do you need?"

Jack sighed in relief. Finally, he was getting somewhere. "I need to know everything you know about tracking runes. Then we're going to Floyd's."

Chapter 30

The throbbing pain in her head forced Adelle to open her eyes. Every inch of her body ached as she pushed herself up to her knees, arms shaking. Through half silted lids, she tried to focus on the dim, cold room. Grey cinder blocks made up the walls and the floor was clean swept cement. There were no windows and a single brown door sat across from her. The damp chill made Adelle assume she was in a basement.

She reached up and gingerly pressed a hand against the back of her head, wincing as it began to throb harder. It didn't feel like she was bleeding though. The ghouls must have slammed her head against the sidewalk. A sad little groan slipped from her lips.

"Dell, are you awake?"

Valerie's whisper pulled her out of her pain hangover. Adelle found her sitting in the far corner of the room legs crossed, her brows furrowed with deep worry. About four feet away, Phoebe was curled on her side, hugging her knees to her chest. Her eyes were open with a vacant stare. Adelle's heart started pounding as she pushed herself to wobbling feet to get to her.

"Adelle, don't-" Valerie started.

The air around Adelle flashed blue and her face smashed into a sold, invisible force. She stumbled back with a yelp and fell onto her behind, clutching her nose.

"What the hell?!" Adelle shouted as she touched her nostrils. She looked to the tips of her fingers, relieved to not find any blood.

"As I was saying," Valerie said, "Don't get up. They put us in fae glass."

Adelle put a hand up, moving it forward until it touched the invisible glass. A blue glow appeared under her fingertips as they pressed against its smooth cold surface. She'd heard of the stuff before. Fae glass was created to contain other creatures of the Wyrd. It was invisible, practically impenetrable, and hard to obtain. Somehow, these mages had managed to get their hands on some. Tony had some powerful friends. Adelle looked to Valerie again.

"Where are we?" she asked.

Valerie blinked then leaned forward. "What?"

Adelle furrowed her brow and said louder, "I said, where are we?"

Valerie continued to stare at Adelle with confusion until she shook her head. "Shit. It looks like they put a silence spell on your cell. I can't hear a word you say."

Adelle frowned. Apparently, Tony didn't want to chance her being powerful enough to break through fae glass. That meant that she probably could. The question was how much force was it going to take?

"You were out for a while. A day or two, I think. I was getting worried," Valerie said.

Adelle gritted her teeth then glanced back over to Phoebe who was still catatonic. She pointed to her and looked back to Valerie who shook her head.

"I think she's in shock. The ghouls came to life. There was some magic slinging and she just couldn't handle it." Valerie bit her lower. "She'll be fine. She's a strong kid. But we have to get her out of here."

Adelle wholeheartedly agreed on that point. Phoebe had to get out. They all did. How, was the question. The door creaked open and a crack of light spilled out across the room and into Adelle's eyes. The sudden brightness made her wince and she lifted a hand to shield her eyes as Tony walked into their prison.

"You're awake," he said, closing the door to the light behind him.

Adelle scowled, wanting to let loose a string of curse words at him. She held them back only because she knew he couldn't hear them.

Tony leaned his cane against the wall by the door then walked over, kneeling down beside Adelle. His hand pressed against her fae glass cell, causing it to glow. Cast in that humming blue light, he looked tired. Tired and afraid. His shirt was half untucked, his trousers were wrinkled, and his dark hair was hanging in his face. The haggard appearance set Adelle's already frayed nerves on edge and the hairs on her arm stood up in warning.

"How are you feeling?" he asked her, rubbing his fingers along the bridge of his nose.

"How do you think she's feeling, jackass?" Valerie snapped from across the room. "You almost killed her."

Tony turned his dark gaze to Valerie. "You always did exaggerate, Val. It's just a bump on the head."

A bump that felt like a fat guy was standing on her neck. Adelle shook her head and leaned away from Tony, pulling her knees up to her chest.

"I don't care if it was a paper cut," Valerie said. Her voice was low, calm, and deadly. "You hurt my sisters. You're a dead man."

"Val," Tony said. "If you didn't have the nerve to kill me when Cybil died-"

"A mistake I intend to fix. And you're never allowed to call me Val again."

"Out of respect for what we had-"

"Had. That's the key word. You're nothing to me now."

Tony visibly winced at Valerie's words. He looked back to Adelle, softening his gaze to her. "Adelle, I know near the end of things we didn't see eye to eye..."

Adelle rolled her eyes. That was an understatement. Tony and Adelle were known to bicker. After he killed Cybil, it was all out war. The last time she saw Tony, Adelle had shot him in the shoulder with her crossbow and told him to never cross their threshold again.

"We need your voice," Tony said. "A sample is all. Just do what Shadow asks. You do that; you and your sisters will be set free."

Adelle turned a scrutinizing gaze onto him and gritted her teeth. Her face flushed hot and rage began to build inside her, pushing her heart into a fast thrum. Tony sent the vampires after her. He killed their mother. That turncoat son of a bitch was the one who put Phoebe in a comatose state. She could scream and test these walls around her to see if they could contain a siren's rage, then woe betide Tony.

No, Dell. They want your voice. They may even have your cell rigged to collect it. Don't give it to them.

She swallowed down her anger. Instead she extended her right hand, and then extended a middle finger with a smirk. Tony's mouth dropped into a deep frown. He pounded his fist against the fae glass, the small cell pulsing blue from the blow.

"I'm trying to get you three out alive!" he said. "You need to cooperate!"

"You got her answer," Valerie said.

"Stay out of this!"

"Fuck you!"

Tony whirled towards Valerie. "How do you think you and Phoebe are still alive? They don't need you two. They need Dell.

You're alive because I told them to keep you alive. There by the grace of *me* go *you*, Valerie Constance!"

Valerie's eyes narrowed, burning with rage. "You never cared about us! Why the hell would you even want to get us out alive?"

Tony glared at Valerie. He took in a deep ragged breath. "Because… I still lo-"

The door opened again and a click of a switch brought flickering fluorescent lights on overhead. The slender blonde man from the previous battle entered. He looked like the academic type: tall, slender, and clad in a conservative vest, button down shirt, and tie all in somber greys. Under his arm was a clear glass mason jar. The man stopped in in mid step, arching a brow in an impassive curious way.

"What are you doing here, Anthony?" he asked.

Tony straightened his posture, smoothing his hair back from his forehead. He tore his eyes from Valerie, face draining of its passion, masking over with a cold smile. "Good evening, Adam. I'm trying to convince the siren to be cooperative." He reached up, buttoning the collar of his shirt.

"And how is that going for you?" Adam asked.

"Unfortunately, she's chosen to do things the hard way."

Adam watched Tony, his face like stone. "It's a waste of your time. Move along. I will take it from here."

"I thought that Shadow would be here to-"

"Shadow has things to attend to. I will be acting in his stead."

Valerie sat up, pressing her hands against the walls of her cell. "What are you going to do to her?" she demanded.

Adam ignored Valerie as he approached, looking down at Adelle as if examining a new species of insect. There was no soul in those eyes, just two sky blue irises as lifeless as a doll's boring down on her with their emptiness. Adelle bit the inside of her cheek to keep herself from turning away in fear.

"What are you going to do?" Tony asked.

"What I need to do to get what Shadow wants," Adam said, placing the Mason jar down beside his feet. "How I get it is entirely up to her. Are you staying to watch?" He unbuttoned his starched white shirt cuffs to roll them up.

With an uncertain nod, Tony said, "Yes."

Tony's dark eyes shifted to Adelle and he gave her a tiny shake of his head. Whatever this Adam was going to do, it frightened Tony pale. He body went cold.

"Don't you hurt her!" Valerie shouted from across the room. She pounded her fists against the fae glass over and over with angry blue flashes. "Don't touch her! I will fucking end you if you touch her!"

Adam's reaction was only to roll his eyes. He finished rolling his sleeves above his elbow. "Can you please put a silencer on that harpy's cell? I need to concentrate."

Tony strode to his cane, snatched it up from where it leaned against the wall, and headed back to Valerie. With two quick taps of the glass, Valerie's shouts were silenced. The lump in Adelle's throat grew, choking wheezes out from her. Valerie's voice was all she had left to cling to for strength. Now, she would face Adam alone.

Adam waved a hand in front of the cell, muttering a few words under his breath. "You're free to speak now," he said.

Adelle wet her parched lips. "What do you want?"

"It's not what I want. It's what my cabal leader, Shadow wants."

"Who the hell is Shadow?"

A corner of Adam's mouth curled up ever so slightly. "The gentleman you didn't topple over the other night when we came to collect you."

Her memory returned to the mage who had fought his way through her storm of power. Adelle gritted her teeth. "Fine then. What does this Shadow guy want?"

"Your voice. Or just the essence that comes from it. I need you to bring forth that magic so I may collect a piece of it for him."

Adelle looked past him to Valerie. She was still beating her fists against the walls of her cell. Her mouth twisted in silent screams as she tried to fight her way out, to no success.

"Now then," Adam continued. "I have two ways of collecting this from you. You can either scream willingly for me, or I make you scream." Adelle's teeth chomped down on the inside of her cheek, palms sweaty as she clenched them tight. "I assure you, it will not be in a good way," Adam said.

"If I cooperate, will you let my sisters go?"

"Yes," Tony said. He was vetoed by Adam's slow shake of his head.

"I'm sorry. But it is too much of a risk to release them," Adam said. "But rest assured, they will be taken care of quickly and painlessly."

Her heart plummeted to the pit of her stomach. Panic bubbled up in her gut as her mind whirled for an exit, a Hail Mary play, anything, but she could see the verdict in those cold shark's eyes of his. Stalling him was the only option. Maybe Valerie could come up with a plan while she was keeping him busy. Adelle took a shaky breath and steeled herself for the onslaught. She raised her chin, narrowing her gaze one the dead eyed man.

"Bring it," she growled under her breath.

Adam cracked his knuckles and shook out his wrists. He placed a hand on the fae glass and tilted his head, studying her in a placid manner. His eyes flashed white for a brief second. "I need you to scream, please," he said like doctor, asking her to take a breath while he listened through a stethoscope.

Adelle was about to tell him to go fuck himself, when every bone in her body felt like it was twisting and snapping into millions of pieces. Her eyes went wide and she buckled to the floor. The urge to scream rose in her throat, but Adelle bit into her lower lip letting out nothing but a muffled groan.

"One more time, then," Adam said.

Another spasm of agony crashed through her, twisting her guts into knots. Her fingers curled, nails cutting into the palms of her hands. Her teeth chomped harder into her lower lip. Blood dripped into her mouth and onto her tongue, warm and metallic. She slammed her eyes shut as tears rolled down her cheeks. The seconds felt like hours as he continued to bring convulsion after convulsion of misery through her. Yet Adelle still refused to scream out loud.

Don't give in. Do it for Val. Do it for Phoebe. Please Val, think of something!

"The subject is strong willed," Adam said.

"She was always the stubbornest of the three," Tony replied.

"Once again."

It felt as if someone had taken hold of her spinal cord and yanked it from her body. Sweat poured down her face as her breaths came is short, desperate hisses through her teeth. Adelle writhed on the ground, blood dribbling from her mouth, praying for the pain to go away. But it kept thundering through her. Her eyes were on fire. Her flesh burned and sizzled from the inside out. One scream and the pain would stop. Everything would stop.

No!

"Seems you have a tall threshold," Adam said as he continued to twist her body in unholy ways. "We could do this for hours. Would it be faster if your sisters took your place?"

Adelle's prickling eyes opened. Her heart pounded so hard, she was convinced it would explode. She clenched her jaw tight, threatening to break all of her teeth as she shook her head.

"No?" Adam asked. "You don't want that?"

Adelle let out a strained moan as she shook her head hard again. Beads of sweat whipped from her cheeks and splattered against the invisible cell walls as her body pulsed in torment. She arched as if her ribcage had burst open, the heels of her bare feet scraping over the rough, cold concrete until they were raw.

"No," she whimpered.

"I'll start with the younger one then," Adam said.

"No," Adelle repeated, begging him. "Please."

"She seems to be awake enough now to comprehend what she'll be going through," Adam said.

"No!" Adelle screamed.

The tortured power burst from her chest, exploding in the air with blinding flashes. White waves of light flowed from her mouth, seeping through the fae glass around Adam's hand. Adam closed his eyes as the power formed into a glowing white orb. He curled his fingers around it, then stooped down, picked up the Mason jar, and placed it inside, screwing the lid back on.

"Thank you," Adam said, admiring his work. "Shadow will be pleased."

With a snap of his fingers, the pain stopped. Adelle flopped onto her back, panting hard, her face drenched with sweat and tears. Choked sobs of relief spilled from her bloody lips. Her eyes flicked to her sisters, praying Valerie was fighting her way out of her cell. But she had not committed a grand escape. Her sister was too stricken with horror, tears streaming down her face. Phoebe had come to now, pale and shaking. They were trapped. They all were going to die.

Adelle rolled onto her stomach, still struggling to breathe. Anger heated her blood and she gritted her teeth. She pushed herself up, leaving bloody handprints on the cement under her.

"Like hell, we will," she snarled under her breath.

Her rage surged forward, eyes glowing white, fingernails dragging across the cement. She hunched her shoulders and threw her head back, letting out a hate fueled screech of fury. The walls shook like paper and the floor rippled, sending Tony and Adam stumbling. Even Adam looked surprised by the sudden force of her wail. White and blue mist whipped about her in a tornado. The fae glass webbed with glowing cracks and shattered, crumbling down around her in pulsing shards.

Adelle climbed to her feet, dragging her aching body towards the mages one slow step at a time, growling, snarling, voice twisting with menace. Magical clouds of her anger whirled in a frenzied storm as she lumbered forward. Adam lifted a hand with the promise of another pain curse but the spell didn't penetrate the force that swirled around her.

"Don't touch my sisters," Adelle hissed as she balled her bloody hands. Her eyes were orbs of white light, crimson hair floating off her shoulders like wild flames.

She was a siren's fury.

Tony pointed his ivory cane, shooting an arc of lightning towards her chest. Adelle threw her hands up, forming a dense shield, deflecting the bolt into the walls. Sparks flew and the lights flickered. Another mighty scream cracked the air, making the concrete undulate like water. Valerie and Phoebe had just enough time to cover their heads before their fae glass cells shattered over them.

Valerie jumped to her feet and lunged for Tony with a shout. A triumphant grin curled around her lips as her fingers caught his cane. She yanked it free from his grip and swung with relentless ferocity, missing Tony by centimeters as he dodged, desperate to get away. He stumbled back into Adam, pushing them both into Adelle's path.

Adelle wanted nothing but to feel the cold satisfaction of tearing them apart, limb by limb. She'd start with Adam so Tony knew what was in store for him.

It would be slow.

It would be painful.

It would be glorious.

Tony reached down into his shirt collar and pulled out a gold amulet on a chain around his neck. The chain snapped with a yank of his arm.

Adam snagged a hold of Tony as he said, "Code Romero."

At those words, Tony held the amulet in the air and shouted. "Eo Ire Itum!"

With a loud crack and the smell of sulfur, they vanished. Valerie threw the ivory cane, trying to nail one in a final blow, but it passed right through them, breaking in two as it hit the far wall.

"Dammit!" Valerie screamed. "Goddamned sons of a bitches got away!"

When the mages vanished, the storm evaporated in the air. Adelle's insides felt icy as black and green spots swam about her eyes. She pressed a hand against the wall to steady herself.

"Phoebe," Adelle whimpered. "Where's Phoebe?"

No sooner did the words leave her mouth; she spotted her little sister huddled in the far dark corner of the room. Phoebe was curled up on her side, eyes shut tight. Valerie was beside her before Adelle even could move. It was a good thing too, she felt like she would collapse if she took one more step. Taking her into her arms, Valerie hugged Phoebe close, rocking her back and forth. Phoebe buried her face against Valerie's shoulder, fingers curling into her shirt sleeves.

“It’s all right Pheebs,” Valerie said. “It’s all right. You’re going to be fine.”

“Is she okay?” Adelle demanded, trying to stay up on shaking legs.

Phoebe raised her face up from Valerie’s shoulder. She looked between her sisters, face pale, body trembling. “That was kind of cool,” she whimpered.

Valerie grinned and smothered Phoebe in a tight bear hug, stroking her short hair. “She’s good!”

A cross between a sob and a laugh trembled from Adelle’s mouth as she slipped to her knees. Her vision tunneled as she felt herself falling. Every ounce of adrenaline in her body drained and her cheek hit the cold concrete. The room faded into nothingness.

Chapter 31

The heavy smell of smoke was thick in her nostrils. Adelle groaned and opened her stinging eyes to find she was hanging a good six feet off the ground, her body draped over Valerie's shoulder. Valerie had one arm hooked over Adelle's waist as she sprinted up a tall staircase. Phoebe was directly behind them, clutching Tony's broken ivory cane in both hands, taking two steps at a time to keep up with their long legged sister.

"What the hell?" Adelle groaned.

"Hi Dell," Phoebe said giving her a timid wave of a hand.

"You were out for five minutes," Valerie said, reaching the door at the top of the stairs. The smell of smoke grew stronger. "I would have let you rest if those assholes didn't decide to torch the place."

Adelle shook off the fog in her head as the ashy stench grew stronger. "What?"

Valerie kicked open the door. Dense clouds of smoke billowed in, shrouding the three sisters in black, followed by an intense heat and the sharp crackling of flames. Adelle coughed, trying to get the oily vapors out of her lungs. Valerie deposited her onto her feet and guided down to her knees below the haze.

"You strong enough to crawl?" Valerie asked.

Adelle's vision swirled. She pressed a hand against her head, eyes watering from the smoke. "Crawl?" She gasped as another unhealthy dose of smoke entered her lungs. Over Valerie's shoulder she spied a large modern living room engulfed in tall orange flames.

"Under the smoke. Can you crawl?" Valerie said through the coughs and sputters.

Adelle was feeling too woozy to crawl through that heat. If they waited on her, they would all burn in no time. Adelle looked between her sisters, then back to the blazing living room. She clenched her jaw then snagged both of their arms.

"Wait a sec. I have a faster way," she said.

Phoebe and Valerie had just enough time to look surprised before Adelle sang a cracked, yet loud trill of scales and summoned her powers back. Her magic rose around the three, clearing their air and diminishing the burn. Standing, she pulled her sisters up, singing her scales over and over. Adelle jerked her head to signal them to start walking. Flames licked around them, threatening their flesh with its blistering heat as they dashed arm and arm through the flames towards the foyer and the front door. Phoebe let out a little squeak of fear as they pressed on. Smoke bowed away from the white and blue tornado that protected them. Valerie kicked the front door open and pulled them all out to the blissfully clean, cool air outside. They fell onto soft grass, panting and coughing.

With a deep breath to clear her lungs, Adelle looked over her shoulder and saw a beautiful two story home smoldering from the inside. Yellow and orange flames flickered within the windows. Soon, the whole structure would be consumed. The courtyard they sat in was surrounded by a tall wrought iron fence. The gate to the gravel drive stood a good one hundred yards away. A quick look to the left and right showed no neighbors within earshot, just rocky hills surrounding them.

"I didn't know you could use your powers as a shield too," Valerie panted beside her.

"Until today, neither did I," Adelle said.

Valerie gave her a smirk then pushed herself to her feet. "My sword is probably still inside there. I can't leave without it,"

"What?" Phoebe cried, "Are you crazy? You're not going back in there!"

Valerie stretched her hand high above her head and in a commanding voice shouted, "To me!"

One of the bay windows shattered as Valerie's silver bladed sword crashed through the glass, hilt first. The metal was still steaming when she caught it effortlessly in her open hand.

Phoebe gasped, pressing her hands against her mouth; her blue eyes wide. "Did you... Did you do that?"

Adelle shook her head. "Show off."

Valerie rolled her eyes then nodded to the gates. "I can probably hotwire one of the cars out front to get us home. I think we're somewhere in Jamul judging by the hills. Those assholes should have had a better contingency plan. I'm guessing Code Romero means torch the bitches in Latin or something."

"Val," Phoebe said. "Isn't Romero the guy who did all those zombie movies?"

Phoebe's words turned on a gruesome light bulb. Adelle lifted her head and took a good look across the courtyard. Hundreds of ash piles were scattered around the lawn ominously illuminated in the flickering firelight from the house.

"Oh, shit," Adelle whispered. Her stomach felt as if someone had just pushed her off a forty story building.

Hundreds of ghouls began to rise. They moaned and stumbled, arms reaching for them. Adelle's heart pounded as she watched the horde surge forward.

"Oh shit is right," Valerie said. She raised her sword ready to strike. "And I don't think they're on a capture mission this time. Phoebe!" She jerked her head to a tall tree only a couple feet away. "Get up there, now!"

Phoebe didn't question Valerie, only dashed to the tree and shimmied up it like a squirrel. She let out a terrified squeak as she straddled a high branch, clinging to the ivory cane pieces and ready to swing them if a ghoul learned how to climb. Then she gave her a shaky thumbs up.

"You up to this fight, Dell?" Valerie asked. She locked on the first wave of hollow eyed dead lumbering toward them.

"Nope. But I don't have a choice."

What with the blow to her head, the torture, and the fight with Tony and Adam, Adelle was functioning on fumes and sheer will alone. She closed her eyes tight, willing another adrenaline rush to hit her. Valerie only gave a grim nod.

Adelle struggled to her feet. Her teeth were grinding with a fury as she clenched her bloodied fists. The ghouls grew closer, arms outstretched, grabbing for them with cracked yellowed fingers. Valerie let out a fierce scream and charged. She swung her sword and took the heads off three ghouls. Their bodies disintegrated only to be replaced by three more standing behind them.

Adelle braced herself on the grass as she called forth the power deep inside the earth. The forces were rich on this land. She could feel the vibrating pools of magic with the soles of her bare feet. This must have been one the mage's homes, to have this much power congregating underneath it. She took a deep breath then let out a scream that cracked the chilled night air in two.

Wind and light burst from her mouth, knocking down a large patch of ghouls and exploding them into dust. She turned and took down another patch before she was cut off with an exhausted cough. Her storm evaporated as Adelle tried to recover.

Another wave of ghouls moved their way, tightening their circle around the sisters. Adelle's energy was almost depleted. Sustaining long notes was impossible, so she concentrated her voice in small sharp bursts of sound, picking ghouls off one by one. Between the two of them, they managed to clear a circle around them. But the two of them wasn't going to be enough to fight this undead army.

"Pheebs," Adelle called toward tree. "We're going to need your help."

"My help?" Phoebe said in panic. She was perched up in the tree, whacking ghouls that crept too close with half a cane. "What can I do?!"

"You have to use your powers!"

"I don't have any powers!"

Adelle turned to Valerie, the line between her brows deepening from the frown she wore. "You *still* haven't told her?"

Due to their circumstances, she figured Valerie had broken the news to Phoebe in the basement. Granted, it would have been awkward but done.

"Told me what?" Phoebe cried.

"You couldn't tell her in the five minutes I was unconscious, Val?!"

"I was preoccupied with saving your ass, okay?!" Valerie growled as she cleaved a ghoul right down the middle. Ash exploded, covering her head to foot and she snarled with an angry curl of her lip. "This is not the time to be arguing this, Dell!"

"Tell me what?" Phoebe demanded as she whacked another ghoul to dust.

"Dammit, Val!" Adelle shouted, shattering two ghouls. She had to break the news to Phoebe. And there was no time to sugar coat the long kept secret for her poor baby sister.

"Phoebe," Adelle said in between explosive yelps. "You're not human."

"I'm not?"

"Not completely!" She screamed the words at a ghoul that reached for Valerie's head and sent it flying back into a pack of others. They evaporated in swirling clouds of grey. "Neither is Valerie. Neither am I."

"Well what am I?"

"You're half Dryad."

"What the hell is a Dryad?!"

"It's a wood sprite!" Valerie grunted as she chopped and sliced her way through four more ghouls.

"I'm a fairy? I'm a fucking fairy?!" Phoebe screamed.

Adelle groaned. She put her hands on her knees to catch her breath. "Phoebe, please."

"What am I supposed to do?! Sprinkle those things with fairy dust and tell them to think happy thoughts?!"

"Dammit Phoebe! Listen!" A ghoul's head popped into dust from the Adelle's anger. "You control nature! All of it! You're a powerhouse, trust me! Just try! Think about the tree you're in and what it can do to save us. Then make it do it!"

Phoebe went silent.

"Pheebs, you can do this. Don't be scared. Don't be like I was."

Still no response.

Adelle turned to make sure Phoebe was all right when gnarled fingers curled into her hair. They yanked her head back, tugging so hard she feared a chunk of her scalp would tear off. Valerie raised her sword, slicing through the grey flesh with a protective roar. Adelle grabbed at her hair, screaming loud enough to take out a few more ghouls that reached for her.

The ground rumbled, knocking Valerie off balance and thick tree roots, blackened with earth rose from the ground. The tendrils snaked around the ghoul that held Adelle and squeezed it so hard it popped into dust. Adelle stumbled forward as her hair was released, almost running into the tree face first. She let out a triumphant cackle and shouted, "That's my girl!" up to Phoebe.

Phoebe's hysterical voice answered, "I did it! I can't believe it!"

Clumsy roots crawled up from the dirt tripping and smothering the ghouls. Grey dust spewed into the air as more were mowed down. Phoebe's wild strength bought them enough time to regroup for the next wave, but her powers were raw and unrefined. No matter how hard they fought or how many they destroyed, the waves of the undead kept coming. Phoebe couldn't keep control and the roots disappeared under the soil, going dormant.

Piles of dead ash surrounded them but a hundred more lined up to take the place of the fallen. Adelle's power waned, only able to conjure up slight squeaks and whistles from her raw throat. Valerie was the last one standing, fighting tooth and nail. Adelle caught Valerie's eyes and saw the grim glint in them. Her stomach dropped when the Valkyrie shook her head. Adelle knew then this was their last stand. With a warrior's cry, Valerie charged forward into the sea of dead limbs, sword raised and slashing.

"Val! No!" Adelle screamed.

Her voice cleared a path for her sister before she was swallowed up by the army. That was the last of Adelle's power. Her voice faded into a pathetic scratchy whisper as she watched Valerie vanish into the fray. Ghouls crept toward her and Phoebe's tree, relentless on their path to kill. Adelle clenched her fists tight, holding her breath. All she could do was wait for the tidal wave of ghouls to consume her.

"I'm sorry, Phoebe," she whispered.

Four giant, scale covered feet slammed down, shaking the ground with a force that threw Adelle backwards against the tree. Ghouls toppled over like dominoes and Adelle looked up to see a huge red dragon standing between her and death. A shot of hot steam, a flap of giant black wings, and he reared up onto his hind legs, bearing dripping long fangs. He opened his maw and let out an enraged roar that shook the night sky.

"Jack!" Adelle whispered, her heart beating again.

The vibrations from Jack's roar uncovered Valerie from the swarm that swallowed her. She was alive, crouching on her knees, still swinging at any foolish ghoul that got too close. Adelle ran to her, hooking her arms under her sister's shoulders and dragging her to safety. Jack snarled and slashed at the remaining army, reducing them to useless clouds.

Valerie looked up at Adelle with a delirious smile. "Remind me to kiss your boyfriend for this!" she said with a hysterical laugh.

"Stand in line," Adelle replied.

Jack mowed them down with his black claws, stomping the ashes into the grass, growling and roaring with an anger that rivaled no other. When only twenty ghouls remained, the great red dragon opened his jaws and shot out a stream of yellow flame, burning them to smoke.

"Is that a dragon?!" Phoebe asked in awe.

Adelle was so entranced by the carnage she forgot her little sister was up in the tree. "Yeah. That's a dragon, all right." Her heart swelled at the sight of the glimmering scaled beast.

My dragon.

When it was all over, Jack dug at the dirt with his claws, scattering remains. Adelle pulled herself away from the tree and staggered up behind him.

"Wait! Dell! Don't get close!" Phoebe said.

"Trust me. She'll be fine," Valerie replied between weary breaths.

"But it might eat her!"

"I seriously doubt she'll mind that, Pheebs."

Adelle placed a hand on the warm scales of his hind leg. At the touch, Jack spun around and reared up, ready for another fight. His amber eyes widened when they saw Adelle standing there, hands offered to him, palms up.

"It's all right! It's just me!" she said.

Jack seemed to wince then lowered his head to her, nuzzling Adelle's side with his cheek. She let out a tired laugh as she petted the spot between his long black horns. The red and gold scales began to ripple, sinking down into his flesh. Black wings folded into his back, melting into his spine. His form shrank to human size and Jack unfolded himself, in his bare human form, brow knitted over those penetrating amber eyes.

"Hey, Buttercup," he said.

"Hey, Jack," her quivering voice answered. Tears burned her eyes as the corner of his mouth lifted into that crooked grin of his.

"You didn't call me for a couple days. Got a little worried."

Adelle let out a choked laugh of exhaustion. "How did you find us?"

Jack's black fingernails tapped the string of runes that were freshly tattooed onto his chest, close to his heart. He gave her a sheepish grin and a shrug of his shoulders. "I figured it was worth a shot." A frown pressed down onto his mouth. "You're hurt."

"I'm fine," she said. "Just a little banged up."

Jack nodded as he looked Adelle over, taking in the blood on her lip. In one swift movement he pulled her against him, and sealed his mouth over hers. Her lower lip stung only a moment before the healing power of his kiss soothed the pain away. She slipped her arms around his shoulders, pressing herself close, never wanting to let go.

"Val," Phoebe said from her tree branch.

"Yeah, Pheebs?" Valerie said.

"Is our sister kissing a naked guy?"

"Yes she is, Pheebs."

"Was he a dragon a minute ago?"

"Yes he was, Pheebs."

Phoebe let out a little sigh. "...Lucky."

Chapter 32

The bright light of morning pressed against Adelle's eyelids, forcing them to open. She gasped and found herself in her own room. Jack and her sisters must have gotten her home last night. Adelle shook her foggy head, looking down to her hands. Her palms had healed. She smiled, sensing Jack behind that. After his kiss, all her energy had drained and it had taken a herculean effort to stay standing. The last thing she remembered was Jack scooping her up into his arms and carrying her across the courtyard.

Soft voices spoke from behind her closed door, followed by clinking of plates and glasses. Phoebe's giggle finally roused her into sitting up. The deep sound of Jack's voice rumbled shortly after. Adelle kicked the blankets off and padded her way towards the kitchen, pajama clad and eager.

When she arrived, she found Jack sitting at the kitchen table with Phoebe, two bowls, a box of cereal and an almost empty box of donuts between them. In an instant, his attention was on her. There he was, in all his rugged, buck naked glory. Her eyes traveled down to find a hot pink *Hello Kitty* beach towel draped over his lap. She looked back to him with a little smirk and he rolled his eyes with a scowl.

"It's the biggest towel you females own," Jack said.

"Where's Val?" Adelle asked.

"She went to pick up a pair of pants for your… friend," Phoebe said. A giddy grin spread across her face as she looked between Adelle and Jack, then she spun back to Jack, fists wiggling in the air. "Oh my God, are you really a dragon?!" She vibrated with giggles.

"Yup," Jack said.

"Do you breathe fire? Do you have a hoard?"

"Yes and yes."

"Do you know any hobbits? Oh my God, I love dragons so much!"

Jack jerked his thumb over at Phoebe. "Is she always like this? I've been getting questions for about an hour now."

"Worse usually," Adelle replied.

Phoebe let out a little snort. "I've been through a traumatic experience. I have the right to be a complete dork."

Phoebe put on a lot of bravado but Adelle could see in her big blue eyes that she was shaken from last night. A little bit of her innocence was now lost, like Adelle's, like Valerie's. Adelle had mourned that loss when it happened to her but she'll be damned if she let Phoebe mourn.

"She's always been completely obsessed with your kind," Adelle added. "See, Pheebs? An upside to this traumatic experience. You met your first dragon."

Phoebe gazed at Jack with adoration as she giggled again. "I read *Flight of Dragons* over a hundred times when I was a kid."

Jack let out a sigh and rubbed his temples. "Oh, good God."

"You think I could ride you some day?"

Jack opened his eyes, looking at Adelle with his brows raised. "Sorry, that's your sister's job."

"Jack!" Adelle snapped.

"Aw, lucky!" Phoebe said.

"I'll say," Jack replied.

Adelle buried her now blushing face into her hands. "Jack, shut up!"

Phoebe looked between the two a moment, her smile dropping from her face as the innuendo sunk in. She turned bright pink and slid back into her seat.

"Oh, you guys are gross," she said.

The front door opened and Valerie swept in, a couple of white and red bags in her hands. "There you go," she said as she plopped the bags down in front of Jack. "A couple jeans and tees for you. Some boxers and socks and a pair of sneakers."

"Thanks," Jack replied. He dug out the pack of boxers, pulled open the plastic wrap with his teeth, and yanked out a pair.

Valerie looked to Adelle and smiled. "Oh good, you're awake! How are you feeling?"

"A little bit better. It's nothing a few days in a coma can't cure," Adelle replied.

She thought back to the night of the attack and the church burnings. Adelle wanted nothing more than to forget that the last few days had happened, but she couldn't. Not with something as big as a holy relic at stake. The mages had gotten a hold of her voice. Did they get the Spear of Destiny too?

"Look, I'm sorry to bring up shop talk after we just had our asses almost handed to us, but what did you find at that church?" Adelle asked.

"A priest who I'm sure isn't human," Valerie said.

"Did he say anything about the spear?"

"Only that we won't have to worry about that or his church burning down."

"Did he say where it went?"

"Nope," Valerie rolled her eyes. "Stoic little prick. He wouldn't tell me anything else. I'm also more than a little miffed that he didn't come out to help us."

"Shove over, I'll take a piece of him too," Jack growled.

Adelle shook her head with a sigh. “Well, they now have part of me, and I’m afraid of what they can do with it.”

“Whatever they do, we will stop them.” The cold determination in Valerie’s voice was enough to bring confidence back to Adelle. Valerie peered back at Jack. “Hope I got you the right size.”

“Close enough. Besides, I’ll have my own stuff shipped over soon,” Jack said.

Adelle’s eyes widened. “Your own stuff? Jack, how long are you planning on staying?”

Jack shimmied into the boxers under the *Hello Kitty* beach towel, wriggling and writhing in an awkward dance. “As long as it takes,” he replied.

“As long as it takes to what?”

He pulled the tag off a pair of crisp new blue jeans and shimmied into them too. “As long as it takes for you to stop these bastards.”

Adelle’s heart did a giddy somersault but held back the excitement as reality set in. She bit her lower lip, eyes narrowing. “Jack. A word with you in private, please?”

Phoebe grinned and sang, “Oh, someone is in trouble.”

Jack pushed himself to his feet then pointed a finger at Phoebe. “Do *not* eat that last donut. It’s mine.”

The fierce bravado was no match for Phoebe’s puppy dog eyes and his tough guy visage melted. He sighed then shook his head, following Adelle into her room.

After closing her door, Adelle spun to face Jack. “You know you can’t interfere with this type of business.”

“Who said I was interfering? You three can do whatever the hell you need to. I’m just here to protect my mate.”

“Jack, you’re going to get yourself-”

Jack silenced her by placing his fingers over her lips, pressing them closed. “I did a little research,” he said. “See, I can’t help you fight, but I can keep my mate safe. There's nothing in the rules against that." He gave Adelle a cocky smile. "Tested that theory out last night and here I am, still ticking."

Granted, he was alive after that daring rescue but it still made her uneasy. "Jack it's not that I don't want you to stay. God, I want that more than anything, but if you even set a little toe into this, karma would have you for breakfast."

"I'll be careful. I'm good at being careful."

"But what about your hoard?"

"Val said I can move some of it in the attic."

"Having half a hoard to sleep on will diminish your powers."

"Only a bit. It might make me cranky but you're used to that by now, right? Isn't that the reason you fell for me?"

"Dammit Jack! I'm being serious!"

Jack snagged her by the shoulders, kissing her hard. Her eyes fluttered closed as her arms snaked around his waist. The touch of his lips was so seductive after months of being denied them. She had missed him so much, the touch of his warm skin and the safety of his arms. She had missed his grumbling voice, his deep laugh, and his smart-ass smile. Jack stroked a hand down the length of her tangled curls, pulling away. He gazed down at her, chest heaving as he caught his breath.

"Nothing you say is going to send me back, Adelle. I can't protect your sisters, but I can protect you and I'm going to." His thumb whispered against her cheekbone as he leaned in close and murmured into her ear. "You are mine. And I am yours. You're stuck with me, Buttercup."

She studied his handsome face and those wonderful amber eyes. "Are you sure about this?" Adelle asked.

Jack's mouth curled up into another grin. "I have never been surer of anything in my entire life."

Adelle closed her eyes as she let out a happy, quivering sigh. So many factors told her that it would be foolish for him to stay, and yet she would do anything to keep him. Now fate had just dumped a solution right into her lap. She'd be the biggest idiot in the world if she didn't accept it. Again, she kissed him, a feathery, brief touch of pure love against his mouth.

"Well, who am I to change a dragon's mind?" she smiled.

Jack chuckled. "Oh, I don't know. You did a pretty good job before. Hell, you almost convinced me to stay up in Whitmore." His mouth twisted into a smirk. "Almost."

Adelle laughed, her heart swelling with love. He was her equal. Her mate. Her dragon. She sighed as she pressed her cheek against his shoulder. "I love you," she said.

His lips brushed across her forehead. "I love you, too."

There was a knock at the door and Valerie poked her head inside without waiting for a "come in". She cocked a brow.

"So," she said. "Since I heard no screaming or animal noises, I'm assuming that you two have come to a fully clothed agreement."

"Jack's going to stay for a while," Adelle said, not bothering to pull away from his embrace.

Valerie didn't seem phased by the news. "Good. I'll clear a space in the attic." She smiled. "Just keep the hot monkey love noises down at night and it's all good."

Jack shook his head. "I make no promises."

Adelle gave his chest a good, hard swat.

"I'll buy earplugs," Valerie said. "Put some pants on, Dell. That priest that isn't human just showed up at our doorstep. And we all need to chat." She pointed a finger at Jack. "Don't beat him up. We need this guy for a while."

Jack rolled his eyes and snorted, giving a reluctant nod.

After Valerie retreated, Adelle chuckled, heading towards her closet to toss some clothes on. "Are you sure you can live with this family of mine?" she asked.

Jack ginned as he leaned over and gave her backside a firm swat. "Buttercup, you're worth every breath."

The future was a mystery, but having Jack by her side gave Adelle the courage she needed to face that uncertainty head on. After all, she was the siren that tamed a dragon. And nothing on earth made her feel more proud.

The *Wyrd Love* Series

"Funny, touching, and just a smidge bawdy"-- Wyrd Love delves into the unseen fantasy world that lurks just along the edge of our own. Dragons, mages, Valkyries, and many others collide, some-times violently and sometimes with steamy results. Wyrd Love offers women with strong personalities, men with tender hearts, and a world where consent is always sexy.

Siren's Song

Valkyrie's Spear

Dryad's Vine

Alchemy's Hunger

Starting Fires

A Witch's Want

ABOUT THE AUTHOR

Since she was a child, Cynthia craved anything that featured heroines with strong personalities. Now she writes books for sassy nerds with a sharp sense of humor. Starting her adult life in theater, she earned a Masters of Fine Arts in Costume Design, but her first love was telling stories. After some encouragement, she dove down the rabbit hole and created the Wyrd Love series.

When not telling tales about hot dragons and werewolves with tight behinds, Cynthia is an SCA geek and an amateur artist. She resides in sunny San Diego, California with her trickster fae husband, two cats of varying intelligence, and a ton of goldfish.

www.CynthiaDiamondAuthor.com

Made in the USA
Middletown, DE
14 March 2022